DEATH CANAL

MICHAEL HARTNETT

Black Rose Writing | Texas

ISBN: 978-1-68433-881-8
PUBLISHED BY BLACK ROSE WRITING
www.blackrosewriting.com

Printed in the United States of America
Suggested Retail Price (SRP) $20.95

Death Canal is printed in Garamond

*As a planet-friendly publisher, Black Rose Writing does its best to eliminate unnecessary waste to
reduce paper usage and energy costs, while never compromising the reading experience. As a result,
the final word count vs. page count may not meet common expectations.

Cover art by Sean Mahoney

Advanced Praise for *Death Canal*

"A brilliantly crafted and wry, sardonic look at life, death, and reality itself in the unreal reality of the Age of Kardashians"
–Len Boswell, author of the *Simon Grave Mysteries*

"Vivid, vivacious and memorable, *Death Canal* is another gem from one of the best contemporary novelists around"
–John Vance, author of *Secret of the Chimes*.

"Global Warming, Murder, Sex —Only Michael Hartnett!"
–Joe Edd Morris, author of *The Prison*.

*To my parents Jerry and Bridget, my wife Amy,
and my children Brittany, Patrick, and John*

DEATH CANAL

Dirk Wall Paralyzed in Crash

By Russell Pines,
exclusively for *The Herald*

Fitness guru and reality show star Dirk Wall has been reportedly paralyzed from a car accident on the Grand Central Parkway late last evening, according to medical officials at Mount Sinai Hospital. Wall crashed into a median on the way back to his Gold Coast mansion in Sands Point on Long Island.

Wall had first achieved modest celebrity status for his workout videotapes in the 1980s. His fame soared after his marriage to his wife Suzie, who had been previously married to high-powered sports agent Frankie Pisano. Their marriage and merging of families led to the development of the reality television show *Peepin' on the Pisanos*. The couple's workout videos of wife Suzie and husband Dirk became a staple on sports and shopping networks. Meanwhile, *Peepin' on the Pisanos* emerged as the number one rated show on the X Network.

"He is one of the great personalities on television," said Suzie Wall. "He is an absolute national treasure."

Wall became renowned for his inspirational words of encouragement. His most famous saying was, "Imagine yourself as a fly. Then imagine yourself stepping on that fly. Why be the fragile wings when you can be the big foot?"

The accident comes on the heels of last week's tabloid stories that Dirk Wall's marriage with his celebrity wife Suzie was on the rocks, with numerous reports of affairs (and accompanying paparazzi shots) engaged by both marital parties.

Over the past decade, Wall's popularity had been eclipsed by that of

Suzie's, given her dominating and domineering performances in *Peepin' on the Pisanos*. In addition, the three daughters on the show have also garnered more attention, especially the supermodel and entrepreneur Heather Pisano, who has become one of the world's most famous celebrities.

Police said the circumstances of the crash were being investigated. "We don't know the cause," said Nassau County spokesperson Gila Cohen. "The investigation is continuing." Hospitals officers said Wall remains in serious condition.

CHAPTER 1
THE RISING OF WATERS

After his bosses subverted the season finale script, Flanagan decided to quit his job. Out of morbid curiosity, he watched the filming anyway. He stood just outside the frame of the camera to witness a staged rescue, one he had envisioned to transpire in a less contrived way. In Flanagan's original script, the loyal Diaz servants would have been saving the beautiful Pisano women from the collapsing artist's shack just before it fell into the Long Island Sound. Dirk Wall would have helped in the rescue effort.

But Suzie Pisano had overruled the plan. She liked the rescue, but what if she and her bikini-clad daughters saved the Diaz servants instead? Wouldn't that be wonderful? Flanagan argued the Suzie's version presented a troubling scenario: the wealthy, strong American royals saving the poor, weak, lowly immigrants. "Anyway, even for our show," he said, "it would stretch credulity."

"Do they even know how to swim?" asked Suzie.

Flanagan wasn't sure. Still, he didn't like where the storyline was heading. The origin of the script came from a talk he had with the Pisano daughter Heather, who wanted to integrate a global warming theme into the episode. For years, Flanagan lobbied for an episode about how the rising waters of the Long Island Sound threatened the foundations of the Pisano Mansion. During this week's high tide, the waves rushed onto the floor of the low-lying artist shack on the estate's shoreline. Built a hundred years ago, the shack, nicknamed the "Crab Cave," had been impractically situated as close to the water as possible by the eccentric wife of a robber baron. Since the shack's construction, the Long Island Sound levels had risen about a foot, enough to lap up the shingled sides. Propped on rickety pilings deep in the shadow of the Pisano mansion, the shack could be easily demolished by the currents ... with some help from production engineering.

Flanagan liked how the shack's dramatic destruction, especially if the Pisano family was trapped inside, would provide the melodrama required for the season finale while letting elements of the outside world creep into the fantasy lives of the Pisanos. In other words, Flanagan would be able to incorporate some reality into the reality television series, even if he had to do much manufacturing and manipulating to achieve the desired effect.

Flanagan's script had called for the Pisano women to gather in the artist's shack, sprucing it up for a painting party. Engineers would snap the pilings, the shack would tumble into the sea, and the Diaz crew would pull them from the water, a signal that even the most famous family in America was not immune to greater forces threatening humanity. Flanagan was certain the near-death experience would turn the season finale of *Peepin' on the Pisanos* into ratings gold.

Suzie saw great script advantages of Dirk being incapacitated for the finale shoot. "Don't you see, Arthur," she said to Flanagan, "this episode will be about women's empowerment."

Under Suzie's revisions, the Diaz family had to move out of the mansion basement and into the artist's shack, which she pretentiously called a cottage. "According to your script, Arthur," said Suzie, "the high tide should be at one o'clock, which is perfect. We will all be in our bathing suits at the beach working on our tans."

"Shouldn't you give Dirk a role?" asked Flanagan. "He has been recovering. Don't you think it would be insensitive to ignore him in this episode, especially after the accident?"

"Oh, why don't you have him up on the veranda?" Suzie suggested. "He can see the cottage collapse first. He can call me and we can spring into action."

As the cameras rolled, Flanagan stood beyond the shadow of Dirk's wheelchair. The three daughters made their way down to the beach, each explaining to the others what bikini brands they were wearing. The youngest daughter Nora wore make-up beyond her 19 years. The 30-year-old Tiffany had her fair share of make-up on too, but that was employed mainly to blend in the fading lines of recent plastic surgeries that made her alarmingly beautiful. Despite how lovely and famous both Nora and Tiffany had become, the eldest daughter Heather garnered the longest minutes and tightest framing from the camera. With an army of Instagram followers greater than the population of Texas,

Heather had become the standard by which all others were judged. Trailing behind to make her own dramatic entrance, Suzie carried a pitcher of green liquid and wore an artfully tilted hat. She called out to her daughters to make sure they took off their tops to avoid tans lines.

"Don't worry," Suzie assured with motherly warmth. "No one can see us down here."

Flanagan never liked when the Pisano women stripped, since their exposed virtues would be blurred out for the television episode and the overall aesthetics came off to his trained eye as messy. Whenever he objected, Suzie would argue, "The notion of the nudity is important even if the audience won't be able to see anything. They will look very hard and that is what we want."

Flanagan was sick of the whole business. He should've known that even with Heather supporting the idea of introducing global warming into this episode, such a concept was far too alien to the sensibilities of *Peepin' on the Pisanos* to find its way into the storyline. Instead, he watched Dirk point to the collapsing shack, call Suzie on his cell, and yell out "My God, it's coming down."

The shack lurched toward the sea, bending downward. The choppy Sound waves rushed into the A-frame and the Diaz family yelled, "Ayudame!" Although the entire Diaz family, even grandma, spoke fluent English, Suzie insisted that the cries be in Spanish.

Then the Pisano women sprang into action, tying back up their tops as quickly as they shed them – the rehearsals had paid off. The cameras were in place as wiry teenager Paco was saved by Nora and Tiffany rescued Mia, the housekeeper. Then more dramatically, Suzie climbed into a collapsing window to find the old cook Alma, who was terribly disoriented, sobbing and groping her way across the tilting floor. As he checked the monitors in the mansion's production studio, Flanagan could not help but admire Alma's restrained acting. If he weren't leaving the show, he would certainly get more use out of her. Alma initially resisted Suzie's assistance, not wanting to cross the waves to be delivered to the beach's safety. Alma's opposition gave Suzie the chance to reveal the results of her exercise regimen as she heroically lifted the slight grandma over her shoulder and carried her onto the designer blanket.

Of course, Heather had been given the greatest spotlight as she had to rescue the butler Felipe. A couple of inches taller than the other women, she carried off the Diaz husband with a statuesque certainty that seemed otherworldly.

How theatrical.

Even for Flanagan, who'd scripted his share of outlandishly staged scenes, the rescue was over-the-top. Dirk's injury and this perversion of his finale script guaranteed his resignation. His tolerance had deteriorated as his suspicions elevated. The high tide and the low-lying artist's shack had been an opportunity to give *Peepin' on the Pisanos* a currency that the show had consciously avoided, from its silly series name to its supercilious family. If the destructive tides of climate change landed even on the Pisano shores, they couldn't be ignored, right?

After she placed a grateful Felipe on the shore, Heather turned to a camera to say. "These rising sea levels could be the death of us all." Flanagan knew the audience would be too busy looking at Heather in her wet bikini to listen to what she was saying. Hell, he could hardly hear a word himself, and he wrote the lines. He predicted that Heather's warning would be cut in favor of testimonies by the other sisters about how the flexibility of their bathing suits made the rescue possible; those endorsements would have a more immediate impact on their financial portfolios.

But the series was no longer his problem.

He returned to the veranda to say goodbye to Dirk Wall.

Staring up at Flanagan from his wheelchair, Dirk said, "Nice try, kid." Dirk called him kid, even though Flanagan was in his late thirties. "I see what you were trying to do here."

"Yeah, well, Suzie had other ideas," said Flanagan.

"Does she ever," Dirk said. "So, are you really leaving for good this time?"

"I am," said Flanagan.

"Suzie's not going to like what you have in mind," said Dirk smiling.

"You almost sound happy I'm doing it," said Flanagan.

"Even I'm curious about your investigation of the family and I'm not interested in much besides push-ups," Dirk laughed. He had a self-deprecating quality not found in the other family members. "Do me a favor, don't get caught up in my accident. You have bigger things to explore."

Though Dirk's accident had haunted him the last couple of weeks since it fit into a pattern of family tragedies, Flanagan knew Dirk was right. When investigating the family, it was easy to get off track. *Peepin' on the Pisanos* had been America's distraction and had so preoccupied Flanagan that he could not remember the last time he had a worthwhile thought. As he started to disentangle himself from the Pisanos, he realized what truly intrigued him was a Pisano-related accident that happened thirty years ago. At the time when he died,

Senator Jimmy Doherty had been a big deal, although his affair with Suzie Pisano had been downplayed. Now, as time passed and distractions multiplied, Doherty had been nearly forgotten. Yet Flanagan sensed he would learn much more about what mattered to him if he investigated Doherty's death.

"O.K.," said Flanagan, "but you're not trying to hide something from me, are you?"

"I am," said Dirk, "but they are small secrets not worthy of your efforts."

Flanagan frowned.

Dirk continued to smile at Flanagan; he was an incredibly happy man for someone who'd just been given a lifetime sentence in a wheelchair. "I promise, when I do tell my little secret, it will be only to you," Dirk said.

"Good," said Flanagan.

"Don't look so satisfied," said Dirk. "Whatever I can tell you, it won't be much. You run along now and dig up some dirt on my wife's former lovers."

Flanagan obeyed. As he left the grounds in his Lexus, Flanagan hoped that the shallow frivolity of his past dozen years as scriptwriter for *Peepin' on the Pisanos* would give way to graver investigations into the Pisano's dark family history. He knew he had secrets to unearth. Next, he would have to figure out how to make a living out of delivering those revelations.

CHAPTER 2
THE OILING OF GEARS

Every time Flanagan entered Kartik Reddy's offices he wondered if he were walking into a scam. The facilities were so spare and makeshift that they reeked of those fly-by-night organizations that will stay in business just long enough to take your money before their front-door letterhead is replaced by a For-Rent sign.

Kartik would explain to him, "I don't have time for appearances. If you want my place to look like a traditional studio office, I can always green-screen in the image for you."

They had become friends on *Peepin' on the Pisanos,* where Kartik made his initial fortune as co-producer with Suzie on the show. Then he made his real money, producing films based on comic books. Surprisingly, Kartik never moved out to L.A., and he always kept in touch with Flanagan to catch up on family gossip. "It is my guilty pleasure," he'd tell Flanagan.

"I thought superhero movies are your guilty pleasure?" Flanagan would ask.

"No, that America's guilty pleasure," Kartik said, "although I'm not certain about the guilt part."

Flanagan always wondered how he became friends with Kartik. While his fine, dark Indian features across his tall frame and his piercing chestnut eyes gave him the look of a Bollywood star, Kartik's defining quality was a fast intelligence that intimidated many. He could even set back on her Gucci heels someone as formidable as Suzie Pisano. Although he now realized that most of Kartik's comments to him were tinged with mockery, Flanagan could tell the wily producer liked him, perhaps viewing him as one of those cartoonish sidekicks so popular in the movies he produced.

So when he showed up at Kartik's impossibly austere office, Flanagan was unsettled. He steeled himself for Kartik to peer down at him with his hawk nose, a nose that was strikingly handsome, although one millimeter larger could well have led to tragic results. Kartik didn't help matters by starting the conversation with, "Oh, Artie, you are meeting me at my office and not at a restaurant, which can only mean one thing, you want money. Didn't you save any from all those years writing for the show?"

"No, I have money," said Flanagan. He decided he better be blunt. "I want to pitch you a documentary."

"Oh," said Kartik, "so you do want money. What documentary?"

"Dirk Wall's accident is the third one that befell a man connected with the Pisano family."

"Besides Frankie, who's the other one?"

"Jimmy Doherty in 1989," said Flanagan. "He was having quite the torrid affair with Suzie Pisano."

"So what's the documentary going to be about?"

"I wanted to start with Doherty's accident and see what I find?"

"Who cares about some guy who died thirty years ago, especially when his last name isn't Pisano?"

"He was a really big deal at the time, a popular Senator, a former basketball star," Flanagan said. "Many people thought he might be President one day."

"Now if he had been President, then you'd have a good documentary on your hands."

"He died right at the peak of his popularity."

"I don't know. People don't go for stories about Senators, especially from long ago. They don't remember the Senator from last week, let alone from the '80s."

"But this documentary won't be about a Senator," Flanagan said. "It will be about sex and murder and as many links as I can find to the Pisanos."

"That sounds a little bit more like it, but I'm not certain you know what you're talking about."

Ah, thought Flanagan, he wasn't too sure himself. Best to go off on a tangent. "Look, you can't deny how popular these murder investigation documentaries have become. Think of the success of podcasts like *Serial* and documentary series like the *Tiger King* and the one on O.J. The best thing is that none of those shows really proved anything. They just presented enough intriguing evidence to engage the audience."

"So how are you going to get this intriguing evidence?" asked Kartik. "What kind of crew do you have?"

"Right now it's just me," said Flanagan, fidgeting and swaying. "I want to do all the preliminary work. I'll record everything and send it to Mehnuma." Mehnuma was Kartik's most trusted employee who served as an intermediary between the boss and those trying to get to him. "How about if she looks at the footage and she can tell you what she thinks?"

"No crew whatsoever?" asked Kartik.

"I can have Edmund J. Coppa shoot atmospheric footage to flesh out some of the scenes."

"Coppa?" Coppa had worked intermittently on the set of *Peepin' on the Pisanos*, doing camerawork that the average contractor would be unwilling to take – in awkward spots in the middle of the night where getting beaten up was a strong possibility.

"My pitch for the documentary is what I deliver to you," assured Flanagan. "I will continually send you footage with accompanying scripts."

"And what do you want from me?" asked Kartik.

"That if you think it's good, you'll produce it," Flanagan said. "That would mean you'd have to clean up all my footage and sound, reshoot where necessary, get the crew together and the editors. In other words, do all the shit you know how to do and I don't."

"That's because I know everything and you know nothing."

"But I have the interest, the time, and the connections to get this story," said Flanagan, sounding more confident than he could possibly be.

"Yes, and what happens when the Pisanos get wind of what you're investigating?" asked Kartik. "I don't imagine they'll be too friendly then."

"Maybe not, but the Pisanos are not known for shying away from scandals."

"That is correct, but those scandals, Artie, generally involve nudity and sex."

"So, I'll just have to make sure those are elements in the documentary," said Flanagan.

For the first time in the conversation, Kartik smiled. "This little investigation might be worth it just to see what Suzie does to you."

"I'm guessing it's nothing she hasn't done to me before," said Flanagan.

"I wouldn't be so sure about that," said Kartik, those dark eyes registering surprise at Flanagan's naivete. "Over all these years, you have not been someone worth Suzie's attention. You might finally get her attention with what you're doing."

Flanagan wondered if he were delving into this sordid past for that very reason. All these years he managed to put words in the mouths of the Pisano women without ever being noticed. "I'll be able to handle Suzie," he assured.

"Uh huh," said Kartik, pausing for a few moments to let his skepticism sink into Flanagan's spine. "What type of initial financing do you need from me?"

"None, right now," Flanagan said. "I will use my savings."

"Good answer," said Kartik. "Then why even come to me with this proposal."

"I want your assurances that if I deliver a compelling story with compelling footage, you'll fully finance the documentary."

"But I could tell you yes now and renege later," said Kartik.

"You could," said Flanagan, "but you are my friend, and I don't believe you would do that to me."

"You have clearly been writing in an alternate reality for too long," said Kartik.

"Which is why I need to make this documentary," said Flanagan.

Kartik grinned. "You know, for the first time since I met you, I think you're right about something."

Flanagan laughed. "Are you telling me after all of those words I have written for the Pisanos I have never been right?"

"Of course not," said Kartik. "Do you think if you had ever been right they would have kept you around for so long?"

Before Flanagan departed, Kartik gave him a cinema-quality Red digital camera. "Don't lose it or break it," he said. "That camera's worth more than you earn in a month."

"How kind of you," said Flanagan.

"Don't thank me," said Kartik. "If I made Mehnuma scan footage that looked like it was shot in a snowstorm, I'd never hear the end of it. Anyway, if you frame decently, I won't have to send my crews out to reshoot everything."

"I'll keep that in mind," said Flanagan. "I have been working for the past few weeks lining up appointments, so I should have something to you pretty quickly."

Kartik stared at the camera like he had stopped listening to what Flanagan was saying. "The sound on this camera is very sensitive, so don't breathe too heavily," he warned. "I know how you get around those Pisano women."

CHAPTER 3
AN EDGING TOWARD THE MEDIAN

Artie Flanagan had been around the gossip mill long enough to hear of Suzie's ongoing affair in the '80s with the late, great Senator Jimmy Doherty. He died in an auto accident. Indeed, three of Suzie's lovers, including her two husbands, had severe auto accidents. Frankie Pisano, her first husband, crashed into a storefront out in the Hamptons and was killed instantly. Now, Dirk Wall had smashed into a median. The pattern was curious, given Suzie's proclivities ... sufficiently curious that Flanagan thought it would provide the backbone of his documentary.

Over his dozen years as the lead writer on *Peepin' on the Pisanos*, Flanagan had regularly heard whispers from Suzie's beautiful daughters about the fate of Jimmy Doherty ("You see what happens when you sleep with Momma"). But those insinuations were complicated by rumors about Doherty's death that had nothing to do with the fabulous jealousies of the former Suzie Jansen who would become Suzie Pisano who would then become Suzie Wall who would now become ...?

Environmentalists often claim Doherty as an early martyr of the Green Movement, which gave him a gravitas not usually associated with the Pisanos. Given the Senator's relationship with Suzie, Flanagan had made inquiries about Doherty's death before. He had to confess that investigations around this family were a bit of a hobby of his. Flanagan told himself this research was necessary for his script writing, but he knew better. He sensed terrible secrets lurked.

Now he traveled out from Queens to the Sands Point mansion just as he set in motion radical changes in his life. He would return the Lexus he was driving to the dealer. He had already sold the condo and quit his job. He dropped off of Twitter, Facebook, Instagram, and TikTok. He no longer compulsively pulled his phone from his pocket. As he wended his way through the leafy, windy North Shore roads, he told himself his actions did not signal a midlife crisis. No, they pointed to the evolution to a better Flanagan, a man who finally extricated himself from the golden handcuffs of *Peepin' on the Pisanos*.

As with everything on the show, Flanagan's departure became the source of drama. He possessed secrets the family members coveted. It started with Flanagan's scandalous intrusion into the bedroom of the Pisano's highest money earner and therefore top goddess, Heather. Given the family history of sex tapes and nude pictorials, one might think the scandal derived from prurient behavior. But for the Pisanos, sexuality was a bedrock commodity. If Flanagan walked in on a woman in her underwear in another household, she would be embarrassed. Not in the Pisano home. When Flanagan entered with a script update, he ignored the impressive state of undress, knowing the labradoodle Merrill merited greater attention.

Suzie once explained to Flanagan, "You are so much a part of us that you are not really here at all." When Flanagan objected that he did not believe "it was supposed to work that way," Suzie laughed and told him, "With us it does."

And yet in the past year, Flanagan saw what everyone in the family agreed he should not have witnessed. Unlike the rest of the women in the household, Heather had of late been closing her door. When Flanagan noted that door was slightly ajar, he entered to explain what she should say about sister Tiffany's new botox ("You will look gorgeous once the swelling subsides"). Even though she was fully clothed, Heather stared at him with great alarm and a shadow of shame. "Get out!" she commanded.

Tail between his legs, Flanagan obeyed, shutting the door behind him. Not knowing what to do, he waited in the hall, figuring she would summon him when ready. Hovering near the entry, he now allowed himself to take in what he had spotted in the room. Strewn on the floor were books and papers. In place of the usual assortment of the finest facial products, her makeup table had a laptop. If Flanagan didn't know any better, he would think serious scholarship was transpiring. But such activities in the Pisano household? Ridiculous.

About fifteen minutes later, he was summoned into Heather's room where she spoke to him like nothing happened. The laptop, the prints, and the papers were gone. He noted one book remained in the far corner of the room. The casual observer would have thought that Heather simply missed putting away the book. However, Flanagan knew Heather did not make such mistakes. She made certain that the direction of the spine would give maximum readability. Noting the title *Seeing the Light*, Flanagan wondered whether Heather was having a religious conversion. Clearly, she wanted Flanagan to know about whatever she was up to.

Flanagan decided to probe further next week when he arrived at the ajar door with holy verses to be inserted into the script. The scene of books, prints, and papers repeated with Heather's accompanying shock and order to "Get Out!" When he was summoned twenty minutes later, she rolled her eyes at the biblical scripture and said to him in his departure, "Tell Deja, I said hi."

Flanagan realized by Heather's response that she learned he was even denser than she had previously perceived. He played back this week's scene in his head, slowly realizing that the books on the floor were technical rather than spiritual in nature. And if he couldn't put together anything from that evidence, Heather's mentioning of Deja certainly gave him a few ideas. He had been dating Deja on-and-off for the past few weeks … funny, right about the time he stumbled upon Heather's secret activity.

That Deja worked at Columbia's Earth Institute and was deeply involved in Climate Change offered more clues. From there on, Heather's interests in the goings-on at the Earth Institute would become a regular topic of his date nights with Deja. In the months before he left *Peepin' on the Pisanos*, Flanagan only had one substantive conversation with Heather about her burgeoning interests and that was centered on the rising waters storyline of Flanagan's script for the season finale. For now, and perhaps forever, his knowing she cared about something beyond her image as a beauty who built a media cosmetic empire would be enough.

And yet, that Flanagan – piddling, irrelevant Flanagan – knew something that Suzie did not gnawed away at the matriarch. While Heather was indifferent about Flanagan leaving the show, Suzie was angry since he might be taking valuable information with him. Despite his efforts to remain non-threatening, Flanagan had become sadly formidable, a position no one was happy about his earning. An observer would not accuse Heather and Flanagan of being kindred spirits, yet each had newly craved something greater than could be satisfied on the set of *Peepin' on the Pisanos*.

He turned onto one of many roads without a street sign. The absence of such guidance was typical of the Gold Coast: only the mansion owners knew the road names. Communities without navigational signposts tended to keep the riffraff out. In his longstanding role as glorified household servant, Flanagan knew the territory well. He understood with his new project that he would be stepping back from the Pisanos, but not completely stepping away. In his investigation into the death of Jimmy Doherty for what he hoped would be a blockbuster documentary, Flanagan eyed Heather Pisano as the perfect source for information, since she was a closet Green Party member and intimately familiar with the Pisano family secrets. As always, Heather tended to tease more than deliver. "I believe," she told Flanagan, "it was vehicular manslaughter. From what I hear, Doherty was stirring up problems." After a sphinx-like smile, Heather shifted her focus to her hips: "Do you think they're getting too big? I know it's always a close call with me." Flanagan tried to get her back on Doherty. "What about Al Gore? Why wasn't he killed?" Heather just rolled her eyes and smiled: "No, really, I think they might finally be too big, no matter how small my waist is."

On his way to Suzie's house in Sands Point, Flanagan had been cut off twice. In less alert moments, he could have suffered a serious accident. Dismissing the idea that he might be targeted, he struggled to figure out if the near-misses were good or bad omens. He had two valid reasons to visit the Pisano compound: 1. To check up on Dirk, who was the closest to a friend Flanagan had of the on-air talent; 2. To officially let Suzie know that he was leaving the show. She always said the show really wrote itself, so he figured she wouldn't exactly be heartbroken by his departure.

After clearing the guardhouse, he made his way to the massive cobble-stoned roundabout. Then he opened the wrought-iron foyer door and knocked on the hulking mahogany portal, only to be held up by the butler Felipe. Flanagan waited outside twenty minutes before he was led into the parlor to see the lady of the house. As he stood in the unusually strong late August sun, he could sense the swelling humidity of hurricane season now upon them; three storms had already moved up the coast and had wreaked havoc in Florida and the Carolinas. While Flanagan was mulling when they would get a direct hurricane hit (this year at least one seemed inevitable), Felipe granted him the precious access to Suzie. Although quite beautiful for her age, Suzie frequented the surgical repair shop often, which regularly left her countenance in different stages of adjustment. Flanagan had seen Suzie at her roughest moments, what he called her "low tide phases," ones instead of the smells of the sea featured the swells of the mien. Mercifully, today landed on the right wax of the lunar cycle. Indeed, she glistened with the roar and sparkle of high tide. If he didn't know she was deep in mourning over Dirk's grave injuries, he might have conjectured that she was on the prowl for a mate. No matter, Flanagan was certain of one thing in life: he was not worthy of the attention of Suzie Wall, formerly Suzie Pisano, *née* Suzie Jansen.

"How is Dirk?" Flanagan asked, in a tone flush with sincerity.

"He won't be able to walk again. It's horrible, just horrible."

"Let me know if there's anything I can do."

At this offer, she frowned at him. "Well, from what I hear you're leaving us, so there really won't be time for that."

"Just because I don't work on the show, I could still stop by and help him."

Her stiff shoulders made clear that Flanagan would not be stopping by to help. Yet she signaled Felipe. "Get me a chilled bottle of the Pouilly-Fuissé and two glasses." From there she prattled on about how she would have to find a new business niche for Dirk, since he clearly could no longer push fitness equipment. "Dirk'll need to keep busy. That's the only thing that will do him good."

Flanagan did his fair share of nodding and "yessing" while Suzie told him how she learned so much from her early days running a candle store ... about finding the right business to suit the skill-set of the individual. Flanagan had the good manners not to ask what Dirk's skill-set would be in his current condition. He struggled to cut off the inner monologue flowing through his brain and the notion that he was in this moment a bit actor in a reality television scene.

Flanagan had long wrestled with his perceptions of Suzie. He wondered whether he was prejudiced by the role he had scripted for her – of the domineering, ruthless matriarch of the family. Did he write that narrative because she was indeed that person? Did she ultimately become the person he had written for her? Or was Suzie merely playing the role, a most lucrative part at that.

She served him the chilled white burgundy and spoke of Birkins. As she sprawled on the divan like a maja of old, Flanagan fiddled with crystal figurines scattered on the endless end tables. After lifting each one up, he made a point of returning these figurines just a bit off. Once directed north, the unicorn horn now pointed east. The tail of the dragon stopped swishing toward the fireplace and now threatened the chandelier. By the time Flanagan had his fingers around a delicate Pegasus, Suzie rose from her glorious repose to methodically redirect the figurines and set the universe back in place.

For every figurine she straightened, she made sure to bend over intently to remind Flanagan of what sorcerers plastic surgeons can be. By his count, she had two breast augmentations and three lifts in his time writing for the show. In her defense, however, *Peepin' on the Pisanos* had an impressively long run. As she offered a pendulous shrug of her tight You Just Be You blouse to fix the unicorn, Flanagan contemplated whether the act was one of dominance or seduction. When she provided a reverse angle as she corrected the dragon, he grew more nonplussed. The mirrors about the room conjured up an alternate theory: perhaps, she was not bothering to send Flanagan a message (even if that message was that he was not worthy of her carnal manipulations); all of Suzie's posturing simply might have been for her to get better views of herself.

"So Arthur, what will you do now?"

"I don't know, maybe make a documentary on an old crime," Flanagan could have said anything, but what was the point of coming over to say goodbye if he didn't get to gauge her reactions? "Those seem to be quite popular nowadays."

"Mmmm," Suzie's eyes hardened the way they might if Flanagan had thrown the unicorn across the room. She was back sprawled on the couch as if she were offering an invitation to someone who wasn't him. "That sounds rather dangerous, don't you think?"

"I don't know." Flanagan leaned into the chair cushion, trying his best to look relaxed. "I think when things get rough, I'll get the law involved."

Suzie took a sip of her white burgundy, the cool sweat beads on the glass now mostly evaporated. "Well, that's the funny thing, Arthur, isn't it? Before someone even realizes things are getting rough, they're already dead."

Shrugging his shoulders, Flanagan tasted the wine. It was such a good wine that he focused more on its complex minerality than on Suzie's warnings. "I appreciate your telling me that as a friend."

"Well, how else would I tell it?" she said.

To lighten her accusatory tone, he answered, "It's the only way you know how, which is one of your many graces."

"Oh, Arthur, you always were the charmer." She put down the glass, stretching her arms and arching her back in what most would characterize as an erotic way. Flanagan had seen Heather perform that slumbering seduction dozens of times on the show. He could not remember her mother ever doing it for the camera. He felt obtusely privileged, slightly stimulated, and profoundly disturbed. As Flanagan contemplated too many possibilities, Suzie, while still in that pose, shifted gears verbally. "And Arthur, by the way," Flanagan nodded to indicate he was still listening, "if you even think of writing a tell-all book, your meager wealth that you gained as our servant will be swallowed up in legal fees."

A bit disarmed by the baldness of the threat, Flanagan laughed. "Suzie, you are savvy enough to know that tell-all books are written by those who know something."

Rolling her eyes, she resumed her languid repose on the divan, "You'd be surprised."

"You don't have to worry about that."

"Do I look worried?"

"Even if I wanted to write a book, I wouldn't be able to stomach the appearances on all of those talk shows. You know what a terrible scandal a book would cause."

Returning to the burgundy, she arched an eyebrow. "Not really. I don't think your story would draw any attention at all."

Sensing it was time to leave, Flanagan again offered best wishes to Dirk, polished off his burgundy, and said with a Suzie-level of sincerity. "I truly hope everything goes wonderfully for you."

Suzie rose and leaned toward him, hardly wondering whether the cut of the blouse was a bit indecent and whispered, "I do too."

As he drove off, Flanagan was never so fearful he might run into a wall.

CHAPTER 4
THE KILLING OF A SENATOR

Flanagan had waited for a long time to have a meeting with Sean Clarkin. With his broad shoulders and his imposing presence, he was a formidable monument of a man. However, Clarkin's inimitable scale led to problems. Every time Clarkin walked into the type of bars he liked to frequent, a few little gnats would antagonize him into the inevitable fight – usually two gnats at a time, sometimes three.

Repeatedly, Flanagan had invited Sean to his apartment, but Sean refused. "We do a Guinness elbow to elbow or nothing." Flanagan had decided a few years ago he was getting a little long in the tooth for bar fights. A generation older, Clarkin should have been too. But his stubborn nature was generally his greatest virtue. For the past month Flanagan had been hectoring Sean to talk to him about the legendary senator Jimmy Doherty. Sean and Doherty had been friends since the late 70s when they were Beta Theta Pi frat buddies at Columbia and bonded on the basketball team.

Clarkin served as advisor and bodyguard during Doherty's years on the Knicks, and then followed him right into politics as his chief of staff. After Doherty's death, many political operatives said big Sean should've run for his seat. Instead, he quit the business and became a chemistry professor at a community college for the past thirty years – possessing enough fame and beloved by enough students for the administration to look past his indiscretions, barroom and otherwise.

Now as they walked together into the Pint O'Plenty, all six-foot-eight inches of Sean was challenged by two men each a head shorter. Without receiving his response, they jumped him, furiously kicking at his legs and punching at his belly. Neither achieved the desired effect of moving him; the deadening thuds of their shots might have been promising if Sean had been willing to offer an encouraging groan. Instead, he elbowed each in the skull. When they staggered and fell forward, he smashed them in their backs and spread a size-fifteen shoe to step on each of them.

The skirmish in front of the Pint O'Plenty was so commonplace – especially Sean's involvement in it – that he did not provide an explanation to Flanagan; he just opened the bar door. Realizing now was not the right time to ask questions, Flanagan followed him. Ordering two Guinnesses with Bushmill chasers, Flanagan let Sean's breathing settle before he started his interview. He knew he'd only have so much time until a couple of wee fellows would antagonize Clarkin into further combat.

Flanagan had already spoken to Clarkin informally, but this time would be the first he would go on the record. He was hoping that Clarkin would hand him Doherty's day planners from his Senate years, but he saw that the big man carried no backpack, suitcase, or envelope. "I thought you were going to bring documentation," said Flanagan.

Clarkin pointed to his head, "The documentation's right in here."

Flanagan frowned. "Stories about illicit affairs are much more credible if they have exact dates," he said. "No one's going to trust a documentary if it just tosses out rumor and innuendo."

Clarkin took a sip of his Guinness. "I can get that for you. It just takes me minute or two to work backwards. That's all. It's kind of like reverse engineering."

"Yeah?" Flanagan did not hide his skepticism. "When did Doherty last sleep with Suzie Pisano?"

"Well, let me see," said Clarkin, his eyes faraway, his brain percolating. "That was three days before Jimmy's death. He died on a Friday night, so that would make it Tuesday night, November 16, 1989. It was at a friend's house. I would know, since I was that friend. He had to be real careful, since going to the Pisano mansion for a carnal rendezvous had always been a bad idea, and now he was really being watched. They even had a pre-dawn breakfast of bacon and eggs with toast." Clarkin took a healthy sip of Guinness. "How's that for documentation, my priggish little filmmaker?" Then he added with a shrug, "Oh, there's even speculation that he saw Suzie on the night of his death." He smiled shrewdly. "But that's only speculation."

Even when Doherty slept with Suzie on the sly, Sean always knew what was happening. Sean needed to know since Frankie Pisano was a serious hothead, and, if the tryst was discovered, Sean would be the one to snap the baseball bat that Frankie tried to connect to Jimmy's skull.

From the time he was on the Columbia basketball team with Doherty, Sean seemed to understand the role he would play in the star's life. While Doherty was the smooth shooter who'd glide about the perimeter, Sean pushed every opponent out of the paint and, when some Harvard prick had the temerity to give Doherty a hard foul, Sean would render the foe so bruised and violated that his good friend would not be touched again.

The relationship between Clarkin and Doherty was forged as much by intellectual pursuits as it was by those athletic. It was Clarkin who had introduced Doherty at Columbia to the geochemist Dr. Wally Broecker, not the other way around. When Sean embraced Wally's exciting new theory of how an excess of carbon dioxide was causing the earth to heat, so did Doherty. And when Wally convinced Sean that the ocean circulated the earth's heat, then Doherty would also believe.

The professor and his star pupil quickly understood that in Doherty they had the perfect vehicle to convey their ideas to the larger public. Broecker told Sean that Doherty possessed that rarest of gifts: to communicate with strangely assuring emotion. And when Doherty's silky jumpshot led the usually hapless Columbia Lions to a Final Four, his reputation as a renaissance man of his age was established and the public was ready to listen to him; Doherty's four glorious years with the Knicks before his knee blew out only burnished that reputation.

However, in his conversation with Flanagan, Clarkin wasn't thinking about global warming, the term Broecker had popularized, or about how its future once rested in the soft, firm hands of Doherty. No, Clarkin was thinking about Doherty's preoccupation, an obsession which jeopardized so many bright and shiny prospects.

"Suzie Jansen complicated matters," said Clarkin. He brushed the rim of the Bushmills like he was grazing the edge of a memory. "Jimmy's twin brother Kevin, the more famous one of the family, told me on a night much like this one his theory on why Jimmy kept going back to Suzie." Flanagan had a pretty good idea of what Kevin might have told Clarkin, since anyone who had watched a nature program for the past forty years knew that every theory Kevin expressed explained human behavior as consistent with that of less evolved animals. In his full professorial mode, Clarkin lectured to Flanagan about philopatry: an animal's return to a specific area to breed. "Kevin said when it came to Suzie, Jimmy seemed to possess the geomagnetic imprinting and olfactory cues common in other species, like pacific salmon and sea turtles."

Flanagan shook his head. "But don't those creatures swim to where they were born?" he asked. Surprised at his rediscovered capacity for logic, Flanagan threw in, "I don't think he was shacking up with Suzie at the site of his birth."

"That's very good, Artie," said Clarkin, with the encouragement he normally delivered to a prized student in his chemistry class. "You must remember that Kevin and I were many whiskies in at the time of this discussion. I am telling you what Kevin said to me not for the reasoning of the comparison between the birds and the beasts and Suzie and Jimmy but for what Kevin told me at the end of the night. As he rambled on, Kevin moved from the sea to the sky and was talking about puffins."

"Oh jeez," said Flanagan.

"Exactly," said Clarkin. "He explained that to mate without having to deal with predators, puffins found their ways to the most treacherous places."

"But Jimmy faced a predator in Frankie," said Flanagan.

"Let me finish," Clarkin said. "Like the puffin, Jimmy had landed on the most inhospitable clifftop. He would return to Suzie's nest with his well-developed magnetic homing skills and his sensitivity to the intensity of the earth's field."

"Oh boy," said Flanagan. "Kevin seems like more of a nutjob in person than he does on TV."

"Still, I think there's something to this atavistic connection," said Clarkin, "although I admit, it's also a bit whacky."

Trying to get the big man on track, Flanagan ventured, "Did Suzie ever turn against Jimmy?"

Sean laughed heartily, then laughed again. "Oh, did she ever? Hell hath no fury."

"Did he cheat on her?"

"No, no," Sean shook his head for effect. "Not Jimmy. No, the problem was he fell in love with a cause and Suzie Jansen did not happen to be that cause."

Flanagan moved onto the Bushmills. "And that cause was Climate Change?"

Sean nodded. "It took a couple of months for Wally and me to convince Jimmy — you'd think the illustrious Dr. Broecker would've moved him quicker. But you know that Suzie can be awfully distracting with her geomagnetic pull."

Flanagan told Sean, "I have only heard Suzie talk about Doherty once. You know what she said?" Flanagan waited, tracking Sean's curiosity, watching the big man nod encouragingly. "That Jimmy Doherty was boring. Boring."

"Yeah?" Sean paused, then repeated, "Yeah?" Flanagan got the impression that Sean was preparing to defend his old friend, but then he took a different tack. "Boring? Well, he was boring into her until the day he died, so guess that's what she meant. The primal tug yanked in both directions."

Flanagan smiled. Now they were getting somewhere. Besides his hearing whispers many times over the years, others around the set had spoken of how Suzie had continued to see Doherty right through her engagement to Frankie Pisano, on into the marriage, even through the birth of Heather. "Man, that's crazy," Flanagan said, encouraging Sean to continue.

"Generally, Jimmy didn't kiss and tell, but on the night of Suzie's marriage to the asshole Pisano, he got shitfaced and recounted in detail to me everywhere they had, as Jimmy put it, consummated their non-marriage. They were in closets, on kitchen tables, against bookcases, on rugs, over park benches, across countertops, in bathtubs, on hills, over dales, through meadows, along streambeds, before obelisks, against sheetrock, enmeshed in plaster, even over a boombox."

"Ah, the 80s," said Flanagan, of a time he really didn't know. "So just to get this straight, even when they broke up, they continued to fool around for years later."

"Up until the day he died."

"You keep saying that, which makes me rather intrigued."

Right then some muscular young punk with a mustache and too much cologne intentionally bumped into Sean, knocking over his drink.

"Excuse me?" said Sean.

Pungent mustache man scowled. "You have a problem?"

"You spilled my Guinness."

"Yeah."

"An apology is in order."

"Yeah. Tough shit." Then moustache man shoved Sean.

"Well, that answers my question."

Sean walked outside and moustache man followed. They found an open spot in the alley behind the Pint O' Plenty. Just as moustache man faced off with Sean, three other young guys jumped the big man and moustache man started swinging. Sean fought the men, who were half his age, as well as he could. Slightly embarrassed to stand around watching the ambush, Flanagan joined in. He tackled moustache man, to get the main puncher out of the picture, and improve the odds. Grunting and breathing like an aging mastiff, Clarkin pushed one after another away, but the young guys kept charging. Flanagan clung onto moustache man desperately, knowing the punches would soon rain down on him.

Fortunately, the fight was over in a few minutes. The barback had run outside and threatened to call the police – the manager knew having Clarkin out of commission would be bad for business. As the four young men took off to some other establishment, Sean checked his wounds. He was significantly less damaged than Flanagan, who gained his first bloody nose in two decades and a big bump above his eyebrow.

Sean clapped a big paw on Flanagan, "Ah, you're a good man, Artie. Coming to my aid like that. I'll buy you a pint for that one."

As they drank, Sean was back in 1980s, suddenly abandoning his lowly Irish drawl for the heady scientific analyses those who frequent his chemistry lectures have long come to know. It was as if now that he'd proven himself once again in the hard-scrabble, rough and tumble world, he could climb atop the Ivory Tower. Clarkin told Flanagan that both he and Doherty had been around at the right place at the right time. First, they were mentored by Dr. Broecker, who had been pretty much ahead of everybody on the climate change issue. Yet while Broecker's papers captured the ominous possibilities with startling prescience, the Columbia professor liked neither to bask in the limelight nor to engage in political activism. Fortunately for the socially conscious Sean and his policy driven friend Doherty, Dr. James Hansen was just a few sidewalks away. Hansen headed up the NASA Goddard Institute for Space Studies, also conveniently situated on Columbia's campus. Sean and Jimmy followed Hansen down to the Capitol in 1986 and more centrally in 1988 when Hansen stripped away all niceties about just what type of future humanity was facing.

Clearly, Hansen was in Sean's head when he flexed his bruised knuckles and pronounced, "The heatwaves of the decade piled up evidence of the greenhouse effect for anyone who carefully studied atmospheric composition. With Broecker laying the groundwork and Hansen leading the charge, Jimmy found his voice, one that spoke with the inspiring eloquence of Winston Churchill under siege, of Martin Luther King under oppression."

Flanagan had gone through the newspapers of the time. More than a few columnists and political pundits were calling on the Dems to dump Dukakis as their presidential candidate and draft Doherty – a figure whose charisma the party hadn't witnessed since Jack Kennedy. "Do you think Doherty had a chance for the nomination?"

"No one can know for sure, but most of us were pretty certain he would have figured out how to forge the first cap and trade legislation in the Senate. And once he got that into place, man, Doherty could have changed the mindset. He might've kept us out of the shitty spot we're in right now." Sean no longer bothered with the Guinness. He ordered a double Bushmill on the rocks. Flanagan decided it'd be rude not to accept Sean's offer to "make it two."

"He was dead a week later though," Flanagan said, egging him on.

"Yeah, he wouldn't be the last one the oil guys managed to get," Clarkin said. "Across the globe, the deaths of more than a dozen environmental activists over the last thirty years have been tenuously linked to the American Henry Center. Doherty happened to be the biggest fish."

"Do you really think they did it?"

"Well, I don't think it was a normal accident, that's for sure. Jimmy was always a careful driver and he was fairly sober that night."

"Let's say it was intentional. Did it have to be the Henrys? Let's go back to his affair with Suzie Pisano. From what I hear, Frankie had gotten wind of it."

Sean picked up his whiskey, belched, thought better about taking a sip at that moment, and put back down the glass. "Well, if anyone would know about that, it'd be you."

"What do *you* think?" Flanagan asked.

"I've long thought it was the Henrys that got him, but if you had decent evidence that one of those two assholes killed him, I could see that."

They spoke for two more hours before Sean agreed to conduct an interview in front of the camera. After they left the Pint O'Plenty together, the two of them spent 20 minutes making a nook of Sean's apartment presentable enough for filming. He answered questions for another hour. If everybody was as willing as Sean, Flanagan would have enough footage for a documentary in a week. Before he left, Flanagan pressed his luck and asked if he could clap an eye at Jimmy Doherty's appointment books for the last year or two of his life. When

Clarkin looked like he didn't know what Flanagan was talking about, Flanagan chided. "C'mon, I know you got everything of Doherty's and will you look at this place? You certainly haven't thrown anything away."

"Maybe next time you come to the Pint O'Plenty."

"You're telling me I've got to get my ass kicked to get my hands on those appointment books?"

Clarkin laughed. "Don't you worry about the ass-kickings you get on my account. You be careful, Flanagan. All those years writing for the Pisanos you were like the proverbial piano player in the whorehouse – always around the action, but never getting any."

Flanagan shrugged. "I'd like to think I was composing the soundtrack."

"The bottom line," said Clarkin, "is you weren't getting any, and I'm advising you that you don't want any. Like Jimmy before you, you might find yourself perched on that inhospitable clifftop."

"I thought your doctorate was in chemistry, not psychology," said Flanagan.

"Believe me," said Clarkin, "you don't have to be fuckin' Sigmund Freud to figure you out."

Flanagan finally got to bed at 4:30 in the morning. Five hours later, he took a Lyft out to Long Island, finding his way along windy Wheatley Road to catch up with the aging supermodel Cheryl Wood. He had been surprised she was willing to meet with him to discuss the accident. She had been married for twenty-seven years to a handsome equity trader after five years of mourning the tragic death of her fiancé Jimmy Doherty.

Although her Old Westbury mansion exuded the scale, appointments, and mahogany of aristocracy, Cheryl answered her own door. Flanagan was impressed by the docile nature of her plastic surgery. He was so used to the aggressive scalpel work that was a hallmark of the Pisano brand. Indeed, one might even say that Cheryl was aging less ungracefully than most of her contemporaries.

As they sat together in the solarium sipping coffee, her demure elegance lasted through the discussion of Jimmy Doherty until Flanagan raised the name Suzie Pisano. Cheryl's countenance blanched and her mouth tightened uncomfortably. Afraid he might be tossed out, Flanagan quickly explained, "I am investigating whether Suzie Pisano might have had a role in Senator Doherty's accident."

Cheryl delicately placed her cup down onto her saucer, smoothed a pleat along her right thigh, and asked with world-weary exasperation, "My God, what took you so long?"

Flanagan smiled. "I'm slow at putting things together."

"You've been working for that witch all these years and it's taken you this long to figure it out?" Cheryl asked. "I can't say you inspire confidence."

"So you think she did it?"

"She was obsessed with Jimmy, and when he rejected her and picked me, she only became more dangerous and violent."

Cheryl looked quite composed. She'd be great on the camera. One more celebrity like her and he'd have no problem selling the documentary. Flanagan asked, "Would you mind if I filmed you?"

Cheryl hesitated. "I don't know …"

Flanagan put the coffee down and picked up the camera. "I tell you what? I will film and anything you don't like, I won't use." From his briefcase, he passed her a right of refusal form. He figured he was on pretty safe territory, since he would not ask her anything that would make her uncomfortable, like the rumor about Jimmy and Suzie still regularly fooling around even when Suzie was married and Jimmy was engaged to Cheryl. No, he simply wanted Cheryl to say she believed that Suzie was capable of murdering Jimmy, and if he was lucky, that she might suggest Suzie killed him.

Flanagan was lucky. He'd done well in the last twelve hours. Strange, he didn't believe he had any better understanding of Jimmy Doherty's death, but a nice story was coming together.

As he took an Uber back home in Astoria, he had to ask himself, had he really quit his job writing scripts for a reality TV show because it sure didn't seem like it?

CHAPTER 5
THE ROMANCING OF SUZIE

Flanagan had been reading through old clips of the Pisanos: a thousand tedious puff pieces about bell bottoms and dumbbells. Eventually, he stumbled across something meatier – a memoir written by the Pisanos' party acquaintance Stuart Cooper. Cooper had been fascinated with the Pisanos before they had achieved fame, and his account smacked of careful observation uncharacteristic in celebrity bios. Flanagan was happy to see Cooper was still alive, residing in Manhattan, and willing to meet with him. Before they joined up for a late lunch at Pastis, Flanagan thought it wise to at least read some of Cooper's book, *Love in the Age of Excess*.

While he would certainly have preferred fewer classical references and wished Cooper would have reined in his flamboyant writing style, Flanagan was particularly struck by the chapter when Suzie and Frankie first met. He read the chapter twice and hoped Cooper would be willing to record some excerpts for the camera.

From *Love in the Age of Excess*
by Stuart Cooper

Chapter 3: Their Lives Like Candles in the Wind

Suzie Jansen marked the distant throbbing of the disturbingly virile man who entered Candle Me with Care. Although an ardent acolyte of plashy diversions, she

found running the candle shop salubrious.
Her clientele invariably comprised of
hippy earth children groping for the
light. But today Frankie Pisano, clad in
his blue pinstripe suit and his pink
pastel shirt, descended from the planet
Eros. He had been coached in the mores of
fashion by the producers of a new show
called *Miami Vice*. They brazenly assured
him that once the series beamed across
the heartland, he'd be the cock of the
walk.

He also donned a new name. His old one
Puglisi was for the earthborn; his new
one, Pisano, could soar in the clouds. He
embraced the knowledge that he
commandeered his name Pisano from a
Tuscan city whose most well-designed
attraction was a crooked building. He
instinctively apprehended that Frankie
Pisano would scale nearer to the summit
of Olympus than Frankie Puglisi. Back
then, how could he ever fathom that for
many years after he passed from this
cruel, cold orb, his surname would be
screamed out by teenage girls and
muttered inwardly by lusty old men.
Frankie first caressed the word Pisano
when watching *The Godfather*, never
realizing he misunderstood the term *Pisan*
… never grasping from the scene that it
wasn't a last name. Yet, for all his
fallibilities, he correctly knew deep in
the crater of his bowels that Pisano was
the kind of name a beautiful woman would
take as her own.

His fellow nomadic traveler in this ever-turning world, Dave Gilmore told him about the woman in the candle shop. "Frankie, that girl is wicked. If my wife wasn't with me …" Frankie had never set his famished eyes on a candle shop before; such waxy establishments weren't stops on his circuit, which generally consisted of racetracks, big sporting events, and unconscionably long business lunches. The firm let him indulge in those lunches because his client acquisition rate from them was equal to great Thor's success with a hammer. That he had cut a luncheon short to make a special stop at Candle Me with Care signaled just how intrigued he was by Gilmore's description of this "wicked" girl.

To Frankie's nose, the shop delivered an odor that was alluringly compromised, as if angels had eructed. An embarrassment of luxurious smells competed and coalesced. Trying to play it cool, like wily Odysseus before Circe, he lifted up a bright red candle and drew it toward his nose. "Mmm. That smells like French Toast at the coffee shop," he announced, loud enough for everyone to hear, and by everyone that meant the only one, the only other panting lungs in the store – the dizzying and dazzling nymph behind the counter whom he had yet to properly inspect. By this first furlong of life's journey, Frankie had become so adept at ogling women that he managed to watch her floridly flounce to him in slow

motion. Like a puppy trapped in panty
hose, her red floral jumpsuit was
impressively snug. She emerged as a
diurnal beacon of more … fending off the
lunar tides of less. The shoulder pads
framed her raven locks, blown and teased,
projecting an aura of nascent power not
regularly emanating from candle store
clerks.

"It's the cinnamon," she said, nodding
to the candle. "It tends to arouse the
senses."

Frankie smiled, surprised that after
so many conquests he was as dumbstruck as
Echo gazing upon Narcissus. "That it
does," he said. Not knowing what to do
with his rakish hands - he'd be
unpardonably branded as sheepish if he
stuck them in his pockets - he picked up
a dark green candle and inhaled like
Zephyrus. "Mmm. Smells like a forest."

"The pine tends to bring the outside
in," Suzie, the lovely dove, cooed. She
leaned a bit into him, not half the length
of Odin's beard … just enough to make
Frankie want to grab her. Then her vocal
chords fluttered again. "It's perfectly
natural that you like it. Most strong men
do."

"Oh, I really do like it," Frankie
spouted with the conviction of Achilles
ringing the walls of Troy.

Suzie tracked him through the aisles
of the store, giving his comments untamed
affirmation, rendering him swelled like
Neptune's trident. Late in his noble

quest, he arrived at a beer mug with a wick on the top of it. Frankie could recognize that the golden contents were a good approximation of a lager. A precocious Icarus dabbing the wax of Daedalus' wings, Frankie stuck his pinky in the beer to make sure it was fake. Frankie constantly verified that earthly constructions were counterfeit. He gained a fingernail full of wax for his strenuous exertions.

The fiberglass in the drop ceiling convulsed. Suzie waggled her finger to admonish Frankie's naughtiness. "No, no, no. Our candles don't itch, so please don't scratch." A sire much learned in the arts of plagiarism, Frankie was certain she had stolen that clever reproach, which made her as alluring as Aphrodite in a fishnet nighty.

For Suzie's part, a man-sighting in the store this time of year was rarer than spotting Bacchus at an AA meeting. The hirsute, masculine sex usually only appeared during the week before Christmas when, desperate to find a gift for an inamorata, they would buy like drunken Argonauts, plundering anything and everything left on the shelves. Suzie opined that a little flirting never hurt the size of a sale. That approach was validated by Frankie bringing candles up to the counter, not only the pine and cinnamon, but also vanilla, potpourri, and blueberry. Frankie studied the elaborate wax sculptures of castles and horse heads and banana splits. A Hercules at his labors, he dropped a large waterfall on the counter. Eventually, Frankie eyed up the most expensive item in the store, examining it as if it were a caryatid at the Acropolis. "Now, that's something," he said. He pointed to a magnificently wretched sculpture of a wizard.

"Indeed, it is," answered Suzie, who wasn't lying.

Blessed with a luxurious beard, the hoary wax figure sported a pointy hat dotted with half-moons and stars above his long, stringy hair. On his shoulder stood a spooky owl, and by his gnarled fingers rested a skull atop an ancient tome. At the center of this tableau was a glowing orb ("That's where the candle lights, silly"). It was the grotesque uncle of those velvet paintings of the era, the ones featuring heavy metal guitarists riding lachrymose griffins. This wax relic was not an object a participating member of society would covet, unworthy of even Pluto's saturnine lair. The only possible shelf for such a creepy sculpture belonged in the dorm room of the lugubrious co-ed who never seemed to run out of lotus flowers.

Frankie triumphantly hoisted up this Wizard of Vulcan and placed it with all of his cousinly spoils on the counter. "O.K., I guess you can ring me up." Frankie flashed a roll of hundreds. The charge was $97.95 - a price in jellie-

step with the early '80s. With the care of Penelope weaving Laertes' shroud, Suzie wrapped up each candle in brown paper. Introducing himself, Frankie seized her name much the way Jason had seized the Golden Fleece. He repeated the name back to her. "Suzie, here's my card. Do you like sports?"

"Yes, I do," said Suzie. Like Pasiphae before a white bull, she tended to say yes to most questions.

Frankie puffed gallantly. "Well, I'm a sports agent and I have access to a lot of big events. I could take you to one, if you'd like? There's a major tour golf outing at Shinnecock this weekend. It's one of the most beautiful courses in the world. I could take you, if you'd like?"

In the distance a box fan whirred ceraceous bouquets. Suzie offered the crestfallen look of someone who became terribly disappointed when she had to disappoint someone else. "That sounds so nice. I am so sorry. I'm busy this weekend, but I have your card. Maybe some other time."

"Well, that wasn't a no," thought Frankie. Maybe, he mused, he should have waited until he gave her the gift. Sensing it was the right time to go, Frankie lifted the massive wax wizard sculpture and bestowed it unto Suzie. "By the way, this is for you."

He strode toward the door as if to indicate that such an impressive gift was no big deal, a mere lightning bug in a vast cloud of thunderbolts. "Oh my God," said Suzie. "Thank you so much!"

As the door shut behind him, she frowned. Why would he ever think she would want such an abomination? She never understood why anyone would buy a clerk gifts from the store where she worked. It would be akin to donating a Trojan horse to a lumber yard. Still, Frankie's wallet tapped a yearnful dirge to Suzie much in the style of Orpheus's song to Eurydice. Frankie might not have been lying about being a big sports agent. Yes, aping that trickster Sisyphus, Frankie may well have had a roll of ones behind those first couple of Franklins he was flashing. But she knew what clothes cost, and that blue pinstripe suit alone was a few hundred drachmas. Those tan leather Armanis were not from the bargain rack either.

During his whole time in the store, she had managed, like Psyche before Eros, to be in Frankie's presence without ever really seeing him. Now with him gone, she decided he was a fairly handsome man, not an Adonis, but a Theseus … he could have been a few inches taller. She already possessed her Olympian, a former Knick and a Rhodes Scholar, not a threshold mortals could pass. Frankie was a tad swarthy - she guessed he had the chest hair of a minotaur - yet he possessed a feral quality that Jimmy lacked. In a simple stroll around a candle store, Frankie conveyed moral limitations that were vaguely exciting to Suzie. He had made clear to her that no rule existed he wouldn't break to be with her. And those shoes clearly were a fortune.

Frankie returned the following week, this time wearing a powder-blue monochromatic linen suit with a black t-shirt. A man made for garish effulgence, he confidently pulled off this unusual outfit. He bought a single cinnamon candle ("It will make my penthouse smell like breakfast is cooking all day long") and handed Suzie a jewelry box. Fecundity oozing from his pores, he gave her another card and mentioned that he had courtside seats to the US Open in Flushing Meadows if she were available. As he headed toward the door, Suzie spoke in a whisper, since she did not want to betray excitement, "Don't you want to watch me open it?"

"I think people should be alone with their gifts," Frankie said.

When he left, she decided it was a good thing he did. She didn't know what to make of the SeidenGang ring. The gold was greenish and the thick, rough front looked like something that a concubine from ancient Rome might wear. Clearly, Frankie's taste tended toward the philistine. Yet the ring was a big hunk of gold and its brutish, squarish face was elegantly rounded and encased by delicate diamonds. Still, she decided she would not join him courtside to watch John McEnroe throw temper tantrums.

Frankie, like Hercules prepared for another feat, was back yet again the following week. Now he wore a spotless white linen suit with a powder-blue t-shirt. Maybe it was the outfit, but Frankie seemed to become more attractive with each visit. He bought a vanilla candle this time ("I think the penthouse needs to waft of dessert all day and all night. We all deserve dessert, don't we?"), and gave Suzie a jewelry box slightly bigger than the previous one. Then he handed her a ticket to the finals of the U.S. Open. "It's McEnroe versus Lendl. That's like watching fire battle ice: two gods on the court of combat. I'd really like you to come with me. If you decide not to come, you don't have to return the ticket to me. I will just stare longingly at your empty seat."

Suzie thought about calling to Frankie as he walked out the door, but she knew it would be better to keep her own counsel. Given the first two gifts, she thought she was well prepared to open the box. This time a huge chunk of gold had been expertly crafted into an alligator bracelet, the tail whipping around ovally back toward the head, every part of the outer flesh of the reptile obsessively designed, startlingly detailed scales, its four clawed feet gently perched on the front of the wrist. She read the tag, Barry Kieselsten-Cord. Whatever she thought of the two pieces of jewelry Frankie had given her, they were much more than a few months of earnings at Candle Me with Care.

Staring at the bracelet which she had
to admit looked strangely beautiful on
her wrist, she decided it was time she
watch John McEnroe throw that temper
tantrum.

As he put down *Love in the Age of Excess*, Flanagan recalled a little nugget he had stumbled upon years ago in a book – in the pre-Pisano time when he used to read regularly. The word *sincere* meant *without wax*. Back in the day, sculptors would hide their imperfections with wax. He liked the idea that Frankie and Suzie's relationship was founded on wax almost as much as he liked the idea that this *without wax* origin of the word *sincere* might be false, since what could be better than being *insincere* about the word *sincere*. He braced himself for such unstable wordplay in his meeting with Stuart Cooper, who beyond the Pisano biography had a long-run as a gossip columnist and a movie critic.

When he sat down with Cooper at Pastis, Flanagan ordered the duck and a Kronenborg. He always ordered the duck. Cooper selected a salad off the specials board and a *rosé*. Flanagan felt underdressed especially compared to the dandy Cooper, who managed to pull off a bow tie and a pocket square without seeming stiff.

"I really like your chapter in the candle shop," said Flanagan. "Right from the beginning, the Pisanos seemed to have a relationship that was, how shall I say it, transactional."

"Well, if you liked that, you'll really like the labyrinthine twists and turns in my new book. Revelations of epic proportions." Cooper pointed to Flanagan's camera. "I think it might be a good idea to start filming."

Flanagan didn't have to be told twice, so he pulled out his tiny, portable video camera, setting it to its highest resolution and supporting it against a water glass. He couldn't exactly prop up a tripod in the middle of the Pastis café tables.

Once Flanagan indicated he started recording, Cooper didn't even wait for a question. "What you have to understand is the timing of Dirk Wall's accident is very disturbing ... as suspicious as snakes in the crib of the infant Hercules. The marital troubles recounted in the tabloids are just the beginning. Behind the scenes, the situation is much worse. The family is as cursed as the house of Agamemnon, or better yet, the Kennedys. Alas, at the heart of it is not emotion, loyalty, or love, but fame and money, and, when those two core values are at stake, these family members respond in extraordinary ways."

"What do you mean by extraordinary?"

Cooper smiled and sipped his water. "What I am saying by extraordinary is that there is nothing, and I mean nothing, certain family members wouldn't do to get what they wanted. They possess the ruthlessness of Ares."

Flanagan did his best not to roll his eyes. "Give me an idea of what they would do."

"They would, they would," Cooper suddenly struggled to breathe and looked at his water glass. "Quick," he said to Flanagan. "I've been poisoned. Take me out to my car."

Flanagan pulled out his phone. "I'll call an ambulance."

Cooper clutched his throat and said through gritted teeth and tightened larynx, "No time for that. I feared this would happen and I'm pretty sure I know what poison they used. I keep an antidote in the car. Please take me there."

Flanagan threw three twenties on the table and reached to turn off the camera.

"No, the world should see this," said Cooper, growing ghastly pale. "Hold me with one arm and record me with the other."

Once outside, Cooper pointed to a lime green Jaguar parked illegally on Gansevoort. The poisoned man was lucky he didn't get a ticket. The door was unlocked. The poisoned man was also lucky his fancy wheels didn't get taken.

"Where's the antidote?" Flanagan asked.

"The glove compartment." His breathing became more labored. "Take me to the passenger's side." Cooper collapsed in the seat. "Sit on the driver's side." As he reached in the glove compartment for a labelless bottle, Cooper pointed to the camera and told Flanagan as he struggled for breath: "I think you better shut that camera off, since there are certain people who shouldn't see what comes next."

Flanagan clicked off the camera as Cooper eyed him with great discomfort and focus. Cooper took a couple of deep breaths. "I sure hope you got all that." He no longer appeared to be in a slow state of painful suffocation.

Puzzled, Flanagan asked, "Are you feeling better?"

Cooper laughed. "Of course I'm feeling better. Can I get a copy of that video? I want to release it on my website. It should also do wonders for your documentary."

Flanagan cursed to himself, anger building. "Was there any part of what I just witnessed that wasn't fake?"

"Of course, the most important part was real. The turbulence in the family, the major motives for Pisano women to push patriarch Dirk Wall out of the picture, and the opportunities for foul play with Dirk's car are all true."

"But the poison bit was complete theater, right?" asked Flanagan. "You never even felt remotely ill at the restaurant."

"No, I did not," Cooper confirmed.

"I'm sure Pastis's management is thrilled with that performance," said Flanagan.

"I specifically made reservations in the lull between lunch and dinner," said Cooper. "Plus, we got out of there before I made too much of a scene."

"I still don't understand, faking or not, why you didn't let me call an ambulance. The recording would have been much more dramatic if the EMTs came in and took you out on a stretcher."

"Alas, dear fellow, they would've figured out I was faking," said Cooper. "And what's worse, is once the police got their hands on me, I would've been in a peck of trouble. Do you have any idea how rare poisoning is? My precious bones could have been dead on the tablecloth and they still wouldn't have believed that I was poisoned. Poisoning only happens in mystery paperbacks."

"Then why did you fake a poisoning when no one would believe you?" asked Flanagan.

"I didn't say no one," said Cooper. "I said the police. Millions will believe I was poisoned – thanks to your recording – because most people love a good poisoning, and they particularly love to consume it like lobster thermador when it involves America's favorite families, the Pisanos and the Walls."

"I hate to break this to you," said Flanagan. "I don't think I'm going to give you the recording. I think it will ruin my reputation."

"Honey, you've been the lead writer for the past decade for *Peepin' on the Pisanos*," Cooper offered an affected chuckle, "and you're worried about ruining your reputation." It occurred to Cooper that this approach might not be the best way to procure the recording from Flanagan. "Can you drive me back to my apartment? I want to show you something."

"You trust me driving your Jaguar?"

"I don't think I have much of a choice, now do I darling?" asked Cooper. "How would it look if I was seen driving my Jaguar when I'm supposed to be rapidly approaching my maker from the mysterious poison?"

Cooper lived only about fifteen blocks away in Tribeca, right on Hudson. For anyone who might have been watching, Flanagan gingerly led Cooper into the building and onto the elevator. Only back in his apartment did a spring return to Cooper's step.

"Give me a minute," he said, slipping into his bedroom and shutting the door. He returned with a blue folder and removed six sheets from it. One was a map with spots plotted all over the city and Long Island. The five pages were running, time-and-date-stamped logs of locations.

"What is this?"

"A detailed description of everywhere Dirk Wall traveled in the past month." Flanagan rubbed his chin. "Don't you see? Dirk's movements were being tracked. That certainly makes it much easier to cause an accident."

"I don't get it," said Flanagan. "Where did you acquire this information?"

"Deep inside the Pisano-Wall family computer network." While Flanagan looked confused, Cooper seemed a bit flabbergasted. "How do you think I was able to write an unauthorized biography of these sneaky bastards if I didn't get someone to hack their systems?"

"Can I get a copy of that printout?"

"Sure," said Cooper, smiling, "once I get a copy of the restaurant recording. I'd advise you to remember that if you want to swim along the shores of Pisano Island you must be as deceptive as the wily Odysseus."

Now knowing where he stood, Flanagan got up and headed to the door. "I'm sure we'll talk to each other soon," he said.

As with everything else lately, Flanagan wasn't sure if he was being truthful. No matter, he was more honest than Cooper, given today's shenanigans. Could he trust the GPS printout any more than Cooper's breathless asphyxiation? When he embraced the idea of this documentary, Flanagan was hoping he would finally wash away some of the lies and deceptions he'd been living all of these years. Now, he was not so certain. To get to any truth, he'd have to sift through more lies than ever. He had learned at least one thing in his years on the set of *Peepin' on the Pisanos*: put a camera in front of people and the lies grew exponentially. For this documentary, he knew he would get a story. Hell, he would get many stories. The question hovered over him, like some poison just real enough not to be perceived, was whether he'd ever approach the truth.

CHAPTER 6
THE RUNNING OF THE CHICKENS

Kartik summoned Flanagan to his austere office, and then the two traveled back through an impressive web of studios. Each of the large soundproof rooms featured costumed actors and little else besides a green screen. Computer-generated imagery would later build elaborate worlds behind the actors' exclamations and gesticulations.

When they arrived at Studio 7A, Kartik's top assistant Mehnuma and his burly nephew Arnav stood in front of a green screen. Mehnuma wore a Suzie Pisano wig and Arnav sported a Frankie Pisano mustache.

"When we do this for the reenactment, we will hire beautiful actors to play the Pisanos," said Kartik. "Not that Mehnuma and my nephew are not spectacular in their own right."

"Does that mean you're going to recreate the scene at Candle Me with Care?" asked Flanagan.

"Yes, but we are going to spice it up, so that the audience will be riveted," said Kartik.

"I thought the scene the way I scripted it was revealing about their characters and the future of their relationship."

"But it breaks three key rules: it doesn't advance the story, since we are no closer to knowing how Senator Doherty was killed; it doesn't have sex; it doesn't have violence."

"You don't give the audience enough credit," said Flanagan.

"And you suddenly are giving them too much," said Kartik. "It's like you've forgotten how you've made your money."

Although he knew he wouldn't like the answer, Flanagan could not avoid asking, "So how do you plan to spice up the scene?"

"Well, Artie, that's why I have my two younger friends here to block out the movements," said Kartik. From a big cardboard box, he lifted a life-size bust of a wax wizard, one just as hideous as Cooper described, and handed it to Mehnuma. "For this first part, Suzie will lift the wizard and the sleeve of her blouse will drop, exposing her lovely shoulder. Frankie will ask to see more, and Suzie will respond. O.K. Mehnuma, go ahead."

Mehnuma smashed the wizard down on Arnav's big skull, the wax cracking, breaking right along the beard. Stumbling and groaning, Arnav rushed out of the scene.

"The subsequent interactions will feature increasingly forward requests from Frankie. Suzie will counter with slaps in the face and kicks to the groin."

"So let me get this straight," said Flanagan, "you want to take my script drawn from Cooper's trashy account and make it trashier."

"I wouldn't say trashier," Kartik qualified, "just streamlined to fit our documentary."

"But that's not what happened," said Flanagan.

"If Suzie looks good in the reenactment, she won't mind. I just wanted to let you know so you can better tailor your script to the overall product."

"Look Kartik," said Flanagan, "I am doing this documentary because I wanted for once not to create something cheesy and second rate."

"So, you'll have to keep me honest," said Kartik. "Speaking of honest, that big man Clarkin overstated his claims about oil lobbies assassinating environmentalists."

"The point is the American Henry Center does appear to have a hand in the killing of Doherty."

"But they didn't kill anyone else," said Kartik. "Mehnuma checked and she doesn't miss anything."

"That's what makes the story extraordinary," said Flanagan. "That the Henry Center would go that far and that one of the Pisanos might have been involved in the murder is what will make the documentary have so many implications that still haunt us today."

Kartik shook his head. "Even with reenactments, we can't expect the audience to stay tuned with so little violence."

Flanagan laughed. "We can't just start knocking off people to make the documentary work."

"Mehnuma's going to weave a rainforest angle into the storyline," said Kartik. He glared at Flanagan. "Don't frown at me. You want all this global warming nonsense in the documentary? We're going to need some scenes with Amazon environmental activists."

"In God's name, why?" asked Flanagan.

"Because those activists tend to get assassinated," said Kartik. "They will make for great scenes."

"You have to depict those scenes accurately," said Flanagan with uncharacteristic firmness. "Otherwise, you cast everything else we present in a bad light."

Mehnuma took off her wig and moved away from the green screen. "I will be the one doing it," she said. "Everything I do is accurate." She spoke with a conviction that Flanagan admired.

"We will reenact great stuff," said Kartik. "This guy Chico Mendes who fought like a madman to preserve the Amazon had two gunmen following him around for months until they just vanished. A week later, Mendes walked out his back door and was blown to bits by a 20-gage shotgun. Even better, another Brazilian activist Wilson Pinheiro was shot right through the window while he was watching TV – a crime movie. How cool will it be to reenact him being shot as he is watching someone get shot on TV? That'll keep people awake while you have some egghead talk about rising carbon emissions."

As Flanagan tried to absorb Kartik's suggestions, he couldn't help but notice that hundreds of chickens were herded into the studio across from them. Arnav walked out and entered the poultry-laden room. He pointed to the director and the camerawomen, surveying the chicken herd in front of an enormous green screen. When the director gave a thumb's up, Arnav smirked and then charged toward the chickens, a shadowless menace. The panicked birds clucked frantically and bumped into each other, seeking shelter in that glowing dayglo wall.

"What the hell?" asked Flanagan.

"Just stippling in a scene for *CaterpillarMan*," said Kartik, offhandedly.

The trade publications promised that *CaterpillarMan* would be the next classic superhero film. Since he knew he could not inquire about the hush-hush nature of the plot – and how, pray tell, it involved this fowl mob – Flanagan asked what he thought was the next best question: "Couldn't you have used CGI chickens?"

"What kind of operation do you think I'm running here?" asked Kartik. "We've got class."

Though Flanagan could have been depressed by this meeting with Kartik, he was strangely heartened. Yes, Kartik was committed to making this documentary as trashy as necessary to get enough eyes glued to the screen. But Flanagan could tell that Kartik decided to go to such extremes because he realized some heady, meaningful material percolated below the surface. Hell, the man would gather hundreds of real chickens to make a scene ring true.

Flanagan understood he only had to worry so much about making his storyline appealing. He could unearth what was important and let Kartik worry about the rest.

For his part, Kartik was not worrying at all. He would simply replace Flanagan if the scriptwriter's increased capacity for ethics reached unsustainable proportions.

CHAPTER 7
THE BIFURCATION OF HEATHER

Flanagan had sold his car and had moved into a basement apartment, so he could stretch the respectable nest egg he'd accumulated over his many years scripting *Peepin' on the Pisanos*. Besides his daughter Michelle and his sometimes girlfriend Deja, he didn't expect visitors. He certainly didn't expect the woman who four times was named by *People* magazine as "The Sexiest Woman Alive." Yet when he opened the beaten-up cedar door, Heather Pisano smiled and bent toward him for a hug.

"How are you?" she asked. Heather clapped twice. Flanagan noticed this quirk on the set of *Peepin' on the Pisanos*. While she would never clap on camera, Heather would constantly do so between takes. Here, the double clap could be interpreted as a request – as in "chop-chop, get me something, boy" – or as an act of self-approval.

Too discomfited to venture an interpretation, Flanagan instead wondered how she managed to find his apartment. Yes, upon his departure from the set, he left a forwarding address. But even if Heather got her hands on it, she would still have to know that once on the property she needed to walk to the side gate, pull the string latch from behind, meander down the sidewalk, skirt around the fig tree and the broken statue of Aphrodite, and then find the door in the alcove that led to the basement steps. And yes, while her arrival was a mystery worth exploring, what really mattered was the reason for her appearance.

Clearly, Heather's stylist had been hard at work this evening. In his years hanging around the set, Heather had never fully given her eyes to Flanagan the way she did now. No, he did not believe she was coming on to him. She was simply making sure he would be receptive to anything she asked. He had one bottle of dry riesling in the refrigerator that he thought worthy of serving her and found two blessedly clean wine glasses. His multi-purpose living room/kitchen/dining room had looked worse, even if the sturdy linoleum floor and the functional formica tops stubbornly refused to dazzle guests. Overall, the presentation was as happy as his sorry situation could project.

Fitting for her foray into the mean backyards of Astoria, Heather wore ripped Lindsay jeans. Naturally, the tightness emphasized her substantive hindquarters, a global force that had received more written contemplations and encomiums this past decade than Shakespeare's plays. As always, her hippy backside teetered on the edge of what most with peripheral vision might describe as excessive.

Her tight blouse was not out of the ordinary except for a dazzlingly airbrushed image of Heather Pisano imprinted on it. Wherever Flanagan stared, he felt he was violating the rules of decorum. He was unhappy with the realization that he was more attracted to what was on the shirt than what was behind it. He imagined the day when Heather would wear a shirt that was a picture of her wearing the shirt. To talk to the Pisano women was to peer more deeply into the voyeuristic vortex than should be permitted by law. Drawing near to him, Heather discomposed Flanagan's thoughts.

As he passed her the riesling, Flanagan asked, "So to what do I have the honor of your company?" He would have preferred smoother phrasing.

Heather took a minute to figure out what he was asking. "Oh, I had a couple of questions about the show."

"Well," said Flanagan, "I'm out of the game, but I can try my best to help you anyway I can." He wondered if she was going to ask him to return for the upcoming episodes.

"I wanted your thoughts on what you think we should be doing this season."

"You could go a lot of ways," said Flanagan at first noncommittal. Heather studied him as if daring him to demonstrate worthiness. "You can't keep going to the wedding well. The novelty has worn off. None of you sisters can play the princess anymore with all those divorces under your belts." Heather smiled in tacit acknowledgment. Now, Flanagan was starting to warm up. "Still, you're going to need suspense and conflict, but the stakes have to be high. The hook-ups have to mean something. It would generate drama if two of you could be interested in the same guy."

"You mean like me and Tiffany," said Heather. "That would work out great, especially if he preferred Tiffany." Heather had an intriguing thought here. She had always been considered by the masses to be the most beautiful and desirable of all the sisters – at least until the youngest, the now 19-year-old Nora Wall, blossomed. Tiffany's new look, with the dramatic and extensive plastic surgery she'd had in the past year, could make the twist additionally spicy, by allowing her to vault past Heather in the esteem of this boyfriend. Indeed, given her comprehensive physical overhaul, it was almost as if Tiffany were no longer Heather's sister but a beautiful alien from another planet. Tiffany could well win out simply because she had transformed herself into the newest model on the scene.

Flanagan was struck by Heather's acumen, but more importantly by her sense of self-possession: she was comfortable with losing this battle to her sister. "That would really work," he said. "Make sure whoever you cast for the part is devilishly handsome."

"Cast? I thought I'd just start dating someone and see if Tiffany also likes him."

Flanagan frowned. "No, no, no," he rolled his eyes. "That won't work. This guy will need an entire series of screen tests. He better pop on camera. And he needs to be a little strange. It will make his embracing of Tiffany both surprising and inevitable."

"And when I find out that he prefers Tiffany, do I cry or throw a fit? Or do I attack the boyfriend? Or do I attack Tiffany?"

"Yes, yes, yes and definitely yes," Flanagan nodded. "You should get mileage out of this one, since it will dominate the season and it's a really big deal. When have your sisters ever stolen the limelight from you?"

Heather took a sip of her riesling and smiled. Such a scenario was unthinkable.

Suddenly disturbed by this display of smugness, Flanagan hit Heather in her weak spot. "I have another idea. How about Nora steals this young stud from you?"

Heather frowned. "I don't think that will work."

Nora's burgeoning sexuality and consequently her burgeoning success as an entrepreneur eclipsed Heather's over the past year. The rise was meteoric. Even at 16, Nora had been augmenting both her figure and her Twitter feed. At 18, once it became fully unstatutory to follow and to ogle, her Instagram account exploded and her long awaited Now Legal line of smells, pumps, and thongs sold as if leering was just legislated as a tax write-off. Nora really did possess the bloom of youth, even if those blossoms had been pared, pruned, and fertilized with ruthless zeal by the tree surgeon. Heather remained beautiful, but while her figure endured as a wonder to examine (how could she have so much shapely flesh and so few ribs?), the observers who couldn't stop observing had given her a decade and a half of their lives. They were not willing to allot the next decade to her, knowing that Nora would vie for their attention. As a TV personality, Heather possessed a blandness that comforted her enormous audience. That blandness gave the impression that she was open to many possibilities, so accepting of others that a fantasist might even read compassion in her expressions. But as impossible as it seemed, Nora came off even blander than Heather. Oh, to be young and mild.

Flanagan noticed the upshot. In the past, Heather had always been shrewd about building allure and image, even if that meant some timely forays into sex tapes and bombshell midnight drops of nudity for her legion of fans. Now a measure of desperation crept into her calculations: Heather's wardrobe malfunctions grew bigger and her bikinis grew smaller. As he thought through these tectonic changes in the Pisano/Wall family dynamic, Flanagan felt shame rattling about his bones. That Nora comment was unworthy and over the past couple of months, with the help of his sometimes girlfriend Deja, he had come to understand that Heather had much more on the ball than she was willing to reveal. He *knew* that she *knew* each year would be slightly less kind to her. As he prepared an apology and what he hoped to be a heart-to-heart talk, Heather – as she was wont to do – took control of the interaction.

Tapping her heels on the linoleum floor, she rose and crossed Flanagan's sight lines from numerous angles. As she bent over to pick up a copy of the *NY Times* from the floor in the snug room corner that might be charitably described as the den, her backside faced Flanagan, her movements choreographed to those of a model shoot. Boy oh boy, thought Flanagan, an awful lot was going on there. She continued to play her role, now examining the paper like the *Times* was a relic of another age: it might as well have been a phonograph or a rotary phone. Outside of the context of reality TV, none of Heather's cavorting aligned with the patterns of everyday behavior.

Flanagan struggled to reconcile these gyrations with Deja's detailed description of another side of Heather Pisano. Deja steadfastly told him that Heather was actually quite scholarly and dedicated to ecological causes, that her voluptuous cluelessness was merely a requirement for her brand. Smart he could believe; scholarly required Deja to deliver proof. Typical Deja, she provided proof. Then Deja expressed her disappointment in his lack of trust in her and left his life for three weeks.

In Flanagan's defense, Heather's being a closet environmentalist strained credulity, especially given her tendency to discard valuable cloths and furniture like they were flotsam and jetsam. Indeed, Heather's behind-the-scenes involvement with the political efforts on climate change might have been interpreted as another poser grabbing onto a *cause célèbre*. Yet Deja provided the reports to Flanagan that Heather had written with NASA engineer Jim Hansen, reports of details and acumen delineating that her Columbia degree was not mere window-dressing. As Deja said, "Look at that family. She's the only one to go to college. That says something about her."

In retrospect, Flanagan realized he might have provoked a longer period of exile due to his juvenile suggestion that Deja had a crush on Heather. Now the wrong woman occupied his attention.

He let Heather and the *Times* stop all of that gyrating and sit back down before he said to her, "Now that I'm out of the reality TV business, can you tell me just what your involvement is with the Earth Institute?"

A bit surprised by the turn in conversation, Heather asked for more riesling. "What do you mean?"

"I realize that you must have your reasons for keeping it quiet, but I know you've spent more time than you'd care to admit at the Earth Institute. In fact, you've been hanging around Columbia for years. Rumor has it that you even have a Master's in Climate and Society from there, although given your schedule, I don't know how." Deja had been at the Earth Institute for a dozen years and she said that Heather had been around for most of them. Heather had even donated money to numerous climate restoration programs. It was uncharacteristic of a Pisano, particularly Heather, not to publicize everything she did, especially contributions that would win over a new demographic of fans, which would translate into a new demographic of consumers.

Heather put her finger to her lips. "This has to be our little secret." Her eyes hardened. For a moment, she exuded the ruthlessness of her mother Suzie, intimating if the secret came out, she would ruin Flanagan.

"But why? Your fans would be proud of the good work you're doing."

"Our focus groups have made clear these activities do not suit our brand."

After holding his tongue for too many years, Flanagan would speak his mind. She was the one who came to his hovel after all. "Let me get this straight, your fans can deal with sex tapes, endless infidelities, unconscionable surgeries, filet mignon feasts for terriers, and exotic enema therapies. And they're going to draw the line at climate change?"

Heather wrinkled her nose. "It doesn't exactly fit our lifestyle. Our family releases more carbon than Rhode Island. Let's just say my efforts at the Earth Institute balance that out. But if the public ever gets wind of this, I'll be seen as a hypocrite."

"But aren't you?" Flanagan thought he'd gone too far.

Still, she answered. "I can afford to be one in this room, but not on *Peepin' on the Pisanos.*"

Flanagan wasn't done with her. In rapid fire, he spit out a season-long plot scenario where Heather keeps running off mysteriously in most episodes until the big reveal in the season finale when she emerges as this major climate change activist. "A march could be set up so that you're arrested in front of some oil corporate offices on the very day of the finale."

For a moment, Flanagan thought she was considering her idea. But then she put down her glass, picked up her bag, and told him, "I think I'll stick with Tiffany stealing my boyfriend."

Flanagan shrugged his shoulders and said, "Before you go, could I just ask you a couple of questions in front of the camera?"

Heather sighed, pretending to be put out, and said, "I guess so, but don't bother asking the questions, since I think I know what they'll be." When Flanagan looked like he might interrupt, she added, "Remember, I'm the one with the degrees from Columbia."

"The degrees I can't talk about."

"Exactly. And I know you won't." By now, this conversation being the longest she had ever had with Flanagan, Heather knew she could read him through and through. No, he didn't want what other men wanted from her (still she was amazed how more of them wanted to forge a business relationship with her than a romantic one), but his sad remnants of ethical idealism would be enough to keep her secrets safe.

Flanagan set up the camera. "So we're rolling."

"In our family, no death is simply a death," she began. "Intrigue enshrouds us. There is so much more betrayal in our family than you know. Our greatest defense is that everyone thinks we're all too shallow to have deeper motivations. There are reasons to dig. But you first have to find your way behind the curves." Heather waved for him to shut off the camera. After Flanagan obliged, she began clapping, which she did after every shoot. As he had with the other crew members on the set, Flanagan now joined in the applause. Satisfied with the adulation, from herself and from her cameraman, Heather asked, "How's that?"

"Wonderful," said Flanagan. What else could he say? "Did you mean any of it?"

Heather laughed. "You think I really came to ask for your advice about next season? I knew what was going down for that season two years ago. Suzie knew it three years ago." From the way he peered into the lifeless camera in the need to do something, she knew she wounded him. Heather began clapping again, clearly happy with this exchange, though regretful Flanagan was not still recording. Heather knew her former scriptwriter deserved the shade. Still the visit was strangely comforting. "This was fun," she said. "I may stop by again."

CHAPTER 8
THE RUNNING OF THE OLD BACKDOOR PLAY

Flanagan was in luck. Red Schultz, the assistant coach of Jimmy Doherty's old Knick basketball team and confidant during his political years, was still alive and willing to speak. Even better, he was just two hours away in Cutchogue. The one unknown was whether Red still had his wits.

Flanagan picked up a rental car and drove out to the wine country of Long Island's North Fork. He found the smallest house in town for the man famous for being the smallest man on the Knick bench. Back then, Red was 5'7"; now at 90, he of hunched back and shrunken spine, 5'4" would be generous. To say that he didn't smell would be another act of charity.

Thankfully, Red ushered Flanagan right through his dark and dingy home to the backyard, where the unusual September heat was tempered by the breezes off of Peconic Bay. Sitting at an old wooden table, Flanagan asked him about Jimmy Doherty. Red first would only talk about Jimmy's basketball career. "He could shoot, he could shoot. We made plays to let him shoot. We'd set a pick and two screens. He could shoot. From the corner, always from the corner." Red struggled to get out the next words. "He could shoot."

Oh jeez, Flanagan muttered inwardly. He took a good half an hour to pivot Red to Jimmy's Senate career. "On the bench, we'd talk politics. Just me and Jimmy. No one else cared. When he ran, he come talk. I told him, Kennedy, Kennedy. He was the next Kennedy. President Kennedy. President Doherty."

Then another half hour passed before he could get Red onto Jimmy's climate agenda. "Big deal, big deal. He saw future. Cap and trade. Cap and trade." Red must have repeated the words "Cap and trade" a dozen times.

Just to advance the conversation, Flanagan suggested, "Carbon tax?"

"No! No! Cap and trade. Cap and trade." Out of breath, Red sunk his bald skull into his hands. Flanagan feared he had fallen asleep. But a minute or so later, he lifted his head and smiled. "Yes, carbon tax."

Flanagan was struggling here, so he thought he might as well come out and ask it. "Do you think Jimmy Doherty was murdered?"

Red nodded so vigorously that Flanagan feared his scrawny, veined neck might snap. "Yes, yes, of course he was. He was. Big money. Big oil. Big Henry. Big Suzie."

Flanagan took out his camera. "You mind if I record you?"

Another furious bobble-head nod. Although he turned on the camera a bit sheepishly, for the ethics of this act was worthy of a Pisano, Flanagan knew in Red's phrase blender was a concoction he needed to consume. The camera actually slowed down Red, focusing his attention. He repeated his answer about Jimmy Doherty's death and then added more. "The accident, you know, Rusty's Auto Investigators, they go Rusty's, they go Rusty's, to the highest bidder."

"Why would anybody want to kill Jimmy Doherty?"

"That's easy. That's easy. Jimmy wanted money for carbon. He got the idea from Columbia eggheads. Jimmy wanted money for carbon. Henry didn't want money for carbon. Karl the Sausage, big trickster. Jimmy dead.

"You said Suzie before," said Flanagan. "I'm guessing you are talking about Suzie Wall, who was Suzie Pisano at the time?"

"Yes, yes. Suzie, she was something. She was something."

"What was her connection to Jimmy Doherty?"

"She was something. She was something. She and Jimmy. I set picks for them. She was something."

"Do you think she was involved in Jimmy's death?"

"Oh, she was something. She was something. Jimmy was scared. Got lots of death threats. No names though. Jimmy was scared. He thought it was Henry."

"When you say Henry, are you referring to the American Henry Center, the group that opposed efforts to fight climate change?"

"Yes, yes. Henry, he thought it was Henry."

"Why did he think it was the American Henry Center?"

"Money to lose. Money to lose. I set picks for Jimmy and Suzie."

Flanagan tried to calculate just how many hours would be required to edit this footage. He might have to buy Mehnuma lunch. "Do you know anyone else who believes that Jimmy Doherty was murdered?" he ventured, looking for leads.

"Everyone thinks so. Jimmy should've been president. President. Everyone thinks so."

Flanagan kept running the recording. He had no idea why. When Red returned to his basketball analysis ("Backdoor, for Jimmy, we always ran the backdoor"), Flanagan contemplated the two-hour drive from the North Fork back to Astoria.

After the taping ended, Red out of nowhere started to talk about Suzie again. Flanagan had stopped paying attention until he heard Red's last words.

"His nose," said Red. "His nose. Did you ever notice that Jimmy Doherty's nose is on the TV?"

Flanagan was tempted to get further explanation, but his interview with Red taught him that the conversation would only get muddier from here.

As he drove along the Long Island Expressway, Flanagan realized that Red had provided at least one lead. After he arrived at his basement apartment, Flanagan poured back over Doherty's 1989 accident file. The investigators of Jimmy's Honda Civic were indeed from Rusty's Automotive Center. He spent much of the rest of the day chasing down a number for Rusty Sansone, the former owner and accident report writer. Flanagan got the wife on the phone, who told him Rusty was very ill. Flanagan explained to her what he was inquiring about and asked, if Rusty felt better, that he call back.

Over the past month, as he had prepared to depart the show, Flanagan had lined up many interviews so that he'd be up and running quickly on the documentary, and so, in turn, he could impress Kartik with substantial footage. However, now Flanagan found himself with the rest of the day empty, which, as always, left him desolate. That the storyline for the documentary seemed more muddled and confusing by the minute didn't exactly improve his mood.

He picked up his phone and scrolled for Deja's contact. He couldn't figure out why he hadn't put her on his list of favorites. She certainly ranked with other such invaluable presences as Othello's Deli. For the past three weeks, Deja had been out of communication after he said something stupid, as Flanagan invariably did. This time it was, "I think you have lust deep in your heart for Heather." Deja, who was quite the hothead, stormed out, with middle fingers raised high and her voice raised higher. He remembered something about his being "a juvenile voyeuristic jerk;" then she added something he could no longer remember, then something else, then finally, "I hope you and your sex doll have a nice life together." That last comment bewildered Flanagan, since he had never even entertained the idea of a sex doll.

Deja's leaving him was a bad business on two fronts: 1) Deja served as his richest and most reliable source of Heather's activities at the Earth Institute and at Columbia; 2) Loneliness washed over him during these three weeks, and Deja embodied the one voice whose whispers made sweet echoes across the hollow corridors of his thoughts. Plus, he wouldn't mind seeing her on his green futon.

"I miss you" was his opening text to her.

He watched the three dots roll about on the reply rectangle for two minutes (Deja was a notoriously slow texter) before he received, "Who wouldn't?"

To which he responded, "I know, right?"

Five minutes later he finally got back, "You and every other red-blooded American male."

He was tempted to write back "and female," but remembering the past blow-up, he ventured, "I heard the Peruvian men are mad for you too."

And then nothing.

Not even anymore dots.

Flanagan wondered if he said something wrong. Did Deja have a secret animosity toward Peruvians or had he managed to insult Peruvians in his text? He figured whatever follow-up text he could offer would only add to the damage. Instead, he took out a pen and pad and tried to figure out what he had gathered so far in his documentary.

There was the pattern of the three accidents, which allowed him to start with Dirk Wall's paralysis, preceded by the decades earlier death of Frankie Pisano, and then to go even further back to the 1989 mysterious circumstances of Jimmy Doherty's demise.

The difficulty came from the realization that he knew the story really had to be about Jimmy, since it was the only territory he could inhabit all on his own. It was far enough away and for some reason had never been picked up as central to the Pisano legend. Through Jimmy's ongoing relationship back then with Suzie, Flanagan could make that connection, especially given the recorded comments of Sean Clarkin, Cheryl Wood, Red Schultz, Heather, and even Suzie herself. Indeed, he stood on shaky ground here, since he would have to insert enough Suzie into the documentary to get wide distribution and attention. Yet, if Suzie didn't like what Flanagan discovered, he well understood she could shut down the production. Then there was the climate change angle. Sure, it might give the documentary some gravitas, yet, and he hated to admit it, climate change could be boring and drag down the story.

He always knew the narrative would focus on Jimmy's death. Since that accident was the one furthest away, he'd have greatest access to free footage, especially since Doherty had been a prominent public figure with the Knicks and in the Senate. To zero in on Frankie Pisano's death would have meant dealing with the family lawyers and a headache's worth of copyright issues. And to center on the Dirk Wall accident would have meant the same problems, plus dealing with active, harried, and very wary police. The detectives on the case of Jimmy's death were either in coffins or very old. Ancient, retired detectives were usually willing to talk, since many of their conversations reverted back to stories of old run-ins and cases anyway. Sure, there was always the possibility the detective would be as articulate as Red Schultz. He hoped tomorrow's meeting with former NYPD sergeant Paul Murphy would clarify a few issues. The retired detective sounded on the phone like he still had his wits. Plus, Murphys and Flanagans had a long history of fruitful conversations. He figured meeting Murphy downtown at the Killarney Rose for a Guinness and a bite at the carvery might help too.

As he tried to organize his questions for Murphy tomorrow, Flanagan found himself continually returning to his conversation with Red in all its fragmented glory. The recorded interview yielded more on repeated viewing, but it was Red's last comment off camera that bothered him. He thought a bit about Jimmy's nose still being on television. He laughed at the notion. Could Jimmy have been a nose model used in sinus commercials? Taking out his laptop, Flanagan stared at picture after picture of Doherty. Indeed, the man had a fine nose, strong and straight and noble. But what the hell was Red talking about? After a while, he shifted on his laptop to looking at images of Suzie, particularly during those early years, eventually moving on to Heather and Tiffany. Of the lot, Heather's nose was closest to Jimmy's, but he knew his perception might have been influenced by his staring at two very attractive people and his desire to make a connection between them.

During these musings, he became distracted and returned to the crux of the documentary. He'd have to figure out how to get Heather Pisano more time in the narrative. Her quick cut he recorded at the apartment would be nice and could appear prominently in the trailer, but if he could finagle a way to get her an expanded role (and perhaps sneak in a cameo from Nora Wall) that would put the documentary in the big leagues. He only saw one way in and that was through Heather's climate change activity, since it would link her story to Doherty's. Talk about conflicted: place the snoozefest of global warming up against the titillation of Heather Pisano. Perhaps, she could proselytize to the masses, pontificating about green energy in skimpy lingerie. He knew what his next move was.

Flanagan took out his phone and started again with Deja.

"I miss you."

More dots, this time four minutes passed. "Where have I heard that before?"

No sense in messing around this time. "I need you for your brains."

This time he waited seven minutes, but in Deja's defense, it was a longer text. "Of course you do. I know what you need, so tell me what you want."

"I want you on my futon."

This time Deja took so long to respond that Flanagan feared she had shut down for good. The dots eventually returned and she refired up the chat the way a plumber might an ancient oil burner. "I guess I'll stick with what you need."

"Does that mean you're coming over?"

"At least my brain is."

"I don't understand."

"You'll understand soon enough."

Flanagan waited patiently for soon enough.

CHAPTER 9
THE FORECASTING OF DEJA

Deja accepted a peck on her mocha forehead, but that was all. Clearly, they would not find their way to the futon. Too bad, Flanagan thought. He'd been thinking about Deja far too much lately, especially since the summer months got her out of those damn lab coats and into tank tops and shorts, her glistening dark skin a wonder of lithe tonality. Although her figure had been in Flanagan's visions, what made Deja most attractive to him was an energetic intelligence imbued in every facial expression, a consistent awareness and acceptance of absurdity that relegated her to many fits of laughter and few of weeping.

"You've got anything to eat in this place beside bacon?" she asked. "I'm starving." Just before they first met, Deja had become a vegetarian, a very unhappy one at that. She would tell Flanagan that she knew the decision was right for her health and for the planet. Although Deja didn't complain, her scowl when she worked through a bowl of kale threatened that she just might tear off Flanagan's arm and gnaw away to satisfy her meat cravings. Her hunger never ceased.

Flanagan knew he was giving the wrong answer, but couldn't help himself, since Deja could be entertaining when antagonized: "I also have a hunk of soppressata and a stick of pepperoni."

"You should be dead the way you eat," said Deja.

"Something about the subcutaneous fat fills me with joy to press onward from one day to the next," said Flanagan.

"Uh huh," said Deja. "I can't say I've missed you at all."

"Still, I'm glad you're here," he said.

Deja understood that Flanagan was the boyfriend equivalent of junk food. He was bad for her and bad for the planet. When she first spotted him across the great hall at a Columbia alumni mixer two months ago, she was engaged in a riveting conversation with Claudia Bowman about oxy-fuel combustion carbon capture. Deja overheard Flanagan passionately endorsing the superiority of Coke Zero over Diet Coke. She excused herself from Dr. Bowman to contribute to Flanagan's assertions, saying that Canada Dry had the best diet ginger ale. "Now you're talking," Flanagan told her. "Isn't it amazing when something can be both so artificial and so true?"

Deja had been seeing Flanagan on and off ever since. She was never happy when she was with him and unhappier without him. And all he had in his dumpy apartment were cured meats. She ignored her hunger pangs and tried to look on the bright side. Flanagan had quit his frivolous job and embraced at least the concept of making a serious documentary.

"Tell me everything that you've learned so far," she commanded, her afro giving her an authority that Flanagan often sensed in individuals with big hair or bald heads. When he was done recounting his documentary research, Deja signaled with her hands, "Get up."

"Where're we going?"

"To Columbia. We'll stop in at the Earth Institute."

"Why?"

"Sounds like you need to know much more about global warming."

"Why would I need that when I've got you?"

"I'm not making the documentary. You are."

"But you can be my expert witness."

She grabbed his arm. "You listen to me. You're not going to treat climate change like one of those sex tapes on *Peepin' on the Pisanos*. For once, you stepped into something meaningful. Even Heather Pisano knows that and it's about time you found out."

On the way to the subway, they stopped at Othello's Deli, where Deja grabbed parsnip crisps while Flanagan would not deny himself the kettle chips. To his credit, he knew to add on two diet Canada Dry ginger ales. While the parsnip crisps weren't horrible, Deja felt her shoulders tighten as she watched Flanagan obliviously crunch away.

They took one of those looping subway odysseys New Yorkers often endure, riding the N out of Queens across the East River and then across town, only to head south to Times Square so they could transfer and head north on the 1 train to arrive forty minutes later at Columbia's campus. What was familiar to Deja, after all it was her workplace, washed over Flanagan with nostalgia. One had to go far uptown to find a college campus in Manhattan. Usually, they were merely big buildings like those at Hunter College crisscrossing avenues along Lexington or like Pace's by Park Row in the shadow of the Brooklyn Bridge. The craziest of them all was NYU which shared Washington Square Park with throngs of locals and tourists and then took all forms of military-like incursions into the East and West Villages, planting its flag between falafel joints and high-end cheese shops.

To get his dual major in English and business, Flanagan decades ago had commuted yet another 30 blocks uptown to the City University where he was greeted by raucous faux-gothic structures. When he transferred two years later to Columbia, the mood was simultaneously more serene and imposing, the domed Low Library anchoring a leafy campus with its Pantheon majesty. To get to the Earth Institute, they practically had to walk back out of the campus onto 114th Street. As they made their way along the brick herringbone paths, Deja explained how Heather became sucked in. "She had been an alumnus from a decade earlier and had even gotten her Masters in Climate and Society."

Flanagan laughed. "O.K. You've got thirty seconds. You want to explain to me what a degree in Climate and Society entails? Do professors explain how people in Miami sun themselves on the beach and those in Denver climb mountains?"

In only a slightly playful tone (with Deja, he never could tell), she told him, "You need to shut the hell up and let me tell you what you need to know. Anyway, unless she was out of town for a model shoot or a store opening or a special appearance or a perfume launch, Heather would attend the steady stream of alumni association confabs and fundraisers. Even when she was in other countries, she made a point of Skyping in."

"What do you think was the attraction?"

"I think it all started with Jim Hansen. He was a legend around here. He'd worked for NASA. He'd been there at the beginning, sounding the alarm about climate change in the 1980s. And he hurt his reputation with some scientists by becoming an activist and getting arrested. He was the closest thing to a climate change badass you're going to find in an old guy."

As they made their way across campus, the late September heat continued to surprise them even though it had been cooking their backs since May. Fall was supposed to arrive in New York by now, but Summer refused to relinquish its grip. Flanagan and Deja had not contemplated consigning their shorts to drawers. Working up a bit of sweat, they crossed their fair share of hexagonal pavers before they finally reached 114th Street and Broadway, ascending the modest staircase of the Earth Institute. Framed above them by an iron railing, a small balcony served as a tempting venue for big speeches. She ushered him to her office, where she sat behind her desk and he scrunched into a folding chair like he was a grad student breathlessly waiting to hear his professor's verdict.

"From what I've been gathering," said Flanagan, "Hansen had also been a tremendous influence on Jimmy Doherty. Hansen and Wally Broecker. Funny, Jimmy also hung around Columbia like Heather, long after he graduated."

Deja pointed south. "A block down on Broadway is the Goddard Institute where Hansen worked for NASA during Jimmy's time. Hell, he was still there a half dozen years ago until Columbia finally figured out how to lure him here. Heather used to visit him at Goddard."

"She sounds like a bit of a stalker to me," said Flanagan flippantly, to make sure that the sometimes prickly Deja would know he was joking.

"Typical man. A woman shows an interest in ideas and she's a stalker. A man does the same thing and he's an intellectual. Heather kept visiting because, like most of us, she needed to keep looking at the science and hearing about how terrible the situation was again and again for it to sink in."

Deja eyed Flanagan in an unacademic way, a soft smile emerging as she rose out her chair, shifted near him, and propped herself on the desk in front of him, offering a view of those dark, shiny legs that had taken many long summer walks along Riverside Drive. He constantly struggled to figure out what Deja was doing or thinking and he kind of liked that. He knew enough that anything he did or said in acknowledgement of her actions would destroy the possibility of romance. He'd just have to take in the view and keep asking questions. "Why won't Heather become a face for the climate change movement?"

"So many reasons," she said, leaning toward Flanagan. "Let's start with the fact that she feels like many of us in the scientific community, that we're lukewarm about the Green New Deal, since we've always been fans of options like carbon capture and carbon pricing as major components of cutting emissions. For Heather, it's a bigger issue. You see, Hansen wasn't the only major influence for her here at the Earth Institute. Claudia Bowman gave her a new focus about how nuclear power could play a larger role in climate change."

"Where the hell did that come from?" he asked. "People are scared shitless of nuclear power."

"Not so much in the scientific community, and I know this sounds strange to you, but I will tell you from the bottom of my heart that Heather Pisano is a scientist in her soul."

"You mean the celebrity of sex tapes and selfies?"

"A scientist." Deja professed this assertion with a finality and sanctity that brooked no argument. Confusing matters was the way Deja drew closer to Flanagan, her legs now touching his in accidental proximity. "If you follow her movements in Europe and even out west, you'll find she would disappear for an afternoon here and there."

"I figured that was to get something waxed or pruned or plumped."

"No, that was to tour nuclear power plants."

"Son-of-a-bitch," he said. Deja stood over Flanagan and then dropped down on top of him in the thankfully armless chair. She sat on his lap, face-to-face, gently caressing his cheeks with her hands. He knew not to kiss her. He could tell she wanted him to keep talking, but man was focusing a challenge. So he babbled about what a curious decision it was for Heather to turn to nuclear power. Meanwhile, Deja, who by now was pressing her chest into his, explained how a cadre of climate scientists see nuclear power being an essential component in the mix of getting to carbon neutral. She whispered in his ear seductively. "She knew that nuclear was not being given its due."

Still trying to figure out how this mating ritual worked, Flanagan whispered back in her ear, "Heather has always been about finding her own lane," he said. "It's a daring move." He let that comment sit for a minute. Seductions in academic offices were not exactly acceptable in the 21st Century. To distract himself from the temptation of slipping his hand inside her top, he managed to concentrate enough to return to the conversation. "Everybody's going to embrace solar and wind, but nuclear, that scares people."

Intensely staring at Flanagan, Deja grabbed his cheek with one hand, tugged the back of his neck with the other, and pulled him in for a kiss that she guided through what had to be a dozen happy, hushed groans. Then she drew back from his lips, breathing a couple of times to regulate and resume the conversation.

"People could let go of Three Mile Island – it was further back and didn't cause much damage, but Chernobyl, you're right, that scared the hell out of people," she said. Flanagan was listening carefully, although he had no idea why and how. "And even if you shrugged Chernobyl off to Soviet communist era gross incompetence, Fukushima really turned people off." The last words Flanagan wanted to hear right now were about turning off. "How does a nuclear power plant protect itself from a tsunami?" She laughed at the absurdity of the global predicament. Flanagan laughed too, but it was about the absurdity of his personal predicament. "And what's ironic is that nuclear power will be more endangered by extreme weather events because of the very problem it's trying to address – climate change."

Flanagan's head was spinning. Deja was leaning back into him, but they were still talking and he knew if he had any chance of the chair becoming a chariot of love, he'd just better let her stay in charge and for once not do anything stupid. She explained the nuances of the new Small Modular Reactors (which Deja kept calling SMRs, like Flanagan was a member of the Nuclear Regulatory Commission and was comfortable with such abbreviations), specifically how they were safer and simplified by their scale as they linked together in chains. Meanwhile, his thoughts returned to practical matters. How in God's name was he going to make these ideas about climate change and nuclear power intriguing in the documentary? He knew it somehow connected back to Doherty's death, but man oh man, the audience might just start snoozing in their chairs. Should he transform the climate change material into an entertaining, zany cartoon? That would cost money and delay production. He understood that the climate change layer would give the documentary implications that the mere vehicular manslaughter of a beloved Senator would not possess, but he was stretching much further beyond the bounds of *Peepin' on the Pisanos* territory than he had imagined. Admiring the arch of Deja's back as she pontificated so beautifully, he sighed, deciding he'd better get more of the whole story first to figure out how to present it.

Somewhere after a comment about concrete protective layers, Deja returned to kissing Flanagan and they started rocking back and forth in a way that signaled the time had arrived.

But then it did not.

Deja rose from the chair, breathing heavily, and returned to behind her desk. Flanagan managed to keep his "What the hell" to an internal monologue.

"So, you see what just happened here," said Deja.

Flanagan tried to compose himself. "I'm not sure what happened here."

"We just had these incredible moments of passion and excitement among all the talk and planning," she said. "And now what do we have? Achingly painful frustration. That's what it's like every day at the Earth Institute. We feel the potential for something great to happen, but all we end up with is a few come-on kisses that get us worked up about what's coming next ... and then nothing."

Still unable to douse the fire in his trousers, Flanagan offered, "You might have simply explained that to me without the demonstration."

"Well, I'm a scientist after all. Would you have rather I explained it to you?"

"God no."

"I have to admit," said Deja, "our conversation was more wonderful and horrible than I imagined."

"I'm trying to figure out whether I should say thanks."

"Funny," said Deja, "I was trying to figure out whether I might one day like to spend more time with you."

"No time like the present."

Deja laughed. "Down there, killer. For today, why don't you escort me to the Cathedral of St. John the Divine? It's my favorite building in the world."

Flanagan rose from the chair. "I didn't think you eggheads were much for houses of worship."

"I like places that still make me wonder," said Deja. "C'mon."

Flanagan leaned toward Deja. "You have no idea what you do to me."

"Yeah, yeah," Despite her dismissive tone, Deja's face warmed. She decided she would disappoint the planet and herself just a little bit. "I tell you what. After we're done at the Cathedral, we'll go across the street to this wonderful Hungarian pastry shop."

"Yeah?" asked Flanagan, perking up. "What's it called?"

"The Hungarian Pastry Shop."

"Go figure. Hey, this feels like a date."

"Shut up or you'll ruin it," Deja warned.

"Ruin what? After what happened in your office, what's there to ruin?" Before Deja could say anything, Flanagan kept going. "Do you think they have strudel? I think I want strudel."

CHAPTER 10
THE INTERMINGLING OF MOTIVES

Eating his take-out strudel from the Hungarian Pastry Shop, Flanagan spent the next morning reading through another chapter of Stuart Cooper's *Love in the Age of Excess*. With its obtuse references to Greek mythology, the book was quite the fascinating piece of trash, heavy in high fashion and fornicating, but if it could provide at least some clues of what was Jimmy Doherty's connection to the Pisanos, then it'd be worth the hours invested. Finally, at Chapter 7, Flanagan hit paydirt.

From *Love in the Age of Excess*
by Stuart Cooper

Chapter 7: Is It True What They Say
About Ballers?

Like Odysseus gazing upon the shores of low-lying Ithaca, Frankie had been anticipating the American Henry Center gala for months. Beyond the waltzing waters and the mermaids twirling sparklers as they rose from the waves, Henry's oil-drenched maestros feted a feast worthy of Trimalchio. Every year Frankie would fatten his clients there with boozy schmoozing, so they could be sacrificed upon the holy altars of commerce. When this year Suzie suddenly came down with severe migraines the day before the gala, Frankie found himself as suspicious as Menelaus over Helen's duplicitous crossing to Troy. And when Suzie hissed softly to him on gala day that she "simply was not up to attending; please send everyone my well wishes and regards," Frankie knew he had an Agamemnon-level problem.

Indubitably, a problem bad enough for Frankie to step out halfway through this most lucrative of bacchanalia to see how Suzie was "feeling." Apparently, she was feeling fine enough to writhe ecstatically about their satin sheets *in flagrante delicto* with a former basketball star and a present-day senator, swirling about like Francesca and Paolo in hell's second circle. That day Frankie glumly discovered the answer to the age-old question, "Do all basketball players dribble before they shoot?" From what Frankie could discern, as he barged in like Ptolemy upon Caesar and Cleopatra, Jimmy Doherty appeared to be ready to hoist up a three pointer.

Years earlier, when Suzie was still engaged to Jimmy and their wedding was a mere six months off, it was Jimmy who found Frankie and Suzie in such an amorous, contorted embrace, an Eloise and Abelard without any silly monk's cloaks obstructing the rhapsodies. That night, Frankie had wept for the first time since his bulldog got run over by a taxi

(Frankie made damn sure that bastard driver lost his cabbie license), wept like the children of Oedipus.

But this time, Frankie wasn't crying; he shook with the rage of Ares brandishing his spear. Unlike this interloping, orb-hoisting Atlas, Frankie didn't have a mere flimsy engagement with Suzie. They had been married for two years and had already borne a noble offspring. Caught in the act of two backs and no conscience, Jimmy only offered a meager quartet of words, "Wow, this is embarrassing." He had the courtesy not to intimate for whom mortification prevailed. Akin to Zeus with his thunderbolt, Frankie responded by throwing a Waterford crystal vase at Jimmy. To truly relegate matters to Tartarus, Jimmy, still quite the athlete, caught the vase. What a pair of hands he had on him. He grasped the ten pounds of leaded crystal like a fig cut from Aphrodite's orchard. The vase would have brained a lesser man.

Wrapping a satin sheet around his waist, a regular Diocletian at the baths, Jimmy nodded to Suzie and said, "I think I better go." Suzie shrugged, as if to say "if you must." Deciding not to return a hallowed weapon to Frankie, Jimmy took the modern amphora with him, only feeling safe putting it down in the driveway as he stepped into his humble chariot, his Honda Civic. He looked like too much of a man to drive that little economy car, an Achilles pedaling a tricycle.

As he backed out of the driveway, Jimmy could hear Frankie shrieking in cacophonous cadences worthy of a harpy, "You said you had a fucking migraine! I'll give you a fucking migraine." The last sounds Jimmy heard as he pulled out onto the road were those of the cherub Heather sobbing.

Like the blind grey sister of fate, Frankie knew he could destroy Jimmy Doherty's future, but at what cost? Frankie would be known as a cuckold and his virile aura which often sealed so many contracts with top athletes would vanish. No, he'd find another way to clean this Augean stable. For now, he turned his attention to Suzie.

She was staring at him, her lips glistening. Frankie couldn't believe this siren was trying to lure him again to the rocks. Was she actually giving him bedroom eyes after what he had just witnessed? She spun around on her stomach, lifting her shapely frame by her elbows just to give Frankie an eyeful of what two expertly managed augmentation surgeries hath wrought. Her body twisted like the crank on a bubblegum dispenser in a dugout full of little leaguers. Her delicate fists holding up her chin, she cocked her head at him in a manner the vulnerable would consider irresistible, though one might be wise to check first for snakes in her hair.

Recalling the scene ten minutes earlier, Frankie rubbed the growing horns on his head and rejected her advances. "I am taking everything," he said. "I'm cleaning you out."

"You can have most," said Suzie, "but not everything."

"What?" The nerve of this troubling Pandora, thought Frankie. "No, I'm taking everything." But, after pacing back and forth and watching her hips wiggle involuntarily and seeing the way her creamy calves rose restlessly, he grew curious. Man, those calves pumped like she could squeeze enough olives to fill an urn with extra virgin. What could she possibly want? "You don't deserve anything."

"I want the Dirt Devil."

"Dirt Devil?" Frankie scratched his head like he was trying to solve the riddle of the sphinx.

Suzie was amused. "It's the little hand vacuum."

Huh, thought Frankie. "What the fuck you want with that? I've never seen you vacuum anything a day in your life."

"It's not just good for vacuuming."

"You are unbelievable. You know that?"

She rose slowly, like Aphrodite from the waves, again making sure Frankie would not miss a single twist and slipped into the closet. Frankie first feared she'd lock herself in there. But she came out with the Dirt Devil. "Let me show you." She didn't turn on the Dirt Devil until she grabbed a good firm hold of him and Frankie forgot what he was thinking

> about. Then she switched on that sucking
> machine of romance.

Certain of where Cooper was heading, Flanagan could not read another word. He felt dirty after perusing that passage, but he had discovered more than he expected. Surprisingly, the information came in the first line. He had not known about Frankie's connection to the American Henry Center. He did not believe anyone investigating the accident had known about the relationship. Only Cooper, who was too busy centering his narrative on sex toys to notice, had that.

Flanagan found former detective Murphy deep beyond the bar at the Killarney Rose, in the back by the dart board. Flanagan had to get his ass kicked in darts for three games by Murphy, who was quite the ringer, before they could sit down and talk. Then he had to hear Murphy's tales about being a sergeant in the bad old seventies ("I remember one time driving with one of the new guys in East New York, and we heard gunfire, and the rookie asked if we should check it out. I said to the rook, nah, that I didn't hear nothing. No use in getting shot today when you could wait till tomorrow").

Finally, he got down to talking about Doherty's accident. "That was quite big news back then," said Murphy. Flanagan sized up the former detective, whose mutton chops and stout figure really made him look the part. The only thing that didn't fit was his drinking red wine, and at the Killarney Rose, their mags weren't usually easy on the heartburn. Murphy was three glasses in and Flanagan two Guinnesses before he was interested in answering questions about the American Henry Center.

"Given all the public battles they had with Doherty over his carbon tax proposal, we thought they were worth a look, even though they seemed like a longshot."

"Why a longshot?"

"First of all, it was a car accident. Generally, we find most of those cases are just that – accidents. Killing someone by car accident is as rare as murdering someone with a train or a plane."

"But the timing and the circumstances of Doherty's death had to bother you. The Democrats were already grooming him for a presidential run, and Bush didn't exactly have Reagan's popularity. Plus, he was not the kind of guy who crashes into the Gowanus Canal."

"Tell me, Mr. Filmmaker, what is the type of guy who crashes into the Gowanus Canal? Sounds like anyone and everyone to me."

"You know as well as I do that he was thought of as a careful driver."

"There are lots of careful drivers in accidents." Taking another sip of the red wine, Murphy decided to take a break from busting Flanagan's balls. "I'll give you this. We found out more unkosher stuff about the Henry group than we expected."

"Yeah?" Flanagan took out his video-camera.

"Our financial investigative team back then was not what we have today, mind you," Murphy said in all modesty. "But I can tell you some surprisingly rough characters were associated with Henry, not the usual types connected to these think tanks."

"Guys capable of doing such a job like setting up a fatal crash?"

Murphy smiled. "They were capable of many other things. Why not that?"

"So what happened?"

Murphy sighed and warned Flanagan, "You're not gonna like it." He finished his red and signaled Flanagan to get another round. While he waited for his Guinness pour to settle before the top off, he brought back the wine, signaling Murphy to continue. "Once the case started to get some juice to it, they pulled me off. From what the Captain said, the orders came from way up top. Even the FBI backed off. The conclusions of the investigation would be that Jimmy Doherty died in an auto accident under completely unsuspicious circumstances."

Flanagan grabbed his Guinness from the bar and asked Murphy, "Just out of curiosity, who were the names that stood out on the Henry Group?"

"Oh, you're not going to like that either."

"Why?"

"Because one of the big names is dead, and the other is spending the rest of his life in prison."

"And they are …"

"Tony Fratiani, aka the Elbow, and Karl Hoffman, aka the Sausage," said Murphy.

"Organized crime figures?"

"I wouldn't say organized, but our files have them linked to a number of homicides."

"And what happened to the one who's dead? Natural causes?"

"Unclear," Murphy sipped his wine. "Tony the Elbow was in his sixties, but natural deaths are not always the case in his profession."

"How about the lifer, Karl the Salami?"

"That's Karl the Sausage," said Murphy. "His lips are tighter than a rat's ass. He hasn't told us anything from the minute he landed in the clink. The man's always been trouble. Quite the trickster and smart as a whip. When he used to talk, he'd always try to confuse you. No one could figure out what he was saying. Now he's shut completely down. Not that it matters."

"What's Karl the Sausage in for?" Flanagan asked.

"Homicide," said Murphy. "Seems he killed a stockbroker who owed him 800 grand. Says he's innocent. Go figure."

"And he won't talk."

"Won't even say hello."

"What a mess," muttered Flanagan almost under his breath. "Did you ever investigate Suzie Pisano or Frankie Pisano?"

"More Frankie. Suzie was never a suspect, but now after all of these years watching *Peepin' on the Pisanos*, I could definitely see her do it."

"Did you know about Frankie Pisano's ties to the American Henry Center?"

"Ties?" Murphy stared into his red wine. "No. What ties?"

"He regularly attended their galas and would get clients from his schmoozing."

Murphy smiled. "That's pretty interesting. I'm certain we would have found that out soon enough if the higher-ups didn't close down the investigation."

Flanagan pivoted. "What do you think of Frankie? Could he have done it?"

"Nah. I don't think so. Too much of a lightweight."

"But from what I hear, Jimmy Doherty was screwing his wife right up to the time of the accident."

"Boy for someone who looks pretty clueless, you've been hearing an awful lot."

"I've got big ears."

"Big ears, huh. If you would've been talking like this back then, your ears might've been stuffed in an envelope and mailed to your Momma."

Flanagan pressed his point. "Do you think Frankie could've done it?"

"I'll think about it."

"While you're thinking, could you tell me where this Karl the Sausage guy … what's his last name?"

"Hoffman," said Murphy.

"Yeah, Hoffman," said Flanagan. "What prison is he in?"

"Attica," said Murphy, "but you'll waste your time trying to talk to him. I'm a pretty stubborn guy. I've taken that seven-hour ride ten times to talk to him. Hoffman just looked at the floor. I know this may surprise you, but he was unsympathetic about how far I traveled to talk to him."

"Will you call me if something else comes to your mind?"

"Call you?" asked Murphy. "Why would I call you? I tell you what." He lifted a dart with a red feather. "You hit the bullseye with the dart, and I'll call you when I come up with something."

Flanagan cleared his throat. "You just played darts with me for an hour. I didn't hit the bullseye once. There's no way I'm gonna hit the bullseye with that dart."

"Of course not," said Murphy dismissively. "Not the first time or the tenth time or the hundredth time. You get as many chances as you like. You just won't get anything from me unless you hit the bullseye."

Flanagan kept tossing the dart and retrieving it. He left holes in much of the board and in much of the board's surrounding environs. Fortunately, he beat the law of averages, hitting the bullseye after twenty minutes, earning a sarcastic round of applause.

"See what happens when you're motivated," said Murphy.

"True that," said Flanagan, "just don't down too much of that red swill. Otherwise, your head will never be clear enough to give me what I need."

"Yeah, like what you need is in my head."

Now three Guinnesses in, Flanagan cut across Hanover Street and wandered down Beaver over to Delmonico's, with its façade that stuck out like a mighty proboscis sniffing the money from nearby Wall Street. He found Stuart Cooper already at a table beneath an elegant Gilded Age mural.

"You feeling all right?" asked Flanagan. "We're not going to have any choking incidents, are we?"

"Not today," said Cooper.

"Good, 'cause if you keep doing that, you'll be *persona non grata* in every restaurant in Manhattan."

"Now we can't have that, can we?" said Cooper. "Otherwise, you'll be forced to buy me dinner in Brooklyn, or, egads, Queens."

"Hey, I live in Astoria."

"So *you* understand."

They had ordered drinks. Cooper had a rosé and Flanagan, deciding he might as well go to hell tonight, had a Manhattan.

Since he was in no mood to repeat the slow dance he just performed with Murphy, Flanagan followed the second rule of interviewing: when you are getting nowhere, compliment an author on his book and say you are intrigued about something. "I am getting a real kick out of *Love in the Age of Excess*. It really made me curious about the upshot of all the crazy affairs."

"Indeed," said Cooper, standing a little straighter in his chair now. "It was quite the wild time."

"In your book, you said that Frankie had to find another way to make Jimmy Doherty pay for screwing his wife. Do you know if he ever found a way?"

Cooper was coy. "I know you have a documentary to produce, but I've got another book I'm finishing."

"Your appearance in the documentary might sell you many copies. Look I'm going to give you the choking recording (it's right here), and I don't even want the GPS information about Wall's driving records. My focus is on the Doherty accident, which I am guessing is far away from what you're researching, so I could use some of your expertise. In *Love in the Age of Excess* you wrote that Frankie went regularly to the American Henry Center galas. Did he have a deeper connection with those guys?"

Cooper polished off his rosé in good order and peered about for the waiter to procure another. "I think you're barking up the wrong tree."

"Why's that?"

"You might be investigating the wrong Pisano."

"You think so."

The waiter returned. Making sure this consultation was worth his while, Cooper ordered the 45-day dry-aged prime porterhouse for one. He added the whipped potatoes and the spinach to guarantee that his plate hit the hundred-dollar mark. Meanwhile, Flanagan, trying to figure out how he could manage on his *Peepin' on the Pisanos* savings, opted for the Amish Brick Chicken, which came in at a quarter of the cost of Cooper's dish. Deciding to stop messing around, Cooper ordered a bottle of rosé. Countering with another Manhattan, Flanagan decided he liked Cooper. He played his role of an obsolete gay stereotype with gleeful authenticity.

Cooper would make sure both would get their dinner's worth out of the meeting. "Let me tell you a little story about Suzie's older sister Barbara Jansen, who, unlike Suzie, was too good to work in the candle shop."

"No one's too good to work in the candle shop," said Flanagan.

"Barbara was," said Cooper. "She was the pretty one."

"Wait," said Flanagan, "unless my appreciation of beauty has been terribly distorted by all those years and procedures on *Peepin' on the Pisanos*, I was under the impression that Suzie was quite the looker, still is."

"Indeed, Suzie seems ravishing until you meet Barbara."

"And why haven't I ever heard of her?"

"She was a recluse," said Cooper. "She was last seen at the end of the 80s."

"Right about the time Doherty died," said Flanagan.

"You're getting ahead of yourself," said Cooper. "Drink your Manhattan. Shut up and listen."

Flanagan obeyed.

"Suzie had spent her teenage and college years trying to emerge from Barbara's shadow," said Cooper. "She finally thought that happened when Barbara married Lars Key."

"The software guy?"

"If you mean by the software guy, one of the richest men in the world, yes. After she married Lars in 1986, Barbara spent most of her time on their yacht traveling the exotic islands of the world. The gorgeous sister was no longer a daily visual reminder of Suzie Jansen's inadequacies. And things stayed that way for a few years until the yacht arrived in majestic New York Harbor."

"Did Barbara come to visit her little sister?"

"Not really," said Cooper. "Barbara came to see someone who Suzie was seeing."

"Frankie?"

"No, silly. She was married to Frankie. If Suzie were seeing Frankie, then maybe Barbara would have come to New York to see Frankie."

"So … Barbara came to see Senator Jimmy Doherty."

"Bingo."

The food arrived – Cooper's porterhouse distinguished by great fanfare (one waiter accompanied by two adoring food runners) and an elegant *au poivre* pour while Flanagan's Amish chicken engendered a more paltry presentation. Cooper was happy to let the waiter fill up his glass with zealous consistency. Flanagan stared into his Manhattan patiently waiting for Cooper to stop chewing and start talking.

"No heterosexual man could resist the charms of Barbara Jansen, now crowned Barbara Key," said Cooper, a homosexual man who happened to be an expert on such matters. "In a note claiming she was deeply interested in his campaign to fight global warming, she invited our virile Senate prince to the penthouse of the Waldorf Astoria. She requested he bring no staff with him, since she valued the opportunity to get the measure of him as a man. She made clear if she were to contribute so much to his campaign, she must know that he was a trustworthy advocate for such a noble cause."

Feeling he was offering too much without enough compensating nourishment, Cooper polished off his glass of rosé and tucked into his porterhouse, heretically dabbing it in his mashed potatoes. Rather than take offense, Flanagan decided to focus on the doleful puddle sitting at the bottom of his cocktail glass. Trying to move the story along, Flanagan prodded, "So she made sure Doherty would come alone. I assume she too was alone."

"It depends what you mean by alone," said Cooper. "A bit of the Amazon rain forest was with her. To show her devotion to the cause, she greeted him at the door in a few choicely positioned draped vines about her enchanting figure. Adam had a better chance resisting Eve and she was the only game in Eden. What did it matter that handsome Jimmy had a superstar mistress and a supermodel fiancée? He fell into the arms of a goddess and did he ever fall. For the next forty-eight hours, it was cancel all my meetings and hold all my calls. The polar ice caps could swamp Staten Island for all Doherty cared. The Waldorf Astoria penthouse became Mount Olympus and he fired his thunderbolts into Aphrodite's charmed cave. When Doherty finally made his way down the private elevator, he walked like a polio victim, which was somewhat appropriate since he would claim grave illness as the reason for his absence."

"So that was the end of the affair?" asked Flanagan.

"Almost," said Cooper. "Perhaps, Doherty was not only staggering from two straight days of connubial bliss. He was also carrying around a million-dollar bank note to pay for lobbyists in support of his climate legislation. But the nugget that might interest you more comes from a letter Barbara posted just before she returned to her yacht. It was to her dear sister. Barbara had written on a card, 'I am so sorry I missed you when I was in town.' Suzie found the note disconcerting since she did not even know that her sister's yacht had docked in New York Harbor. But what really shook Suzie was the enclosure of a fig leaf. She did not need to put it to her nose for her to recognize the fragrance rising from its stem. Doherty was the only man she sniffed who wore Kouros by Yves Saint Laurent."

Flanagan digested this tale while Cooper digested his meal. Maybe it was the booze or the information overload, but whichever the case, Flanagan felt dizzy. He stared at Cooper, tried to concentrate, and started talking. "Let me get this straight. Senator Doherty was engaged to the supermodel Cheryl Wood while he was cheating on her with Suzie while he was cheating on Suzie with her sister Barbara." Flanagan whistled while Cooper nodded and grinned. "Ah the '80s," said Flanagan, "when you could be a philandering rat bastard and still be the most appealing of presidential candidates."

Cooper lifted his glass. "To the good old days!"

"So are you suggesting that Suzie killed Doherty because he slept with her sister?"

"You have no idea how jealous Suzie is," Cooper said. "And there are so many other reasons: that he never let her help with his campaigns when they were dating, that he didn't buy her the Brooklyn Heights townhouse she begged him for, that he picked the supermodel over her to marry —"

"But she's the one who cheated on him with Frankie. You wrote that yourself in your book, and she chose Frankie over him to marry."

"If you're going to use logic and reasoning in this discussion, we're not going to get anywhere," said Cooper drily. "Suzie had a passion for Doherty that she never had for anyone else."

"Let me ask you something," said Flanagan. "If you're so certain that Suzie planned out Doherty's car crash, why isn't it in your book?"

"You think I'm stupid," said Cooper. "I can earn much more money being on Suzie's good side than her bad side. The woman is a freaking ATM."

"Then why are you telling me all this?"

Cooper laughed, killed the bottle of rosé, and said "Because I'm curious to see what, if anything, you're going to do with it."

CHAPTER 11
THE SELLING OF A DOCUMENTARY

Although Flanagan sent in his footage to Mehnuma religiously, her responses were limited to polite thank yous. Flanagan decided to check in with Kartik to see if he had any thoughts about what had been cobbled together so far. In preparation for their meeting, Flanagan sent Kartik a tentative outline of the preliminary script and gave him a list of possible interviews, including what he hoped to draw out of those discussions.

Flanagan saw it as a good sign that he didn't have to wait long before he entered into Kartik's plain office. One look at Kartik told him there might be a strategy behind the austerity: the producer wore an exquisitely tailored blue suit. In such surroundings, he stood out even more … as if he possessed one dimension greater than his environs. Kartik's height and strikingly dark features told all who observed him that he could be as easily in front of a camera as behind one. Nothing impresses a movie star more than movie star good looks. Even Flanagan was tempted to focus his lens and figure out how to fit him into the documentary.

Kartik's burly nephew Arnav stood in the corner. After Flanagan acknowledged his presence with a wave, Arnav grabbed a large manila envelope labeled *Confidential!* off of Kartik's desk and walked out. Kartik loved his theatrics. Arnav always seemed to be on a special mission, about which Kartik revealed just enough to perpetuate a steady buzz of office intrigue. Now that he made sure Flanagan witnessed Arnav's maneuvers, Kartik addressed the business at hand.

"You've been a busy boy, Artie," said Kartik. "Perhaps you are less shallow and lazy than I thought."

"Oh, tell me more," said Flanagan. "Your gushing compliments make my knees weak."

Kartik frowned, not having time for Flanagan's sarcasm, and got down to business. "I like this Clarkin guy," said Kartik. "Can you get some images of him fighting?"

"I'll send Coppa to the Pint O'Plenty," said Flanagan. "He won't have a problem going there since he practically rents the back room of the place."

Kartik reached into a drawer and took out another small, high end camera; the same Red model Kartik had given Flanagan a few days earlier. "I trust Coppa with this camera even less than I trust you," he said. "If he breaks it, you're paying for it."

"Yeah," said Flanagan, "I'm figuring out that making this documentary means I pay and then I pay some more."

"I'm pleased you are finally learning something useful," said Kartik. He stared down at Flanagan's outline. "The Heather Pisano footage is good. Can you get some of her wearing a little less?"

"Than what she has on in the interview?" said Flanagan. "There's not much fabric there to begin with."

"Maybe you can get Coppa into one of her swimwear shoots. He can ask her those questions on the beach."

"Would you let Coppa into a swimwear shoot?" Flanagan asked.

Kartik just laughed. "Mehnuma has already been able to scrounge up some stock footage of Suzie's sister Barbara on that yacht," he said, "which should go nicely with her alleged rendezvous with jaunty Jimmy. After Lars bought her an old Gold Coast mansion, Barbara also did some Home and Garden show features where she gave a tour of her lovely estate. Too bad she died a few years ago. Putting her live in the documentary would be some get for you."

"It'd be an even bigger get if we could summon her from the grave," said Flanagan. "Do a whole metempsychosis thing."

Kartik ignored him. "It's a shame she died of cancer," he said. "A car accident would have been wonderful. Even a boating accident would have been a nice nugget to insinuate into the narrative. And by the way, what's the deal with this Stuart Cooper character. He's quite the ham, isn't he?"

"I'm guessing his choking scene at the restaurant is destined for the cutting room floor," said Flanagan.

"That's a pretty good bet, Artie," said Kartik, "unless it works for comic relief. We could put it in right after Suzie says something particularly outrageous. And I was going to ask you, why haven't you interviewed Suzie?"

"I wanted to wait for that, until I get all my ducks in a row," said Flanagan.

"Oh, just as I figured," said Kartik, "you are scared of her."

"I'm not scared of her," said Flanagan.

"You should be scared of her," said Kartik, "if you're going to accuse her of vehicular manslaughter."

"There are many more angles to this story than Suzie Wall," said Flanagan, "and many more suspects."

"That may be the case, but no matter who the suspects are, the real subject of this documentary is Suzie Pisano. She and her daughters are always the story – don't ever forget that."

"Even if Suzie didn't kill Jimmy?"

"Definitely," said Kartik. "The likelihood of Suzie wiping out Jimmy is too great of an uncertainty."

"But what if the Pisanos don't have enough connection to the Jimmy's death?" asked Flanagan.

"Then Jimmy's death will take a backseat to whatever this documentary ends up being about," said Kartik.

"That sounds like an awful mess to me," said Flanagan.

"Whose idea was this documentary anyway?" said Kartik.

"Hell if I know," said Flanagan.

Mehnuma came in with 8X10 pictures of two surly looking fellows.

"So who are these specimens of American wholesomeness?" asked Kartik.

"Allow me to introduce you," said Mehnuma, "to Tony Fratiani, aka the Elbow, and Karl Hoffman, aka the Sausage."

"They sure fit the part, don't they?" asked Kartik.

"And what part is that?" asked Flanagan.

"Whatever part we need them to play," said Kartik. "And by the way, we are going to do some serious editing on that Red Schultz footage."

"He doesn't draw the clearest of lines between two points, does he?" said Flanagan.

"He doesn't even draw the clearest line between two pointlessnesses."

"Still, he and Clarkin offer some intriguing connections to the American Henry Center," said Flanagan. He turned to Mehnuma. "Can you see what kind of dirt you can dig up on them? I'll be doing my own research, but I get this feeling you are better at this than I am."

Mehnuma looked at Kartik. "You never said he was good at manipulating people."

Kartik answered her, "He's getting better at it." Kartik had been used to being the smartest person in the room until he hired Mehnuma, a pretty wisp of a girl who couldn't be older than 25. Not only quick on her toes, Mehnuma carried around an encyclopedic knowledge of the shallow and the deep. That meant she could pontificate with equal facility about the Pisanos as she could about string theory.

"I'll poke around," Mehnuma said. "but we've got to be careful about not getting carried away with the global warming issues and the American Henry Center. That's a rabbit hole which could drag down the entire documentary."

Kartik turned to Flanagan. "She'll find out what she can about the lobbying groups and the oil companies, especially the awful Roy Crowne fellow who ran the Henry and many other oil lobbies. But you better keep delivering more celebrities. Cheryl Wood was a pretty good get. Remember the trailer is going to do most of the selling for the doc. The more famous faces you give me, the more likely you'll get a high-end production."

Flanagan left the meeting with his head spinning. He had completely forgotten why he had come to visit Kartik. Oh yeah, he wanted to find out if Kartik thought he had the makings of a documentary. Apparently, he did. Just not the one Flanagan thought he was creating.

CHAPTER 12
THE PLANTING OF THE FAMILY TREE

Flanagan regularly saw his 15-year-old daughter Michelle on weekday nights for a hot chocolate at Il Bambino. Every Saturday night she would stay over. After leaving his luxurious accommodations in a waterfront Williamsburg high rise, Flanagan had to rejigger the sleeping arrangements with him now slumbering on the futon while Michelle slept in his bed. He adjusted his routines, changing the sheets on Saturday morning and cleaning off the dressers so for a day the bedroom truly felt like Michelle's. Over the headboard, he put up a poster of Pete Alonso, Michelle's favorite Met, to make the place homey.

Yet his efforts had not removed Michelle's anxiety. "Dad, are you alright? I told Mom where you're living and that you quit your job."

Flanagan exhaled, hiding a few thoughts behind a smile. "Tell Mom I have stored away enough for child support for at least a couple of years, if that's what she's asking."

Flanagan and Sophie broke up soon after Michelle was born: his work at *Peepin' on the Pisanos* made their relationship initially untenable and ultimately unbearable. After scratching out each other's eyes for the three years surrounding the divorce, they settled into a somewhat pleasant rhythm of sharing approaches on how not to ruin Michelle's life. While he understood that his sudden career change would cause Sophie consternation, Flanagan had his own parental worries. Michelle had started to put on makeup in a strikingly similar style to that 19-year-old Nora Wall. Occasionally, Michelle would ask in what she probably thought was the most nonchalant manner possible what Nora was like in real life. Flanagan would invariably answer, "Michelle honey, you are watching her on reality television. How much more realistic can it get?"

Michelle would laugh and press ahead. "She seems like she really has it together with all those clothing lines and perfume brands."

"Is that what you want to do?"

"No," she said, giving him a look like "how could you even …"

Flanagan was a little relieved by her answer. She had seemed to be cast under that Pisano/Wall spell that enchanted so many teenage girls. But Michelle's slight look of horror at following in Nora's entrepreneurial footsteps comforted him. "So what would you like to do?"

"I'm too young to know," said Michelle, giving the answer she had been told by many adults, "although I have some ideas. Promise not to think I'm stupid if I tell you."

"Don't worry," assured Flanagan. "I already think you're stupid, so I won't think any less of you." Michelle kicked him in the shin. One day, Flanagan would have to talk to her about those kicks. They were always at the shin, and man they stung. Yet he was secretly happy that she lashed out more now. She had spent early adolescence often withdrawn, chewing her fingernails to the nubs and lightly twitching when anyone approached her. Her opening up about her dream had to be a positive, right?

"Dad, I know this sounds corny," she trembled a bit, "but I'd really like to help fight global warming."

"I think you should shoot for something less ambitious, like fixing the Iranian-Israeli conflict or getting the North Koreans to give up nukes."

"Don't be a jerk. I think I want to be climate scientist."

"That's a noble calling," said Flanagan, secretly overjoyed. Of course, he knew that Michelle would probably explore twenty more career paths by the time she left for college: he had prepared himself for anything from politician to plumber. He naively feared his time on the show may have had a deleterious effect on her worldview. He was fortunate that she, like many teenagers, had no interest in seeing her parents as role models.

"I'm glad you feel that way," said Michelle, "because I was hoping we could go to the community garden and plant something today."

Flanagan was thinking of having a softball catch with Michelle and watching one of the movies that they had seen together too many times. Oh, thought Flanagan, so she told me about this new career goal just to make this community garden thing happen. He figured there must be a cute boy there. "Do we have to bring anything?" he asked. "A shovel?"

Michelle snickered and then added in a sheepish plea, "I was hoping we could bring a tree with us."

Flanagan grumbled something about trees costing money.

His daughter countered, "You know the best way to capture carbon is through trees."

Ugh, here we go, thought Flanagan, another Gen Zer saving the earth one tree at a time. "Is that so?" he asked, unwilling to commit further.

"We could get a lovely oak."

"I hate oaks. They drop too many brown leaves and they're really not very pretty. No wonder people like to cut them down."

"How about a nice white pine? No leaves."

Flanagan knew his daughter was a determined little bugger. If he kept badmouthing one type of tree after another, she'd be espousing the virtues of birches and beeches, spruces and sycamores, hornbeams and hickories. "How much is this going to set me back?"

"We probably could get a good deal at Verni's Garden Center."

The next thing Flanagan knew he was in Elmhurst propping up six-foot pines in burlap for Michelle's inspection. "How about those smaller ones over there?" he asked.

"Dad ..." said Michelle. "Those will take too long to grow. We need to help the world faster than that."

"Well, all I know is that bigger trees will cause a more drastic climate change in my wallet."

"It's forty dollars more. That's means you won't drink as many beers. You will not only save the earth, but save that belly of yours."

Michelle really didn't fight fairly. Flanagan was nearly proud of her. They purchased the six-foot pine that looked least likely to die ("Dad, Astoria can be tough on trees"), dragging it to the abandoned neighborhood lot where the young and beautiful were filling up construction bags with the last of the random concrete. The lot still looked horrible, but soon a truckload of mulch was dropped off and partially covered fifty years of urban sin.

Flanagan found himself cursing his daughter as he dug the hole for the pine, finding so many surprises of asphalt, iron, and assorted fill. The Gen Zers took one look at the tedious task before Flanagan and decided their energies would be better placed spreading mulch. Flanagan hoped there would be some celebrity waiting in the wings to hand him a fatherhood trophy at the end of this nightmare. In her defense, Michelle jumped into the hole to pick out concrete chunks during those moments when her father stopped, leaned on his shovel, and wondered whether that tightness in his chest might be the beginning of a heart attack. Not helping matters was the cursed heat. Though October had begun, it felt like late July. The weathermen spoke of unseasonable temperatures, but how unseasonable were they when the heat remained unchanged during what should be pumpkin picking time?

Knowing he would embarrass his daughter if he started bitching about the current state of affairs, Flanagan concentrated on digging and breathing. He wished he knew less about planting trees. He didn't like the fact that proper procedure called for the width to be three times greater than the root mass. This white pine would have to settle for two times greater. On the bright side, he also remembered that the depth of the hole did not have to be any lower than the root mass. In fact, the top of the root mass should be a bit above the ground. The bottom line was the white pine was dropped into the hole with the absolute least amount of excavated debris possible.

As he backfilled the dirt around the tree, he whispered to Michelle, "This saving the earth shit is very hard. I can now say with utter certainty that we have no chance of making it as a species."

Exhausted, Flanagan found a concrete wall to rest his back on and took a zen-like nap while Michelle flirted with boys who exuded the feral aura of global righteousness. He only slept for a few minutes because he couldn't stop himself from eavesdropping on his daughter's conversations. He was struck how she deflected the compliment about the softness of her hair and somehow redirected the discussion to creating microforests in urban areas. "It's really part of the ancient tradition of Japanese temples," she said. "We just need to get a variety of seedlings and plant them tightly. The key is to use fast maturing, native species. If we do that in every open lot in the city, we will make a quite a dent."

"Wow, that can really save the planet," said a teen Flanagan imagined in his closed-eye state as having perfectly coiffed messy hair and skinny jeans that rode well above his ankles.

"Well," said Michelle. "Let's not make too much of this. Research says if we plant a trillion extra trees – not a billion, but a thousand billion – we might remove about a quarter of the carbon dioxide in the air. After all that, a quarter. We should still do it. The tree planting helps and reminds us to stay active and focused on the needs of climate change. But the stuff we really have to do will be much harder than sticking a tree into the ground."

Yeah, thought Flanagan, you might feel differently if you just broke your back digging a hole through the merciless urban rubble. Still, his daughter sounded sane. He sensed he could pretend to awaken now since skinny jean/sloppy hair boy had slyly procured Michelle's number by offering to text her a blog on bamboo.

Grabbing some shawarma on the way home, they settled into his basement apartment. All Flanagan wanted to do was rest; all Michelle wanted to do was talk. Her skull was exploding with climate change data; data dispirited Flanagan.

Oddly, Michelle sounded awfully chipper as she made such devastating pronouncements as, "Everything rests on the next decade. If we don't cut carbon emission in half in the next ten years, it's all over." Or this little sweet sentiment: "A million species will go. We'll follow."

Flanagan was curious exactly how much Michelle, this teenage punk, really knew. "Why only a decade?"

"That's when we'll get right up against a 2-degree centigrade rise in temperatures, which most of the scientific community sees as cataclysmic and irreversible. With so many of the past twenty-five years posting new worldwide high temperature records, the models extrapolating the results are really scary."

Flanagan liked how measured his daughter sounded when delivering all of this doom and gloom. "So what's your answer?" he challenged her. "Do you really have that much faith in solar and wind?"

"I'd like to have faith in governments delivering large-scale efforts for solar and wind," she said. Flanagan stared at her, waiting, making clear she hadn't really answered his question. "No, I don't really have enough faith in them. The technology hasn't moved as quickly as anyone would've hoped. Plus, the energy collection and storage is not what it needs to be, and right now these technologies take up too much space for what they yield."

Flanagan nodded. "It sounds like you've been researching in between those long hours putting on makeup." Michelle gave one of those "oh Dad" frowns. "What have you been reading?"

She laughed. Flanagan might have heard a little condescension in its lower register. "Dad, nobody reads anymore. I watch videos." Flanagan groaned. "You know TED talks from climate scientists and panel talks on the YouTube channels."

"Those talks give you any insight into how to get out of this mess? Please don't tell me they suggested planting trees in abandoned city lots."

"No, silly, that was just to get you off your butt and spend some quality time with your wonderful daughter."

"And give my daughter a chance to exchange digits with some boys who've got a little global warming their pants." Reflexively, Flanagan retracted his shins.

"Do you have to turn all of our conversations into an episode of *Peepin' on the Pisanos*?"

"I'm sorry," said Flanagan. "I haven't written any other type of script in a while. I'll try to shift the plotline. So since you are not sure that solar and wind are going to completely cut it, do you have any alternatives?" Curious, Flanagan threw out, "How about nuclear?"

"Funny you should mention that. I've been watching a lot of videos from Claudia Bowman."

Flanagan knew he should have played dumb, but he was desperate to demonstrate relevance so he tossed in, "You mean the Columbia scientist?"

"Yeah," said Michelle, trying not to act surprised. "How do you know about her?"

"I read," Flanagan lied.

"Anyway, Dr. Bowman thinks nuclear has to be part of the solution."

"And what do you think?" asked Flanagan.

"At first, I was skeptical," she said. "Nuclear is pretty scary. If things go wrong … Bowman calmed me down a little bit. But what really changed my mind are these NukeMan videos."

"NukeMan?" Flanagan chuckled.

"Yeah, he's great," she said. "He waddles around in the grass dressed up as a nuclear reactor."

"Boy, he must have some figure."

"It's all about the base, Dad. Here let me show you." Michelle took out her phone, tapped and slid her index finger along the screen for a few seconds, turned her screen sideways, and handed Flanagan the phone.

The video opened with apocalyptic visions of nuclear destruction and then cut to a man who was indeed in this incredibly well-designed costume of a nuclear reactor cooling tower, the bottom steadily and elegantly expanding near his Nike-sneakered feet, where the base rounded at his ankles. The off-white color of the entire costume was faded in spots to give the impression that the reactor had been in use for a while. A steady stream of white steam rose from his neck. As he stood in the grass framed by hedges, he appeared to be constantly emerging from an ancient mist. To further accentuate the point, NukeMan's face was mainly covered with black hair, long and scraggly atop, thick mustache in the middle, mangy beard below. Anyone who saw him knew he had walked over many mountains and crossed endless streams to reach this very point.

"When I was just a wee lad, a nuclear holocaust used to be the scariest prospect possible," he said in a voice older than his presence – perhaps the sloping suit took years off of his appearance. "It is time to put away these childish fears. Now comes the stuff of adult nightmares." The camera quickly cut away from NukeMan to images of rising waves and flooded cites, forest fires and burnt villages, dried creek beds and dead puppies.

When the camera returned to NukeMan, he stood in the distance, the smoke rising from his head, looking like nothing less than inspiration. As the camera zoomed in, NukeMan blew away the smoke and his arresting eyes gleamed (even Flanagan had to acknowledge they were beautiful peepers). He spoke with the clarity that only the absurdity of the situation and the madness of the man could hope to produce. "So isn't it ironic that the thing we were most afraid of must be the only thing that can save us now." NukeMan let the smoke rise a few moments and then he exhaled, blowing the cloud toward the viewer. "I exaggerate. Nuclear power can't save, but it can be the stones of the bridge to get us to the other side."

Now the screen cut to a sophisticated animation of a stone bridge construction evolving into a steel-cabled suspension span on the far edge of the riverbank. The "camera" dropped into the river where old-fashioned bulbous alarm clocks floated downstream. As the clocks tumbled into a waterfall, the mist welling up from the plunge basin transformed into the steam rising out of NukeMan's neck.

"Nuclear power gives us back the one thing we seem unable to regain: Time. We need the time for solar, wind, biofuels, and batteries to save us. If we just wait for them, it will be too late. Don't get me wrong. Let's erect every turbine we can, install every panel, employ every clean energy technology we can put on the battlefield today. But don't forget nuclear. Because right now, our scariest weapon happens to be our best one."

The screen cut to nuclear plants across the planet as classical music – Flanagan thought he might have detected Bach's "Jesu, Joy of Man's Desiring"

– serenaded soothingly. With the softness of the camera lens, the images of the wafting white steam from the crests of the cooling towers resembled the geysers of Yellowstone.

"I am NukeMan. I speak for the trees. I live in the forest. I am not happy that we must go nuclear, but these are desperate times, my friends. I have learned to live with this smoke swirling around my head. It is time you do too."

As the screen cut to black, Flanagan saw that NukeMan offered many more videos, so he started clicking and watching. Five minutes into the sequel, which was even better (the cooling towers danced like Disney hippos in tutus and then NukeMan sauntered along in such stylish goofiness that Flanagan audibly chuckled), Michelle poked her father, "Can I have my phone back?"

"Oh, sure," he said, passing hers over and picking up his phone. For a good half hour, Michelle watched her father watching NukeMan videos. When she left him, he continued clicking from one to the next, addictively. Something about NukeMan was familiar. Excited and disturbed, Flanagan spent the rest of the night on the futon gazing at NukeMan videos.

As she slept soundly in what was usually Flanagan's bed, Michelle decided she might actually not hate her father.

CHAPTER 13
THE BLUDGEONINGS OF CHANCE

After talking with Michelle about NukeMan for many hours and dropping her back at his ex-wife's, Flanagan decided he could use another conversation with Clarkin, which invariably delivered him to the entrance of the Pint O'Plenty. In light of the number of revelations about the late Senator, some of those rather randy, he figured Clarkin offered the best chance to contextualize the last few months of Doherty's life.

Flanagan did not make it to the front door before two guys in Yankee caps said they wanted to talk to him about Heather Pisano. "I'm not at liberty to say anything about her," he told them. "They made me sign Non-Disclosure Agreements."

"Yeah, don't worry," said the taller one, jocularly. "We don't want no trouble." Then he pushed Flanagan back while the other Yankee cap charged into him like a right guard for the Giants, blocking him into the alley. Not the best of fighters, Flanagan took a swing at the blocking guard and luckily caught him on the jaw. That slowed the pressure of the bull rush, but just then the taller Yankee cap punched Flanagan in the gut with a hard right fist, sending him down on a knee. The blocking guard now collapsed on top of Flanagan and tall Yankee cap was kicking him in the ribs with ruthless efficiency.

Flanagan gasped for breath in too much pain to figure out how to defend himself beyond a lame curling of his torso and a covering of his face with his arms. He now became determined only to save Kartik's fancy Red digital camera. Eventually, tall Yankee cap had stopped kicking him, although the blocking guard angrily smacked Flanagan on the top of the head a couple of more times, clearly unhappy about the sock to the jaw. Flanagan thought less and his skull reverberated more with each whack. "That's enough," said tall Yankee.

The two stood over Flanagan and listened with satisfaction to his labored breathing. "You need to stop what you're doing," said tall Yankee. Flanagan was starting to wonder if the blocking guard was a mute. "If you continue, we won't be so nice next time." Tall Yankee dropped to one knee and leaned his head down, so he could be eye-to-eye with Flanagan, who unfurled a few fingers from his face out of morbid curiosity. "You understand," said tall Yankee.

Flanagan nodded.

"Good," answered tall Yankee. He patted Flanagan's back, which made his curled, prone body flinch. "Like I told you, we don't want no trouble."

Flanagan heard the two of them walk out of the alley and down the street. Apparently, they would not be imbibing at the Pint O'Plenty. After many minutes when he was pretty sure that the Yankee caps were long gone, Flanagan moved out of his curled state, muttering to himself that he couldn't even get the fetal position right. He cradled Kartik's camera which came through the assault much better than he did. He did not try to stand, instead swiveling his ass and leaning his back against the alley wall.

To alleviate the throbbing in his ribs, he attempted to focus on breathing, often not succeeding. He touched his lower lip, pulling his finger away to gaze at the blood. That minor injury was collateral. His first suspicion was that the attack was ordered by the American Henry Center. Sure, the obvious perpetrators would be the Pisanos, but he had worked with them for more than a dozen years, much of Michelle's lifetime. He could not imagine them attacking him. Yet when he touched his nearly pristine countenance, he could not come to any other conclusion than the Pisanos were behind the assault. Only the Pisanos would allow for contingencies that his face might need to be clean for any filming they were planning. But filming what? None of it made sense to him. Though he had written the scripts, he could never figure out those damn Pisanos.

As he started ruminating about his damaged ribs, Flanagan spotted an enormous man stepping out of the Pint O'Plenty back door into the alley. Flanagan recoiled involuntarily until he realized it was Clarkin. His slight movement caught the big man's eye, since Clarkin was well attuned to scoping the alley in case other combatants might emerge from the shadows. Clarkin moved closer to Flanagan's slumped figure, his big paw on the back. "That you, Artie?"

"Yeah," said Flanagan.

"What's wrong with you?"

"I got beat up," said Flanagan. "What are you doing out here?"

"I got challenged to another fight," said Clarkin. "But it seems like he decided the better of it and ran off. That happens a lot. This bar doesn't have half as many brawls as you think it does."

Flanagan groaned. "You picked a rotten time to try to convince me of that."

Clarkin laughed and sat down next to Flanagan against the wall. He put his massive arm across his new friend's shoulder and asked, "What happened?"

"Got jumped." Flanagan was in no state to recount the entire incident.

"You know who did it?" asked Clarkin.

"No, I don't," Flanagan answered. "But I'm pretty sure they don't want me to make this documentary."

Clarkin thought for a minute. "Well, that gives me some ideas."

"Me too," said Flanagan. "Can I buy you a drink? I need to ask you a few questions."

"Sounds like you haven't taken the warning to heart."

"Not today," said Flanagan. "Maybe tomorrow it will sink into my thick skull."

"All right," said Clarkin, "but I'll be buying tonight. I strongly believe in buying the loser a drink."

"But I didn't fight you," said Flanagan.

"I believe that for any loser," said Clarkin.

Flanagan laughed grimly. "No wonder you're broke."

Once inside and drinks were served – Flanagan decided it was a Maker's Mark kind of night – Clarkin tried to get Flanagan to play darts. When Flanagan looked horrified and declined, Clarkin said, "I'm sorry. What was I thinking? You're in no condition to do anything but drink."

"It's not just that," said Flanagan. Then he explained the meeting with Detective Murphy at the Killarney Rose, his wrist still sore from missing the dart board so many times.

Clarkin laughed. "The way you're going you'll be broken in six pieces by the end of the night."

"Then, I'd like to get some more information from you before that happens, if you don't mind."

"I don't mind. Shoot."

"I heard a few things about Jimmy Doherty and Barbara Jansen." Clarkin's eyes widened. Flanagan made sure he couldn't play dumb. "You know, the gorgeous recluse married to the software billionaire Lars Key, the one who happened to be Suzie's sister, the one famous for her intergalactic sibling rivalry with Suzie."

"Oh," said Clarkin. He drank half his Jack and coke and sniffed dismissively. "That was not something Jimmy ever confirmed."

"But you think he slept with her?"

"When I asked him directly all those years ago, since I had been there a few days earlier when he received an intriguing message from her and promptly left the office, his answer was incredibly circumspect, even for a politician. I think he didn't flat out say no because he was secretly proud of the conquest, like he had slept with Marilyn Monroe or someone."

"I'm getting the impression Doherty wasn't all about policy decisions."

Clarkin grunted. "It's in the family genes. His brother Kevin has an eye for the ladies himself." He headed off on a tangent, explaining that Kevin, who had spent many years in England, has been linked to everyone from Elizabeth Hurley to Helen Mirren.

Sensing he would not be getting anything else out of Clarkin on this topic, Flanagan moved onto the connection between Frankie Pisano and the American Henry Center.

"I hadn't heard of that before," said Clarkin, "but I can't say I'm surprised."

"Why's that?"

"Frankie seemed to be everywhere in New York at the time," he said. "If there was a plate of food and a potential client, he figured out a way to get on the guest list. The Henrys were big oil and that meant big money, especially back then with Roy Crowne running things, so Frankie would be very interested in getting to know them."

Given the generalizations Clarkin was offering tonight, Flanagan was starting to get the impression that the main thing he would gain from visit to the Pint O'Plenty was a battered torso. Clearly fishing, Flanagan tried one more angle before placing his whiskey glass conclusively on the counter. "Just a hunch, let me ask you about something that's been bothering me. What did Doherty think about nuclear power?"

Clarkin lifted his brow in surprise and smiled. He might have even been impressed. "Funny, he was a closet nuclear lover. No one in his political lane could just come out and say it. I can tell you as his close friend that one of the last things he did in his short life was to meet with the Council of Energy Awareness, at the time the biggest nuclear lobby."

"Did the meeting lead to anything?"

"Besides his death, you mean? Jimmy didn't share his plans with us on what he was doing with the council. He didn't want anything leaked to the press."

"Whoa, hold on." Flanagan picked up his almost empty glass and pointed his index finger at Clarkin. "What do you mean beside his death?"

"I have a sneaking suspicion that the Henry Center was well aware of Jimmy's meeting with the nuke guys since by that time they were following his every step." As the bartender watched Clarkin polish off his drink, leaving only small, melting cubes in the bottom, he dropped a fresh Jack and coke on the bar and signaled to Flanagan, who waved off another. Clarkin picked up the drink, foamy with coke bubbles, but did not yet imbibe. "Once the Henry guys caught Jimmy meeting with their most hated enemy – since back in the eighties, big oil saw nuclear as their greatest and most immediate threat – they considered it the last straw. I think they decided right then that he had to go."

Awkwardly groaning, Flanagan stood up and tried to put on the bar two twenties, which Clarkin returned to his pocket and offered just enough menace in his scowl for Flanagan not to make a second attempt. "Thanks. I am starting to get the feeling I need to do much more research."

"It's about time you came to that conclusion," Clarkin said. He muttered and reached into his backpack. "I've been debating all night whether I should let you borrow these, but you look so damn pathetic all slumped over like you've been through fifteen rounds, even though I'm pretty certain you didn't even last one." He pulled out two appointment books labeled 1988 and 1989. Flanagan lurched toward them. "Slow down there, champ. I want to make absolutely clear to you, if I don't get these back by next week, I will rip your arms out of your sockets and remove at least one of those bruised ribs of yours."

"I can't thank you enough," said Flanagan, picking up the appointment books and leaving quickly.

As Flanagan headed out the door, Clarkin yelled out. "You really are a slow learner, aren't you?"

Flanagan yelled back. "It's taken a very long time for me to figure that out."

Forty-five minutes later, drunk and damaged, Flanagan gingerly found his way onto the dark green futon, shoved a pillow below his head, and picked up his laptop. He noodled around the Attica prison website until he figured how to send an Email to the lifer Karl "the Sausage" Hoffman, since the convict might be the last living connection to Doherty's accident. Despite Murphy's warnings, Flanagan figured what did he have to lose writing to a prisoner who refused to talk. He drafted the Email, preparing himself for another failed effort, which is why he brazenly started his note with "Dear Karl the Sausage." How could he offend someone who was permanently offended?

Flanagan decided to keep the note short and sharp. "I am not a cop. I am doing a documentary about the death of Jimmy Doherty. I think Frankie Pisano was involved and you might have some knowledge of his role. I am offering you nothing. Still, I can't think of any harm it will do for you to tell. You could write me back simply because you might find it's a good way to pass a few minutes among the endless hours of gloom." Flanagan hit send.

He clicked on the remote. Deciding the rib pains weren't sufficient suffering, he listened to the local news for a few minutes as the anchorwoman and then the weatherman spoke ominously of Hurricane Zelda brewing out in the Caribbean, threatening to come up the eastern seaboard. Clicking around on the remote, he eventually landed on an installment of *Peepin' on the Pisanos*. Flanagan knew the entire episode by heart: most of the lines he had written, except for those the daughters had flubbed (Suzie never misspoke a word or was off even a cadence). Entitled "Naked Ambition," this one featured Heather's shoot for *Maxim*, the one where her sisters counseled her to keep on her thong and Suzie encouraged her to be "as naked as the day God and I made you." As he intently observed the comings and goings of the family with the concomitant drama, Flanagan felt strange ideas bubbling to the surface. He knew insights were coming, but damn if he could figure out what they were and when they would arrive.

CHAPTER 14
THE DELAYING OF A SECOND

With his ribs still aching, Flanagan pushed back his appointments and spent the day reading from the comfort of his futon. He perused every word written about Jimmy Doherty, from the *New Yorker* profile to the *Time* magazine story to the *Commonweal* article entitled, "The Man Who Wants to Save the Planet." Flanagan sadly came to the realization that no serious biography of Doherty had been written. Earlier in his career a sports memoir called *From the Corner* was pretty good, and later he received the kind of fluff biographies common for political campaigns.

For hours, he watched archival footage of Doherty playing basketball and making speeches. He spent even more time simply looking at photographs of Doherty, carefully studying his face. He had been infected with the Pisano philosophy that most of what can be known about a person can be discovered through appearance. An impressively handsome man, Doherty seemed to be bred for voyeuristic gazing. Flanagan was struck particularly by his flawless chin and nose. Easily distracted and always willing to go off on tangents, Flanagan read up on the perfect defined angle of a jaw line, discovering that Doherty had possessed the coveted Duchess nose with its straight edge and 106-degree nasal tip rotation. Except for realizing that he could use Doherty's arresting face to help promote the documentary, Flanagan was disappointed that his careful perusal offered little insight.

When he was done staring, Flanagan returned to reading. Perhaps he had been influenced by Clarkin's comments last night, since Flanagan decided that the most curious account came from his Jimmy's brother Kevin Doherty. Although they were identical twins, the brothers took very different career paths. While Jimmy focused on athletics and politics at Columbia, Kevin embraced the natural sciences, studying zoology and geology at Cambridge. Flanagan pondered the significance of the identical twins deciding to make their marks an ocean away from each other.

Since he was as tall and handsome as Jimmy, Kevin attracted much attention, especially for his early fieldwork in the wilds of Madagascar. At the beginning of his career, he was merely interviewed on nature shows; then he became the host of *The Original Kingdom* and, much later, of the still thriving series *Planet Green*. Curiously, Kevin hosted *The Original Kingdom* in London studios, but, shortly after Jimmy's death, he returned to New York, which has ever since served as the home base for his far-flung adventures. To the amusement of his old friends like Clarkin, Kevin continued to affect a lilt of the British accent, although he spent the bulk of his formative years nearer to Kew Gardens, Queens than to the one just west of London. That Elizabeth II figured out how to knight Kevin further conflated both his heredity and his intonations. His autobiography, *Life below the Clouds*, dedicated one chapter to his relationship with Jimmy. Flanagan noted that Sir Kevin studied his brother Jimmy the way he would an exotic creature, like say the Rainbow Lorikeet. Sir Kevin preferred engaging in this scientific distance rather than contemplating his brother as the physical manifestation of his own destiny. Opening his Kindle, Flanagan dove into Sir Kevin's florid prose.

```
From Chapter 12 of Life below the Clouds
          by Sir Kevin Doherty


The death of Jimmy struck me the way the
loss of the northern white rhinoceros
had, the way the extinction of any native
species would, since my brother was the
rarest of creatures. By moving onto
England's green pastures, I found an
ecosystem more suited to my survival, one
that suppressed my compulsive appetites.
Oh, how the rain on the heath dampened
the spirits of those who might frolic
among the heather!
     Remaining in his native territory of
the North American continent, Jimmy
```

roamed the mid-Atlantic coastal moraines much the way the wolverine ranged Vancouver Island from the rolling eastern side to the wet and rugged western edge. Coincidently, the Vancouver Island wolverine and Jimmy suffered extinction at nearly the same time. Both the wolverine and Jimmy were too expansive and voracious to survive. Filled with impulses and a raging intellect that would not be tamed in such a wild political habitat, Jimmy would discover he was threatened by invasive species at every vale and notch.

I remember when Jimmy and I were just two young whelps; no one could tell us apart. The only difference was that Jimmy was slightly faster in his words and actions than I was. That meant as I was ready to say to my father, "Why do we have to eat liver every Tuesday?" the question would already be out of Jimmy's mouth. Initially, I would feel stupid that Jimmy always beat me to making a point, but soon I learned. Father would send his big Irish paw across Jimmy's head. If I had been faster on the draw or Jimmy had not been there, I would have been the one receiving the whipping. Instead, Jimmy always made the point and always suffered the consequences: whether it was the in-school suspensions for telling Mr. Schwartz that he should resign from teaching forthwith since he had no understanding of thermodynamics or whether it was the slap on the cheek for his comments to Kathy Bronzert about the swish of her hips reminding him of the swing of Pleiades.

I learned from observing Jimmy. He faced the consequences that I had avoided. My thoughts and actions were marked by just enough deliberative delay. In our early years, I was only a heartbeat behind Jimmy. As the years passed on, my toddler caution that had initially settled a mere trice behind was followed by grammar school pauses of a moment, in turn followed by adolescent suspensions of a second. Don't mistake me. At Cambridge, the wags of the Footlights said that I was the quickest wit since Oscar Wilde. And when I responded that Wilde attended Trinity and Oxford, never setting foot on this campus, they answered, "Exactly."

I remained rapid fire in my thoughts and pursuits. But my brain and emotions would slow just enough to think a situation through for the second and a half that Jimmy disregarded (the half second being his natural advantage, the next whole second becoming mine). For the first 18 years of my hyperintense life, I envied Jimmy and cursed the ridiculous concept that although we possessed the exact same DNA, Jimmy was a tick faster. I less bemoaned how this condition was unfair, but how that was even possible. Indeed, I was damned with knowing enough about genetics that his advantage came not from the genes, but from either his inexplicable gifts or my inexplicable defects. Whichever, this scenario rendered me hostile: "round he throws his baleful eyes."

As the beatings continued throughout Jimmy's meteoric yet tumultuous adolescence, I came to understand that my suffering was more conceptual. Jimmy endured many a physical bludgeoning for being too smart, aware, and unfiltered; contrary notions could not be permitted without penalties. He would regularly undergo wrath and weeping (I heard his teeth gnashing at bedtime) even if he had too much Irish in him to reveal his misery to any object larger, clearer, and lighter than a pint of Guinness.

A strange phenomenon transpired when we both applied to college. I had been rejected by Columbia and accepted by Cambridge while Jimmy had the same split, only in reverse. For years, Jimmy had been considered the shining light of us twins, and yet, when the colleges acceptances had been handed down, the dozen or so schoolboy intellectuals who weighed each of us daily like we were slabs of prime meat ready for market decreed that my selection by Cambridge was an affirmation of what they had suspected all along. They argued - and I secretly concurred - that while Jimmy's pyrotechnics got all the attention, my measured wisdom was one worthy of donning the black jacket in those hallowed English halls.

Suddenly, I emerged as the brother who was perceived as more brilliant since I could hold my enlightened counsel just a little longer. By that time, no one would perceive that an identical twin could possibly process and think more slowly than his brother. The pause and delays were borne out of humility: the noble tendency to think a matter through on seven levels before a word is spoken. Even before I strolled with hushed dignity along Pembroke Street, the masses had endowed upon me the serene knowledge of the Daoist, the acceptance of inevitable dysfunction by the Buddhist, the long view of the Deist, and loopy ironic posture of the Existentialist. Like my opportunistic brother before me, I knew a prospect when I was proffered one, so I became the Brahmin of the Cantabrigians; I would, in turn, become the Brahmin of the Field Site; then the Brahmin of the European continent; then of the Western World, and then, and then …

Jimmy witnessed my ascension to the apex of the Old World from afar. He would faithfully watch my programs, featuring my concomitant wry hand-wringing of a European culture that had been destroying its forests for millennia. He understood as I did that the populace had no other choice of how to respond to my sermons but by paying and donating and paying and donating until I became the conscience of a citizenry I neither knew nor recognized.

While I, with my one second delay, looked backwards, Jimmy looked inexorably forward. Jimmy's impulsive instincts served him well in basketball, always hitting the spot before his opponent, popping off a jumper without wasting the time to contemplate whether he should. That spontaneous wit and willingness to answer without resorting to old bromides would again do his bidding in politics. He gathered enough attention that shortly before his death he merited a favorable story from the BBC, the correspondent only on a singular occasion asking about his famous brother stationed in London. Naturally, Jimmy's perception of the threat of global warming was once again a step ahead of me. Alas Jimmy, he always knew what needed defending.

When we were fifteen, we tended to roam the woods. Of course, we hardly ever trounced about together since it was in both of our natures to go it alone. Jimmy was a great collector of snakes, picking up rocks all over the island, catching garters and black racers and hognoses. He'd put them in tanks in his room until Dad would come in and find them hidden by the side of his bed, beating him like he had a prostitute there instead. One day I had been digging through the clay looking for Indian arrowheads and paint pots when my small shovel nicked a mole. The mole squeaked and writhed. Initially, I thought I had killed the poor little critter, so marking it was only wounded,

I brought it home with me, stuffed in my sweatshirt pocket so it would stay warm and out of the light. I dug up earthworms and fed them to the ailing fellow, its webbed claws clinging to my finger as its nose rooted about my pocket for the meal, those tiny eyes in a constant state of closure. One day, my father discovered the mole in a shoebox while he was searching our room.

"Where did this vermin come from?"

I prepared to confess, but Jimmy, as usual, was quicker. "I am saving it to feed to my snakes," he said.

Before I could dispute the claim, our father was on top of him, furiously smacking him, clearly fed up with my brother's persistence. When my father left the room, I asked Jimmy, "Why did you say that?"

He answered, "I thought it was the right thing to do."

I didn't know what to say to him. I don't remember thanking him. I do remember never feeling happier to have his DNA. From that day on, I had this sneaking fear that he would die young and I would live to be a very old man. I am ashamed to admit that I was surprised he lived as long as he did. Like the Pyrenean Ibex, Jimmy was destined for extinction, hunted from this world for the temerity of peering from the mountaintop and heading in the right direction.

Flanagan was sure any psychiatrist would have quite a great deal to say about how Sir Kevin depicted his identical twin brother. But for his purposes, Flanagan did not need to make sense of the sibling rivalry. He was satisfied that he detected, underneath Sir Kevin's abstruse Darwinian metaphors, a belief that the death of his brother Jimmy was no accident.

CHAPTER 15
DRIVING TOWARD SOMETHING

Normally, when a top cast member of *Peepin' on the Pisanos* summoned Flanagan, he'd jump right to it. But Flanagan waited until Dirk Wall called him a second time before he responded. He couldn't see how Dirk would fit into this documentary. When it came to his crash, Flanagan saw two scenarios: 1. He truly had a car accident; in that case Dirk's sad suffering merely contributed to the sense of vehicular foreboding for the men who made the poor choice of embracing Suzie Pisano. 2. The car crash was intentional, a narrative which would be coopted by everyone from the police to the Pisano family before Flanagan got his finger on the record button.

In other words, meeting with Dirk Wall could muddy the narrative he was slowly formulating about the death of Jimmy Doherty and the connection of Frankie and Suzie to it. Significantly, Dirk no longer lived at the Pisano mansion. Yes, he showed up there briefly, so the cameras could capture his tearful homecoming. But within a couple of days, he rolled his wheelchair over to the East River to reside in a shiny new Long Island City co-op.

A relatively late interloper to the family, Dirk had once thought his fitness celebrity, featuring his good looks and can-do attitude, would attain new heights with his 21st Century marriage to Suzie. He soon came to realize that when he incorporated Suzie into his workout videos, she immediately sucked all the attention to her. And when Heather became involved, Dirk's role continued to shrink. Eventually, nobody acknowledged that the workouts were his, deciding any activities so eye-catching had to be the brainchild of those Pisano women. Flanagan consciously tried to beef up Dirk's role in *Peepin' on the Pisanos*, incorporating his new exercise routines into the episodes, but his presence in the show steadily deteriorated.

Flanagan guessed Dirk knew that as the script guru, he sympathized with the alleged "man of the house," who endured a steady stream of indignities. The way things were going Dirk's trousers would soon be rolled. Though Dirk Wall was not yet dead, he had clearly been written out of the script. Now, diminished in his wheelchair, Dirk greeted Flanagan on the balcony of his Long Island City penthouse.

As usual, the weather was balmy. Yesterday's October evening dropped down to the 50s, giving the entire sweaty region hope, but the temperature was back up near 80 on the balcony, even with the merciful breezes of the East River. Peering out onto the erector set frame of the Queensboro Bridge, Dirk hollered, "Hey there Artie, how's it shaking?"

Flanagan thought for a man who would spend the rest of his life in a wheelchair Dirk was in an awfully good mood. But then again Flanagan had never seen Dirk appear unhappy. "Doing all right," said Flanagan. "How are you feeling?"

"Oh, I couldn't be better," said Dirk. "I've been yelling for everyone to get off their asses all their lives. Now, I get to see how the other half lives." He laughed so heartily that Flanagan felt obliged to join in. As America's third most famous fitness guru, Dirk was renowned for his joyous motivation. His signature command, "Move!" was delivered so warmly and affectionately that it was positively bovine ... as in "Mooooooooove!"

"I was wondering if I could record you for a documentary I'm doing on the family?" asked Flanagan.

"Oh, please don't record me," said Dirk. "I invited you to come over because I wanted to talk about something deeply personal and private to me, so I'd like it between us."

"Certainly, Dirk," said Flanagan, "what would you like to talk about?"

"I would like you to help me write my life story," he answered.

Oh Jeez, thought Flanagan. Here we go again. Even though he was only a script writer, Flanagan received regular requests from many acquaintances to write these stories. He never knew how to gently deliver the harsh truth that most people's lives weren't worth writing about. Flanagan's best explanation started with the devastating realization that the life least worth recording was his own; that whomever he was now engaging was certainly much more intriguing a subject than he was. He would tell them that, unfortunately, he was so overwhelmed with the demands of writing *Peepin' on the Pisanos* that he was simply incapable of taking on the project. "Anyway," he would say, "your life deserves a much better writer than me."

Usually the man making the requests (for it was always a man) would express grave disappointment, adding that he thought Flanagan would have been the perfect candidate. Flanagan interpreted that sentiment as his being the ideal mediocre writer for his subject's mediocre life. Now, he made similar expressions of regret to the man who had been his boss (well, sort of) for many years.

"That's too bad, Artie" said Dirk, "because I've learned so much from this accident that I want to share with the world."

"Yeah," said Flanagan. "I can't imagine how terrible that must have been. Here's your perfect life suddenly shattered."

"Artie," said Dirk, "let's have some hummus." He tapped out a message on his phone, which Flanagan soon realized must have been "Bring out the platter" because a young Hispanic woman brought a tray with carrots, zucchini sticks, and crackers surrounding a mighty scoop of hummus.

"Wow," said Flanagan. "That's some spread."

"I enjoy hummus more than ever now that I've left the house," said Dirk.

"Is this arrangement permanent?"

"I believe it is," said Dirk, "if I have any say about it." Neither Dirk nor Flanagan was sure he had any say. After dipping a carrot into the hummus and chomping down, he added, "Whenever Rosa put out a hummus plate, the girls would swoop in on it like they'd never eaten before in their lives. Then Suzie would get her claws in it. The only hummus left for old Dirk was hidden under a leaf of lettuce."

During his exercise videos, Dirk was legendary for speaking metaphorically, lines like "just because the caboose is at the end of the train doesn't mean there's anything wrong with bringing up the rear." Flanagan never had to exhaust his limited intellect to figure out what Dirk was driving at. The most devastating diminishment of Dirk's value as a family member and more importantly as a family commodity emerged in the adolescent blossoming of Nora, his daughter with Suzie. Now Dirk understood that he was only selected as a mate by Suzie to create such an offspring. Dirk knew he was a good-looking man, good-looking enough that many people refused to take him seriously, but he could not imagine that someone as beautiful as Suzie Pisano would dismiss him in his own household as just another pretty boy.

Flanagan thought stating the obvious was in order. "Well, there's no shortage of hummus here." Then, he dabbed just a smidge on a cracker as not to intrude too radically on the magnificent bounty.

"I thought after I had married Suzie that I would become a movie star," Dirk said. "I mean big. Not just like the Muscles from Brussels or Chuck Norris. I mean like Schwarzenegger big. Maybe I could have even been the governor someday. Many people told me how much they loved *The Dismisser*."

Flanagan decided many people must have been lying because *The Dismisser* made *Conan the Barbarian* look like *The Godfather*. It featured an inappropriately pleasant Dirk Wall announcing to each of his victims, "Your services are no longer needed," before blasting them to kingdom come. Dirk was too nice of a person and too bad of an actor to play the tough guy. *The Dismisser* became the source of many cruel jokes by critics, including Stuart Cooper's *bon mot*: "At least his targets once contributed something to society ... Dirk Wall's only possible way to contribute to society is to never grace a movie screen again."

"The film did receive its share of attention in its day," said Flanagan.

"I could've been the Rock," Dirk lamented.

"Still, you've had an amazingly successful career," said Flanagan.

"Not really," said Dirk. "Look how Suzie soared and Heather, oh my God, Heather, she's an industry, and then Nora, look at how she's exploded. My God, even Tiffany has had so much more success than I've had!"

"I wouldn't say that."

"I would," said Dirk. "And I'll tell you something else, the best thing I ever did was crash that car."

"Crash the car," Flanagan laughed. "You almost sound like you did it on purpose."

"I did do on it on purpose!" said Dirk gleefully, like he was encouraging his audience to squeeze out one more sit-up. "I'd been thinking about crashing my car for a while, but I had to work myself up to doing it."

Flanagan imagined what rituals Dirk performed to prepare for the accident, featuring many mantras of "you can do it." Perhaps, he shifted his trademark cajoling from "Moooooove!" to "Diiiiiieee!" Damn, Flanagan wished Dirk would have let him record the conversation.

Flanagan put his arm on Dirk's shoulder and asked, "Do you still want to kill yourself?"

"No," said Dirk, "now I'm great."

"Is that because you realized that you didn't want to die and that you had so much to live for?"

Dirk laughed. "No. It's just that now I'm in a wheelchair and the world has lowered its expectations of me. Anything I do from here on will get a lot of attention and make everybody feel good. I've already talked to my agent about it. I'm going to travel around the country inspiring paraplegics to get in shape."

"That's wonderful," said Flanagan.

"All I needed was a good tragedy," said Dirk. "I was already as low as I could go. Getting paralyzed just dropped expectations to better align with my fortunes. You're the scriptwriter. I'm disappointed you didn't think of writing my death scene into the series."

Although Flanagan was well aware that suicide attempts were becoming common plotlines on reality TV shows, he liked to believe he had *some* moral standards. "I'm not as sharp as you are."

"Yeah, that's why you hung around the show so long," said Dirk. "It's good you're out. Promise me you'll think about the biography. We'll write a wonderful book together."

Although he wanted to answer, you mean you will talk a lot and I will suffer the drudgery of writing a book few will read, he ventured, "I'll think it over. Maybe after I'm done with this documentary."

"Remember," said Dirk, "if those Pisano women get too rough for you, keep in mind my advice."

"What's that?" asked Flanagan.

Dirk flashed the joyous smile that made him moderately famous. "You can always slam your car into a wall."

CHAPTER 16
THE NEUTRALIZING OF A REACTOR

It would not be accurate to say that Flanagan constantly thought of the unlikely scenario that Heather Pisano might make another visit to his incredibly humble basement apartment. However, he did have a bottle of $30 *rosé* in the refrigerator, even though he could not tell the difference between it and a $20 *rosé*. He also bought a wedge of Irish cheddar which was twice the price of the cheddar he regularly purchased. Flanagan put out both when Heather arrived in her workout outfit, one that few others would dare of tight short-shorts, a tank top, and elevated pink sneakers. Her face was fully made up – her sweat had been limited to what was required for her appearance – although her hair exuded an artfully conceived wetness.

She sprawled on the green futon like she was doing a parody of a photo shoot for a trailer park magazine. Flanagan shrugged in recognition that she made his basement apartment her own territory the moment she entered. Now a mere observer in his own home, Flanagan sat on a kitchen chair, dropping rice crackers in a bowl. After some bizarre niceties of Flanagan asking about Heather's workout and Heather asking him how he liked the place, Flanagan knew he needed to start filming her. Right now, he felt like he was a viewer of one of those entertainment profiles that teetered on the edge of soft porn. Perhaps with the camera on and some serious questions, he might be able to take the dynamic to another place.

Unfortunately, Heather was not game. "I don't think my agent or lawyer would allow anyone but my photographer or cameraman to shoot me."

Flanagan nodded. "Well, how about this: Can I take out my pen and pad? I just want to write some notes as we speak."

"Okaaaay," she answered as if he'd asked the oddest question in the world and, by that very notion, became intriguing.

"Good," said Flanagan. "So a little birdie told me you have quite an interest in nuclear power. What's that about?"

Flanagan could see Heather's mind going through a few permutations, since she had expected a question of the usual vein, say "How do keep yourself so beautiful?" She came here to find out something. Maybe answering his question would be the right path. "Let's just say I think nuclear power is highly underrated."

Flanagan passed her the *rosé* and clinked glasses with her, "To clean energy conversations," he said. She smiled, trying to figure out if Flanagan was engaged in some obtuse form of flirting. "Don't you think nuclear power is dangerous?"

"A little. But much less than oil and natural gas. Its role in curbing climate change would compensate a hundred times over. Plus, it's gotten safer."

"Alright, say we let Chernobyl pass because the Soviets weren't exactly models of protocol, but what about Fukushima?"

"The problem came from it being an older plant."

"Wasn't the problem the tsunami?"

"They could've handled the tsunami if they had a system that allowed the reactor to cool without power." Heather spotted Flanagan's puzzled look. "The old power plants use electric pumps to move water to cool everything down. The problem with the electric pumps is when the power goes out, you're in big trouble. In the newer plants, the water flow relies on gravity from elevated storage tanks."

"Like the water tanks sitting on top of the city apartment buildings?"

"Yes … although I wouldn't imagine the nuclear tanks are the ones in the wooden barrels with the metal straps around them." Flanagan laughed. My God, a normal conversation with a Pisano was possible. "The truth is the plants are getting safer and safer."

"How about the spent fuel? What about those used rods? You can't do much with them for five years as they sit in the cooling tanks, and then the disposal problems only get bigger."

Heather smiled at him. "My God, you are more than a pretty face. You're so cute when you talk about rods." Flanagan blushed, trying to figure out which of Heather's comments did the trick. "You're right. Storage has always been a problem. The spent rods can end up in caves deep underground and transporting them isn't ideal. But once you've cooled those used rods for the five years you so accurately mentioned," Flanagan wondered if she was patronizing him, "then they can be stowed in dry casks which makes them much less dangerous."

"I got you," said Flanagan, taking a sip of the *rosé*. He was tempted to slap a piece of cheese on a cracker, but wouldn't do so until Heather had one first. "But what about the financial costs? From what I've read, it often takes a decade for a return on an investment in a nuclear plant. That's quite a problem for such a controversial technology."

Heather winced. "If the government supported the nuclear industry half as much as it did big oil, if it supported nuclear the way it did hydropower, the way it does wind, the way it does solar, then no one would be concerned about stock dividends. Nuclear is as commercially viable as we want it to be."

"Wouldn't you say that we don't want it to be commercially viable?"

"I would say that right now," Heather acknowledged, "but people can change their minds."

"Are you thinking of changing those minds?"

"I might help."

"That'd be quite a departure from perfumes, workout clothes, and lingerie."

"What's the matter, Flanagan, you don't like lingerie?"

Man, oh man, he thought, she can turn on a grain of sand, can't she. Flanagan chose to not answer the question, but to have a bit more wine. "I think your knowledge of the subject and your passion could make you a convincing advocate."

"So you like my passion."

"More than I like your flirting."

Heather smoothed out her very small workout shorts like she was smoothing out a pleat on a skirt. She had to know she looked slightly ridiculous. She confessed, "Nobody's ever said that to me before."

"I'm sorry," Flanagan said. "You're awfully bright. You don't have to do that here. You're not in front of a camera."

She rolled her eyes like she was answering an irritating child, "How would you know?"

Flanagan looked around for cameras he could not see. He stared down at his pad. He had a couple of pages worth of notes. For what purpose, he had no idea. Nothing else for him to do but keep asking questions. That's how he and Heather functioned together without that awful awkwardness. "Alright, how about the relevance of nuclear? Solar and wind are getting cheaper. And better batteries are coming for storing them. Once the batteries arrive, nuclear power seems like a bit of overkill, doesn't it? Like you're pulling the sun from the sky to light a match."

"Look who's not only handsome, but also the poet." Putting down her empty *rosé* glass with a finality, Heather got up and offered a hearty round of applause. Flanagan got the impression that for once the claps were not for herself, but for him. Indeed, her applause was so enthusiastic and her outfit so committed to fitness that Flanagan saw Heather's exertions as an exercise of utility. She usually only clapped after a television shoot. As Heather walked out, Flanagan realized he had become the show.

To prevent his thoughts from going in the wrong directions, he pondered what the hell kind of game was she playing. He certainly didn't seem worth playing games over when there were so many rappers and ball players to conquer. He could not convince himself that nuclear power served as an aphrodisiac, the oyster or rhino horn of the moment. He decided it had to have something to do with the documentary. He might just be able to figure out what was the connection if he could get his mind off of the outfit Heather really wasn't wearing at all.

In his search for a distraction from Heather's distractions, Flanagan tapped about his phone, discovering an Email from an entity called JPay. Just before he deleted, he spotted the name Karl "the Sausage" Hoffman and the subject line: In the End, just Four You. Karl's note was brief. "You must be stupid if you think that there'd be a situation where Frankie told us what."

Flanagan shook his head. He did not understand what the hell Karl the Sausage was talking about. In his reply Flanagan indicated no such confusion. "So, just to be clear, Frankie never directed you and Tony the Elbow to deliver Jimmy Doherty's car, and by extension, Jimmy Doherty, into the dark, lethal sludge of the Gowanus Canal?"

If this Email delivery was like the last one, JPay would delay Karl's seeing the message until it was thoroughly examined and vetted. Flanagan would have to wait for whatever frustrating response Karl the Sausage might deliver next. Still, rather than think of Heather, Flanagan muttered, "You must be stupid if you think that there'd be a situation where Frankie told us what." He repeated this doggerel until his eyelids groped for darkness and his head stopped craving light.

CHAPTER 17
THE READING OF A RELATIONSHIP

Flanagan arrived at the door of his apartment to find a small dead rodent dangling over the knob, assuring he'd have to remove the animal to enter. Nailed to the rodent was a printed note: "Don't end up like the chipmunk."

Fearful of contracting a disease, Flanagan kicked the chipmunk off the knob with his shoe and opened the door with his forearm shirtsleeves.

Then, he took off the shirt, grabbed a garbage bag, used the shirt to pick up the chipmunk, and dumped it in the bag. Flanagan tried not to think about how effective the scare tactic was. He buried his memory of the dead chipmunk in the laundry bag next to his shirt. Still, he would not remain in the apartment to dwell on what happened.

Earlier in the morning, he had stepped out to get a sandwich and some groceries, allowing about a two-hour window for the chipmunk to be delivered to his door. Clearly, someone was watching his apartment. For all of yesterday, he had been hunkered down at the dinette table tapping into Columbia's search engines to learn more about the major players in the climate change battles of the late 1980s. He had spent enough hours pathetically and methodically making his way through every scrap he could discover about the American Henry Center to know it was time for him to get out of the house.

His incarceration in his research dungeon wasn't wasted, however, since he had stumbled upon a series of FOIL requests for the Center. The positive of being located in New York for a group like the Henry is access to countless investors, many of whose stock interests aligned with the Center's expressed goals; the negative was that every watchdog group used the Freedom of Information Law to dig up dirt on shady organizations like the Henry. As Murphy had indicated, the Henry Center had longstanding connections with crime figures, although the bookkeeping was so byzantine, even financial investigators weren't sure how these figures were paid and for precisely what services. These considerations were further muddled by the dead chipmunk on his doorknob, since that message felt like something one of those Henry Center crime figures would send.

Shaking off the memory of the chipmunk, its little body still warm even through the layer of the shirt, Flanagan continued to strategize about the documentary. He would have to get one of the watchdog wizards on camera, but not for too long … just enough to confirm that the Henry had rough people at least free-lancing for them, if not on payroll, people capable of planning the death of Jimmy Doherty. The rest of his time at the dinette table had been spent poring over the ProPublica lobbying database and following Columbia's search engines to establish the American Henry Center's connection to the American Petroleum Institute. Back in the early 1980s, the API ran a task force that monitored and even conducted climate research, making some disturbing discoveries. For a brief, shining moment, it looked like big oil might take some responsibility for the climate problems on the horizon and pivot toward cleaner energy. Internal task force memos and correspondences left no doubt that the Henry Center played a vital role in the big-oil's lurch toward climate change denial.

The problem right now was all he had were documents. Like that chipmunk, most of the members of the task force were dead, and the ones still living were on record as skeptical about climate change. Sure, Flanagan could get an articulate, reasoned climate change activist to read through the documentation he gathered and tell the tale of the Henry Center's role in crushing the climate research movement. But someone with an insider's knowledge and credibility would really help.

Simply put, he knew his case and therefore his documentary remained flimsy. The dead chipmunk signaled he was running out of time. He had so much work to do. He skimmed through Doherty's appointment books, but nothing had jumped out at him. He clearly needed to peruse the calendar dates doggedly. He would wait to tackle that when he came back home. Now he needed to get the hell out of Astoria. Curiously, Doherty's Senate papers were given to the New York Public Library instead of Columbia University (he'd have to ask Clarkin about that decision). So he took the subway up to 42nd Street and walked around Bryant Park's perimeter until he made it to Fifth Avenue where the stone lions guarded the magnificent, columned library.

To prepare for his visit, Flanagan thought he did everything right. First, he Emailed the Archives and Manuscripts department, and, after getting a response, he set up an appointment with Sharon Heinz who would let him look at the files as long as he did so on the long table adjacent to her office. During their phone call yesterday, Sharon said, "You'll have plenty of room, but once you enter you cannot leave until you're done with examining the papers." Given his impression that Ms. Heinz possessed a controlling nature, Flanagan wasn't sure if this stipulation was the library's or simply hers.

Yet, when Flanagan arrived at noon like they had arranged, Ms. Heinz told him that she would not have the documents ready until 3. Trying not to lose his temper, he walked away, waving, "I'll see you in a couple of hours then."

He wandered around Fifth Avenue, noting the suspicion that had been bubbling up in him all day since to he took the N train out of Astoria: he sensed he was being followed. Yes, many people near him looked down at their phones, but he caught numerous sideways glances, shifty eyes, askance visions, askew glimpses.

To get off the street and away from peering peepers, he'd figured he'd head around to front entrance of the public library and pore over the Doherty's appointment book in the majestic wood-paneled reading room. Flanagan no sooner scaled the steps when he heard, "Arthur, is that you?"

Flanagan looked about until he caught vision of someone he almost recognized. With her face and figure receiving a complete renovation, Tiffany Pisano offered the observer both wonderment and seasickness. The latest Tiffany was, objectively and conceptually speaking, quite attractive. Yet she attained that tipping point where the creator's hands had been so savagely amputated through ruthlessly efficient and effective procedures that arousal was tempered by repulsion.

Still, Flanagan had a soft spot for Tiffany, whose greatest crime came down to her not being her older sister Heather and, of late, not being her younger sister Nora. Plus, she was the only family member who got the jokes he embedded in the script – Heather was mighty smart, but often presented the single-minded business acumen that could render her humorless.

"Hey," he said. "It's so great to see you." For the moment, he decided to forget that she only showed up here because someone paid by the family had been following him. He was intrigued by the strangeness of the entire dynamic – God, a Pisano at a library, who would have ever thought it possible? Might have made a good fish-out-of-water episode.

"You going in too?" she asked the obvious since Flanagan had already queued on the security line. "I had always wanted to see this place."

"I'll show you around if you'd like."

She smiled every millimeter that her tightened skin permitted, using her thick red lips to help out, "Gosh," yes she really said gosh, as if she'd been watching old Marilyn Monroe movies, "I'd love to." Before the surgical overhaul, she had her father's looks and her mother's steely resolve. Now, she emanated a modest aura of mystery, like the latest version on an I-Phone.

"I'm guessing you haven't been here before," said Flanagan. He was tempted to say he was guessing that she had not been to any library, but good manners and great self-interest held his tongue.

"No," she said, and added with what seemed like sincere enthusiasm, "But I'd love to see it."

They strolled across the cavernous lobby of grand stone arches, light gleaming through the high windows. Tiffany and Flanagan rose a couple of flights until they arrived at the third-floor rotunda with a red marble surface so soft in tone that it appeared some of the color had been washed from the stone. Emitting admiring oohs, Tiffany drew close to the dark wood. It was framed by Corinthian capitals, finials, and moldings, competing with painted narrative panels, which told noble tales. Tiffany pointed up to the fresco in the barreled vault.

"I think that's Prometheus," she said.

"Yeah," said Flanagan. "He brought trouble."

"He brought fire," Tiffany corrected. "He brought light."

"Sometimes we're better off not being able to see."

Tiffany rolled her hands, her forearms in a downturn, the way gameshow models reveal exciting new merchandise. "Not here," she said. "Not now."

Flanagan wasn't sure if she were referring to the rotunda or herself. They followed the herd into the enormous reading room. At the oaken book delivery desk, they broke left, deciding to check out that south hall of the room first, since that was the only part where pictures could be taken, and, alas, what would Tiffany do if she were unable to snap a selfie. Above the levels of bookcases framing the sides were arcades of massive windows and above their heads loomed tiered chandeliers. They stared at the ceiling's painted clouds in a room that suffered from no shortage of light.

Tiffany took out a plastic baggie, pinched a substance, and popped it into her mouth. "You want some?" she asked Flanagan. The uninitiated would have assumed Tiffany was offering drugs. But it was actually a wad of clay. "It'll get rid of the toxins in your body," she assured him.

"No thanks," said Flanagan. "I like my toxins."

Tiffany laughed and said, "Suit yourself." About a year ago, she started eating clay. Tiffany swore it made her feel pure. Flanagan had his doubts.

Given the architectural opportunities, Tiffany must have taken two dozen selfies with varied backgrounds of hushed opulence. As he looked on, Flanagan catalogued her physical changes even from last season's episodes: her lips thicker, her nose thinner, her eyes bigger, her chin smaller, her hair lighter, her skin darker, and her eyebrows (not to mention her breasts) higher.

To Flanagan's chagrin, Tiffany cajoled, "Come take a selfie with me?"

"If I'm in it, isn't it no longer a selfie?" asked Flanagan. "Maybe it's a Twoie or a Pairie or a Twinie or perhaps a Duetie?"

"C'mon. I want to see how we look together."

Why on earth, Flanagan wondered. "O.K., prepare to be disappointed."

"Oh, I won't be disappointed." She pulled him tightly toward her various surgically enhanced parts.

Flanagan tried to suppress his internal frown. Great, more Pisano games. Twelve years of working with Heather and Tiffany Pisano, the only words they exchanged with Flanagan were the ones he put in their mouths. Now, the sisters spoke to him with a familiarity of many long, intimate conversations they never had. What made the exchanges with Tiffany all the more startling was that Flanagan was speaking to a face he could not recognize, although the voice he had at least heard through the television screen.

Knowing he was being played, he had to get Tiffany out of the library because all he needed was the Pisanos to know he was scouring Jimmy Doherty's Senate papers. "This place is intimidating," said Flanagan. "You want to step out? Go get a cup of coffee or something?"

"I would love that," Tiffany answered, her excitement so palpable that Flanagan realized he didn't give her enough credit for what a fine actress she was.

They headed down one grand staircase after another, regularly turning ninety degrees along the way until they finally made it to the outside steps that led them off this erudite plinth. All the way, Tiffany held Flanagan's hand like she had proprietorship of it. After 12 years of his being on the payroll, she may well own his arm and his leg too. She didn't talk, just giggled and smiled, a technique more common at sister Nora's age than hers.

As they strolled in Bryant Park, Tiffany suddenly squealed. "Oh, Wafels and Dinges! Let's sit there. I love this place."

Flanagan shrugged and walked with her onto the kiosk line. After going back and forth on what to order, Tiffany landed on the Brussels wafel with spekuloos crumble and Flanagan opted for the throwdown wafel which was topped with spekuloos spread and whipped cream. Tiffany carried the two coffees to the café table while Flanagan took the waffles. Even what they carried struck Flanagan as revealing: the act of not completely carrying one's own total meal and instead divvying it up was more characteristic of couples than of friends merely enjoying a snack. The mid-October weather was so unseasonable that Tiffany was sweating, a metabolic function no Pisano women performed without motive.

Flanagan knew he needed to keep the subject matter as light and breezy as possible, as if there were no meaning to their interaction. "I get the Wafels, although someone better teach these Belgians how to spell, but what in God's name are Dinges?"

"Oh," said Tiffany, her hands flying about and her fingers counting off as she listed terms, "a dinges is a whatchamacallit or a whosiwhat or a thingamajig or a doodad or a gimcrack or doohickey or just a plain old thingie."

"Ah," said Flanagan, chuckling, "that clears up matters. So what do Dinges have to do with waffles?"

"The Dinges go on the waffles."

"Like syrup or butter?"

"Sort of, but really whatever you can imagine putting on a waffle," Tiffany said. "I've heard that some people put avocado on a waffle."

"That sounds like your type of crowd," said Flanagan.

"Yeah?" Tiffany challenged. "I've put mac and cheese on a waffle, who does that sound like?"

Flanagan knew she was the only family member besides Dirk who was willing to take on so many carbohydrates at once. "Now quit waffling about these Dinges," he chided. "What are the Dinges on these particular waffles we are eating right now?"

"You see that stuff on top of your waffle that looks a bit like peanut butter," she pointed. "That's spekuloos spread. That's a Dinges."

"So Dinges is spekuloos spread?"

"Not all of them," she said. Flanagan could tell that Tiffany was losing her patience. "Spekuloos spread is a type of Dinges. In this case, it's anything you put on a waffle."

"Kind of like a condiment."

Tiffany wrinkled her nose. "Not really. It could be a condiment, it could be a spread, it could be a topping, it could be an add-on, it could be anything, what it is is a whatchamacallit."

"I am starting to feel we are getting somewhere and nowhere at the same time," said Flanagan.

"Eat your waffle and shut up," said Tiffany.

He liked this Tiffany much better than the bubbly one. "Shall I eat my Dinges too?" When she did not answer, the two dined in peace for a few moments. After he had polished off most of the waffle, Flanagan thought it was high time to steer the conversation in another direction. With still some coffee to sip, Flanagan decided he might as well try to dig up more dirt on Suzie. "Can I ask you a question I've been asking everyone I know lately?"

"That's an intriguing way to get me to answer, as if to indicate to me that anything you ask will be perfectly normal, since you've been asking everybody," said Tiffany. "If I didn't know beforehand, the last ten minutes have told me that I might not like the question. But ask me anyway. As I said, I'm a little intrigued." She crossed her legs, arched her back, and ran her fingers through her hair. Flanagan was struck by this return to coquettishness. It was as if for the previous conversation she had completely forgotten that she was supposed to be seducing him. "Shoot," she said to him as she puffed into the coffee like it was a cigarette.

"O.K." said Flanagan. "What is the meanest thing anyone has ever done to you?" Now this question was quite risky given the parade of self-absorbed jackass boyfriends who had marched through Tiffany's life. But Flanagan calculated none of those guys had the hold on her that her mother did.

"It was my sixteenth birthday," she said.

"Ah, sweet sixteen," Flanagan drawled encouragingly.

"Nothing sweet about it," she said. Flanagan sipped his coffee and waited. "It all started the week before when I was picking out dresses with mother for the party. She decided to also buy a few dresses for herself. I thought I would be nice and told her, 'Wow Mom, I hope I have a body like yours when I'm your age.' My mom laughed and told me, 'Tiffany dear, you don't even have a body like mine now. How do you expect to ever have a body like mine when you're older?' I was a little chubby then."

"You were not," Flanagan objected. "There's nothing wrong with having a little meat on your bones." He considered her, some twenty years later, and calculated with the work now done, she might indeed look like mother did all those years ago.

In response to Flanagan's supportive comment, Tiffany's smile was just crooked enough to look sweet. "Then there was the event itself. All the boys kept asking me if my mother was going to be at the pool party, which really was a big deal with ice sculptures everywhere, DJ Tito, and a ginormous chocolate fountain."

Flanagan grinned. "Sounds like a typical Pisano gathering."

Tiffany laughed. "I forgot who I was talking to. Anyway, I thought the boys would be disappointed when I told them my mom would be there, but they seemed very happy. I figured most of them would ask me if Heather would be there because by then she was already starting to become a bit of celebrity. It was odd that more of them asked about my mother.

"On the day of the party, I found out why. First of all, while I'm wearing my pink tube top, lavender capris, tan Uggs, and pink Von Dutch hat, what does Mom wear? A one-piece bathing suit, but not any one piece. I don't know how she managed to keep that thing on, but it had a plunging neckline, a cut-out to show off her firm belly, and a thong back."

Flanagan nodded. "So that's why the boys were asking about her?"

"Well, there's more to it," said Tiffany. "What I found out from my friend Ronnie the next day was that she had just been in a spread for *Shape* magazine wearing that very bathing suit. My friends knew about it, but Mom hadn't told me."

"So your Sweet Sixteen party wasn't really about you."

"Not so much." Tiffany pulled back out her bag of clay and took a pinch. Flanagan thought to himself, I guess it's better than smoking. Tiffany slid another wad into her mouth. Flanagan sure hoped she had a spare bag, since she was running through clay like she was making a vase.

Flanagan stood up. "That's horrible. Look, I would love to stay here and talk to you all day, but I have to go pick up my daughter." Flanagan was impressed by how casually he lied. Being with a Pisano tended to bring out his most insincere qualities. "I'm going to the Times Square station. Would you like to walk with me?"

"Why not," said Tiffany. As they crossed Sixth Avenue at 42nd Street, she put her hand over his shoulder. Yes, he knew she was manipulating him, but why did he feel in her touch genuine affection?

"Anyway," Flanagan said. "I hope by now you know how attractive you are, and I'm not just talking about your looks. You can be pretty funny when you want to be."

"Yeah, funny looking," she said, crossing her eyes and sticking out her tongue. When they arrived at the Crossroads of the World, she took selfies, ate more clay, and watched him head toward the N train. Flanagan did indeed get on the N, but in the wrong direction, for one stop to Herald Square, where the transferred onto the D train for one stop uptown to Bryant Park, so he could stroll into the library and back to Archives and Manuscripts department where with any luck Ms. Heinz would have the Jimmy Doherty collection out and waiting.

Ms. Heinz did hand him a folder when he arrived. "Is this all of Doherty's Senate papers?"

She laughed. "No, there are a couple of hundred more where that came from. I didn't want to overwhelm you."

"That's all right. I figure I'll be able to weed out a lot of material. Could I get them in twenty folder installments?"

Ms. Heinz did not answer, but she did return with a stack of folders. As Flanagan slogged through the material, all he could think about was Tiffany. He laughed at the absurdity of it all. He had spent much of the afternoon with someone who was the closest to a cyborg that he had ever met, and yet for that day she was his Dinges.

He kept running through his mind her Sweet Sixteen party. One of the reasons he could write the scripts for *Peepin' on the Pisanos* was that he never got trapped in the pathos most of the audience embraced – along with fierce, cultish admiration – for these poor little rich girls.

But he hated to admit the melodrama of that scene of a blossoming 16-year-old Tiffany eclipsed by the matriarch captivated him much more than the folders before him. Flanagan smiled and cursed to himself. "Shit man. It's your turn to stop waffling."

CHAPTER 18
THE REDRESSING OF LANDSCAPES

Flanagan had spent the last three days perusing Doherty's Senate papers with little to show for the effort. Yet, he had the sneaking suspicion he was missing something. He had the same suspicion during the evenings when he combed through Doherty's appointment book. He grew so frustrated that he loaned the appointment book to Michelle to see if she could find something. Father and daughter had been sitting at the table eating bacon, eggs, toast, and hash browns when Michelle chided Flanagan for once again serving breakfast for dinner: "What do you eat for breakfast? Turkey, mashed potatoes, and stuffing?" This exchange was a running game between them where she would offer her question with a new breakfast suggestion – last time it was chicken cordon bleu with rice and asparagus. Usually, Flanagan would play along, answering with a traditional luncheon plate, like, "Of course not. I made a chicken avocado club with a side of macaroni salad and a pickle."

But this time the reply was darker, "I feast on the bitter cud of the vilest bile that fills the belly of the weak and damaged."

"Whoa," said Michelle. "I only have a couple of hours with you tonight and I've got to read 'The Monkey's Paw' and write something about the problem with wishing. So, you want to tell me what's up?"

In a life of circumspection, Flanagan always appreciated Michelle's bluntness. "Sounds like you're likely to do a much better job on your homework than I've been doing with mine." Then he spent the next hour explaining his first day at the library and the previous evening's careful examination of the Doherty's appointment book. Steadily, he filled Michelle in on Doherty's activities back in the late eighties when he lined up support for his climate change legislation. Although she would not care to admit it, Michelle thought for the first time that her father was doing something worthwhile with his life.

With the same determination Flanagan noted when she just *had* to plant a tree, Michelle appealed to him: "Let me take the appointment book for the next couple of days," she said. "Maybe a fresh set of eyes would help."

Flanagan wanted to object with arguments like she wouldn't know what to look for, especially since in the age of cell phone calendars, she had never seen such an artifact. Plus, he was thinking of letting Deja take a crack at it. But, really, how could he say no?

Now, two days later, he hoped that Michelle had come up with more than he had in perusing Doherty's Senate papers. A dark thought rose in his head of Michelle losing the appointment books. His vision cut to Clarkin removing his arms from their sockets upon hearing the news of the missing books. To further complicate matters, he lately feared that Pisano henchmen would show up at his apartment and ransack it. That's why he kept the laptop and all his files on his person while also sending his notes and footage into the I-Cloud. Still, his cautious measures only made him more fearful that he would be jumped, this time with much greater brutality than the assault at the Pint O'Plenty. That led to him fearing that a Pisano thug would attack Michelle. He hoped that the Pisanos would not think he was so stupid to give his teenage daughter the appointment book.

Besides the one he scripted, Flanagan had watched far too many bad television series.

His thoughts returned to Clarkin, flashing to memos the big man had sent to Doherty in early 1989. He tapped in "Federal Election regulation" on his screen after remembering that Clarkin had written a report about the fundraising of six U.S. senators for the '88 campaign. Flanagan hadn't thought much of the report previously since three of the senators were Democrats. During his first run-through of the stack of folders, he had not even read the summary. Doherty's papers were so voluminous that Flanagan had to cheat somewhere to plow through the material – he did not have intellectual stamina and doggedness of a researcher. Yet, why would Clarkin – Doherty's most valued staffer – spend so much time on that report?

Flanagan now proceeded to read through the 73-page document from beginning to end. Although he found useful accounts of contributions to the Senators from the American Henry Center, he wished he had jumped to the conclusion ... like Doherty clearly had. If Ms. Heinz wasn't lurking in the background to make certain these documents were returned to her in the exact condition received, he would have underlined the following: "The contributions from the American Henry Center in their various incarnations – including those from the Lexington Trust and Concord Foundation – were clearly designed to influence the voting patterns of Senators Siegelman, Frazier, Stone, Addison, Cruise, and Hunt. While each of these incumbent senators raised between two and three million dollars, the American Henry Center through its many affiliated groups contributed more than twenty percent of the total to these campaigns. Although the nature of these offerings cannot be considered outright bribes, a clear and direct case can be made that these senators are beholden to the oil lobbying interests. The compromised positions of the senators should be made clear to them before impending votes on Bill S1927."

If Flanagan had learned anything in his three days of reading through Doherty's documents, he knew that Bill S1927 was the United Carbon Amelioration Initiative, a plan that had been gaining steam in 1988 and still had its fair share of supporters in 1989. The Democrats had majorities in the House and Senate. While the legislation was unlikely to become law with the old oilman George H. Bush in the White House, Doherty certainly seemed to be on the brink of making much noise and causing even more trouble. Flanagan surreptitiously snapped pictures of the concluding remarks and the report's cover page. He'd have plenty of opportunity later to blow-up and highlight the key points for the camera.

Even as he considered the consequences of these revelations and how many more people might have wanted Doherty dead (was he already squeezing these senators at the time of accident?), Flanagan fretted over how to present this material in the documentary. While the information was important, it would be as visually exciting as watching him shuffle folders and turn pages. Maybe he could have Clarkin do a little reenactment. Better yet, he would pay his old buddy Edmund J. Coppa to go hang around the Pint O'Plenty (which for Coppa wouldn't exactly be a hardship) to film Clarkin's nightly fights. Interspersing those fights would enliven the revelations and if he could get Clarkin to talk on the camera with a few whiskies already into him, some entertainment value might yet be possible.

Then it occurred to him that the bastard Clarkin had once again held out on him. Flanagan knew he needed to talk to Clarkin again, and this time it couldn't be at the Pint O'Plenty. His bones were not up to another visit. Realizing that five o'clock was approaching, he passed back the folders to Ms. Heinz, left the library, headed down 42nd Street, and caught the N back to Astoria. When he got there, Michelle had already let herself in.

"It's about time," she said.

"Sorry," Flanagan answered and then took out bowls, bread, eggs, and links, proceeding to slap together some French toast and sausage. As he dropped the sausage and the battered bread into the frying pan, Michelle sprinkled cinnamon and asked, "What did you eat for breakfast? Filet of sole stuffed with spinach over a bed of quinoa?"

"Of course not. I made a cold tuna salad plate with a side of cold slaw and some chickpeas."

Michelle appreciated his keeping with the healthy motif. "In a better mood, huh?"

"You could say that." Flanagan filled Michelle in on his discovery.

"That's great," she said. "I think I might've found something interesting in the appointment book."

"Yeah?" asked Flanagan.

She hesitated, "I'm not sure, but this entry on October 30, 1989 – it's just an address. I don't think he'd put only address unless he was hiding something from his staff."

Flanagan decided not to explain to Michelle that, given what he had learned about Doherty, he may well have only left the address because the destination could have been for yet another lover, or at the very least a rendezvous point for Suzie. Still, it was always possible the hidden address could have to do with S1927. Besides his emergence as quite the Lothario, Doherty must have also been a political animal, comfortable with playing hardball and dirty dealing.

"That's three weeks before his death." Flanagan read the address aloud. "239 5th St. Apt. 3B (by 2nd Ave)." He frowned. New York had its share of 5th Streets – he figured one in each borough. That the apartment was next to Second Avenue was a helpful clue though. He typed in the address on Google and found the first one that popped up was in the East Village, right by 2nd. He blew air out of his cheeks, grateful that sometimes research could be easy.

"There you go," said Michelle.

"That's great," Flanagan said. "I'm depressed I missed it and impressed you found it."

"No one can be both a great chef and a great investigator at the same time."

"True, yet one can successfully be a failure at both."

After watching more NukeMan videos late into the night, Flanagan woke up the next morning with news that Hurricane Zelda was heading directly for New York and would make landfall by the following night. He had heard warnings about the hurricane the past couple of days, which he promptly ignored, since so many of them blow off in another direction. But now with Hurricane Zelda becoming a more disturbing prospect, he decided to alter his plans. Rather than going back to the library for more torture, Flanagan took the W train early in the morning out of Astoria and rode its snaky bends down to the 8th Street stop near Astor Place. From there, he had a mere ten-minute walk to 239 5th Street, which was indeed right on the edge of Second Avenue. Flanagan wanted to get to the apartment early enough to grab the entrance door from those going to work, so he wouldn't have to randomly buzz; he also wanted to catch people who lived in the apartment before they took off for the day.

He climbed up the three flights of stairs with some optimism that the occupant might still be there, since the place had all the markings of rent control and residents tended to hold onto these cheaper apartments until the day they died. But, the mysterious entry was from more than 30 years ago, so who knows. He didn't count on waking up the tenants with his knock. A cranky woman answered and Flanagan quickly offered an innocuous lie about his working for the housing department and that he was trying to track down tenants from the 1980s who were entitled to benefits that the city was required to pay out following a class action suit.

"Doesn't the city have records of who lived here?"

"I'm embarrassed to say that those records were lost in a water main break twenty years ago."

The cranky woman tittered, mumbling something about typical. "I moved in here two years ago, so I can't help you. You might want to talk to Lupa. She's the super."

"Lupa, the super," Flanagan laughed.

Cranky didn't. "She's a pain in the ass. She's usually outside smoking with a broom in her hand. I don't know why she holds the broom. I haven't seen her sweep anything since I've been here."

After saying his thank yous and farewells, Flanagan trudged down the stairs and copped a squat on the outside stoop leading to the sidewalk. He waited about ten minutes. Lupa's cigarette smoke arrived before her. Relatively young and reasonably heavy, she smiled at Flanagan.

"You Lupa?"

"Yes. I'm Lupa, unless you want money. Then, I'm nobody." She laughed and smiled.

"I'm from city housing. I'm just trying to find out who used to live in 3B. I mean a while ago, say 1989."

Lupa made some strange noises from her tongue that might be interpreted as exasperation. "I can't help you with that. But my mother might. She's up in 6B. Her name's Georgette. She's more talkative when you bring her flowers."

Flanagan took off to the bodega and grabbed a fall bouquet of mums. Typical that the old lady lived on the top floor of a walk-up. Flanagan had seen so many of the city elderly trudging up the steps with their groceries barely huffing while he was currently trying to figure out whether that numbness in his arm might the beginnings of a heart attack. By the time he knocked on 6B, the flowers weighed fifty pounds. Once he told Georgette that he was looking to find out who used to live in 3B in the late 1980s, she offered him a chair and started talking. Over his labored breathing, he tried to listen as Georgette spoke of Alice Germond in 3A who had the Pekinese and the Martyns in 3C who left pizza boxes in the hall and the Rosarios in 3D who played salsa music late at night. Occasionally, she'd mention Chuck Herbert in 3B, how heavy he was and all he did was eat. "We always thought he'd die."

"Did he?" asked Flanagan.

"Not here," Georgette. "He didn't die here, but that was two years ago, so he may be dead now."

Georgette was not a day under eighty. She could be dead now too. "He was here up to two years ago?" asked Flanagan.

"Yeah," she said. "He moved to a beach house on the Jersey Shore. I never thought of him as the type to stroll along the boardwalk." Georgette smiled. "I never thought of him as the type to stroll anywhere."

Two years ago? That was a bit of bad luck. "Do you know what Mr. Herbert did for a living?"

"The Martyns said he was a nerdy mathematician. I could never see it. He was kind of a slob. More likely to have a sleeve of oreos in his pocket than a calculator."

"Mathematician, huh?" Flanagan would have preferred that Herbert was a scientist — maybe a meteorologist or an astronomer or a physicist. But it's a more promising position than a stockbroker. "By any chance, do you know where he moved?"

"No, I don't," Georgette said. "He told me he was going to Bradley Beach, but I didn't believe him."

"Why?"

"I don't trust him."

"Why not?"

"I just don't."

They spoke for a while longer, but from that point Flanagan learned much more about the Rosarios than he did about Chuck Herbert. Still, he had a name and town. Back down on the front steps of the apartment, he caught up with Lupa, wanting to get a clue about why her mother didn't trust Chuck Herbert.

She took a puff and said, "She really doesn't trust anybody, even me."

From there, Flanagan walked a few blocks down 2nd Avenue across 8th Street to the old brick Ottendorfer Library to get a wifi signal for his laptop. He took all of five minutes to track down an address and a phone number for Charles Herbert of Bradley Beach. Flanagan called, hoping that Chuck, like most old bastards, still answered his house phone.

Chuck did.

Flanagan explained that he was conducting research for a documentary on the Senator Jimmy Doherty. "Did you know Doherty?"

Flanagan could sense Chuck's hesitation until he answered, "A little."

"Would you be willing to talk to me?" said Flanagan. "I'll buy you lunch." He knew how much old people loved lunch.

"I guess that would be all right," said Chuck.

"Can I come today? I can take the 9:46 out of Penn Station and get to you in about three hours. I could meet you at the lunch place."

"Can we go to Marandola's?"

"Wherever you'd like."

"I'd like to go to Marandola's."

"So I'll see you there about one."

Flanagan had no idea whether Chuck could tell him anything, but he knew he'd rather take three-hour train ride than have another stab at the Doherty papers under Ms. Heinz's austere gaze. As always, the slow train ride, in this case to Long Branch before the quick bend to Bradley Beach, gave Flanagan time to think. Why wouldn't Doherty want his staff to know that he was meeting with a mathematician? Considering how much he left transparent, the wily senator must have had his reasons.

When he arrived at Marandola's, Chuck was already sitting at a table. Georgette's description of Chuck being "somewhat tall, but very wide" served Flanagan well. Though it was unlikely to attain the heights of Delmonico's tab, Marandola's was pricey. Flanagan envisioned his savings being drained by such gourmands as Stuart Cooper and this glutton who had already ordered smoked mozzarella fritters for the table and was eying up the pork chop giambotta for the main. Still, he was grateful that Chuck picked an indoor table. With the unrelentingly heat of this fall, Flanagan felt like he was in Florida where the old people sought the refuge of air-conditioned booths to escape the brutal sun, just as New Yorkers used to huddle to dodge the January frost.

Chuck greeted him with the usual niceties and Flanagan explained what he was researching (in the broadest and most innocuous terms necessary). Not until he was halfway through his bucatini amatriciana did Flanagan finally get deep enough in the conversation with Chuck to ask substantive questions. "So you're probably wondering why I wanted to meet with you," said Flanagan.

"I have my suspicions," Chuck answered.

"Your address was in Jimmy Doherty's appointment book for October 30, 1989, three weeks before his death. I was curious what he wanted to discuss with you."

"I actually contacted him," Chuck said. "I had kept my mouth shut for years before Doherty came along. But when he started speaking up, he seemed committed to doing something about this climate change problem and had the power to get things done."

"But I heard you were a mathematician," Flanagan asked. "How were you involved?"

"I'd been hired by Exxon years earlier to lead the Mathematical Sciences Laboratory at their research department," said Chuck. "I ran models on climate change."

"Let me get this straight," Flanagan said, shaking his head. "Exxon actually hired you to study climate change."

"Sounds crazy right," Chuck said, "but during the early 80s Exxon took climate change seriously. I wasn't alone in thinking we were in trouble. A number of the astronomers and atmospheric scientists were in agreement as we all saw how temperatures were on a trajectory to rise at least one and a half degrees within 50 years, although I don't think they were as confident that human activity was the root cause."

"And you were," said Flanagan.

"I ran the models again and again," Chuck said. "I couldn't come to any other conclusion. When Exxon started creating task forces to deny climate change and hired think tanks to spread the word, I knew the truth would not be coming from them, so I returned to the university."

"Until you decided to talk to Doherty."

"That's right, and you see how that turned out. I handed over every bit of research I had, so he could use the graphs, data, and charts to make his case."

"I'm guessing he never got a chance to make them public," said Flanagan.

"When I handed him everything, he seemed like he was calculating a larger plan," Chuck said. "He told me that what I gave him would make a huge difference. I guess he was right, but he didn't know that the huge difference was whether he'd be dead or alive."

"Did they ever come after you?"

"Nah," Chuck said. "After Doherty was dead, I did my own calculations and came to the conclusion that I would keep my mouth shut about this matter."

"Until now," said Flanagan.

"It was a very long time ago."

"Can I send someone by to record you?" Flanagan asked.

Chuck thought for a minute. "Why not? That's if you get me dessert too. The oil industry isn't the powerhouse it used to be, and I can't imagine they'd be concerned about this old news. I'm surprised you are."

"You were there from the outset of a tragedy," said Flanagan.

"Tragedy? What tragedy?"

"That's what I'm trying to figure out."

CHAPTER 19
THE RIDING OUT OF HURRICANE ZELDA

The flurry of texts messages from Deja made one point clear to Flanagan: she did not want to be alone at her parents' ancestral home in Hamilton Beach during Hurricane Zelda. Since Deja's decision to hunker down in a flood zone during a category five made no sense, Flanagan naturally wanted to join her more than ever. He took the A train all the way out to Howard Beach and then walked the rest of the way to her house, a backpack strapped across his shoulders carrying his necessities – clothes and a liter of Bushmills. He wasn't sure if he was just being used by Deja, another wooden support to prop up her house. But he was hopeful such a cataclysmic event could draw them together and make her forget or at least forgive much that was wrong with him. When they arrived at the house, the storm surge had already begun. The white caps grew angry and spit on the crowns of the pilings.

"Hasn't everyone evacuated?" he asked.

"There are a few thickheads who refuse to leave," Deja said, hiding no contempt in her voice.

"Like you?"

"Oh please," she said. "You have never been manipulated by my mother." Deja's mom was in a nursing home going through rehab. She made her daughter promise to take care of the house during the storm. Under the best of conditions, Hamilton Beach flooded. Hell, the tides sent water into the street if the moon was full and the time was right. Now the time was very wrong.

"Couldn't you just lie to her?" asked Flanagan. "Tell her you stayed, but had to clear out after things got rough?"

"That might work if Mr. Rizzo two houses down and old lady Cioffi across the street didn't have their old hawk eyes peering out of their windows." Deja then proceeded to tell her family's history in Hamilton Beach as the only blacks in the neighborhood, one, like the adjacent Howard Beach, filled with Italians. More than a few efforts were made to kick her family out, from the pettiness of leaving fish heads on their porch to the more serious beatings her father endured. She said it wasn't until her father helped save the Cancelleri bungalow during Hurricane Gloria back in '85 that they were accepted into the community. "Then the riots happened after Michael Griffith was killed in Howard Beach, and we figured that the neighbors would come after us."

"Did they?" asked Flanagan.

"We saw a lot of small gatherings down the block," Deja said. "But they never came."

"Why not?"

"We weren't sure then, but later on we heard it was because a lot of the old guineas thought that," here Deja raised her fingers to make air quotes, "we were some of the good ones. It's a stupid label that angers me now. But back then, when I was a little girl, we were just happy they didn't burn our house down. All that work holding onto the place in those early years has my momma obsessed with not letting anything happen to it."

"Ah," said Flanagan, "I imagine you have seen the irony in you, a climate scientist, pretending that you're not fighting forces much greater than yourself."

"It might have occurred to me," she said. "We are Z already in the storms count." Each hurricane season, the storms are given names alphabetically, one per letter. "It's the earliest we've gotten to Z. I wouldn't be surprised if we make it through the Greek alphabet this season too."

"So you attribute this storm to global warming?" Flanagan asked, continuing to cobble together how this climate change angle would fit into his documentary.

"Not necessarily," said Deja. She was one of these professors who never liked to overstate the science. She was much less reckless in her profession than in life, which made her a rotten interview on camera and a thrilling girlfriend. "The number, pattern, and scale of these hurricanes I think we can attribute to climate change, but not any one individual storm. We've had major hurricanes for centuries."

"But not as severe," Flanagan pressed, "and not as often."

"I think that might be the case," she said.

Jeez, Flanagan thought, not much of a definitive statement there. Deja had a clearer vision of how to prepare the house for the storm. Fortunately, the old bungalow had been lifted after Hurricane Sandy beat the hell out of it. Unfortunately, the extra six feet of elevation might not be enough with tonight's storm surge. That meant carrying many sandbags in the tropical heat.

Flanagan grabbed one after another and trudged up the stairs, slightly ashamed that Deja was moving a little faster than he was. But hey, she'd been running five miles along Riverside Park for the past decade. During that period, Flanagan's exercise consisted of strolling back and forth to the Pisano set trailer to ravage the few slices of bacon and rations of hash browns pushed to the corner of a buffet dominated by tofu and kale.

The fortress of sandbags was no joke as they stacked layer upon layer and Flanagan huffed, his once-crisp blue button-down shirt (which he had hoped Deja would find appealing) now soaked to the point that the burlap holding the sand looked better. By the time the perimeter walls were stacked three feet high, Flanagan began to wonder if the supports could hold all the weight. He suspected the pilings groaned much the way his back did. Thank God they ran out of sandbags.

They clambered over the sandbag barrier to scramble into the entrance like Great War soldiers negotiating trenches. After shutting the door with a finality of those who were ready to hunker down, they drank glass after glass of water until Flanagan had enough of that and pulled out the Bushmills. He poured a few fingers worth in each of two jelly glasses. "Here's to one enchanted evening," he toasted.

After taking a sip, Deja said, "You should shower before things get rough."

"Things are going to get rough?" he asked playfully.

"Just get in the shower," she said. "You look like a beached porpoise."

"Considering the marine creatures you could've selected, I'll take that as a compliment." The shower head pulsed into his bones, both soothing him and reminding him what type of pain he would be in tomorrow. When he got out, he noticed the candles, matches, flashlights, and lanterns Deja had set up. "I didn't even know you could still get kerosene."

"Around here it's still popular," she said. "I'm going into the shower. Why don't you watch the news while we still have power? Maybe there's an update of the forecast. And charge your phone."

Flanagan got to watch about three minutes of news – yes, the storm was coming right at them and there would be big and bad surges along the coast – when the wind picked up and the electricity flew away with it.

Deja showered in the dark. From what Flanagan could discern, she came out damp in fresh clothes. Lighting the pilot on the gas stove without blowing up the house, she put trays of eggplant parm and pasta in the oven; comfort foods from the local market for nights like these. Flanagan was relieved that this dinner would not be one of those health-food nightmares he had endured with Deja in the past, heavy on quinoa, beans, and chard, brutally light on butter. Stacked on the cupboard shelves were dried seaweed packs. He had feared that his meal might have been consigned to nibbling on those stiff green vessels of salt, food too close in nature to what washed up on the shore to be to his liking. He sensed that tonight Deja might loosen her strict adherence to wise and healthful decisions.

Ignoring the rushing surf, the howling wind, and the flying debris outside, Deja asked for an update on his documentary research. While Flanagan offered some heady material about political machinations, scientific environmental studies, and climate models in the 1980s, the conversation ended up where it always did: the Pisanos.

Flanagan always struggled to understand Deja's fascination with the Pisano women. Was it a guilty pleasure for this egghead intellect? Was she fishing for information to see if he was interested in one of them? Would such interest make her jealous? Or just confirm that he was shallow? With so many questions swirling around like the gusts outside, he couldn't figure out if the truth was a good idea, even though he wasn't sure what the truth was. He peered into his evaporating glass of Bushmills, the flickering candles casting shadows about the amber liquid.

"Both Heather and Tiffany have visited me." Flanagan didn't want to get into the details about Tiffany's *coincidental* appearance at the Public Library. "I'm starting to worry that they're looking to destroy my documentary."

"I would think they're too busy to care about your documentary, especially since you've stayed away from investigating the Dirk Wall accident."

"I figured the same thing," Flanagan said, "which is exactly why I decided to focus on Jimmy Doherty."

"Maybe they're sweet on you," she said teasingly. "You can be somewhat attractive when you're not acting like an asshole."

"Believe me, that's not the case," said Flanagan. "I have the wrong bank account, the wrong personality, the wrong attitude, the wrong shoe size."

"Maybe, that's it," she said. "You're so wrong that you're right. You're a bad boy."

"Not a bad boy," said Flanagan, "but a dull boy. You can't be a dull boy and be with the Pisano sisters."

"That's true," acknowledged Deja. "You only get to be dull if you're a very beautiful woman with very few clothes. You clearly are wearing too many clothes. But I'm sure you're much less dull to them with that camera you've been dragging around."

"You don't have to worry," said Flanagan. "They have no interest in me. And I certainly don't have any interest in them." If Flanagan were honest, he might confess a smidgen of interest. They were Pisanos, after all. Quite perceptive, Deja should've picked up this discrepancy, but she was too focused on Flanagan's "You don't have to worry" assurance.

"You're damn right I don't have to worry," said Deja. "What do I have to worry about? You're not my boyfriend. You're just some guy getting me through a storm."

A bit wounded, Flanagan quietly picked at his eggplant and pasta. In what Flanagan might have interpreted as a peace offering, Deja uncorked a bottle of red and placed it with two wine glasses on the table, pouring heavy and high. They drank and chewed and swallowed, peering through the candlelight and listening to the waves. After his plate was clean, Flanagan grabbed the dishes and washed them in the sink. Deja sidled next to him, towel in hand, drying the forks and plates and refilling Flanagan wine glass. She leaned up against him and pushed into him as she returned the dishes into the cabinet.

"Oh, excuse me," she said. A part of Flanagan wanted to say, you don't have to say excuse me to a guy just getting you through a storm. But that part of him was shrinking as other parts of him were swelling. After Flanagan cleared the sink and Deja put away the dishes, they stood inches away from each other and killed off the rest of the wine.

Yawning, Deja said, "Boy, I'm tired. I think I'm going to bed. You want to come?"

Flanagan nodded and followed her candle through the dark corridors. When they found the bedroom, Deja blew out the light. They discovered the mattress and each other in the darkness, awkwardly groping for spaces to land softly. Flanagan simply held Deja for a while, eventually repositioning his way to spooning and gliding his right hand along her back and shoulders. He rubbed tenderly and gently until he found a knot or two to squeeze, receiving approving groans from Deja. Soon his hand branched out further into the suburbs, gliding over hills and dales, receiving muted approval for his travels from Deja. By the time he'd wandered out to the country, Deja made clear with her twists and turns that he might want to move beyond merely employing his right hand.

He obliged and the wind whipped and the rain lashed and the foundations moaned and the sandbags wondered why they had to always be commandeered for the endless battle against the tide. The darkness shrouded their intimacy. They knew that no words would be shared, not now, not later.

Instead, when Deja spoke again, it was to predict the damage done to the neighborhood where she grew up. "The boats that haven't been dry-docked are gone now," she said. "Half the houses will be ripped off their foundations."

"Any good news, you think?" asked Flanagan.

"I don't smell smoke, so maybe the neighborhood isn't in flames, like what happened in Breezy Point during Sandy," she said. "And we still have a roof over our heads."

As the winds calmed and morning arrived with more sun than had once seemed possible, Flanagan pointed out two cracked windows and a hanging gutter. After boiling water and brewing coffee in the French Press, they took their mugs, opened the front door, pushed back a few sandbags, and inspected the block. The Rizzo's house was tilted a bit on its side. Only the Palmieri's foundation, the neighboring house to its left, prevented it from flipping, since the bungalows were so squeezed in here that the rickety structures didn't have much room to break away. Still, the Rizzo's house angled sharply enough, pressing against the Palmieri's piling, that both bungalows wedged slightly up; the crooked houses looked like they belonged in a fairytale. As they walked to the edge of First Street, they picked their way past gas grills, buoys, torn awnings, vinyl siding, and other sodden debris. The floodwaters rose halfway up many a door and Deja could already anticipate the mold.

Most of the houses along First Street had taken advantage of the much longer warm season by edging their properties with palm trees in massive pots. Usually, by now, those palms would have shipped off to an atrium of a nearby office complex. Given the balmy October weather, the homeowners had grown confident that the palms would make it through the winter … as if Hamilton Beach had magically been transported to the Amalfi coast. The presence of flying fish in their canals – a species usually found down in the Caribbean – confirmed that as long as the floods didn't rise too high in the streets, their changing climate had many advantages. But true to what hurricanes wreaked in southern climes, the palm trees were now down, and the broken pots had strewn shards of crockery onto the sidewalks.

Flanagan opened his arms wide. "How many years do you think this place has got left?" he asked.

"I don't know," said Deja. "I thought it was done after Sandy. But my best guess now is ten."

Flanagan suddenly grew very sad, like he had lost a friend. He was mad at himself for this reaction. Last night was the only night he'd ever spent in Hamilton Beach. Sure, it turned out to be a good night, but if he started to lament every neighborhood that would be under water in the next twenty years, he'd be boohooing like a teenage girl watching a boy band.

They hadn't returned to the house for more than fifteen minutes before Deja announced, "I have to get to Columbia."

"I don't want to surprise you with this notion Deja, but I believe classes are cancelled today."

"I'm not going there for the classes, dumbass," she said. "There's work to be done."

"Can't it wait until tomorrow?" Flanagan asked.

"Tomorrow, they'll be even more data," Deja said, stress starting to accumulate in her throat, an anxiety that oddly had not been present during the life-threatening storm. "Feeding the model every day gives me what I need."

"What's that?" asked Flanagan. "Clarity?"

"God no."

"Then what?"

"A little stability. I like the continuum when all else has fallen apart."

He too wanted to return to his own work, but given the current state of the city, he did not think the Public Library would be opening. He hoped his electricity was on. The good news was that the A-train was running. They travelled together for an hour all the way to Times Square, where they parted – Deja transferring to the 1-train uptown while Flanagan picked up the N. Just before they pulled into Times Square station, Flanagan received a text from Heather: "Can you come over to the compound at 1 today? We need to talk. Felipe will let you in at the gate."

He managed to neglect to tell Deja about the text. He tried to measure what storms were brewing around him and inside of him. He was not ready to characterize it as catastrophic, but, unlike Deja, he was not monitoring his situation with any degree of care.

CHAPTER 20
THE BRACING FOR TSUNAMI PISANO

As he approached the mansion, Flanagan could see very little damage from Hurricane Zelda within the compound walls, besides a few freshly cut trunks. Good thing the season finale got rid of the artist's shack before Mother Nature inflicted her wrath. On this coastal estate, the lights that had flickered and blew out much of the city had been kept humming by a squadron of generators. After all, how could a Pisano survive without a fully operational straightening iron?

Wearing a sympathetically tailored salmon button-down and crisp trousers, Flanagan appeared to be in much better physical condition than he actually was. He had reached the age where unenhanced muscle structure and gravity supported him for the last time. He knew the price of luxuries such as carriage and posture would soon be paid. Anyway, the Pisano sisters were far too busy examining every last line and curve of their own figures and faces to inspect him or anyone else too carefully. They needed to summon their powers of attentiveness to see the way he saw them. That knowledge relegated Flanagan to a self-consciousness that resulted not from staring at them, but from wondering whether he was staring at them in the proper manner.

As Heather's text promised, Felipe showed him in and guided him up the stairs. For this meeting with Heather, Flanagan felt less intimidated than usual: ever since he left the show, he continued to write whole scripts of *Peepin' on the Pisanos* in his head. If he were more prone to introspection, he might have found this lingering habit revealing. But on this occasion, the plotting of scenarios replete with dialogue had its virtues. His latest conjured episode imagined his friend Professor Ralph Coleman as a suitor for the hand of Heather Pisano. Dr. Coleman's expertise was literary theory. In the type of fish-out-of-water scripts that often provided a dash of zany humor to the show, Dr. Coleman would wax poetic about Heather's neck, a covetous neck that would serve as a stand-in for some other body part for which the most famous of all the Pisanos was justly notorious.

Flanagan had been summoned to Heather's bedroom where she sat in a satin white robe before the makeup mirror. The tying and the hanging of that robe about Heather's figure was one of those Pisano miracles of seamstressing and silicon. The lapels along the uniformly tanned cleavage hung on bravely and the bottom edge of the robe splayed provocatively. Flanagan decided that much double-sided tape participated in this dubious state of unreveal.

The three-sided mirror guaranteed that whatever Flanagan missed of Heather directed before him was reflected behind him. Rona, her makeup artist, had finished up with her, but Heather remained before the mirror anyway, fiddling with her contour brush, dabbing the palette. After greeting her and not wanting to appear like a servant summoned, Flanagan did his best to play Dr. Coleman's role. Anyway, what Pisano could resist a conversation about her body parts?

"I know your neck, but I don't understand it," he said, as if they had been talking about the subject for hours.

"You don't have to understand," she said, "but I'd like you to at least try to misunderstand it." Not bad, thought Flanagan. Had he written lines so long for Heather that she reflexively knew what to say? He tried not to consider the more likely scenario: that Heather had always known what to say without his silly dialogue.

Still Flanagan pressed on. If their conversation would be academic, he might as well delve further into the conceptual. "My problem is I feel that the only way I can understand the nape of your neck is if I understand your entire neck."

She waved a wand that had blender on it. Flanagan could not figure out if it was highlighter or concealer. Heather ventured, "Would it help to caress it?"

Flanagan tried not to gulp. "I fear that might confuse matters more, my dear." The "my dear," was exactly the way he wrote Dr. Coleman's line. Flanagan surmised that this entire scene was being filmed. He knew enough not to scan the room, but all those years with the show taught him when a scene had been fully staged. Considering what Dr. Coleman would do in his situation, he thought it best to ask questions grounded in theory rather than practice. "What is your intention by having such a neck?"

Heather laughed, amused by the direction the conversation was taking. "You would think it would be to make people look at it."

"It isn't?" asked Flanagan, mildly surprised.

"Yes, it is," she answered, reversing herself. "But what I really want is for people to talk about my neck."

"What do you want them to say?"

"Where does it lead?"

Flanagan asked, "I'm not sure that's what they're asking."

"Ah," she said. "I find myself constantly disappointed that the interpretations of the masses rarely meet my intention." Heather must have spent more time in Columbia's semiotic circles than Flanagan had imagined. She twirled her brush, feathering out from her cheek bones.

Warming up to his role as Dr. Coleman, Flanagan leaned against wall. He wished he had a pipe and a herringbone jacket with elbow patches to complete the look. "Most of the conversation about your neck tends to center on whether people like it or don't. From what I've heard, people really, really like it or really, really don't. You have a very polemical neck."

Heather sighed and put down the brush, staring at the mirror with an approval that must have been reflected in Flanagan's eyes. "I don't care whether they like my neck or don't, but I hate when they just stop there. Does the size of my neck evoke a visceral reaction or does it inspire cool aesthetic analysis?"

Confused, Flanagan found himself reaching toward his mouth for a pipe that refused to appear. He murmured to himself, "This is not a pipe," and then asked, "From what milieu does your neck derive? Suzie's genes? Glandular implants? A bit of both?" He'd written enough scripts to know that whatever umbrage Heather might take to his provocative questions was dwarfed by her desire to keep the conversation about her neck going.

"My neck is borne by the zeitgeist of our time," Heather said. Flanagan was coming to understand that Heather's reading of her clippings stretched far beyond the tabloids … her phrasing smacked of her perusing scholarly journals, right down to the footnotes. "If my neck didn't exist, someone would have to invent it."

Heather picked up the wand and further blended the edges of the contour makeup from her chin onto her neck. Looking into the mirror, Flanagan positioned himself just off to the right, where, if the camera was installed at the spot he thought it would be, his upcoming speech should be captured in sympathetic lighting.

"Every time I turn away from your neck, I erase my memory of it," he said. "Then I reconstruct it in my mind's eye. I can never figure out whether it's your neck that seems surprisingly familiar or is it my recollection of your neck that gives me this sense of déjà vu?"

Heather smiled knowingly. "I'm good with it either way as long as you keep deconstructing and reconstructing my neck. But we're not really talking about my neck here, are we?"

For the first time, Heather turned away from the mirror and offered Flanagan a profile, so she could deliver a little side eye. The effect before him served up a fourth dimension of Heather, the other three faces delivered from the various angles of the mirrors. "How elegantly you provide your reasons to stare, your justifications to ogle." Heather frowned. She picked up her eyelash curler, then glancing in the mirror, thought it better not to overdue her preening. "Doesn't all of this talk about my neck make it ripe for mockery?"

"Your neck is a vehicle for entertainment," Flanagan said. "You can control who laughs, who faints, who sighs, who cries. You have to be excited that they entered your carnival when so many other bright lights are flashing before them."

Heather stared seductively at the mirror, directly into Flanagan's reflection. "So now that you have fully entered the carnival, have you come to juggle, throw balls, or ride the whirligig?"

Flanagan breathed in deeply, steadying himself on the bedpost. "Now I'm the one who no longer believes we've been talking about your neck."

"Oh, thank God," Heather said in feigned relief. "Imagine how horrible this conversation would have been if we had talked about what was really going on here." For the first time, Flanagan saw that Heather was looking at the mirror without bothering to find him in the reflection. Then she proceeded to clap continually for thirty seconds. Although Flanagan was slow to realize it, the shooting of the scene had ended. Heather's applause expressed her satisfaction with her performance. Although Heather's self-congratulations would never be recorded, Flanagan knew he would hear that clapping in his head, an echo for her to relish and for him to endure.

Heather put away both her brush and Flanagan. "If you will excuse me, I have to get dressed," she said. "Tiffany asked for you to stop by her bedroom after you were done here."

Flanagan said, "Sure," and left. As he wandered toward Tiffany's room, he still had no idea why Heather had been invited him in the first place. In their time in front of the mirror, she made no request of him, issued no directive, imparted no command. He was smart enough not to ponder the unthinkable: that she merely wanted him to look at her.

When he arrived in Tiffany's bedroom, he was surprised to see all chairs removed from the entire space. He was happy Tiffany was not in front of the makeup mirror since he was tired of seeing a Pisano and himself through a reflection. However, her position on the bed, sprawled out diagonally, half twisted in a relatively modest lacy lavender lingerie, did raise other concerns. Propped up by an elbow on the bed and a hand under the narrowed chin, that new face of hers brightened and smiled at him.

She signaled for him to sit next to her on the bed. Instead, he sat on the floor near her pedicured toes, sparkling a cool purplish azure (it's not every day a girl matches her toes to her lingerie). Bowing before her, he dropped himself so low that he hoped his decision to be positioned at the heel of her bedside would be taken as one of deference rather than aggression.

"I've been thinking about you ever since we shared Dinges," she said. Flanagan had to give Tiffany some credit; Heather would have never said anything that would leave her vulnerable. Even the much younger half-sister Nora might only go so far as to say to someone, "I was thinking about how much you must be thinking about me."

Flanagan understood that this middle child required the standard rules of decorum not usually applied to the Pisano women. "So have I," he said.

Then she added, "I remember how good the Dinges smelled and how lovely the waffles smelled and how wonderful you smelled."

Oh boy, thought Flanagan. The Pisanos were olfactory entrepreneurs, with the largest perfume sales in the country, but no one could ever consider them a bunch of sniffers. Tiffany writhed out of the bed and crawled over in a feline prowl to Flanagan, who had thought he had been prudent by sitting across the room from the bed. He discovered that true discretion would have been jumping out of the window. He worked mightily to suppress a laugh. He also worked mightily to suppress arousal. He weighed whether Tiffany or he was the more absurd creature. She stared at him with her large eyes. Only her eyes and her lips were bigger in the renovation. The rest of her face was dramatically smaller. With her jarringly diminished nose, she sniffed him and groaned with predatory wantonness. Again, Flanagan sensed the cameras zooming in on the action. If he were writing the script, he would entitle the episode *50 Shades of Pisanos*.

Unfortunately, he had yet to write such a scene – if he had, he was sure he would have been fired – so he didn't know how to play out what was transpiring. He was pretty sure Dr. Coleman would not offer him a theoretical construct for this encounter. He just kept his mouth shut and let her sniff away, smiling at her slightly embarrassing noises of approval. Flanagan had to say one thing about Tiffany; unlike the other sisters, she was willing to throw herself out there.

"I've been working on a fragrance for the last year that I believe I've finally perfected," she said. "I have dabbed some on my neck. Could you lean in and tell me what you think?"

On her neck, eh? Did Heather text her? Or had she watched the previous scene on her phone sitting before the makeup mirror. He remembered the discussion he had with Heather in his basement apartment about plotlines for the upcoming season, specifically having Tiffany steal Heather's potential boyfriend. His being the boyfriend did not seem credible.

Unless … unless … Heather liked the idea of the scriptwriter on the show now becoming a love interest. Before today's conversation, he would not think that Heather's proclivities bent toward the meta, toward the postmodern. Only at this moment did he come to realize that *Peepin' on the Pisanos* had always been at its core a reconfiguring, an absurdist parody of what not only a reality show could be, but what reality itself could be.

Flanagan leaned in, so he could inhale the aromas just below Tiffany's gorgeous shrunken head. "An alluring aura emanates from your neck."

Tiffany groaned again and climbed onto Flanagan's lap, rising above him, her nape pressed against his lips. "Taste it," she said. "I made the fragrance edible."

"Oh my." He put his tongue to her neck. It had the flavor of a warm breakfast bun. He pulled his lips away, but she pressed further into him. As he kept pulling back further, she leaned more toward him. He knew she would land on top of him if he did not make an impolite maneuver. He turned to the side and let her flop past him onto the lush pink rug. "Hey, hey," he said. "You don't want to be going there. You're too good for that. You smell too good for that."

He followed her crestfallen posture, suddenly as diminished as her head. He dedicated himself to telling her anything as not to hurt her further. He spoke sweetly and softly. "Your openness is wonderful, but you don't need to seduce me. I already think the world of you. You are the Pisano with soul."

"You rejected me," Tiffany said.

"I did not," said Flanagan. "In fact, I am asking you right now to go out on a date with me tomorrow. I want to learn all about your dinges, your whatchamacallits, your whosiwhats. I want to know the things about you that could never surface on an episode of *Peepin' on the Pisanos*. I cannot write those lines. Only you can."

Tiffany sniffled and nodded. Then she crawled to her nightstand, pulled out a baggie, and nibbled on some clay.

Flanagan, feeling terrible, kept pouring it on. "We will go to the Park Side in Corona and watch the old men toss bocce balls. We will eat pasta and drink chianti and speak of your childhood and how you managed to find your way in this craziest of families." Tiffany cried and he held her softly. She ate some more clay. Eventually, they walked out of her room and down the stairs.

Suzie waited for them on the divan. "Oh, there you are Arthur," she said. "I have some papers for you to sign."

"Yeah?" he asked. "What are they?"

"Oh, just some non-disclosure agreements."

"I signed them before I started working for you way back at the beginning of *Peepin' on the Pisanos*."

"Yes, but that was for writing on the show," she said. "Now that you left the show, we need this agreement for the role you will have in future episodes."

For once, Flanagan understood immediately the implications of what she was asking. If he signed these NDAs, not only would he be unable to talk about the show, but they would also interfere with all of his documentary work. "Look Suzie, I'm sorry, but I can't sign them."

"You know what a great opportunity this is." With Tiffany still sitting next to him on his left, Heather sidled up on his right, intimating an interest he had heretofore not witnessed. Despite the advances of the sisters, Flanagan was sufficiently grounded to understand that he might as well be a moderately pretty chambermaid to their lords of the manor. Flanagan offered them the familiarity, the easy access, and the absence of consequence that historically made longstanding servants attractive targets.

"Oh, I know, but I am going to have to reject your generous offer." He rose from the couch and could immediately perceive the sisterly desire for him wane.

Suzie said to Felipe, loud enough for Flanagan to hear, "you can bring in the next boyfriend candidate now."

He couldn't help but feel a bit hollow that he failed the audition, nor was he convinced that Tiffany would show up for tomorrow's date. He liked the idea of a clean break with Tiffany, considering his hopes with Deja, but as always, Flanagan never felt good when he left the Pisano household.

As he headed out, Flanagan noted that the rapper MeatDad Catharsis had arrived. MeatDad had been Tiffany's boyfriend during seasons 2 and 3 and drew high favorability ratings from focus groups. Even Flanagan had to admit, his return to the show made more sense than a scriptwriter's appearance before the camera. Heather came to the door to greet Mr. Catharsis and offered a distracted farewell to Flanagan. The focus in her lovely, intense eyes struck Flanagan. Those dark, arresting peepers reminded him of visions in many sleepless nights of late.

He smiled believing he might have stumbled onto something quite valuable, but he would have to wait until tonight when Michelle came over and he had another pair of trusted eyes to help him believe what he had not thought possible.

CHAPTER 21
THE PRODUCING OF A C-SPAN BLOCKBUSTER

Flanagan had to wait an hour before Kartik let him in his office, which he saw as an ominous sign. Since his last visit, the spare, austere lobby had been transformed by film scenes projected on the four walls. The secretaries and security guards in front of those walls gave further dimension to the scenes, not only serving as effective props, but, in their animated answering of phones and staring at screens, providing the impression of a movie inside a movie.

From all angles about the room, strong, superhumanly attractive heroes in tight suits or in mere paint leaped and smashed and hurled and fired. Initially, Flanagan found himself wrapped up in the clangoring tumult; after twenty minutes, the swirling action and flying body parts made him dizzy; forty minutes in, he felt spent, like he had been a loser vanquished by the superheroes; sixty minutes in, Flanagan had dozed off. The secretary had to shake him to tell him that "Mr. Reddy is ready to see him now."

Processing the secretary's information, Flanagan answered, "I bet you like saying Reddy, or is it ready, twice." The secretary acted like she didn't understand what he was talking about. Flanagan shook his head and rose.

In contrast to the sensory overload in the lobby, Kartik's office was as godawful dull as ever. The room was only brightened by Kartik's impeccably cut light blue suit and his shining eyes.

"Artie, what the hell happened to you?" asked Kartik.

"What do you mean?" asked Flanagan.

"You have been spending all your time at the library," said Kartik. "Do you think we are making a documentary that belongs on C-Span?"

"These are important revelations I unearthed."

"Look who suddenly became Bob Woodward," said Kartik. "Three minutes ago, you were writing lines like 'Do you think my butt looks big enough in these jeans?' and now you think you are going to change the world."

"If the documentary has a little meat to it, that might keep the viewers riveted," said Flanagan.

"Speaking of a little meat, where is the footage of all the beautiful people?" asked Kartik. "Plus, everyone I have watched in the last batch of footage is wearing far too many clothes, for which I guess I should thank you because these are not the type of people I want to see naked."

"So you would like me to film more people you'd like to see naked."

"Yes," said Kartik definitively. "Where are my celebrities? Where are my Pisanos? I know you're afraid of Suzie, but you could at least get Tiffany doing a lingerie shoot. No one can resist staring at the before-and-after footage of her."

Flanagan recoiled. He knew he should be shooting footage of Tiffany, but something unfamiliar to him – a conscience perhaps – told him not to. "I hear you," he assured Kartik. "I'll get you some sizzle."

Kartik picked up his phone and said, "Can you stop into the office for a minute?" Kartik waited and Flanagan waited with him.

Mehnuma walked in, "What's up?"

Kartik looked back and forth between Flanagan and Mehnuma. "Allow me to reintroduce you to Mehnuma," said Kartik. "That research you've been doing … Mehnuma can do it faster and better than you can."

"She might," said Flanagan. "But I need to go through all of this legwork to understand how to mold the story. I know much of what I am giving you will end up being cut, but I need the time and space to sort this all out. I am certain that Mehnuma can do a better job, but I'm sure her impressive skills would be more effectively employed on more lucrative projects."

"OK," said Kartik. "But if the next batch of footage is anything like the last pile of elephant dung you sent to me, I will have no choice but to put Mehnuma in charge of the documentary."

Flanagan was tempted to protest that Kartik could do no such thing, that this documentary was his baby. Yet, he understood Kartik was using this idle threat to pivot Flanagan back to embracing his trashier tendencies.

"Can I return to what I was doing?" asked Mehnuma.

"Sure," said Kartik. "I'll see you at the four o'clock." As Mehnuma departed, Flanagan thought it was his cue too and moved toward the door. "Where are you going?" Kartik asked Flanagan. "I've got a few more matters to discuss with you."

"What now?" asked Flanagan. "You planning on turning my documentary into a porno?"

Kartik laughed. "Now that's what the documentary needs, a little of the Artie Flanagan attitude."

"Then what can I help you with?" asked Flanagan.

"I've been hearing from the Pisano lawyers," said Kartik.

"I didn't know they knew I was working with you," said Flanagan.

"One thing about the Pisanos," said Kartik, "they know everything everyone else knows about their business. Apparently, you have come to learn a few things."

"Do you think the lawyers could be a problem?" asked Flanagan.

"It's nothing I can't handle," said Kartik, "or at least nothing my lawyers can't handle. I can protect the documentary, but I can't protect you."

"Without the documentary, there is no me," said Flanagan.

"All right, Artie, if you say so," said Kartik. Flanagan wished that Kartik believed him. If Kartik did not believe him, Flanagan realized he probably was lying.

Kartik's nephew Arnav entered through the back door, carrying a big box labeled *Top Secret*. Arnav smirked at Flanagan and turned to his uncle. "I'm sorry, Tauji," he said. "I didn't know anyone was with you."

"That's O.K.," said Kartik. "I'm not so sure either."

Arnav propped the *Top Secret* box onto Kartik's desk. It didn't look too heavy, but, then again, Arnav was so broad it might have been weightier than Flanagan perceived.

"Curious?" Kartik asked Flanagan, "aren't you?" Arnav continued to smirk.

"You two do this act all the time?" Flanagan asked.

"You wouldn't ask me that question if you knew who this was from," said Kartik.

After waiting a few beats, Flanagan asked, "Are you going to tell me?"

"No, not now," said Kartik. "When it's over, maybe."

"And when's that going to be?" asked Flanagan.

"Well," said Kartik, his elbow resting on the box, "that all depends on you, doesn't it?"

CHAPTER 22
THE COMING OF THE NUKEMAN

The landlord knocked on Flanagan's door upon his return to his basement apartment. "I had to sign for these letters," she said. "They seemed important so I thought I should give them to you right away."

Flanagan thanked his landlord, waited for her to wend her way back to her front door, and then opened the envelopes filled with sheaths of legal papers. Reading through carefully, Flanagan did not understand the nuances of the documents, but he got the central message: that he should cease and desist his documentary efforts; indeed, he should stop doing anything that had a connection to the Pisano family. The letters and past experience left no doubt that if he did not comply, Flanagan would be overwhelmed by a blizzard of legal activity that would bury him in debt and render him so busy filling out affidavits and forms, responding to evidential claims, and appearing in court that he would have very little time to pursue even the most innocent of activities.

"Well, that confirms I won't be the new Pisano boyfriend," he said, grimly chuckling.

From these threats, he knew he needed to take a different course than the letters intended. Given the legal onslaught that would be cast upon him in a few days, he would have to work very quickly to accumulate all of the material he could. With the right set of revelations, he might be in a better bargaining position or at least Kartik might interest the right corporation, say NetFlix, to put its resources and legal team behind him. After all, who doesn't covet an explosive documentary, since, like a hydra, it sprouts more heads when attacked, with podcasts and spinoffs always in the offing.

He needed to speak to Clarkin about those six compromised senators that he and Doherty had targeted. Plus, he hoped that Doherty back in '89 had briefed Clarkin about his meeting with Chuck Herbert. Doherty had to be planning a big announcement before he was killed in the accident. His papers, those senators, Chuck Herbert, the shenanigans of the American Henry Center, Frankie Pisano's ties to the group, those two hoodlums (Tony "the Elbow" Fratiani and Karl "the Sausage" Hoffman) employed by the Henrys, Doherty's ongoing love affair with Pisano's wife Suzie, Suzie's jealousy of her sister Barbara's rendezvous and of Jimmy's engagement to supermodel Cheryl Wood, Jimmy's secret infatuation with nuclear power, including his clandestine meeting with the industry's biggest lobbying group … All this lurid stew bubbling over as the future of Climate Change hung in the balance.

He called Clarkin and managed to convince the big man not to meet at the Pint O'Plenty. "I've been followed lately," Flanagan explained, "and threatened with aggressive legal action. My bones are not ready for another trip there right now."

"OK, you big baby," said Clarkin, "you can come over my house tonight at 9. Just bring some Guinness."

"I will," assured Flanagan. "Yeah and I better not get over there only to watch one of the neighbors challenge you to a fight."

That issue addressed, Flanagan picked up Michelle, who would help with the next item on his agenda. He started making pancakes with ham. That led to the usual patter. "Hey Dad," Michelle said, "what did you eat for breakfast? A rack of ribs, rosemary potatoes, baked beans, and cornbread?"

"Of course not," Flanagan answered. "I made a bacon double cheeseburger with a side of onion rings and a fried apple pie for dessert."

Flanagan needed a couple of minutes to push past Michelle's talk about planting more trees in Astoria – he promised he would buy another white pine and help her dig the hole on Saturday – before he could get her younger vision on his current obsession: Heather Pisano's eyes. After Flanagan popped her image on the screen, Michelle looked at him and she said, "I'm starting to worry about you. You're too old to be obsessed with a Pisano."

"You really studied her eyes, right?"

"Yeah Dad," she assured. "What is it you want to know?"

He punched up a NukeMan video. "Don't look at the cooling tower outfit, don't look at the beard, and don't look at the moustache. Look past the rising steam. Just look at the eyes."

"Wow," said Michelle. "Maybe, they're related."

"Related, my butt," said Flanagan, always a little prudish with his language around his daughter. "Those eyes belong to Heather Pisano." Flanagan pulled his screen next to Michelle. Yes, arresting was their main feature. Big dark pupils, flecks of iridescent sparkling through her irises, almond shaped with a slight downturn.

"Eyes are not fingerprints, Dad," Michelle said. "They're not that distinctive. I'm sure Heather Pisano is not the only one with those beautiful eyes."

"Perhaps," he said. "But she's the only one with such eyes I'd imagine who has expressed sympathy for the nuclear power movement, she's the only one with such eyes with a budget to make these extravagant NukeMan videos, and she's the only one with such eyes who would put on those pink Nike sneakers to accessorize the Cooling Tower costume."

Michelle laughed. "Now what are you going to do with that information?"

"I'm trying to figure that out myself," he said. He didn't think blackmail was a good idea.

Lifting her chin, Michelle said, "She should've worn color contacts."

Flanagan shrugged. "I truly believe she did not think anyone who saw her on magazine covers and on *Peepin' on the Pisanos* would be the type of person who would watch NukeMan videos. If there were a Venn diagram for each group, the two of us might be the only ones on the line with both."

"Boy, Dad, are you clueless," she said. "Yes, the NukeMan may have a million or so followers worldwide, but Heather Pisano is followed by everybody. I mean everybody."

Flanagan didn't appreciate being called clueless by his daughter, especially after he thought he'd been damned perceptive in spotting Heather Pisano behind the hair and the smoke and the gender. He kept staring at Heather's image to tell Michelle even more about her eyes. Yet he then started gravitating to Heather's nose. It was suddenly familiar in ways that had nothing to do with her incredible overexposure. When he had glanced at Heather's nose earlier as they spoke in the bedroom, he sensed ideas stirring. Still, he just thought her presence made him dizzy and daffy.

His study of that straight nose with a small, soft button of a bulb, the envy of Hollywood, reminded Flanagan of one of the stranger comments Red Schultz had said to him. Yes, everything Red said was odd, especially with his tendency to repeat clipped phrases. But he remembered Red's last comment as Flanagan walked out: he still sees Jimmy Doherty's nose "on the TV" as Red quaintly put it. The exchange might not have returned to him now if he hadn't been studying Heather's face so carefully. He turned his gaze onto photographs of Jimmy. The resemblance of their magnificent noses could not be denied. Could Heather's nose be an exact replica of Jimmy's? Could Heather Pisano's nose be the one part of her body that hadn't been touched by a scalpel?

Again, he called upon Michelle's younger vision to consider his comparison. He began with side-by-side screens of Jimmy's nose and Heather's. He even managed to get an image of each of them in their early thirties, so they would match up age to age as well as nose to nose.

Michelle whistled, "That sure looks like the same snout to me."

Then, Flanagan moved back in time. The great advantage of researching the Pisanos was that they have been public for so long, especially the girls, who have had their faces recorded for the tabloids from infancy forward. Flanagan would be able to spot whether a nose job had been perpetrated – he figured that would have happened around sixteen or seventeen. His greatest fear is that crazy mother Suzie might have had Heather's nose sculpted to resemble her dead lover. The idea only made sense if you knew Suzie.

Yet picture after picture revealed that Heather's nose had remain unchanged. "See," said Michelle. "I told you Heather was more down to earth than you thought."

"In theory, yes," said Flanagan, thinking of his last conversation with Heather.

Now, Flanagan knew how to proceed. He texted Heather. "I would like to talk to you about NukeMan, and I would consider it a great favor to me if we could meet this evening."

Flanagan immediately saw the response text dots, but for minutes he received no reply. He understood that Heather would always be booked for some event tonight. He also knew that Heather cancelled her appearances at many of them. Some of that was strategic; as the most famous of the Pisanos, she could not ever appear to be too accessible. He wondered who knew about NukeMan. He was certain not Suzie, or she would have put an end to it long ago.

From the delay in the response, Flanagan could tell that Heather did not fully understand him; she was quite accustomed to walking into a situation with a predetermined outcome. Soon she texted back. "Park Side Restaurant in Corona at 8. Don't be late or I'm gone."

Son-of-a-bitch, thought Flanagan, that's where he was supposed to meet Tiffany tomorrow night. Although he figured, given how badly his visit ended and the stack of legal threats from the Pisano clan, that Tiffany was unlikely to show, he was continually amazed how well the Pisanos played their games. The text was a simple reminder that whatever Flanagan held over her head, Heather would be in charge of what transpired.

Flanagan had no choice but to call Clarkin and push back his visit for an hour. He arrived at the Park Side early and managed to snag a great table in the garden room – dropping the Pisano name had its advantages. He looked up at the glass panels into the darkening sky and tugged on his last good shirt. It was ironic that Flanagan would have to purchase more nice clothes after leaving the Pisano show, mainly to become presentable to the Pisanos in what the family liked to call the alternate life.

He had to stretch his budget to order the Black Label Gavi di Gavi that ran 85 bucks a bottle. He probably should have ordered red, but then he would have been tempted to get the Coppola that was less than half the price – for what Italian, especially a Pisano, could resist vino from the director of *The Godfather*. Instead, he delusionally thought ordering the Gavi was his independent decision, one that would give him some measure of control as to how the night would go down.

Flanagan was soon disabused of this notion when Heather arrived (her signature scent perhaps a few beats before the click of her heels), garnering long stares, double takes, whispers, and general approbation. The response would not have been more animated if the President had walked in. Heather wore what could be characterized as a traditional floral dress. Yes, it hugged curves more lasciviously than most dresses. Still, for Heather, the outfit was downright wholesome. She leaned across the table and offered a cheek for Flanagan to kiss. He timidly obliged. He noted the taps of many camera phones.

"You sure you want to be seen here with me?" asked Flanagan.

"I only show up where I want to be seen," Heather answered.

"But I think a few people are taking pictures."

"Of course they are," she said. "And some of them are on my payroll."

"I think I'm being set up," said Flanagan.

"So says the man who sends me a text that smacks of blackmail." The waiter filled Heather's wine glass with Gavi. She lifted it and whispered "Cheers."

"Cheers," said Flanagan. "First of all, I know better than to blackmail a Pisano."

"You should," said Heather, "but I'm not really sure how smart you are."

Flanagan wanted to say that he felt the same way about her, but after years of clearly underestimating her intelligence, he was coming around to understanding he might be overmatched in the brains department. Still, he pressed ahead. "Second of all, none of the Pisanos should be concerned about what I am doing with my documentary since it is strictly focused on the 1980s."

"Oh?" Heather challenged. "So what am I doing here?"

"You seem to share an interest in climate change and nuclear power with Jimmy Doherty, the subject of my documentary."

"And you seem to be under the impression that I am NukeMan, which means you are even more obsessed with me than I thought."

"I take pride in my research."

"I bet you do," she said. "Just how many pictures of me did you have to look at to make the connection? I bet you were looking at those pictures night after night. And I bet you were wondering why it was necessary in your research to study me wearing bikinis and lingerie when you were comparing me to a frumpy nuclear power mascot."

Flanagan turned quite red. He wanted to say that he hadn't been up all night studying her to make the connection, but he knew no matter how he worded it, his remonstrations would sound lame. All he could do was redirect. "What made you decide to disguise yourself as Nukeman?"

"I'm not going to pretend you're curious," she said. "You already know the answer, so let's get down to business. You can have a recurring role in the series this season. You might be in three or four episodes, but you don't get to be Tiffany's boyfriend and you definitely don't get to be my boyfriend. You get to be the pathetic loser who hangs around and tries too hard."

"Wow," Flanagan said. "That shouldn't be too hard to play."

Heather laughed. "And you have to sign the NDA."

"Look," Flanagan said, "I don't want a role and I won't sign a non-disclosure agreement."

Heather laughed again. "You better sign that agreement," she said. "Mother almost had a stroke when you didn't sign the last one."

"Admit it," said Flanagan. "You were happy I didn't sign it."

"A little," she said. "You are slightly harder to figure out than I thought. So what *is* it that you want?"

Flanagan smiled. "I want to do you a favor."

The waiter came. Flanagan asked for the fettucine carbonara while Heather ordered the walnut salad with a side of broccoli rabe – the marvels of medicine alone could not maintain her figure. Inwardly, Flanagan calculated that the princess of the Pisano family happened to be a cheaper date than either Stuart Cooper or Chuck Herbert.

"Where were we?" asked Heather. "Oh, I remember. Where we left off, you did not want anything at all from me. In fact, you wanted to do me a favor."

"Yes, I did," Flanagan said bravely. "I would like you to take a DNA test."

"For what?" Heather asked.

"To find out who your father is," he said.

"Don't I know who my father is?" Heather said in a playful tone. She too had heard whispers that she might not be the daughter of Frankie Pisano. The whispers made her more exotic and intriguing. In the Pisano world, to be a bastard would not damage a career; like a timely sex tape, the revelation might ironically father forth a fiduciary windfall. She mused. "Let me see. Do I know who my father is …"

"Do you?" asked Flanagan. "I think if you knew the identity of your father, it might explain a few things."

"I thought your documentary was limited to the 1980s."

"You mean, the decade when you were born?" asked Flanagan. "Yes, it is."

Their meals arrived and they spent some time much the way two people might on their first date, discussing their favorite foods and where they would like to travel. The one exception to the usual date fodder: the subject of their families did not come up. Flanagan had to slow down his twirling of his noodles to stay at Heather's disciplined, glacial eating pace. When the waiter finally cleared the plates and they ordered espressos, Flanagan returned to the situation at hand.

Flanagan whispered discreetly. "Let me make clear to you that there is nothing connected to my request for you to take the DNA test as far as my discovery that you are NukeMan. I am curious about NukeMan and when you are planning your big launch of whatever you will be doing as far as climate activism, but even a fool like me knows that I am going to get nowhere on that subject tonight." Heather killed off the rest of the Gavi in her glass. Flanagan assured her, "Honestly, I'm not going to tell anyone about NukeMan because I know what hassles I would have to deal with if I opened my mouth."

"So if I don't get the DNA test, you are not going to do anything about?" asked Heather.

"No, I won't do a damn thing," said Flanagan.

"Then why even ask me?"

"Because I think you would like to know too, and I am currently collecting some DNA that may provide you with some answers."

Heather laughed. "Where are you going to get DNA from? Unless you think we're related? That would be crazy, huh?" Suddenly, he could see how happy Suzie would be to throw a nice incestual plotline into the season. It was Flanagan's turn to chuckle, since for all of the uncertainties of this investigation, he knew one thing for sure: that he was in no way related to the Pisanos. "I can't imagine anyone handing over a swab to you."

"That's hard for me to believe either, but let me worry about my swab and you worry about yours."

Heather batted her eyelashes. "Are you trying to get me to swap swabs?"

Again, Flanagan turned red, ashamed with how easily she could make his ligaments vibrate with the merest suggestion of something other than business. "All I ask is for you to think about it," he said.

She bent across the table and touched his hand. "I will," she said, as at least one of her photographers snapped a picture. After she pulled her hands back, they ended up under the table to issue muted applause, so that only Flanagan could hear what she was doing. Another scene in the fabulous life of Heather Pisano had been documented for posterity. The muffled claps could not hide a gleeful jauntiness in her aspect. Oh, the satisfaction of performing an act that only her singular target audience could perceive.

Their expressos arrived. Heather downed hers like she was taking a shot of tequila. Already sufficiently emasculated, Flanagan was not about to respond by sipping his, so he hastily delivered the espresso down his gullet and turned over the cup onto his saucer, hoping future fortunes resided there.

Heather rose. "Don't get up," she said. "I'm off to make a serious deal."

Deciding not to consider the implications, Flanagan stood up. "May your identity always be yours and only yours," he said.

Then he and everyone else in the restaurant watched Heather Pisano leave. Flanagan promptly paid the bill and headed off to a bodega, hoping to find

Guinness. Luckily, they had the tall cans with the widget that enlivens the pressurized nitrogen. When he arrived at Clarkin's with three four-packs, the big man was not unhappy to see him.

"What the hell happened to you?" asked Clarkin. "I thought the idea of meeting me here was so you wouldn't be beaten up."

"I had an encounter with a Pisano."

"Say no more."

They popped the top of a couple of Guinnesses and waited for the nitrogen to do its work. Flanagan sat on a vinyl kitchen chair and threw his elbows across the formica table. Clarkin grabbed pint glasses from the cabinet and slowly poured.

"You ever hear of Chuck Herbert?" Flanagan asked.

"Don't think so," said Clarkin, rubbing his two-day old beard with his meaty right paw. "Who's he?"

"Chuck worked for Exxon," said Flanagan. "He led a laboratory that ran models on climate change in the 80s. It seems like he gave Exxon news they didn't want to hear."

"So why should I know him?" asked Clarkin.

"He met with Doherty three weeks before his death," said Flanagan. "From what Chuck told me, he gave our good senator an earful about what the oil industry knew and how they would formulate their denials."

Clarkin took a slug of Guinness. "Well, I'm embarrassed to say, I knew nothing about that. I thought I was the only one Doherty didn't keep secrets from, but I guess he even kept secrets from me."

"He was a curious man, your friend Doherty," said Flanagan.

"He was indeed."

"Oh, by the way," Flanagan said casually, taking a sip, "I noticed you never told me about those six senators who took received substantial campaign funds from the oil industry."

Clarkin nearly spit out his stout. "How'd you find out about that?"

Flanagan smiled. "From many miserable hours at the Public Library poring over folder after folder of Doherty's Senate papers."

Clarkin smiled. "It seems like you're more tenacious than I figured. Are you sure you just wrote scripts for the Pisanos?"

"I know, I know," agreed Flanagan. "My newfound devotion to brute research doesn't exactly fit my profile. But tell me about those senators. What was Doherty planning on doing with your damaging findings?"

"Immediately, nothing," said Clarkin. "He was waiting for the right time. I believe Doherty would only use that information if he'd gathered enough support so the legislation was close to passing. With Bush in office, Doherty would have to craft that legislation just right to get enough parties to sign. One of the last things he said to me was that he would have to put some sweeteners in for the petroleum industry if he wanted to get any traction."

"Too bad the boys at the American Henry Center didn't know that," said Flanagan.

"Indeed," said Clarkin, polishing off his Guinness, "it might have saved his life."

Sensing Clarkin's melancholic mood, Flanagan knew to shut his mouth. He wanted to ask what types of sweeteners. As he had come to understand from the files, Flanagan knew the wily senator would not simply throw money at them. Sure, the money would be there for big oil, but it would be for the producers to pivot toward solar and wind. Doherty would assure them that they'd be in on the ground floor of the clean energy industry and government funds would pour into their coffers as they let solar and wind become their focus. Hell, knowing Doherty, he'd offer them monopolies on the clean energy industries if the oil producers just played along. The possibilities made Flanagan almost as sad as Clarkin, but in a multitude of different ways. What the hell did it matter now? Doherty was long dead.

They moved on to their second stout.

"I need another favor from you," said Flanagan.

"How many favors does one man need?" Clarkin asked. "Why should I give you yet another favor?"

"Because I think I amuse you," Flanagan said.

"Yeah, you amuse me much more when you're getting your assed kicked," Clarkin said. "I knew we should've met at the Pint O'Plenty."

"Next time," Flanagan promised, "just give me a few more days for my ribs to heal."

"Pussy," said Clarkin. "What is it you want now?"

"How close are you to Jimmy's brother Kevin?"

"Like he is my own kin. Why?"

"Could you get him to take a DNA test?" Flanagan asked. Clarkin raised his eyebrows. "I just got Heather Pisano to agree to take one. I believe the results might tell us a lot." Flanagan raised his pint of Guinness to Clarkin and muttered, "Cheers." After he took a hearty pull and wiped the foam from his lips, he conceded, "It's not the traditional way to get a paternity test, but since Kevin and Jimmy are identical twins, they will have the same DNA. Anyway, I don't think it'd be easy to get a swab from Jimmy, now would it?"

"Where are you going with all this?" asked Clarkin. "I mean besides the obvious – that you might get a few headlines for your documentary?"

"Well, I wouldn't mind the headlines, but Jimmy Doherty being the father of Heather Pisano would further Frankie's motive to kill him off."

Clarkin stroked the stubble on his chin. "I'm surprised I didn't think of that myself. All these years of just teaching chemistry has made me less devious than I used to be. Most of the bonds I deal with nowadays are either ionic or covalent. I'm no longer used to bonds being this unstable."

"So will you ask him?"

"I'll think about it," said Clarkin.

"Damn," said Flanagan. "That's the second time I've gotten that answer in the last two hours."

"Better than two Noes," said Clarkin.

"Unless the *I'll think about it* is just a way to brush me off instead of directly saying *No*."

"I don't believe that's the case," said Clarkin, "at least with me. And it might not be the case with whomever Pisano you propositioned – given the smell of you, my money's on Heather – she might be as inclined to say *Yes* to you as I am. But seeing how often it is you ask for favors, those you're asking might think it wise to string you along for a while."

"What for?"

"First of all, you can't underestimate how enjoyable it is to make you suffer," Clarkin said. "You're a bit of a twitchy wreck. Plus, you're less likely to ask either of us for another favor before this one is settled."

"So will you get Kevin to take the test?" chided Flanagan.

"You're an asshole, you know that?" said Clarkin.

"I'll think about it," said Flanagan.

When he left Clarkin's in an Uber, Flanagan tapped around his phone until he stumbled upon another Email from JPay. Karl the Sausage Hoffman had finally decided to answer Flanagan's follow-up message. The subject tag was the same strange one as last time: In the End, just Four You. Clearly, Attica didn't offer spelling lessons as part of its rehabilitation program. The new Email was as brief and insulting as the last. "You must be an idiot to think we'd ever want a car to make go." Flanagan feared that Karl the Sausage might be too inarticulate to be understood. Yet by the time he returned to his green futon and wrote back, he remained hopeful that one day Karl's responses would make sense. Flanagan's reply signaled that he was in no position to take offense. "I might be an idiot because I am failing to understand what happened the night Jimmy Doherty crashed into the Gowanus Canal. I think you know. Could you have pity on an idiot and help me to understand?"

He hit send and considered that most of his conversations were riddles delivered by sources with little incentive to tell him the truth. Still, he found his tongue rolling over Karl's words – "You must be an idiot to think we'd ever want a car to make go." As the message reverberated, most of the time Flanagan never made it to the second half of the sentence, getting stuck on the "You must be an idiot" part, saying the words with a gentle lilt that soon had him off in slumbers. Even in his dreams, he repeated those words, grinning, knowing that if Deja were in the bed next to him, she might believe he was capable of introspection.

CHAPTER 23
THE RECKONING OF AN OLD STORY

Flanagan returned to his apartment door after grabbing a bacon, egg, and cheese sandwich to confront a new set of problems. He was greeted by a dead squirrel on his doorknob with another printed note attached: "Don't end up like the squirrel." Triple the size of the chipmunk, the squirrel had been wedged tightly between the knob and the jamb, so Flanagan had to actually take off a shoe and pry away to dislodge the critter. As with the chipmunk, Flanagan removed his shirt to open the door, so as not to get a handful of disease.

Flanagan decided a second dead animal was much harder to ignore than the first. He considered calling the police, which he rejected, since he didn't want to consume the time of filing a report and trying to explain what activities led to these threats. Then he thought about contacting Kartik, but again rejected the notion, fearing his potential producer might bail on him. He considered setting up a surveillance camera, but he could not imagine making such an investment given his compromised financial state.

He pondered who might be the deliverer of these bad tidings. While he still suspected someone from the oil companies, he knew Pisano involvement was increasingly likely. Perhaps they decided legal papers did not send an urgent enough message. Whoever perpetrated the act had been carefully observing his activities, since Flanagan's trip to Othello's Deli left him out of the apartment for fewer than 20 minutes. As he contemplated the odd rodent threats, a text from Tiffany Pisano delivered his next reason for anxiety.

When Tiffany confirmed their dinner at the Park Side, Flanagan knew he was in deep doo-doo. He sighed and took the two subways to Columbia, so he could preemptively face the wrath of Deja. He considered the dead squirrel a minor problem compared to Deja.

When he arrived at her office, Deja looked pleasantly surprised to see him, perhaps still humming a bit from their gathering on the darkest of evenings during Hurricane Zelda. That night belied his visions of her: though he had not witnessed the glisten of her mocha skin, the sloping elegance of her strong thighs, and the intelligent awareness of her countenance, he saw it all in his memory as clearly as he had heard her excited breaths. Bracing himself for what he had to tell Deja, Flanagan knew the good vibes would not last. On the way to Columbia, he had considered buying her a dozen roses, but ultimately decided in the end the flowers would only enrage her further: he had concerns about being punctured by the bouquet's innumerable thorns.

"To what do I owe the honor of your presence," said Deja, uncharacteristically playful. "Do you require a primer on this season's storm models and their relationship to global warming?"

"No," said Flanagan. "I just wanted to give you a heads up about something."

Deja's demeanor markedly darkened. "Oh, what might that be?"

"I just wanted to let you know I've been seeing a lot of the Pisano sisters lately."

"When you say sisters, do you mean all three of them?"

"Well, no. I don't mean Nora."

"Of course you don't. I can't imagine she'd want anything to do with you. But I can't imagine why the other two morons would want to see you either."

Flanagan immediately wanted to defend himself, arguing that their advances to him were unsolicited. But he thought that would be an awful strategy. Instead, he went for a merely bad one. "I thought you told me that Heather was really smart."

"That's because you don't listen," she said. "You only hear what you want to hear. I only told you that Heather wasn't completely stupid; you heard that her IQ was as big as her ass."

"Hey," said Flanagan, on the verge of blurting out unintentionally provocative comments. "I didn't bring up her ass."

"No," said Deja, "but you sure couldn't wait to talk about it the minute I brought it up. So what do you mean by seeing a lot of?"

"I've been over their house."

"I'm sure they want to use you," Deja said. "There can be no other reason."

"Maybe they like me."

"My God, you're dumber than they are. Anyway, they are not the issue. The fact that you came running over to their compound like a little lapdog tells me what you're after."

"I came there hoping I could get footage for my documentary."

"You came over there hoping you'd get some footage of yourself starring in a sex tape."

"That's not true." Even Flanagan was taken aback by how lame he sounded.

"What bothers me most is you don't have a chance with the Pisano girls." Flanagan did not like that Deja called them "girls." They were grown women in their thirties; she made his visitation sound statutory. He wanted to object, but Deja's voice grew louder and she was now seething with rage. "You don't have a chance with those girls, but that you are trying to get them is really disappointing. You might as well try to sleep with a pyromaniac who every day burns a couple of acres of Amazon rain forest."

"What?" said Flanagan. Not knowing what else to say, he added, "What?"

"I have work to do," she said.

All the time he spoke to Deja and even now in this respite of silence, Flanagan's phone kept beeping, buzzing, and vibrating like a smoke detector in a barbeque joint. It took great restraint not to check the phone, although part of him was curious to see how Deja would respond.

"I just wanted to let you know what was going on, Deja," he said. "I didn't want to lie to you."

"That's good since lying to me might confuse you considering how much you are lying to yourself."

As he got up to leave, Flanagan tossed out, "Oh yeah. I just wanted to let you know, I went out to dinner with Heather last night, and I'm going out to dinner with Tiffany tonight."

"What!" Deja yelled loudly enough that by now those in the offices around them who were trying to save the world might be a tad distracted. When Flanagan earlier said "What?," it spoke of muddled exasperation; Deja's "What!" delivered incredulous fury. "I can't believe I wasted my time with a fool like you."

As Flanagan headed to the door, he said, "I think you'll understand when I have finished the documentary."

She fired her copy of *The Uninhabitable Earth* at him. It clipped him on the right ear and a clenching shoulder, stunning him momentarily. He wished she had hurled a paperback instead of a hardcover. He was hoping her savage act would render her apologetic. Instead, she peered at her bookshelf for her next weapon.

As Flanagan shut her office door, he yelled out, "I don't know why you're so upset. All you keep telling me is that you don't want to see me."

When Flanagan got back onto campus grounds, he checked his phone. The first text was from Michelle asking if they could go out to dinner tomorrow night. She playfully added, "although I will be devastated not having your specially cooked breakfast for supper." The next was from Clarkin, who said that Kevin Doherty had submitted a DNA swab and that the results should be back in three or four days. The final five texts and three phone calls were from retired detective Murphy.

When Flanagan called, Murphy made clear he wanted to meet right away, or as he phrased it, "while I still feel like talking to you." More extraordinary than the time of his request was the location: on Sackett Street right by the Gowanus Canal, the spot where Jimmy Doherty plunged to his death more than thirty years ago.

Flanagan and his camera made another one of those absurd subway journeys, first on the N train, then transferring onto the 7, and then onto the G which staggered through Queens and Brooklyn, zigging and zagging like a drunken hipster for 16, count them, 16 stops until he arrived at the station that sat at the corner of Smith and 9th Streets. Then he had to follow the canal almost to its headwaters, reaching the corner of Sackett and Bond Streets. Since Murphy had yet to arrive, he walked along the cobblestoned block toward the most toxic body of water in New York City. The dead end was marked by a little sign that read: **Green Zone, bringing nature back to our streets.** Basking in the unseasonably strong sun of this late October afternoon, he sat on a small park bench next to a dying shrub, staring at the churning brown water. He hoped the color derived from the pumping station stirring up mud.

Minutes later, Murphy sat down next to him. "Boy," said the former detective, "doesn't this place just warm your cockles?"

"Too bad I hadn't visited this canal years ago. We could've set a season of *Peepin' on the Pisanos* here. It could've had an industrial chic feel."

"Uh huh," said Murphy. "Let's walk back up the block to where the car was parked."

"Not the kind of location I'd expect to find Jimmy Doherty," Flanagan said.

"Let me ask you something," said Murphy. "If you think there was foul play behind Doherty's accident, how do you think it was done?"

"I figured someone cut the brake lines," said Flanagan.

Murphy laughed. "You really do live in a TV world, don't you?"

"What do you mean?"

"That might have worked for cars long ago, and I mean back in the 1960s, and even then it would've been hard to pull off without the driver noticing that something was wrong."

"We are talking about a crash that happened in '89."

Murphy smiled condescendingly. "Doherty would have had to have a very old car, which he didn't. But even then, the driver would have had to have not noticed that his brakes were all screwed up when he started driving and would have had to immediately accelerate, racing at a high speed to fully drain all the brake fluid. Only after all of that, he would hit the brakes. Not a likely scenario, especially the idea that the driver had never tapped the breaks beforehand to notice the pedal was flat on the floor. Sorry kid. That only happens on bad TV shows."

Disheartened, Flanagan ventured. "But you do have suspicions about Doherty's accident?"

"I do," he said. "The problem is I don't have any hard evidence, just a theory based on the circumstances of the case."

"Well, I wouldn't mind hearing it," Flanagan said.

Murphy stretched his arms across the cobbled street. "Let's start with the indications that the car had sped up before plunging into the canal. That's always bothered me since Sackett Street is a short block from where he was parked by Bond Street."

"What was he doing there?" asked Flanagan.

"From what we can determine, screwing somebody," said Murphy. "It was a really out of the way place, especially at night when all the industries were quiet. It was the type of place you could get some privacy without any pain-in-the-ass reporter sniffing around." Murphy pointed up to the second floor of a brass factory. "If it was like other converted warehouse spaces in the city, the top floor could have made for a spacious loft, quite the love nest."

"Do you know who he was with?" Flanagan asked.

"Hey, this was the '80s. We weren't doing DNA samples, although back then we had our suspicions."

"Yeah," said Flanagan. "I think we might suspect the same partner."

"Anyway, he starts the car and he drives right into the canal," said Murphy. "He must have picked up some speed to break through the guard rail, although I have to tell you that guard rail wasn't going to stop much. It was there for show, but it worked until Doherty's car. In fact, he's the only one who ever died from a car sinking into the canal. Can you believe that? It makes a man wonder. You have a car parked on a street toward a canal with a minimal barrier in front of him. If someone did want to kill him and make it look like an accident, there was a good opportunity."

"But you just pooh-poohed somebody cutting his brakes."

"I think the problem was acceleration, not braking," said Murphy. "Given how short the distance is from the parked car to the canal, his Honda Civic would have had to accelerate for him to shoot into the canal like that. My problem is, I can't figure out how it could be done."

"Maybe it's something we have not thought of," said Flanagan.

"That was always my weak spot as a detective," said Murphy. "I have trouble imagining something that I haven't read about or seen before. Still, I can't imagine Jimmy Doherty just willfully driving into the canal. He only had a little alcohol in his blood. He was under the legal limit. He seemed to have everything to live for. He was certainly getting enough to make any man happy. So that brings me back to someone tampering with the car."

"So you think someone messed with the acceleration to intentionally kill Jimmy Doherty."

"I think it's a strong possibility, although there's one big problem with my theory."

"What's that?"

"The accident report didn't find any foul play."

"Do you think Rusty's Automotive investigation might have been a whitewash?"

"All I can tell you is that there was a lot of pressure from up high to wrap up this case and determine that the death was simply an accident."

"When I talked to you the other day, you seemed pretty skeptical of about this being a homicide," said Flanagan. "What changed?"

"I did some thinking and made some calls," Murphy said. "I found out that those two thugs Tony 'the Elbow' and Karl 'the Sausage' not only had ties to the American Henry Center. According to investigators on the Frankie Pisano accident, they knew Frankie pretty well too. They all worked together in the early 90s. I know that's a few years after Doherty's death, but it raises my antenna. When one of Frankie's star athletes Otis Freeman was in trouble with gambling debts, Tony and Karl made those problems go away. According to my detective buddy, the criminals and the sports agent seemed to have had a falling out about five years later, near the time of Frankie Pisano's accident. The Karl Hoffman connection is the key to the whole situation. Everyone in the business knows two things about Karl Hoffman – the man is brilliant and wherever he goes, trouble follows."

Flanagan held his head. Too much sordidness and innuendo swirled around the Pisano family for him to keep straight. Those whacky Emails Karl sent him just confused matters, and Murphy seeing Hoffman as the lynchpin to the crime didn't make his understanding clearer. If he had a chance of presenting anything like a coherent documentary, he had to stick with the Doherty accident and that accident only. Yes, Frankie's connection to Tony "the Elbow" Fratiani and Karl "the Sausage" Hoffman was of value. But the rest of Frankie's subsequent relations with the two thugs he would not touch.

Flanagan spent the next hour recording footage along Sackett, the canal, and the surrounding area. He interviewed Murphy throughout, who was less forthcoming with the camera on. Still, the old detective had a twinkle in his eye, a deep timbre to his voice, and sufficient suspicion in his tone to intimate that Doherty's accident joined the ranks of those delicious unsolved mysteries.

Even though he showed no sign of it for the camera, Murphy announced at the end of the shoot, "Man, am I sweating. Do you think it's ever going to get cooler?"

"Maybe December," Flanagan offered.

"I'd never thought I'd hear myself say it," said Murphy, "but after this autumn, I'd take some snow for Christmas."

After bidding farewell to Murphy and getting assurances that he could continue to tap into his investigative expertise, Flanagan took the hourlong journey back to Astoria. He had just enough time to clean himself up, find a respectable shirt, and make his way to the Park Side to meet with yet another Pisano sister.

The *maître d'* seemed quite amused to see Flanagan again, setting him up at the same table. This time he landed on a red, a $90 Barolo. It was five bucks more than last night's Gavi, but the two wines were close enough in range that he hoped neither sister would judge favoritism in the selection. Tiffany's appearance gained even more head-turns than Heather's, perhaps because word had already spread around Corona about last night's Pisano sighting.

Compared to Tiffany's outfit, Heather had dressed like a nun. Essentially, Tiffany's black "evening gown" covered only the parts usually required by law. A voile cape provided a sheer screen through which all could view the show. By this point, Flanagan had become increasingly accustomed to being near Pisanos in their various states of nakedness. His demeanor evolved from embarrassed excitement to casual bemusement. Although Tiffany's makeover made her ripe for derision, Flanagan viewed the middle sister with greater sympathy upon each encounter. Tiffany was trying hard, with a desperation that could make a man who was trying for the first time in his life feel for her.

He sincerely wanted to get to know her and like her the way he would his own sister. Her warm collagen-stiffened smile and the sparkle in her lens-tinted eyes told Flanagan that Tiffany was giving authentic humanity her best shot.

"God, this place is wonderful," she said. "It reminds me of the restaurants we'd go to when we were young."

"I'd imagine your father liked this type of place," Flanagan said.

"He used to take us to Arthur Avenue in the Bronx," she said. "To Mario's and Dominick's. We'd leave there stuffed."

Flanagan understood by "we" Tiffany meant she and her father, certain that Heather and Suzie might at best split an eggplant dish. Tiffany, God bless her, not only liked food, but liked to like food. In another Italian family, she might have been adorably chubby. A further issue for her was, unlike Heather, Tiffany was clearly Frankie's child, which might have made her pretty enough for Bensonhurt, but did not make the grade for the Upper East Side. Yet Tiffany was not nearly as predatory as Frankie.

So when Tiffany grabbed his hand gently across the table, Flanagan thought nothing of it.

Until he saw the cell phones lift.

Flanagan was still surprised that he was no less the fool than he was as a pimply 13-year-old. Tiffany had undoubtedly posed for the same photo that Heather had set up last night. He tried not to consider what would come of these

Park Side sisterly photos; he sipped the Barolo, hoping for twenty bucks of flavor out of a $90 wine.

As he started to wallow in misery, Tiffany smiled at him sweetly. To any but the coldest of hearts, that smile seemed sincere. "What I love about you," she said, "is that you have always tried to act like a gentleman, even when I could tell our provocativeness got you all discombobulated. I remember one time you were so startled by the way we were prancing around the parking lot when you arrived that you parked your car, but you never turned off the ignition. You kept the car running all day. I like a man who couldn't hide how distracted we made you."

"Oh, I'm not the only one who you've been known to fluster," said Flanagan.

"You say the nicest things," said Tiffany. "You always knew how to make me feel good. I remember when Heather was doing that centerfold and I put on those short-shorts and that halter top just to get a little attention in the episode. You came over to me and gave me more lines, so I'd have a bigger role. Even as you handed me the paper, you looked down at the marble floor. You treated me like a goddess who was too beautiful to gaze upon."

Flanagan had to be nimble here. He tended to stare at something else when he was near Tiffany because he often felt embarrassed for her on the set. She was constantly craving attention, especially from Suzie, that she rarely garnered. The last thing she needed was pity in the eyes of her script writer. Now he had to compose his own lines for this scene. "Sometimes you realize someone is so beyond you that you keep whatever distance you can."

The waiter came over and Tiffany ordered the veal parmigiana. Unlike her sister, she appeared not as obsessed with her waistline, willing to return to the plastic surgeon if concerns arose. Even though he really wanted to, Flanagan made sure he did not order the fettucine carbonara again, figuring having the same meal two nights in a row at the same restaurant would render him an object of ridicule. He settled on the ravioli.

Tiffany kept smiling. She was ebullient. If she were faking her joy, hell if Flanagan could tell. "I never thanked you for the words you put in my mouth and the ideas you put in my head. I remember when all of Heather's businesses were taking off, you gave me that scene where I pitched the Second Sister brand to my mother."

Tiffany didn't realize that Flanagan wrote the scene for comic relief, knowing what Suzie would say to such a suggestion. Undeterred, Tiffany, God bless her, launched the brand, first as a clothing line and later incorporating a full complement of bathroom products. Having the Pisano entrepreneurial touch and the concomitant name recognition, Tiffany made Second Sister a roaring success. The brand became an emblem for all of those women who never felt good enough. "Tiffany, don't thank me," he said. "You did it with your hard work and your vision. You empowered girls all over the world." Flanagan knew he was laying it on thick, but what the hell else was he going to say.

"Listen to you," Tiffany said, gathering his compliments like gold dust in her palms. "You never like to give yourself credit for anything. You can say what you want, but we both know you came up with the name Second Sister."

"But it wasn't until you expanded the brand to All Sisters that it truly became a feminist icon."

Mercifully for Flanagan, the food arrived. They shifted their praise to the meal for a while as they ate. Tiffany became more animated as she described the burrata at Babbo, the osso bucco at Volare, the meatballs at Carbone. Flanagan had to admit he loved how much she loved to eat. But eventually Tiffany had to return to the one unavoidable topic: *Peepin' on the Pisanos*.

"I almost like putting this veal into my mouth as much as the words you so lovingly place there," she paused, to make certain Flanagan did not miss her flirtatious intents. Still, she could not focus on seducing him because her mind took her to another place. "And yet the best thing you have ever written for me is not the words you put in *my* mouth, but what you put in my *mother's*," Tiffany said. "It was during my hour of greatest need and Heather was trying to steal the episode from me, like she always did. And that's when you had Mother say, 'Heather, honey, you might want to stop taking selfies. Your sister is going to jail now.'"

Flanagan lifted his cloth napkin and wiped his mouth uncomfortably. He desperately wanted to take credit for the most famous line ever uttered in the show, but Suzie was responsible for it. He half-heartedly confessed. "I think your mother had more to do with that comment than I did."

"Oh," said Tiffany, blushing in a way that indicated that she really had a little thing for Flanagan, "you're just being modest, like always, giving us the credit. When I got caught shoplifting, I didn't know what to say. I had no idea why I stole what I did. I certainly could afford the merchandise. Then I spoke your words and it was as if you read my thoughts, even though I didn't yet realize what my thoughts were."

Flanagan had Tiffany explain that she stole the cheap costume necklace and earrings because they made her feel prettier. She was ashamed to buy them because to purchase would be to acknowledge how inadequate she felt. By stealing them, she had hoped to keep those insecurities hidden. "Oh, your feelings were perfectly understandable," he said.

"To you they were," said Tiffany, her tinted eyes staring adoringly at him. "You were the only one who understood. I don't think you realize how important you have been to my life."

Flanagan shifted awkwardly, even more uncomfortable in Tiffany's presence now than in her theatrical seduction at the compound. "How's that?"

"Your words made me realize that I needed to make some changes," she said. "I was unhappy with my appearance. I always felt inadequate. Before you put those words in my mouth, I was ashamed of the minor procedures I had done, a little lip plumping here, a minor breast augmentation there. But your words empowered me to go into the plastic surgeon's office and get everything I wanted. In essence, you made me what I am today."

"That is very sweet of you to say," said Flanagan. "But, honestly, we both know you deserve all the credit." Again, Tiffany took these comments for modesty while Flanagan presented them for holy absolution. He took full measure of Tiffany. Maybe if he had not known her all those years, he would be able look at Tiffany now and come to concede that she was conceptually beautiful. If she had walked by him on the street, would he consider her someone to covet? From a distance, yes. But up close, the dimension and vulnerability of her entire experiment left him sad and desolate.

Oblivious, Tiffany buoyantly smiled, pinching some clay into her mouth. "Nothing cleans the toxins from a fine meal like clay," she said. "Are you sure I can't convince you to try some?"

Flanagan felt he'd be rude to reject her again. "Sure," he said, "why not?" Then he thought to himself, I'll eat some of your dirt.

When Tiffany passed him a wad, he popped it in his mouth. Flanagan found that certain times in his life when he tried something new, he was pleasantly surprised. This occasion was not one of them. "Oh, I can feel those toxins floating right out of my body," he said.

Tiffany laughed. "You joke, but you'll see." Then she ate another wad. Flanagan wondered whether she was the proud owner of a dried-up creek bed where the clay was harvested.

When the waiter returned, they ordered cappuccinos. Soon the coffee arrived, and they each ripped open an Equal. Flanagan tapped in a little; Tiffany poured in the whole packet.

When he returned to his basement apartment, Flanagan was greeted by a text from Dirk Wall. "I heard from a little birdie that you've been seeing a lot of the sisters lately. My condolences."

Flanagan texted back. "It could be worse."

"I greatly doubt that," Dirk answered. "Remember, you can always crash your car into a wall."

"I'll keep that in mind," Flanagan assured him.

That night as he lay awake in bed, Flanagan tossed about trying to figure out whether he was in love with Deja or Tiffany. He muttered to himself, "What if it's both?" To get his mind off the knowledge that Deja would not have him and that Tiffany would only have him within the confines of the reality series, he stewed about his documentary, plotting out his next moves. The demands of piecing together the narrative confused and soon exhausted him, sending him off to slumbers.

He did not know that tomorrow would present challenges he had not heretofore considered.

CHAPTER 24
THE TRASHING OF COURTSHIP

After heading to Othello's Deli for a bacon, egg, and cheese sandwich, Flanagan returned home to find a dead pigeon wedged between his doorknob and the jamb with yet another note attached: "You don't want to be this pigeon."

Flanagan mumbled, "No, I don't." Once again, he removed his shirt to grab the pigeon without contaminating his hands, throwing the bird in the trash and the shirt in the sink. This message felt personal. Although Flanagan hated to admit it, the pigeon was his spirit animal: it fed off the crumbs of others. He sensed that more violent acts would come soon. His ignoring of these dead animals could not be good for his health.

He opened up the parchment paper and grabbed half the sandwich. Damn carcasses were souring his taste for breakfast. Over the past week, Flanagan had managed to keep the mystery of these dead animals out of his head. He was not smart enough to carry around that puzzle in his consciousness along with the ambiguities swirling about Jimmy Doherty's demise. Plus, the dinners with the Pisano sisters left him further disoriented. How many mixed messages could the family deliver to him?

He knew Michelle would freak out if he told her about these cold, stiff presents that had arrived at his door. Since she was coming over this morning, he made sure to put the pigeon in a bag inside of a bag.

Little did he know that Michelle would give him more to ponder.

The minute she arrived, Michelle passed Flanagan her phone. "My father is a mysterious chick magnet," she said definitively.

"What?" he said.

"I guess you haven't been on Twitter."

"Not unless I have to."

"I would say this time it's necessary," Michelle said. "I'll make it easier for you, old man. Here, I clicked on an article in the *New York Post*. I guess I shouldn't call you old man. Maybe I'll call you by one of your many hashtags: twotiming studmuffin."

Flanagan groaned at the headline: "Wordsmith Playa Spreads Sisterly Love." Worse were the two side-by-side pictures. The photos captured Flanagan there at the same Park Side table with Heather and then Tiffany, each caressing his hand and looking adoringly at him. The gossip columnist Mindy Quincy brought home the gravity of the situation.

He read the article.

It appears that the Pisano sisters are vying for the love of the same hunk. The buxom Heather and the bodacious Tiffany were spotted nibbling and snuggling with mysterious scriptwriter Arthur Flanagan, who has known the girls for years on the *Peepin' on the Pisanos* set. But now that he's left the show, the debonair Mr. Flanagan appears to have made his move. The sisters must have suddenly come to realize what a little honey they had buzzing around their flowers all those years.

Flanagan frowned at how even by the low standards of gossip columns, Mindy's mixed metaphors made the skull ache. Yet, what choice did he have but to read on.

Apparently, both are ready to be deflowered by the wine pouring raconteur. Our sources have reported that King Arthur had recently breached the walls of the Pisano mansion and has pulled his Excalibur from its sheath, prepared to show what his legendary sword offers in

courtly conquest. No word yet on whether
older sister Heather has a leg up on
Tiffany, but given the younger sibling's
competitive streak and her recent
visitations to the knights of the
operating table, we figure it will be a
catfight to the finish.

Flanagan's horror about what he was reading was compounded by the
knowledge that his daughter had read the article first. He could also imagine it
might find its way to the research labs of Columbia University, where Deja's
disgust with him may just have escalated to homicidal levels. Unfortunately, the
article did not end there. Mindy Quincy, generally known for her punchy little
items of a few sentences, apparently could not get enough of this story.

Rumor has it that controversy swirls
around the two-timing badboy as King
Arthur is facing impending lawsuits from
the Pisano family over activities that
might expose long-held secrets of their
clan. I guess it's true what they say
about all is fair in love and war. Stay
tuned my loyal followers because given
how hot and heavy King Arthur's
encounters have been with the two fairest
sisters in the land, I am sure that
something or certainly someone will be
exposed soon!

The twitter commentaries were even more troubling, the worst perhaps
being – "Pisano sisters find their caves are being mined by gold-digger. Sure,
Arthur Flanagan offers quite the shaft, but his hammer is no match for the
diamonds between their thighs."

What the hell was with gossipers and their whacked-out metaphors. He
handed the phone back to Michelle and said, "Wonderful."

"I didn't know you had it in you Dad," said Michelle. "Mom didn't either."

"You showed these posts to your Mother?" Flanagan asked.

"Of course not," Michelle assured him. "She shared them with me."

"Even better," said Flanagan.

"I was wondering if we could plant another tree today in the Astoria lot."

Flanagan nodded. Kartik has summoned him to his office at three, but he figured even if the digging process took as long as last time, they'd be done with two hours to spare. "I will plant a whole forest of trees if I don't have to talk about this Pisano nonsense. Just give me a minute. I just have to order somebody flowers."

"Which sister?" Michelle asked.

"Oh God, not you too," said Flanagan. "Neither. And if you keep asking me questions, no tree."

"All right, but hurry up. Last time it took you forever to dig the hole."

"That's because none of your cute boys on electric scooters would help."

"Hey, if I can't ask about the Pisano sisters, then you can't ask about those boys."

"Not quite," said Flanagan. "I'm going to pull out the father card on this one. I have to do my best to make sure you screw up your life a little less than I have mine. Anyway, you keep bothering me, I'll never get the flowers delivered."

Flanagan ordered a bouquet from 1-800-Flowers to be sent today to Deja at the Earth Institute, since the woman even worked there on weekends. He enclosed a note:

The scene the Pisanos set was a stager
My love for you is true you can wager
I am asking you to turn the pager
For I only write bad poems for my Deja

He only hoped the poem was rotten enough for Deja to hate him just a little less. He had to start somewhere. The good news was when she received the flowers, he'd be planting a tree so many miles away from Deja that the vase could not come crashing down on his skull.

Flanagan and Michelle returned to the nursery. This time he decided to buy a flowering cherry. He wanted to be able to walk by the lot with Michelle each spring and see the tree's puffy white buds, an annual reminder to them that life had returned to the big bad city. Since Flanagan knew what he wanted and Michelle was all for a flowering tree, they picked out the root ball quickly and were at the lot in no time. Unfortunately, the spot Michelle selected for planting was clustered with even more chunks of concrete than the last one, which meant Flanagan cursed when he hit hard spots and did more picking and prodding than he had anticipated, relegated often to many unsatisfactorily small shovelfuls.

Sweating his way through the increasingly familiar labor, Flanagan concluded that the heat wasn't the worst of it, even though this Halloween Day registered in the mid-eighties. The humidity was what did him in. By now, dry autumn breezes should have offered some relief. As he looked around the lot, none of the deciduous trees had changed color. The pervasive greenness was unnerving.

Eventually, the hole grew excessively wide and sufficiently deep to drop in the root ball. During that time, Michelle swapped jokes with a few environmentally conscious dudes about one TickTok channel or another. Flanagan didn't mind as he was beginning to find the sweet spot where he could spend time with his daughter and still give her a bit of a social life. To the boys' credit, when he finally got the cherry tree in and Michelle filled in around it with fresh bags of dirt, they applauded.

After he was done, Michelle pulled him to the side. He thought she was going to ask if she could go out for a while with the boys. Instead, she wanted to know if he would take her out to lunch.

"Sure, pumpkin, where do you want to go?"

"I don't know," she said. "I heard the Park Side is really nice." Her mischievous giggle served as a reminder that he should lighten up.

"You know, I could rip that cherry right out of the hole," Flanagan taunted.

"After how long you labored?" chided Michelle, who might have been watching Victorian dramas as of late. "Oh, how you suffered. Would you really remove this precious tree, depriving the world of its carbon capturing virtue, a tree in an army of trees that just might save the planet as we know it?"

"Have you been listening to those pretty long-haired boys?"

"You listen to your long-haired girls, and I'll listen to my long-haired boys. Anyway, I don't think you'll remove that tree even if I dared you because you looked happier digging that hole than I've seen you in months. You might have been complaining about all the concrete, but when you put the root bulb in the ground, tell me that didn't feel good."

He drew no pleasure from how well Michelle understood him. He knew that the tree contributed almost nothing to the cause his daughter so intensely embraced, but compared to his squalid activities of the past week, it was wholesomely refreshing. "So do you want to get some halal and go to Astoria Park?" he asked. "You can stare at the sycamores and I can count all the cars going over the Triborough Bridge."

"That sounds wonderful," she said. "I'm not sure a Pisano would take you up on such an offer, but I definitely will."

They meandered west until they arrived at the edge of the park where the halal food truck had an unreasonably long line. Like everyone else, they waited. It was damn good halal and it would be, by far, the cheapest meal he had out in a week. As they waited, Michelle lobbied that they should start putting up fruit trees next in the lot. "How great would it be to have an orchard in Astoria?"

Flanagan was tempted to point out the maintenance fruit trees required, not to mention all the bugs and the bees they attracted. Instead he told her, "You're right. It would be great." He meant it, especially when he had a shitty morning like, say, this one. Eventually, they came to the front of the halal line. Michelle had chicken, Flanagan had lamb. They found a bench looking over the East River, which Flanagan decided was an even better snag than a table in the solarium of the Park Side. They were entertained by a half dozen white egrets, poking their sloped beaks in the water in search of their own lunch. By now, they should have flown south. But they were as confused as every other New Yorker with the summer that never ended.

As they looked at the bridge and downstream toward Roosevelt Island, Flanagan spoke of his relationship with Sophie. "Your Mom loved to travel and so did I," he said. "When we first got married, we would go to Europe and wander through the small towns. You know how good mom is with languages, so she always got us into situations and conversations that made us feel part of the action." Sophie's Puerto Rican heritage came in handy in Spain, but she switched over to Italian with disarming ease. Since she took French in school, she managed to talk her way across the continent. Flanagan had been dazzled and intimidated and deeply in love.

"So what went wrong?" asking Michelle, posing the question every divorced kid will direct at one point, and then again and again.

"I went wrong," said Flanagan. "I'd written a couple of promising pilots, but they really went nowhere. Then Suzie Pisano got wind of my opening episode of *The Bellini Brothers*, about a bunch of Italian cops who lived on the South Shore of Long Island. Somehow, from that pilot she thought I would be perfect to portray her privileged quasi-Italian family. I wrote a script for Suzie. Then it was picked up. I didn't know what I was getting into."

"Mom thinks you knew exactly what you were getting into."

"I don't believe your mother is right about that," he said. He conceded, "I might have known more than I was willing to admit at the time." At first, his scripts were playful and subversive. This entire reality nonsense had to be tongue-in-cheek, especially given how over-the-top Suzie was as the anything-to-get-my-daughters-ahead entrepreneur. The girls tried so hard to be ridiculously attractive. That they succeeded made the family even more absurd.

As they tucked into their meat and rice, Flanagan tried to explain how he originally approached the scripts. Michelle rolled her eyes and asked, "Then what happened Dad?"

"To really do the scripts right, I essentially had to live at the mansion," he said. "The more time I spent there, the less time I spent with Sophie, I mean Mom."

"And you didn't cut back your hours," said Michelle as a matter of fact, not as a question.

"No, and that was the worst thing I did to your mother, since she actually liked spending time with me. I had found the one woman who liked to talk to me even when we were done talking. Still, I left Sophie until late at night, so I could write that goddamn show. The Pisanos were so driven. They kept working until past midnight. I worked right along with them."

Michelle looked at her dad like she was growing up before his eyes and was trying to calculate whether she hated him or loved him. "Did you enjoy it?"

Flanagan thought she deserved the truth, even at 15. "More than I cared to admit. Nothing was real, but we were living on some sphere of heightened reality that was like a drug. My scripts became less subversive. I wrote without irony. Ultimately, I wrote with great sincerity. Fortunately, a couple of critics thought I had simply become more dry and subtle in my deadpan attacks. They said, 'Flanagan's letting the Pisanos hang themselves … no ancillary commentary required.' They did not know I no longer undermined the sisters and the mother because I no longer wanted to. I was like one of those servants in the British manor houses who had pledged loyalty to his masters because in doing so, just maybe, they would think I was one of them. Pretty fucked up, huh?"

"I'm glad you're no longer working for them," said Michelle. "Will you be angry if I give you some advice?"

Flanagan did not want to say he might become quite angry, so he answered, "No."

"You probably shouldn't go out to dinner with them."

"You are right," said Flanagan. "And since we are trying to talk to each other like adults, I think I should be honest with you. I might go out to dinner with them anyway."

"Why?" she asked. Her tone was plaintive, gentle. "Why Dad, why?"

"I have to finish playing this out," Flanagan said. "Somewhere, in these investigations into the Pisanos, I sense I am uncovering a truth. I'll be honest with you, though, Michelle. I can't figure out if the truth is about my investigations or about myself."

Sensing she should not pursue the conversation any further, Michelle brightened by taking another tack. "What did Heather say about being NukeMan?"

"Not much," said Flanagan. "She didn't deny it. It was funny. When you talk to Heather, you spend so much time defending yourself that you don't get a chance to ask many questions."

Michelle nodded. "That's true if you're a man."

"So how do I correct that?" Flanagan asked, genuinely requesting advice from his teenage daughter.

"Stop being a man," she answered.

"That's not going to happen," he said, "but I think I'm learning. The Pisanos are a distraction, one of so many, like this thing –" Flanagan pulled out his cell phone. "I realize these distractions are a pleasant way to pass the time in our miserable lives. But there is a sinister side to them. They keep us from focusing on what we have to do. Hell, if Heather, the queen of all distractors, realizes this problem, I certainly could come around to this way of thinking, although it might take some time."

"I'll wait for you," said Michelle.

So another afternoon passed without Michelle giving up on Flanagan. She might have viewed him more as troubled friend than as a father, but at least he wasn't on the outs with one person who was important to him. He saved a little bit of lamb and rice for the pigeons that were cooing about the bench. Scattering the food on the grass, Flanagan told himself grim jokes, all the time smiling at Michelle with gratitude.

He dropped her back off at Sophie's, since she was going to a Sweet Sixteen party tonight, which meant hours of preparation before the pictures and the ceremonious arrival at the catering hall.

He returned to his basement apartment with the desolation that Michelle had temporarily kept at bay. To make the day truly special, he received more threatening letters from the Pisano lawyers. From what he could gather, they would soon drag him before a judge. Flanagan was not up to calling Nelsie Spector right now to get legal guidance.

With still two hours before he had to be in Kartik's office, he prowled around his basement apartment. Hoping to escape the world for a while, Flanagan picked up Stuart Cooper's *Love in the Age of Excess*. While he had skimmed most of the book, the only chapter he completely ignored was an early one, "Frankie's Catholic School Years," for obvious reasons. Now, he preferred to read about those glory days than to think about Frankie's daughters or Suzie's lawyers. He cracked open the spine and escaped.

Love in the Age of Excess by Stuart Cooper

Chapter 2: Frankie's Catholic School Years

Perhaps it was the restrictive halls of the all-boys Catholic school where he searched for skirts and all he found were trousers, perhaps it was growing up in 1970s when the sexual liberations of the previous decade had been homogenized into the prurient teases of bikini-clad angels of Charlie and the plunging leotard wonders of women, perhaps it was the small Bensonhurst apartment with four brothers where an aroused adolescent found no quiet place to release his volcanic eruptions pent up in his loins. For whatever reason, young Frankie Pisano struggled when he encountered women.

Yes, for a Catholic boy to be distracted by the beauties of the opposite sex is not uncommon. Yet, Frankie's neighborhood friends acknowledged that his fever, his lust, yes his unadulterated lust, was extraordinary. His childhood buddy Rusty Sansone explained how he took his responsibilities as an altar boy much more seriously than Frankie. "Frankie would always forget to ring the bells when the priest lifted up the Eucharist. I'd have to kick him to get him to pick up a bell and give it a shake. He was too busy checking out the ladies in the pews to focus on the mass."

But Frankie had bigger problems than the kind of dumbstruck magnetism that stunned King David when he first gazed upon Bathsheba. He couldn't figure how to talk to the girls at the Catholic dances. "It was crazy," said his old friend Bobby Lucchino. "We'd go up to a group of chicks, hand them some Orange Crush, and start talking to them about what TV shows they liked. Then Frankie would try to say something. He started out normal like, 'The Rockford Files is a really cool show ...' and then he began to cry, tears streaming down his face. At first, we thought Frankie was trying out a slick move, you know, a come-on, especially when a sympathetic babe would snuggle up to him, drop a hand on his shoulder, and ask what's wrong? But then he would stop crying and start laughing maniacally, like he was a psycho killer. I tell you Frankie didn't do us any favors. The girls took their Orange Crushes and were far away from us real fast."

It got to the point that whenever he noticed a young lady in the room Frankie started boohooing louder than the long-lost Joseph at a family reunion. Frankie was forever running outside, where he would then begin to laugh uncontrollably. He questioned his sanity, and he wasn't alone.

Embarrassed, Frankie decided he must conquer his fear of women. "For a guy who couldn't talk *to* women, he certainly talked *about* them day and night," said Rusty. "He had this crazy idea that the only way he could get over his fear was to have a conversation with not just any woman, but one of the most beautiful women in the world."

Akin to a scrawny Philistine wooing Delilah, Frankie had set his sights on meeting and getting a date with Jaclyn Smith, one of the *Charlie's Angels* goddesses. She was coming into New York to promote an ABC television movie, and Frankie was plotting to be on the scene. He had spent months researching about her before her visit. He listened *ad naseum* to Tchaikovsky, her favorite composer, learning the *1812 Overture* note for note and becoming casually conversational about *The Nutcracker*; he watched her favorite movie, *Gone with the Wind*, five times so that he'd be able to toss off lines from the best scenes; he even swallowed his masculinity to buy a pink shirt, so she would see him in her favorite color.

After so much Job-like toil and patience, the press conference was cancelled. Frankie's friends had to spend the next week talking him out of flying out to California to meet her. Rusty finally got through to him by pointing out that the lusciously lovely Ms. Smith happened to be the same age as his Aunt Millie. "I know you've worked hard to have common interests with Jaclyn," said Rusty, who always had to call her Jaclyn in front of Frankie because by that point the two were on a first-name basis. "But you might want to start with someone closer to your age."

Adopting the hermetic ways of St. Francis, Frankie didn't leave his room for a week after the disappointment of the Jaclyn Smith no-show. When he did emerge from his cave, however, he had a new target of love: Valerie Bertinelli. He started by kissing the television every time she appeared on her hit show *One Day at a Time*. He listened to Elton John's songs after he heard her first concert was at the Bitch is Back tour back in '74. When he learned she was coming to New York to promote her TV movie *Young Love, First Love*, he knew they were destined to meet. She was barely older than he was, and on the TV she seemed like the girl next door, as approachable as

Zipporah was to Moses. Only Valerie was a TV star too. In essence, she was the perfect woman for him to conquer his fears.

Frankie explained years later what happened with Valerie Bertinelli in his interview on the Oprah Winfrey show, his adoring wife Suzie by his side, a Rachel to his Jacob.

"Meeting Valerie Bertinelli was a turning point in my life," he told Oprah. "The week before I was so nervous that I role-played in front of the mirror each night, and every time I cried. For weeks, I would watch the show on Channel 2 on Sunday night, talking through the TV screen to Valerie's character Barbara Cooper. I cried then too. But then on the last Sunday night before I was to meet Valerie, I was watching an episode. I started reciting the lines of Schneider, the building superintendent on the show. With his tattoos and his tool belt, I could never imagine Schneider crying, so I totally took on his character. For the next few days, I became Schneider, talking his macho way, even chewing gum like he did. By then, I had seen so many episodes of the show, I knew all his mannerisms, especially how he leaned back and smirked. Then I realized that I could not just be like Schneider because he was pretty old, and I might come off as weird and creepy."

Oprah laughed. "I could see that."

"Anyway, I thought I should add a little bit of the softness of Parker Stevenson, who was quite the teen heartthrob back then. He was on the *Hardy Boys* and Valerie had made a guest appearance on the show. I noticed her pretty eyes glistened every time she saw him. So I mixed some Parker Stevenson into my Schneider imitation. All of my lines I had practiced suddenly came out great without a tear in my eye."

Here Suzie, who now sounded more like Leah than Rachel, interrupted, "So I fell for this Frankenstein monster version of a teen detective and a building superintendent?"

"You and so many others, my love," Frankie said. After the audience stopped laughing, he explained, "What I learned more than anything was talking to a woman was like playing a jazz instrument during a gig. All musicians have their little runs and fills they practice just like I had all these lines and clever comments I would say to Valerie when I met her. I knew, like every jazz musician does, that there will be moments when you have to improvise. My improvisations would always come back to asking her a question; if possible that question would include something I knew about her, like that she sang in her school vocal group the Peppermint Rainbow. I might ask about her favorite song, and about what kind of music she performed with the Peppermint Rainbow. That would make Valerie talk longer, flattered by my knowledge and interest in her, so I could bide my time to figure out how to return to my rehearsed lines."

Oprah interrupted. "So how'd it go with Valerie?"

"I think pretty well," Frankie said. "I managed to get past her handler and give her a red bracelet, which was the most important thing I could do, since Valerie said those bracelets reminded her to stop and be kind to others. I also wore a yellow shirt, her favorite color. I told her how much I was like her, I loved crossword puzzles and that my mom made me outfits for the school play just like her mom made her outfits for junior high. When she started talking about how she had to get going because her father was very strict, I said I understood because my father was Italian and I was raised Catholic like her."

"Did you ever get a date with Valerie?" asked Oprah

"No, I didn't do that," said Frankie. "Once I started talking to her, I knew how stupid it was to even try. I learned so much there. I learned that before you go out on a date with a woman you need to spend a lot of time with her." Here Oprah's audience sighed approvingly. "I learned that the most important thing is that you must get to really know a woman. And this I must say to all men out here. There's nothing wrong with having a script before speaking to a woman. Hey,

> that's the only way I could meet a woman
> without crying my eyes out."
>
> "No one could believe that today," said
> Oprah. "You seem so confident."
>
> "It's all an act," said Frankie.
>
> "If it is an act," said Suzie, "I love
> your performance. Just keep doing it
> babe."
>
> "I will my love," said Frankie, "one
> day at a time."

Flanagan closed the book. He had read enough. While Frankie's techniques of picking up women were indeed intriguing (talk about making mating rituals reality television before reality TV even existed), Flanagan could not let go of the name Rusty Sansone. He had almost completed the chapter before he realized that Rusty Sansone was the Rusty of Rusty's Automative Center, which had conducted the investigation of Jimmy Doherty's Honda Civic that had plunged into the Gowanus Canal on November 16, 1989.

He took a deep breath. From what his wife had told Flanagan, Rusty had been pretty sick. He called the number again anyway, since Rusty might well hold the key to the entire investigation. Rusty's wife answered. She told him that Rusty was now in hospice and not to call again.

Flanagan stewed for a while about the dead end that had once been a promising Rusty's Automotive angle. He thought about reopening the book, but decided he was in no mood to read about the sexual conquests of Frankie Pisano. He had to be in Kartik's office in an hour. He wondered whether Kartik would chastise or praise him for his dalliances with the Pisano sisters. As each day passed, he had more problems reading people.

After a few minutes of staring up from his green futon onto the ceiling, he received a text from Clarkin: "You might want to get in touch with Barry Rubinstein in Connecticut. He's an old retired senator. He could tell you something you'd want to know."

Flanagan texted back. "Got a number?"

Clarkin didn't answer for a while, like he was thinking about something. Then the text arrived. "If you tell Rubinstein where you got this number, you will not know what hit you. 203-580-3652."

Flanagan texted back, "Thanks. Don't worry. I have no interest in being mauled by you."

On the bright side, Clarkin's number, like Clarkin himself, was true and useful. Senator Rubinstein would be happy to talk about his dear, long-lost colleague Jimmy Doherty. On the murkier side, he wanted to meet for lunch tomorrow at L'Escale in Greenwich. That the restaurant was French and waterfront signaled a painful tab. When he embarked on this documentary, Flanagan had no idea he would be feeding much of the tri-state area. He was discovering, despite his mother's admonitions, people only like to talk when their mouths were full.

CHAPTER 25
THE RECASTING OF AN EXPLOSION

Kartik sat in the front of the Range Rover across from Arnav, his burly nephew and driver. "We haven't involved you in some of the footage we're generating," Kartik explained to Flanagan, who sat in the back, "but we thought you ought to see what we are doing today." Flanagan was certain that when Kartik said "we," he meant Mehnuma who was peering studiously at her laptop in the other backseat.

"So where are we going?" asked Flanagan.

"To the pine barrens way out on the island," said Mehnuma, still not looking past her screen.

"Why would we want to do that?" Flanagan figured he might as well use Kartik's "we" too.

"Because we didn't want to fly to Texas to shoot this scene," said Mehnuma. "It's almost as hot here anyway."

"To Texas?" asked Flanagan.

"You'll see when we get there," said Kartik.

Mehnuma closed her laptop. "We noticed a hole in the documentary," she said.

"A hole," said Flanagan. "And that is —"

"You keep bringing up the American Henry Center, but you haven't done any research about Roy Crowne."

Flanagan frowned. As always, Mehnuma had a point. Roy Crowne had been one of the richest men in America. As the head of the American Henry Center and as a board member of every lobbying group in the petroleum industry, Crowne did more to prevent action on climate change than anyone. Flanagan had avoided investigating Crowne, given the mogul's tendency to destroy people with his money, whether it be their fortunes or their reputations. More importantly, Crowne was not one to physically destroy people as in murdering them or, say, hurtling their cars into canals. He simply didn't fit the profile. Then there was the other minor problem.

"It's harder to contact Crowne now that he's dead," said Flanagan.

Inconveniently, Roy Crowne suffered a massive heart attack on a golf course last year and died right there on the fifteenth hole. Flanagan preferred to have his villains living. "That's actually a good thing," said Mehnuma.

"Why's that?" asked Flanagan.

"Crowne liked to sue," said Mehnuma, "his estate, not so much. From some of the recent stories published about Roy Crowne, it's clear the family doesn't care about maintaining the old man's reputation as much as they care about keeping every last dime they inherited."

"Don't we have enough bad guys with Frankie and those two goons Tony the Elbow and Karl the Sausage?" asked Flanagan.

"You can never have enough bad guys," said Mehnuma.

"That still doesn't explain why we're out here," said Flanagan.

As they exited off the Long Island Expressway and clover-leafed onto something called the William Floyd Parkway, Kartik answered by saying, "We're almost there."

From what Flanagan could see, "there" was the middle of nowhere. They rode through woods of horrible little scrub pines with gangly branches bent over the sandy soil. They stopped in the middle of a parkland where trailers and film crews had already set the scene. "This is a park?" asked Flanagan. "Who the hell would want to preserve this?"

Kartik laughed. "Apparently, these trees and the sandy soil below them make for very clean water."

"So we have arrived in Texas," said Flanagan.

"Indeed, we have," said Kartik. "It's not quite right, but when Mehnuma gets done transforming the landscape, you'll expect a cattle drive to run across your screen at any moment."

"I'm still trying to figure out what this has to do with Roy Crowne," said Flanagan.

"I'll explain after the shoot," said Mehnuma, who promptly walked away and started giving directions to a young couple in a rusty, broken-down pickup truck. Clearly in charge of everything, Mehnuma studied the condition of the corroded pipeline propped out of the ground.

Flanagan followed her, staring down at the damage. "What're you looking at?"

Mehnuma ignored him, yelling out, "We need more steam here."

The tech guy answered, "Steam is not usually visible from gas leaks. You generally just smell the leak."

"Cameras don't have noses," said Mehnuma. "The only way anyone will know there's a gas leak is that they see mist or smoke or steam. So give me some of that."

Two large firetrucks loomed in the distance, their big hoses spraying down the perimeter. Behind those trucks were an armada of emergency vehicles: it seemed like every volunteer fireman on Long Island had arrived at the scene to watch the shoot. To get those vehicles out of the camera sight lines took some maneuvering. After about ten minutes of jockeying and checking, then double-checking, the director yelled action.

As the steam billowed from the pipe, the attractive young couple hopped out of the pick-up. "You smell that gas?" asked the young beauty. The hunky boy nodded in response.

They jumped back in the pick-up and then hunk hit the ignition.

"Cut," yelled the director.

The two young actors left the seats in the rusty truck and were replaced by dummies with heads remarkably like those of the two actors. The dummies were strapped into their seatbelts and then the tech guys came along, checking wiring. After about fifteen minutes, Mehnuma nodded and said to the crew, "I think we're ready." Then she turned to Flanagan. "You might want to step back about twenty feet."

Before he could question her, he noticed that rest of the crew was retreating, so he followed the herd. Then Mehnuma threw in, "When the director yells action, I want a blast of steam, then wait five seconds to detonate."

Flanagan laughed, wondering just what the director's job was on set, since Mehnuma barked out the orders. As he considered what the word detonate might suggest, the director bellowed, "Action!"

The steam spewed from the pipe like a geyser at Yellowstone and as the mist reached the rusty pick-up, the explosion sent the truck off the ground and flames shot up and out.

"BANG!"

"BOOM!"

The camera lingered over the burning pick-up, smoke shrouding the melting faces of the dummies.

Mehnuma had seen enough. She tapped the director on the shoulder, "You got it from here?" she asked. The director nodded and Mehnuma signaled Flanagan to return to the back of the Ranger Rover.

As he rested on the comfy leather cushions, Flanagan asked her, "What was that all about?"

"It's a reenactment," said Mehnuma. "A bunch of years ago these two teens smelled gas outside their mobile home, so they drove over to investigate. They did not know that they were sucking in vapors from a corroded butane pipeline that Roy Crowne would not replace. Their truck stalled as it was enveloped by these vapors. Eventually, when they got the car restarted, the gas tank blew, and the two were burned alive. It's not your typical murder, but with the right voiceover, we can put Roy Crowne in the negligent homicide category."

"Still," said Flanagan, "that sounds like a bit of a stretch."

"Let me show you this interview I conducted with Grace Chen," said Mehnuma. "She's a climate change historian and an activist." Flanagan wanted to say he already knew that and was planning on meeting with her, but he couldn't see any purpose in telling Mehnuma that now. "I think her comments convey what we want here."

Mehnuma passed Flanagan her laptop, and he hit play. In her signature pink lab coat, Grace Chen smiled as she delivered her searing indictment. "When it comes to Roy Crowne, I think it really begins with his Nazi nanny when he was growing up in Germany. He never cared how many people died around him as long as he got his way. That was always his approach to global warming. Jimmy Doherty was in his way. He had to go. Jimmy was like those two teenagers in the pick-up. Stay out of the way of his pipelines or expect to be blown up."

"Wow," said Flanagan, "that's pretty good. It's almost like you scripted it yourself." A disturbing thought struck him, and he turned to Mehnuma, "You didn't, did you?"

Mehnuma laughed. "Remind me what you did for a living before."

"That was reality television," said Flanagan. "This is a serious documentary."

Mehnuma laughed harder. Flanagan tried his best to appear to be neither embarrassed nor angry. Reading his response, Mehnuma decided it was a good idea to keep Flanagan's morale high. "That explosion will guarantee the documentary stays exciting throughout and will also force the audience to puzzle over who is the true villain here."

Peeking in, Arnav smirked at Flanagan, as if he too had been briefed on Flanagan's limitations, and jumped into the Range Rover. Soon following Arnav into the SUV, Kartik turned around to Flanagan. "Well, if it isn't lover boy?" he chided.

Mehnuma chimed in, "Yes, from what I hear, you are a two-timing bad boy."

Flanagan frowned. "Don't believe the gossip columnists."

"Did you hear that Mehnuma?" asked Kartik. "If we stop believing in them, how can we trust anyone again?"

"That's true," said Mehnuma. She tapped Kartik's shoulder. "Shouldn't you advise Flanagan to keep his – what did they call it? – his Excalibur in its scabbard?"

"Yes," confirmed Kartik, "put that sword away, will you?"

"Don't you start worrying about my sword," said Flanagan.

"I won't, believe me," said Kartik. "If I start worrying about Flanagan's sword, Mehnuma, you have permission to put me in that pick-up truck and blow me up."

That Arnav listened intently, trying his best to suppress laughter, didn't help matters. Flanagan thought about throwing himself out of the car onto the William Floyd Parkway. After letting Kartik and Mehnuma prattle on about his "canoodling with the Pisano sisters" for 50 miles on the Long Island Expressway and not rising to the bait, Flanagan turned to Mehnuma and shrugged. "Can I ask you about something else?"

"Why not?" said Mehnuma. "It's nice to hear you have other interests besides skirt chasing."

"I was wondering," asked Flanagan. "Can you send me Grace Chen's contact information? I may need to speak to her down the road."

CHAPTER 26
PERFORMING FOR AN AUDIENCE OF ONE

The first thing Flanagan did in the morning was send a fruit basket off to Deja at the Earth Institute. He couldn't come up with a good poem, so he sent a bad one:

Here's a bough of berries
In red, black, and blue
If seeing you means waiting,
Then I'm first on the queue
Though I may be false,
I know this much is true
That when I go to bed at night
I think only of you.

Flanagan groaned and sent the poem. Even as he tried to find a way forward with Deja, he fretted that Tiffany might try to contact him again. The more he got to know Tiffany, the more he struggled to push her away. He had wished the Pisano sensibility did not focus so deeply on sexuality because for once his feelings for an attractive (if surgically troubled) woman were strictly platonic. He sensed that Tiffany needed a brother. If she contacted him, he knew that dreaded question, "Can we just be friends?" would be insulting – especially with her deigning to entertain a relationship so far below her socio-economic-physiological grade. He puzzled with how he could get her to reject him before he had to reject her.

Pushing his thoughts of Tiffany aside, he refocused his attention on his main interview for the day as he took the subway to Grand Central, hopping off to catch the train to Greenwich. By the time Flanagan had arrived at L'Escale, Barry

Rubenstein, the retired Senator, was camped out on a sunny table looking across at the big yachts and the bigger yachts in the harbor. Rubenstein was sipping coffee. Seasoned with a half century of campaigning, Rubenstein shook Flanagan's hand heartily and asked him if there was any way he could help him with any matter. The former Senator's dentures were quite impressive, white sturdy choppers that made Flanagan want to rip out his bicuspids and get some pearly falsies. After introducing himself, Flanagan asked the Senator if he wanted anything stronger than what was currently in his cup. When Rubenstein said the coffee was fine, Flanagan smiled inwardly that perhaps this lunch bill wouldn't land in the four-hundred-dollar range as he feared.

The waiter took a Diet Coke order from Flanagan and poured Rubenstein more coffee which he clearly didn't need, since the Senator was yapping like dog in front of a postal warehouse. Flanagan didn't even have to ask Rubenstein a question.

"Jimmy Doherty was one of a kind, I tell you," said Rubenstein. "I'm glad you want to talk to me about him. As Cicero said, 'The life of the dead is placed in the memory of the living.' The oil industry had been after Doherty for years and they finally got him."

"How did they get him?" asked Flanagan.

"That I can't tell you," said Rubenstein. "All I know is that Jimmy Doherty scared the hell out of them … all of them, even that Henry Center group that wrecked more than a few politicians over the years."

"What made him so frightening?" asked Flanagan.

Rubenstein sipped more coffee, then lifted his hands, waving them about like he was giving a speech on the Senate floor. "Doherty had built quite a bi-partisan coalition when it came to climate change. I was one of thirty co-sponsors on the bill. All of us, especially the oil companies, knew if Dukakis had been elected, that legislation would've become law and our entire future would've been in much better shape than the shitshow we have now."

The waiter returned. Rubenstein ordered the swordfish while Flanagan got a bacon cheeseburger. "But since Bush won, what were they worried about?" Flanagan asked.

Rubenstein pointed his finger in the air like he was speaking to a considerably larger audience than Flanagan. "As Cicero said, 'While there's life, there's hope.' You see Doherty's legislative skill and what might-have-been were no doubt too close of a call for the oil companies. They saw Jimmy Doherty as a long-term problem."

"Couldn't they have simply destroyed his reputation?" asked Flanagan.

"Yes, that was definitely an option, but it seemed an opportunity presented itself and they took it," said Rubenstein. "Certain parties were highly motivated. One of those parties could create a nice distance between Doherty's death and the American Henry Center."

Flanagan sensed that Rubenstein had phrased his comments in a dead-end cagey sort of way. He had to respond accordingly. "Have you ever come across Frankie Pisano?"

"Peripherally," sniffed Rubenstein. "I may have encountered something about his relationship with certain organizations like the Global Climate Coalition, but he seemed to have had a greater connection to the American Henry Center, a group more inclined to do the dirty work, if I happened to be talking about dirty work, which I'm not."

"Of course you're not," Flanagan assured.

"I'm glad you understand that," said Rubenstein, who was heartened to hear that anything he said was not taken as fact, but might be taken as true. The swordfish and the burger arrived and the two stopped talking for a few minutes, except to remark how happy each was that the food was not overcooked.

As he moved onto his rice, Rubenstein pontificated about how Doherty was a once in a generation politician. "Yes, he could inspire like Reagan before him and Obama after him," he said. "But more importantly he knew how to spread the money around to Republican districts as well as Democratic ones. He always gathered some key little particulars about every congressional hotspot. I remember one day I saw Doherty in the corner talking to Ginny Smith of the third Congressional District in Nebraska. Ginny was almost eighty at the time, but when Doherty started gabbing with her, she might as well have been a giggly schoolgirl. And then he told her about all the funding she would be getting in his climate change legislation for the Cooper Nuclear Station. You think anybody outside of Nebraska in Congress even knew Nebraska had a nuclear plant? And here's a New York Democrat who stood there on the banks of the Missouri and had actually visited the plant and wanted to hand over more money which meant more jobs in Brownsville and beyond. The man had a gift."

"Sounds like Doherty might have been a bit of a con artist," said Flanagan.

"Cicero said, 'If we are not ashamed to think it, we should not be ashamed to say it.' Doherty thought of everything. Then he'd talk about it to whichever constituency would like to hear thoughts that in other places might be embarrassing. To make sure he got Republican support, he wouldn't just spread around the pork, he'd make sure in every couple of lines in the legislation he'd sprinkle in words like 'tradition' or 'Constitution' or 'freedom' or 'patriot.'"

"So, the Democratic leadership was unable to pick up the mantle after Doherty died?" asked Flanagan.

Rubenstein pushed his empty plate to the middle of the table. "Without the measured credible messenger of Jimmy Doherty, the oil companies and all of their front groups like the Climate Coalition and the Henry Center could question the science without enough pushback. You see, as long as no one knew for certain about the impact of global warming, the public was not going to invest in change. That's all the oil companies needed – that and millions of dollars to keep pounding away at that uncertainty."

Flanagan played with a french-fry. Responding to the bluster of the Greenwich Harbor breezes, Rubenstein filled in the vacuum. "Cicero said, 'Silence is one of the great arts of conversation.' What do you think, Mr. Flanagan?"

Flanagan shrugged. "I think you've been reading a lot of Cicero in retirement."

Rubenstein laughed.

Flanagan conducted a preliminary recording and Rubenstein agreed to let a cameraman return to get further footage.

"So do you think Jimmy Doherty was murdered?" asked Flanagan for the record.

That set Rubenstein off again as the waiter poured more coffee and the old Senator gesticulated his way through a long speech. Soon Flanagan felt like Rubenstein was fillerbustering his exit from the restaurant. Only when Flanagan offered his apologies that he had to catch the 3:13 out of Greenwich station was he finally permitted to pay the check and leave.

On the train back from Connecticut, Flanagan received a text from Tiffany: "Can I come over? I want to talk to you about something."

"I'm out right now," Flanagan texted back. "I'll be home in three hours. Do you know where I live?"

"Of course I do," Tiffany texted back, with a smiley face. "I will walk around the back and knock." That last message was capped with an emoji face blowing a kiss.

"Oh brother," Flanagan muttered to himself. Now Flanagan would have to think long and hard about how to handle the situation.

He first had to run through his thoughts about the accident. More and more, he was convinced that Frankie Pisano played a role in sending Jimmy's car off of Sackett Street and plunging into the canal. The fixers at the American Henry Center had a vested interest in keeping Frankie's involvement in the shadows, since he could have implicated at least some of the intermediaries in the plan. That made him wonder whether Frankie's fatal accident years later might have been to silence a man who knew too much, who was increasingly desperate for funds, who had just been served with divorce papers. As always, every time he thought of possible culprits, Suzie returned. She had good reason to want Frankie dead, just as she had good reason to want Jimmy dead.

And now Suzie's daughter would be showing up at his house. Boy, Flanagan really stepped into a pile of shit. On the train ride home, he pulled out his laptop and embarked on the task that had filled his past dozen years. He thought his encounter would go much better if he prepared a script ... not so much his lines, but Tiffany's. Always a good sport, Tiffany would be willing to play along.

To complicate matters, Flanagan returned home to find a dead crow wedged between his doorknob and the jamb with yet another note attached: "We have come to the end." Somewhere in his limited education, Flanagan had learned that a black crow was a sign of death. Going through the now familiar ritual of removing the carcass, he considered leaving the crow on the futon to gauge Tiffany's reaction.

He decided she had no part in these grim visitations. Indeed, this entire form of intimidation did not really fit the Pisano profile. No, the Pisanos would be more likely to spray foul-smelling cologne in his doorway or ensnare him in an embarrassing scandal. This front door behavior was simply too thuggish for America's backdoor royalty. Although this black crow sign was the most ominous yet, Flanagan continued his strategy of pretending none of these dead animals had ever graced his door. He would press ahead and bring his investigations to a speedy resolution.

If enemies would render him as lifeless as that crow, he decided he would leave this world with something better on his ledger than a dozen years of scripting for the Pisanos. He felt a comforting confidence that Kartik would tell his story … that is if Flanagan managed to finish the tale. He knew he had to act with greater urgency and that started with ending this Tiffany Pisano dalliance.

By the time Tiffany arrived at his basement door an hour later, Flanagan had already printed out the script and highlighted her lines for her. In her tight purple tank top, short cut-offs, and five-inch heels, Tiffany was clearly ready for her role. She immediately took up residence on the green futon, reclining in an odalisque pose. Flanagan took out two wine glasses, unscrewed the top of a chablis, and handed a glass to Tiffany, who twisted on the futon the way her acting coach taught her. When Tiffany saw the script on the coffee table, she put down the glass and clapped. "You wrote this for me?" she asked.

"I thought a read-through might be fun," Flanagan said.

"It will be, especially since you'll be playing you instead of someone else for a change," said Tiffany.

"Shall we start?" asked Flanagan. Script in hand, he stood six feet away from her while she remained splayed out on the couch, softly purring.

"You have the first line," said Tiffany. "So whenever you begin, I'll join in."

FADE IN:

INT. FLANAGAN'S LIVING ROOM/KITCHEN/BEDROOM

Tiffany, 31, looking particularly beautiful today, has marked out the green futon as her own. Flanagan, 38, just trying to seem like he belongs in the same room as Tiffany, stands nearby.

FLANAGAN
Are you ever tired of being a Pisano?
TIFFANY
Every day.
FLANAGAN
We can change that.
TIFFANY
How?
FLANAGAN
We can rewrite the script.
TIFFANY

But every rewrite we've ever done just leads to more drama and more complications.

FLANAGAN

Not this time.

TIFFANY

You have piqued my interest, Arthur.

FLANAGAN

You are always so worthy of having your interest piqued, my dearest Tiffany, second sister, but first flower of the Pisano family.

TIFFANY

Oh tell me more.

FLANAGAN

I will, my lovely goddess. Imagine yourself walking through the woods, green leaves are a'falling, where you come across a small cabin of clay and wattles made, where we live together by nine bean rows and the bee-loud glade.

TIFFANY

Sounds romantic.

FLANAGAN

It is romantic, for it has peace and quiet and nature to engender that blessed mood in which the burthen of the mystery, in which the heavy and the weary weight of all this unintelligible world is lightened. It comes from being close to the earth and with someone who cares about you.

TIFFANY

And who cares about me?

FLANAGAN

It is I, Arthur, of course.

TIFFANY

Oh my sweet prince, the one who will rescue me from the tower.

FLANAGAN

So does that mean you will come with me?

TIFFANY

Oh yes, I will. When shall we go?

FLANAGAN

Today, my love, right now.

TIFFANY

But this is all so sudden. What will I tell mother?

FLANAGAN

That you are tired of being a Pisano.

TIFFANY

Will she believe me?

FLANAGAN

Only if you mean it, my dear Tiffany. Do you mean it, Tiffany?

TIFFANY

I think I do, Arthur.

FLANAGAN

Good because once we go, there is no turning back.

TIFFANY

What do you mean, Arthur?

FLANAGAN

Once we go to that cabin we will stay for a year. We will live simply and well. It will be wonderful.

TIFFANY

A year? I thought you meant for a night. Where is this cabin?

FLANAGAN

In the Catskills.

TIFFANY

The Catskills?

FLANAGAN

The Catskills.

TIFFANY

I don't know Arthur. Your offer sounds very tempting, but I have an obligation to my family. And what about all of those girls who rely on me for my Second Sister products. I would no longer be a role model for them.

FLANAGAN

Does that mean that you don't want to run away with me?

TIFFANY

It's not that I don't, dear Arthur, but I can't.

FLANAGAN

I understand.

TIFFANY

I know you're heartbroken, but I have more than myself to consider.

FLANAGAN

I know sweetest Tiffany. I should not have even asked. How stupid of me to want to be with you when the entire world needs you.

TIFFANY

Then I will go now to give you time and space to deal with your sorrow. I am hoping when your wounds heal that we can once again be friends.

FLANAGAN

I would like that.

Tiffany rises from the green futon and walks out the door. Flanagan collapses on the futon, hands covering his face.

Although Flanagan delivered the stage directions for Tiffany to depart, she remained on the futon sprawled out as provocatively posed as ever.

"I think we needed to clear the air," said Flanagan. "I felt something building between us for a while. We had to play this out. I'm glad we did. Are you?"

"I am," said Tiffany. "I never knew you had such strong feelings for me. I suspected, but you never know until you hear it."

"Well, you heard it," he said. "Now I think I better deal with the rest of it alone."

Tiffany leaned toward him, trying to angle herself just right to offer the fullest show possible. "But wouldn't you like to spend some time on the futon with me. I can comfort you."

As he began to feel cramped and excited, Flanagan reverted to speaking like his scripted character. "I am more than certain you can comfort me, most lovely of goddesses, but I know the faster you return to your life of serving others, the better it will be for the world."

"But I am worried about you," she said.

Flanagan confirmed Tiffany was worried by the fact that she took out her clay and started nibbling away at it. He had been tempted to incorporate her eating some clay into the script, but feared she might have taken offense. Now its reemergence signaled that he better be direct or he'd never get Tiffany off of his futon.

"I will survive," Flanagan said. "Now go to your calling."

Tiffany pulled Flanagan close and kissed him. Then, like the stage directions had so stipulated, she rose from the green futon and walked out the door. Also true to the stage directions, Flanagan collapsed onto the futon, hands covering his face.

But he was laughing.

He knew the humble cabin was likely to push Tiffany away, but the fact that it was in the Catskills – not the Hamptons or Park City or Ibiza – sealed the rejection. He believed Tiffany felt better about herself than when she had walked into his basement apartment. He was finally free of the Pisanos.

His joy lasted for a couple of hours until he got a text from Heather. "Have you sent the DNA yet of your mystery man? I've got my workup done. Labcorp is just waiting to see if there's a match?"

Flanagan immediately called Clarkin. "Hey, have you heard from Jimmy's twin Kevin yet?"

"Sure, he already went to Labcorp and had the swab taken."

"Heather Pisano has her tests results and she wants her doctor to look at Kevin's to see if there's a match?"

"So she knows that Kevin has taken a DNA test?" asked Clarkin.

"Not really. She just knows I am getting my hands on some mystery DNA. By the way, you think Kevin will be afraid he could get accused of being Heather's father."

"Are you kidding?" Clarkin said. "He'd be thrilled to have one of the richest people in the world claim he was her father. What's she going to do, sue him? Anyway, everyone knows about Jimmy and Suzie. Besides, I think Kevin was working in London at the time."

"So I can tell Heather she should know if she has a match real soon?"

"Sure," said Clarkin, "Try not to sell your soul to Heather Pisano in the meantime."

"Are you implying it'd be OK to sell my soul to her once the results came in?"

Clarkin just laughed and hung up.

Flanagan quickly dropped off to sleep after that. His cell phone ringing shot him out of bed. He didn't recognize the number, yet he had this great fear that it was one of the Pisano sisters – Tiffany with a fresh thought; Heather with a fresh demand. He picked up the phone anyway.

"Is this Arthur Flanagan?"

"Yes, who is this?"

"It's Angie Sansone," the voice said, "Rusty Sansone's wife."

"Hi, is Rusty all right?"

"No, that's why I'm calling you," said Angie. "He's near the end and wants to talk to you."

"When?"

"Right now."

"It's one thirty in the morning," said Flanagan. "Do you really want me there now?"

"Frankly, no," said Angie. "But that's what Rusty wants, so I'm giving it to him."

"I'll be out the door in five minutes," said Flanagan. "I'll be there as fast as the first Uber or taxi I can get takes me."

He took the address from Angie. The hospice was over in Gravesend, Brooklyn. It was a bit of a pain-the-ass to get to, but what was he going to do? He packed his camera and headed out the door.

CHAPTER 27
THE CONFESSINGS OF RUSTY SANSONE

The Gravesend hospice was a pretty nice place to die. Flanagan entered through a full kitchen with the types of cabinets and countertops fashionable in home makeover shows. Still, the deodorizers could not fully mask what was going on here. Angie greeted Flanagan with a scowl. A skinny Italian lady in her early 60s, she had a fair share of wrinkles because she had neither the fat to fill them in nor the Pisano inclination to iron them out. Angie was done crying for the time being.

She led Flanagan into the dying man's bedroom like she was granting the greatest favor to the least worthy. While she was unhappy to see him, she was infuriated by the sight of his camera. Flanagan told Angie. "I'll ask if I can use it. If he says no, then I'll give it to you to take into the kitchen."

When he entered the bedroom, he was hit with the smell that no amount of washing can cleanse. Yet the dark mahogany headboard and the bureau with ornate brass fixtures gave the room a baronial air. He half expected to see a hunting dog at the foot of the bed and two servants standing solemnly in the corner. One glance at Rusty's state of decay – his greasy salt-and-pepper hair, the sallow pallor of his olive skin, the oxygen mask over his nose and mouth – snapped him back to the urgency of the situation.

"Thank you for seeing me, Mr. Sansone," said Flanagan.

Rusty pulled the oxygen away. "It's been on my mind," he said. "I think I'd like to get this off my chest. My wife said I should talk to the priest. I don't think he'd understand. I hope you will."

"Are you sure you want to take off that oxygen mask," asked Flanagan. "I can come close and listen to you with it on."

"No," Rusty said. "That thing's a pain in the ass. I kept it on as I waited for you to come. I should be alright to talk for a few minutes without it."

"Do you mind if I record this?"

"Why the hell not?" said Rusty. "Maybe it'll make me a celebrity like Frankie." Rusty suppressed a laugh, not wanting to waste his energy.

Flanagan set up the tripod and camera, framing Rusty in the bed, then hit the record button. "So you were friends with Frankie Pisano."

"All my life," said Rusty. "Well … all his life. We went to school together when we were kids. I think that damn Catholic guilt is why I'm talking to you now. I remember Sister Tracy saying, 'You do not want to do anything that you someday will need to confess on your deathbed.' That old witch was right."

"Were you and Frankie still close at the time of Jimmy Doherty's accident?" Flanagan asked.

"Sure, we were close before the accident and we were even closer after the accident, although I wasn't happy about that."

"Why weren't you happy about that?"

"I think you might know why," said Rusty. "Otherwise, you wouldn't have contacted me."

Rusty stuck up an index finger as he struggled to breathe. He put back on the oxygen mask and closed his eyes. Flanagan feared he had fallen asleep. As he waited for Rusty to refill his lungs, Flanagan thought about his owned lapsed Catholicism. He knew if he had a deathbed confession, it'd be a three-hour production, not the mere five-labored minutes Rusty harbored deep in his soul.

When Rusty's eyes opened back up, noting both the interviewer and camera before him, Flanagan said, "While you take your oxygen, I will ask you a question that I hope you'll answer once you're ready; about the accident report you filed on Jimmy Doherty's Honda Civic, was that completely accurate?"

Rusty continued to breathe in oxygen for another minute before he pulled the mask away. "No. I omitted an important element."

"And what was that?"

"It appeared the throttle mechanism was messed with."

"How do you think that happened?"

"Somebody shoved something in the throttle."

"Like what?"

"Like a metal rod."

"That sounds serious."

"It was."

"I presume that would cause Jimmy Doherty's car to accelerate on Sackett Street and plunge into the Gowanus Canal."

"That I can't be certain of," said Rusty. "Jamming the throttle mechanism would not necessarily work so quickly. It would have to be done well, and then for it to work, the person had to be lucky, or in Jimmy's case unlucky. I think Jimmy might have been unlucky."

The explanation took a good deal out of Rusty. He struggled mightily for breath and ended up sucking oxygen for a few minutes before he was ready to answer Flanagan's next question. "Was Frankie handy with cars?"

"He was almost as good as me," said Rusty. "But that doesn't mean he did it himself. He was not at a point in his life when he got his hands dirty anymore."

"Did he ask you to doctor the report?"

Rusty tried to smile, but under his state of duress it came out as a grimace. "He didn't ask me to do anything," said Rusty. "All he said was that he sure hoped that my report came out clean."

"So ..." Flanagan waited.

"So I made sure the report came out clean."

"Did it bother you to do that?"

"Why do you think I'm talking to you now," said Rusty. He pawed back for his oxygen. "Look, I'm fading here. Call in Angie." Flanagan brought her in. Rusty looked at her. "Can you tell this guy about what happened at Rockaway Beach? I think I told you about that."

"About three hundred times."

Rusty looked at Flanagan. "Promise me you will record what my wife tells you," he said. "Promise me that goes into your story too."

Flanagan did not like to promise anything when it came to his documentary, but a dying man's wish was awfully hard to deny. "I promise," he said.

"Now let me rest and listen to my wife."

As the nurse came in to check on Rusty's vitals, Angie and Flanagan headed out and found a seat at the kitchen table. Flanagan said to her, "I know this is awkward, but I'm going to record you."

"And I didn't have my hair done," said Angie. "Might as well make a shitty day worse."

Flanagan set up the camera. "So what happened in Rockaway Beach?"

"It was when Rusty was a teenager and he swam out past the rocks," she said. "He was out of the view of the lifeguards. The riptide was really pushing him about until he understood that he was not going to make it back to the shore, that he would drown out there."

"That sounds awful," said Flanagan.

"From the way Rusty tells it, he had never been so scared in his entire life."

"So what happened then?"

"Frankie Pisano is what happened. He charges into the water and swims and swims until he finally gets to Rusty. By then, Rusty is exhausted and swallowed a lot of water. Frankie hooks Rusty under his arms and starts the slow swim back. After what seemed like an hour, Frankie gets him to the beach and Rusty is unconscious. Frankie gives him mouth-to-mouth and in a few moments Rusty is spitting out water."

"So Frankie saved Rusty's life," said Flanagan.

"It appears so," said Angie. "I always thought Frankie was an asshole, but he did rescue Rusty. Rusty never forgot that. Even if he tried, I don't believe Frankie would have let him forget."

"Did Rusty do favors for Frankie?"

"Oh did he ever," she said. "There are two types of boys who go through Catholic School: the ones who have too much guilt and the ones who have too little."

"And I presume Rusty had too much?" asked Flanagan. Angie nodded. "And Frankie …"

"Well, you already know the answer to that," she said.

"Did Rusty ever feel guilty about what happened to Jimmy Doherty?"

"I'm surprised he took all this time to tell somebody," she said. "For years after the accident, he kept telling me he was going to go to the authorities. But in the end, he told me and nobody else. And when Frankie died, he thought about telling somebody then, but he didn't want to dishonor Frankie's memory."

The conversation started wandering from there. Angie pulled out the family photos and took Flanagan through every baptism, communion, and confirmation, through the colleges ("You know Rusty didn't go to school, but he made sure all the kids did") and the weddings. By the time the grandchildren arrived, Flanagan had shut off the camera while Angie talked and remembered, talked and remembered because sleep was not possible. From an album binder, she pulled out a laminated page with a series of Polaroids of hand brakes and modified steering wheels. "He did these all for handicapped people in the neighborhood, so they could drive," said Angie. "And he didn't take a cent from any of them."

Flanagan was struck that Rusty needed to record his acts of charity for posterity. He had clearly told Angie what he was doing and snapped those photos of his efforts so that she would be able to praise him after his death. For both Angie and Rusty, the importance of his being a good man was essential to a life worth living.

A few hours in, Angie decided she wanted to return to Rusty's bedside. Flanagan followed her and patted the sleeping Rusty on the arm, his oxygen mask sending his lungs rising and falling. As he threw the tripod over his shoulder and headed out, Angie said to Flanagan, "Make sure you don't disappoint me."

Clearly, Rusty wasn't the only one who knew a thing or two about Catholic guilt.

When he arrived back in his basement apartment, Flanagan was still wired by Rusty's revelations. He fooled around on the computer until he found an Email from JPay from Karl the Sausage Hoffman. As with the other Emails, the subject tag read, "In the End, just Four you," which made even less sense than the previous times he read it. But the subject tag line was only an appetizer for the mess that was the actual Email. "You must be the dumbest man on the planet to think we'd care so Doherty'd be gone."

Flanagan rubbed his neck. Just when Rusty Sansone finally brought clarity to the investigation, Karl the Sausage had to gum up the works. Looking back on his Email thread, Flanagan read in succession the three messages he received during the past weeks.

"You must be stupid if you think that there'd be a situation where Frankie told us what."

"You must be an idiot to think we'd ever want a car to make go."

"You must be the dumbest man on the planet to think we'd care so Doherty'd be gone."

Ordering the three works and reading them consecutively didn't help a bit. He wrote Karl back. "I deeply appreciate all you have written me. Now that we have well established that I am not very smart, could you just explain to me why 'we' don't care that Doherty is gone? Who is 'we'? Is Frankie Pisano part of the 'we'? I know you are trying to tell me something. Could you offer me a hint about just what you mean?"

Flanagan knew he would be able to crow to Kartik about his Rusty Sansone revelations. But he decided he would not tell anyone about his Email exchanges with Karl Hoffman. Embarrassed by his inability to comprehend, Flanagan received a jarring reminder of how ill-equipped he remained for the tasks before him. He didn't understand Karl's Emails any more than he understood why small dead critters were jammed beneath his doorknob or why Tiffany beamed lovingly at him while she nibbled on clay or why Heather gave herself a round of applause as she dismissed him. Each day he learned more and understood less.

CHAPTER 28
THE UNVEILING OF PATERNITY

The next morning, Flanagan was awakened by a Heather text: "Dr. Rodriguez said he will have the lab results in a couple of hours. You can hear the results with me if you'd like."

Flanagan texted Heather back, "I would like."

Flanagan called Clarkin first, who made Flanagan promise that he would not reveal the identity of the mystery man. "She just has to know that the DNA is Jimmy Doherty's after all," said Clarkin.

"I think I can finesse that one," said Flanagan. "Maybe, I'll tell her that the DNA had been taken of all Senators in 1980s."

"I know it shouldn't seem like a big deal," Clarkin explained, "but the more Kevin thought about the DNA swab, the more regrets he had. Kev was quite the rascal in his day, like Jimmy, and he doesn't want to deal with a rash of paternity suits."

By the time Flanagan gave Clarkin his assurances, he got a text back from Heather. "Can u come 2 a photo shoot I'm doing at the Gowanus Canal? I'm near Smith Street. U can find me next 2 the cameras."

"Of course I can," muttered Flanagan.

Before he texted Heather back and let the day get away from him, he composed a bit of doggerel and called the Hamilton Deli, placing an order to be delivered to Deja at Columbia. He paid extra so a note would accompany the breakfast.

To date me can be awfully roughin'
To deal with my guffin' and huffin'
But still I offer some stuffin'
So enjoy this banana nut muffin

Flanagan hoped that one day Deja might text him again. In the meantime, he'd keep writing and feeding her. That box checked, he texted Heather back, called another Uber, and set off to Gowanus. As he rode in the small Toyota, Flanagan pondered whether Heather's shoot right at the site of Jimmy Doherty's death was coincidental or intentional. The Pisanos had always been a serendipitous lot, luckily being in the right place at the right time, but they were also a manipulative, enterprising lot, who would spend many hours in front of makeup mirrors calculating what was the right place at the right time.

He arrived at Smith Street, an arched road featuring a wide expanse of debris, detritus, and rubble in front of the most contaminated canal in America. Cameras and lighting equipment were being set up among the not-so-ancient ruins. In her pink fur coat, Heather was not difficult to spot. Flanagan was surprised that Heather was dressing for last year's November rather than the balmy high seventies of today. In her black, laced-high boots, she sauntered over to him, a little extra sway in her hips, which Flanagan understood as a warm-up exercise for her photo shoot. She wore a wig of white bangs, powdered her face to a bloodless, vampire-level pallor, and built up so much black eyeliner and mascara that Flanagan thought of raccoons. And with the pink fur coat, what a disaster.

"Can you come with me to see my personal physician after I'm done here?" she asked.

"I would love to," said Flanagan. He was contemplating just what endangered species had been gutted, flayed, and skinned to give the furrier the ability to stitch together that coat when the chiding image of Kartik entered his head. "Can I let the camera run a bit?" he asked Heather. "This footage might be very useful contextually."

Heather smiled. Flanagan wondered if she thought he was giving her a line and if she had heard the line before. "You can record images of the photographers doing the photo shoot, but don't come too close to me," she said. "I don't think the *Vanity Fair* people would like you stealing their images."

As she walked away, Flanagan went over to the shoot producer and told her that he was filming the scene for an upcoming episode of *Peepin' on the Pisanos*. He knew the magazine would sufficiently covet the publicity to give him some leeway. Flanagan waited around a half hour as the producer and the photographers picked out different locations among the bent rebar and the scarred cinderblock.

When Heather finally removed the pink fur coat, her state of undress was surprisingly disturbing. Flanagan could not fathom that Heather could be anything less than palpably alluring when she was almost naked, but in this rarest of cases ... her usually deep olive skin had turned wan; her nude bodice pushed around her flesh in awkward ways, and her thonged undies could best be described as unfocused. If she were playing a part in a movie, it'd be of Tara the homeless girl dumped on the side of the road by Sid, her abusive, junkie boyfriend.

Flanagan filmed her anyway. What the hell else was he going to do? As she posed in front of storage tanks, scrap metal, and portapotties, Flanagan found himself more entertained by the crew, alternately cajoling and beseeching Heather to pout and bend with what one photographer urged as "desperate sexiness."

He turned the camera on the crew just in time for one sycophant to call out, "We all know you are the most important woman on earth. Now act like you are the last woman too."

Until now, Flanagan had not noticed that except for him only women were on the set. He was surprised that they fawned over her even more than men. "Oh Heather," yelled out one quisling, "you can even make a junkyard gorgeous!" Another boot licker cried out, "Honey, you look so good that anyone would swim across that filthy canal just to get to you."

Heather's boots were as clunky as the rest of her outfit. The orange fishnet stockings didn't do her any favors either. Flanagan tried to figure out whether the praise from the crew for her was greater because she looked so awful, or if they had an entire other level of groveling and flattery when Heather looked every bit of her beautiful, air-brushed self. After an hour or so, the crew's cameras and Flanagan's shut off. He spotted Heather putting her hands together. Unless one was looking for it, this little act of applause was imperceptible. Yet, Heather did it anyway. The crew's flattery must not have been sufficient. A little self-affirmation was required to make it through the day.

He waited for Heather to emerge from her trailer as someone else.

She needed an hour for the transformation, but what struck Flanagan most profoundly was that she washed much of the death from her skin. What type outfit do you wear to find out the identity of your father? If you are Heather Pisano, you put on tight jeans and a tube top like you are a guest on the Jerry Springer Show. Especially since he sensed a solemnity to the impending proceeding, Flanagan tried to hide his amazement at her alteration – clearly certain trashy looks worked better for her than others. Heather's driver came around onto Smith Street to pick them up to go off to her personal physician.

"How did you get your hands on this DNA?" said Heather. "I didn't think it was possible."

"I'll explain it to you if it ends up being a match."

"Let's get some ground rules straight before we go in there," said Heather. "You can record, but you can only make it public with my expressed permission. You are going to need to sign these papers if you want to be in the room."

"Is it another Non-Disclosure Agreement?" asked Flanagan. "You know I won't sign one of those."

"Relax," said Heather, putting a hand on his thigh. "Read it. It just says I have control of what you do with the recording."

Flanagan decided the access was too good to give up. He'd have to do some heavy duty campaigning later with her to allow the tape to be used, or better yet, let Kartik negotiate with her. He signed the papers. When they arrived at Dr. Rodriguez's suite, Flanagan was stunned to be led directly into a medical office without any wait – there's a first time for everything. Yes, he should have known that Heather Pisano would have such frictionless access, but for Flanagan it was jarring to experience the treatment.

After a nurse came in serving coffee and tea, Dr. Rodriguez entered like the star of a top rated medical series. His blue eyes nicely offset his carefully styled blond locks, which were just messy enough to hint that he recently left a love-nest with a rap diva. Almost everyone in the Pisano world had to be beautiful. Flanagan understood that he would eventually be booted from the set of that exclusive club for the crime of tipping too lightly on the aesthetic scale.

After the usual niceties, Dr. Rodriguez got down to the meat of the episode. "I would not usually get involved with confirming lab results on paternity tests, especially since the identity of one DNA was not revealed to me," he said. "However, given my longstanding relationship with your family, I will deliver my findings."

When he did not say anything further, Flanagan inquired, "And those findings are?"

"Before I proceed," said the good doctor, "I just want to ask you, Heather, whether you would prefer I deliver these results to you privately?"

"No, you may present your findings in front of Mr. Flanagan," said Heather.

"In that case, I must tell you the DNA received by Labcorp is that of your father."

"Are you sure?" asked Heather.

"I made the lab check two more times before I called you."

Heather said nothing. Dr. Rodriguez continued to speak to fill up the awkwardness with empowering explanations about how DNA determines less of who you are than your actions. Eventually, he ended with, "I'm sure you have much to think about and to discuss."

With that suggestion, Heather and Flanagan rose, thanking Dr. Rodriguez, and departed, never even sipping their drinks. The driver took them back to the Pisano compound. "Can you give me an hour?" Heather asked. "I just want to shower and change."

"Is it all right if I sit outside on a bench in the garden or out in the car?" asked Flanagan. "I think it would be a really bad idea for me to come into your home."

Heather smiled weakly. "You might be right there."

Flanagan passed the time near a burbling tiered fountain surrounded by geometrically patterned hedges. He thought about what he should say to Heather; he thought about what he should say to Suzie; hell, he thought what he should say to Deja. For someone who should have a damned lot to say, his mind had gone blank.

He sent material off to Kartik, pointing out that some of the revelations that had come to light over the past few days would require intercession and a deft touch. He urged the producer not let the information go beyond him and Mehnuma for now.

When Heather returned, the make-up had been scrubbed from her face, her hair was pulled back in a ponytail, and she wore a loose-fitting blue hoodie with baggie cargo pants. She could have passed for a mom in the PTA, albeit one still trying to dress younger than her age. "Tell the driver to take us wherever you'd like," said Heather, "just make sure it's some place I haven't been."

Flanagan decided to make the choice easy on him. He had the driver drop them off by Astoria Park, so he'd be on his home turf. He grabbed a peasant loaf from the market and then a bottle of Grand Marnier with two snifters from the liquor store. They followed the paths to the north end of the park where they found a bench on the water overlooking the Hell Gate Bridge and Randall's Island.

Flanagan broke off a hunk of bread, poured a snifter of the liqueur, and passed them to Heather. They chewed and sipped, letting the breezes from the East River blow across their faces, slowly cooling some of the tension of the doctor's visit.

"It's been a while since I last knew who I was," said Heather.

"You are a tremendously famous celebrity," said Flanagan.

"I have always been famous for being famous," she said. "Paris Hilton might have done it before me, but she had the Hilton name. All I had were my looks and Mommie Dearest." Flanagan noticed she ate and drank quickly, nervously, almost ravenously, as if her mouth demanded both nourishment and distraction. "For the longest time, I was OK with all of that. I got so much attention, so much money, such a luxurious lifestyle, that I could laugh at the ridiculousness of it all. Nobody *had* to watch the show, nobody *had* to buy the products, nobody *had* to follow me on Facebook and Twitter and Instagram and Ticktock. It seemed like if everybody was having such a good time, including me, then why should I have a problem?"

"Sounds like you really figured it out," said Flanagan.

"Until I didn't," said Heather. "I got tired of people thinking I was stupid. Even when the trollers acknowledged that I attended Columbia, they said I got in because of my money and celebrity."

"So how do you answer something like that?" asked Flanagan.

"You don't," she said. "I just spent more time at Columbia."

"At the Earth Institute," Flanagan said.

"They didn't treat me like a dope there," said Heather. "I'd get a few looks, but I kept reading, asking questions about geoengineering, especially about spraying sea salt particles into the clouds or injecting sulfur dioxide into the stratosphere. I continued to research the latest on lithium ion battery storage and advances in solar panels. But I didn't really feel I belonged until I started working with Professor Bowman."

"Ah, the Nuke doctor," said Flanagan, smiling.

"The Nuke doctor," Heather nodded. "If *Peepin' on the Pisanos* taught me anything, it was to embrace the possible and practical. Nuclear energy was both."

"You have been leading a double life," said Flanagan. "For the cameras, you are a mild-mannered celebrity goddess, but in the shadows you transform into NukeMan."

Heather smirked, drew closer to Flanagan, and stared into his warm eyes. "And now that we have talked around why we're here, are you going to tell me who my father is?" asked Heather.

"I figured you already knew," said Flanagan.

"I'd feel better if you just said it," said Heather.

"Your biological father is Jimmy Doherty, former Knicks star, Senator, and early climate change activist."

"Former Knick, huh," said Heather, "no wonder I've got four inches on Tiffany and Nora."

"Yeah, seems like height wasn't the only thing he shared in his DNA," said Flanagan. "It's revealing that you have moved, if secretly, toward the same cause that occupied the last years of his life."

Heather didn't seem to be listening. "He's long dead, right? So father/daughter dances are out, right? I'm trying to think about him, but I'm having a harder time not thinking that my father all of my years growing up was not actually my father."

"I get it," said Flanagan. "I think Frankie Pisano was your father for all practical purposes. He drove you to school, brought you to the Yankees games, took you to church."

"Yet he was just my stepfather," said Heather. "I still play that hologram of him that Meatdad Cartharsis gave me for my birthday. I have always been a Pisano. That has been my brand, more than anyone else in the family. How can it be my brand when I'm not even a Pisano?"

Flanagan poured her some more Grand Marnier and handed her another hunk of bread. "Let me ask you a question: why did you agree to this paternity test?"

"I have been dissatisfied for a while," said Heather. "I thought the results of the test would give me an explanation for it."

"Have they?"

"I have no idea," she said.

"Would you feel better about it if you controlled the narrative?" asked Flanagan.

"I would," her eyes crinkled, flecks of anger rising in them, "but I already thought I controlled the narrative."

"You will, only if you don't tell anyone else right now."

"You mean Mom."

"I mean when Suzie knows the facts are out, you will have no say in what happens next."

"But *you* know the facts," said Heather.

"Yes, but I don't have much power," he said, "and it would benefit me greatly to ride the wave of how you roll out the narrative."

"You now know two secrets about me that nobody else does: that I am Jimmy Doherty's daughter and that I am NukeMan." Heather eyed Flanagan dangerously. "I don't see how you will survive with so much information."

"Have I betrayed you ever?"

"You've had no reason to be this tempted before."

"I've got a documentary that needs a star."

"You've got a star that requires creative control of the project."

"I've got a producer that I've got to talk to."

"You better slip him more than this Grand Marnier," said Heather. "It makes me not want to murder you at this moment, but it doesn't quite make me trust you."

Flanagan decided it would be a bad time to deliver to Heather another shock to her system: that the man she thought was her father all of the years may well have been the murderer of her biological father. "That will take time," said Flanagan.

"It's not going to happen now," said Heather. "Can I put my head against your shoulder without you reading anything into it?"

"I've got enough to read into without thinking about romance with you," said Flanagan.

"Now I know things are wrong," said Heather. "If I don't have people thinking romantically about me, what is my value?"

"Good question," said Flanagan. "We're going to find that out."

Heather rested her head on Flanagan's shoulder and began to weep softly. He just shut his mouth and let her cry. The next thing he knew she was sleeping against him and then she was snoring. Flanagan's shoulder and arm deadened and he wished he could move. What he really wished was that he could take out his camera. Heather Pisano snoring might be the biggest revelation yet.

She slept on the bench next to him for an hour. When she awoke, she rolled her eyes at him, as if exasperated that he had been sleeping on her instead of the other way around. She called her driver, who must have been nearby because he appeared at the edge of the park in two minutes.

"You want me to escort you home?" asked Flanagan.

"No, I need alone time," she said.

As he walked her to the car, he asked, "Are you going to be O.K.?"

"No," she answered, "but I think I'm good with that."

Then Heather began to clap and Flanagan joined in. They clapped with such vigor and gusto that they sounded like an entire studio audience. And for the first time since he had known her, Heather Pisano truly laughed, hearty and uncontrollable, shoulder-shaking laughter. And Flanagan laughed too.

And neither knew why.

CHAPTER 29
THE LOOMING OF *DEATH CANAL*

Kartik greeted Flanagan in a jovial mood. Flanagan thought the bastard better be jovial after what he sent him. "Only you, my friend Artie," said Kartik, "could finally get inside a photo shoot for the most beautiful woman in the world to find her dressed and made up to be at her least flattering."

"Yeah," said Flanagan who spoke in a confident, feisty state, "and I believe disastrous images of Heather Pisano will make the trailer even better."

"As long as we put it up against a quick cut of Heather at her most alluring," said Kartik. "I've already got the trailer and the posters all worked out in my head. I've even got a title, *Death Canal*."

"*Death Canal?*" said Flanagan. "Isn't that a little cheesy?"

"I think you're confused about what type of documentary you are making," said Kartik.

"But *Death Canal?*" asked Flanagan. "Really?"

"I won't even ask you what you would suggest for a title because you'd give me something like – The Untold Story of the Loss of a Minor Early Figure in the Climate Change Fight."

"Shouldn't you be praising me about now?" asked Flanagan.

"I must admit, you have some very compelling footage," said Kartik. "It's not every documentary that has a deathbed confession. I think you might have something here."

"That's it?" asked Flanagan. "Nothing about my discovery that Jimmy Doherty is actually the father of Heather Pisano?"

Kartik chuckled. "Well, it's not a superhero saving the world, but it might get a headline or two." Flanagan scowled. "O.K., the stuff is dynamite. But we have a few issues."

"Like what?"

"Like how do we get Heather to keep this information secret until the documentary comes out?" asked Kartik.

"I think I've got her to stay quiet for now," said Flanagan. "The bad news is she wants creative control over the documentary."

"That she cannot have," said Kartik. Answering Flanagan's shrug, he added, "But I can collaborate with her and make her believe she has more control than she actually does."

"I hate to say this," said Flanagan, "but I know what has to be done. It's going to require some sorcery from you."

"And that is …," said Kartik.

"The only way is to make a deal with Suzie Pisano," said Flanagan. "She'd have to agree that the documentary comes out right before the season premiere of *Peepin' on the Pisanos.* That way they can get the ratings bumps from their tears, their howls, and their shocked expressions."

"They probably should find out during a mother-daughter swimwear shoot," said Kartik. "I'll work on that. Don't be surprised if you get a call from Suzie soon. I smell a moneymaker as long as everything is kept quiet until the documentary comes out. Suzie and I have a similar nose for such matters."

Kartik proceeded to spill out production details and how he already had a deal with Netflix for six episodes and how he took Mehnuma off the *CaterpillerMan* set so that she could work full time on pulling the documentary together. He assured Flanagan, "Don't worry, we will still be working off of your scripts." Kartik talked about how he would integrate popular period songs into the scenes. "80s music is the big thing in documentaries nowadays," he explained. Then he threw in that he procured permits from the city to recreate Jimmy's accident. "We're getting a stunt guy to slam on the accelerator on Sackett and crash right into that awful canal. He's going to wear a scuba suit below his Jimmy Doherty sports jacket, so his skin doesn't peel off when he hits the water."

Arnav dropped in, smirking as he was wont to do, murmuring just loud enough so Flanagan could hear, "Tauji, when we reenact the meeting of the oil companies in the Niger Delta, the bullets will be flying and the blood will be spilling. Oh, Tauji, it will be beautiful."

Though he wasn't sure what Arnav was talking about, Flanagan was coming to understand that Kartik would be incorporating as much violence as he could conjure into the documentary. Beyond the smirk, Arnav exuded a cavalier brutality in his ensuing conversation with his uncle that scared Flanagan. Despite his recent triumphs, Flanagan sensed he had immersed himself in a world that was beyond him in its calculated depravity.

After Arnav departed, Kartik just kept going, thoughts exploding out of his head. He said that Flanagan's last interview had to be with former detective Murphy. He wanted to be able to have the final scene in the documentary reveal that the police were reopening the case of Jimmy Doherty's accident based on the evidence uncovered in *Death Canal*.

"Is that all?" asked Flanagan wryly. "I have to go pick up my daughter."

"No," said Kartik, "one more thing. How about getting an interview with Sir Kevin Doherty about his twin brother?"

"Can he be in his typical safari clothes?" asked Flanagan. "Or does he have to put on a Speedo to fit in with your desire for every interview subject to wear no more than a loincloth?"

Kartik chuckled. "I don't think having him wearing a Speedo will be necessary. But if you can get him holding a monkey, that would be good."

CHAPTER 30
FERTILIZING DOWN TO THE ROOTS

Flanagan wrote his daily bit of doggerel and called Absolute Bagels. They agreed for a surcharge to include his note in the delivery of the everything bagel with cream cheese to Deja at the Earth Institute.

Each morning when you do your kagel
And your breakfast is snatched by a seagull
Know I'm the man who will finagle
Every day on an everything bagel

An hour later, Flanagan received a text on his phone from Deja. "Hey moron, kagel and seagull don't rhyme." Flanagan was not going to play it cool. He preferred Deja to know without a doubt that he desperately wanted to see her. He jumped right onto a response. "You think that's bad. Tomorrow, I was planning on sending you a croissant, so naturally I would rhyme with savant and détente, but after that I was getting desperate since I don't think Levant has much relevance and *bon mot* might relegate me in the same kagel/seagull problem."

Deja answered soon enough. "My God, your texts are worse than the drivel that you usually send me. With those messages at least I get fed."

Flanagan saw the opening. "I can feed you again tonight, if you'd like. How about Miss Mamie's Spoonbread Too?"

"Did you pick that place because I'm black?" texted Deja.

Man, thought Flanagan, the girl knows how to keep me back on my heels. "No, I picked that place because it is good and it's pretty near Columbia. But if you'd prefer, we can just go to the diner."

Deja responded. "No, I think I'd prefer to have a nice racist meal with you at Miss Mamie's."

"How about I come to the Earth Institute at six?" Flanagan texted back, adding, "I always believe in getting an early start on racism."

Deja shot back, "You are quite the humanitarian, aren't you?"

Flanagan started to type back but decided to quit before he screwed up his dinner date. He had followed his hunch that Deja would be working on a Saturday; otherwise, his bagel with a smear of doggerel would have sat outside her office door for the weekend. For once, momentum seemed to be on Flanagan's side and more of his efforts had yielded dividends than he had ever recalled.

He met Michelle for lunch. True to the moment, he took her to the Brooklyn Bagel & Coffee Company, which paradoxically happened to be in the heart of Astoria, Queens. Flanagan ordered chicken salad and Michelle egg salad on their bagels.

"We'll get the answer to at least one pressing question, won't we Dad," said Michelle, wryly.

"What's that, pumpkin?" asked Flanagan.

"Which comes out first, the chicken or the egg salad?"

Flanagan winced, "That was pretty bad."

"Now, you know what it's like talking to you," said Michelle.

They took a decent length walk to Rainey Park. Flanagan wanted to avoid returning to Astoria Park after yesterday's visit with Heather. Plus, he liked looking across at Roosevelt Island, with its sturdy little lighthouse at its northern point and its haunting octagonal peaks of bygone mental hospitals. Father and daughter found a bench right on the shoreline, cracked open their sodas, and spread their sandwiches across their napkinned laps.

Flanagan filled Michelle in on what had been transpiring in his investigations. She was becoming quite a helpful combination of advisor and sounding board, all at 15 years old. Still, he made her swear to secrecy before he gave her the whoppers about Jimmy Doherty's car being tampered with and Jimmy being Heather Pisano's biological father.

Every other teenage girl he knew might have focused on the paternity issue, but not Michelle. She saw many implications in Jimmy's accident transforming into vehicular manslaughter. She homed in on Frankie's connections with the American Henry Center. "This case could have other victims," said Michelle, "maybe even Frankie."

"Part of the problem," Flanagan explained to Michelle, "is that most of the major players from the American Henry Center are now dead."

"Were any of those deaths suspicious?" asked Michelle, sounding more like her father every day.

"Unfortunately, no," said Flanagan. "There might be a few of the lower-level players at the center who knew something. Some of them are still alive, but Kartik doesn't want me to pursue them right now."

"Why not?" asked Michelle.

"He says the story is perfect the way it is," said Flanagan. "He wants to get the documentary out. Anyway, he says that investigation will take too much time and might even mess up the narrative."

"So, the documentary will have a lot of unanswered questions."

"Apparently," said Flanagan. "Kartik says I can pick up the trail for next season."

"Next season?" asked Michelle. "Isn't one season enough?"

"If I teach you one thing, dearest daughter, a single season is never enough," said Flanagan. "So let's stop talking about what I'm doing. What's going on with you? Still hanging out with skinny boys in hoodies who like to talk about planting trees but don't care to pick up a shovel."

"Boy, have you become quite the cranky old guy," said Michelle. "Are you ready to get up and get moving?"

"In a minute," answered Flanagan. "This chicken salad is weighing me down. Why?"

"I want to show you something," said Michelle.

"How far away?" asked Flanagan.

"It's a lot less than the walk we just took from the bagel store to here," said Michelle. "It's just up Vernon Boulevard a ways, maybe 15 minutes."

"I guess I can handle that," said Flanagan.

They wandered along until they hit the playground by the water, turning onto Main Street. Michelle pointed, "There," she said, "I want us to work here." They arrived at Two Coves Community Garden. The garden had paths and trees and shrubs and flowers and vegetables. Normally, during this time of year only the pumpkins, the squash, and the gourds would be left on the vine, but during this sultry fall, tomatoes still ripened and hot peppers continued to curl into form.

While Flanagan had to admit that the place had its charms with so many blooms and a picnic table to boot, he was not ready to be suckered into another commitment. "Yeah?" said Flanagan. "I have a job and you have homework."

"We also have our phones, which consume much of our time together," she said.

"True, but a phone is much easier to pick up than a shovel."

Michelle started negotiating. It seemed like everyone around Flanagan was negotiating with him lately. "Just two hours every time we see each other."

"One hour," counteroffered Flanagan. "My back and my arteries say one hour works better."

"Then, you can't give me excuses like you're tired and already had a long day."

"I can give you those excuses," clarified Flanagan, "but I'll still show up."

"Deal."

"Don't look so happy," said Flanagan. "Once you start weeding you'll realize how unpleasant all of this saving the earth crap is."

"Some of my friends who do it say they don't mind, especially as long as others are with them to pass the time," said Michelle.

"And who are these friends?" asked Flanagan.

"Just friends," said Michelle casually. "Joy and Rafael and Ramon."

"And who are these Rafael and Ramon characters?" asked Flanagan. "I haven't heard of them before. Handsome guys?"

"Oh, they're just brothers," said Michelle, like it was no big deal. "Nice guys, really into the environment."

"And how old are these nice brothers?"

"I don't know," said Michelle, like she didn't. "I think Ramon's 16."

"And Rafael?" asked Flanagan.

"I don't know," said Michelle, acting a little put out. "Maybe 18."

"If you're going to chat up anybody, make sure it's Ramon."

"Dad," Michelle rolled her eyes at her father's cluelessness. "Just because Rafael's older doesn't mean it's a problem."

"Look at my experience," said Flanagan. "Siblings can be problems."

"What are you saying?" asked Michelle.

"I'm saying, make sure the only seeds they offer you come in little paper envelopes."

Michelle snickered. "That's pretty interesting coming from a Pisano boy toy."

For the first time in his memory, Flanagan felt the urge to lash out at his daughter. He walked over to a corner of the community garden where ornamental cabbages popped out of the ground; the cabbages had clueless, faceless heads. He was no fan of his own amorous dramas and had not prepared himself for a front-row seat in Michelle's budding romances with all the accompanying teenage angst.

Michelle came over to him. "I'm sorry Dad," she said. "I shouldn't have said that to you. It's just you're a little late for the protective father scene."

"What does that mean?" Flanagan asked. "Have you been involved with boys already?"

"Not too much," said Michelle. "I just need to find my own way. If I wanted to sneak around, I wouldn't have asked you to volunteer for the community garden with me."

"You've got a point there," said Flanagan. "Can you allow me to worry a little bit about you?"

"I think I can," said Michelle. "But we've got bigger things to worry about. I'm finding I feel a little less stressed out when I'm doing something to help. I'm not stupid. I know what we'll be doing is really not much, but it's better than nothing."

"And if you end up weeding with a few cute brothers along the way, there could be worse things in the world," said Flanagan.

"Exactly."

Flanagan looked down on the ornamental cabbages. "Can you do me a favor with these brothers? – what's their last name?"

"Espinal."

"Can you and the Espinal boys put something better in this spot than these things?" Flanagan asked. "I think I'm going to have nightmares."

Michelle laughed. "They're not so bad," she said about the cabbages, "but I'll see what we can do." As they walked out of the garden and started heading back to the basement apartment, she asked, "Hey Dad, did you ever think about becoming a vegetarian?"

"No," Flanagan said flatly.

"C'mon, it'd be fun," said Michelle. "We can do it together, and we'd be helping the earth."

Flanagan rolled his eyes. "Tell you what, you get those Espinal brothers to do it, and I'll think about it."

"Deal," said Michelle.

Flanagan had the strange feeling by the speed of her reply that Rafael and Ramon were already vegetarians. That belief gave him a bizarre sense of comfort as if boys who didn't eat meat were less predatory when it came to women. God, his head was filled with too much nonsense. By the time he dropped off Michelle at the library so she could finish up a group project with her friends on the Protestant Reformation, he was in a bit of a panic that he wouldn't have enough time to shave and shower before he met up with Deja. His hair and body were still wet by the time he got into the Uber that took him to Columbia. The journey was a straight shot over the East River and across town to Morningside Heights, so the car got him there much faster than his usual zigging and zagging on the subway lines. Since Kartik was now paying him, he no longer fretted so much about each dollar that left his bank account. He even gave the Uber driver a good tip, figuring he needed to build up his standing on the site. He decided not to tell Deja that he took a less earth-friendly mode of transport to get there.

While Flanagan was indeed on time, Deja made him sit for a half hour. As he curled up in the corner, once again playing the grad student waiting to hear about his research paper, Flanagan received a text from Dirk Wall.

"How are you hanging in there?" Dirk asked. "Reaching the end of your rope?"

"Getting close," Flanagan texted back.

"You know freedom is just one car ride away," Dirk wrote back. "Out on the expressway, there's a wall somewhere with your name on it."

"What are you?" asked Flanagan. "The grim reaper?"

"I'm just trying to help you out," Dirk wrote. "You seem as unhappy as I once was."

"You know," Flanagan texted back, "I don't even have a car anymore."

"Stop making excuses."

Mercifully, Deja finally completed whatever urgent project occupied her attention, so Flanagan ended his tête-à-text with Dirk. "Sorry," Deja said. "I just had to finish sending some numbers off."

"The Earth still burning to a crisp?" asked Flanagan.

"Slowly but surely, rising one hundredth of a degree at a time."

"Then we better eat before the world comes to an end," said Flanagan.

"Why the hell not." They wended their way through the grounds of the Cathedral of St. John the Divine toward 110th Street. "Your girlfriend said you're not a completely awful person."

"Which girlfriend is that?"

"Heather."

"Oh, I wish I would have known she was my girlfriend," he said. "I wouldn't have invited you to dinner. I don't think it would be a good idea for me to cheat on Heather Pisano."

"I wouldn't advise that either," said Deja. "But I like the idea of stealing Heather Pisano's boyfriend. It sounds like the plot of a romantic comedy you would never take me to."

"So let me get this straight," said Flanagan. "In theory, you are saying that I would not take you to this imaginary romantic comedy movie that is based on an imaginary relationship I am having with Heather Pisano."

"And is my relationship with you also imaginary?"

"I sure hope so," said Flanagan. "Otherwise, I'd be having idiotic conversations with you about so many things that haven't happened."

After settling in at Miss Mamie's, Deja ordered the Louisiana catfish with collards and rice while Flanagan asked for the fried chicken with macaroni and cheese and mashed potatoes. "I hope you took some Lipitor before you ordered that," said Deja.

"I have been trying to hold off on adding medication to my daily routine," said Flanagan. "So what were you calculating?"

"I was going backwards in my numbers to try to determine what might have happened with the earth's temperatures had Jimmy Doherty survived," said Deja.

"That's a bit different than your usual calculations," said Flanagan. "So what did you determine?"

"Obviously, there are a lot of what-ifs, but if you take just a fraction of Doherty's agenda and pass it through Congress in 1990 – and I am talking about modest improvements – and you consider how big the United States climate footprint was then and how much their leadership then could have impacted global approaches throughout the 1990s, I'd say we are at least ten years behind and a few hundredths of a degree higher than we would have been if he lived."

"Can I record you saying that?" asked Flanagan. "I think that would bring a good deal of context to what Jimmy's loss meant."

"Sure," said Deja. "Do you really want to interview me? I will be keeping all my clothes on."

"Hey, I'm trying to make a serious documentary here."

"Mmmm," said Deja. "It's intriguing how you have become quite serious about the same time Heather Pisano has."

"Yeah?" asked Flanagan. "And what is my girlfriend Heather up to?"

"Like you don't know," said Deja. "I think she's ready to use her celebrity for something other than making money."

Flanagan was inwardly relieved, initially fearful Heather would undercut his bombshell revelation of Jimmy being her father. "Sounds like she's been spending a lot of time with you at the Earth Institute."

"More with Dr. Bowman than with me."

"So she's going nuclear." Flanagan calculated that he still had viable footage and a compelling angle on her NukeMan story even if she revealed her identity before the documentary came out. "I wonder how the public will react."

"I'm a little concerned myself," said Deja. "Heather's made a career of hiding that brain of hers. The people don't tend to like their sex symbols too intellectual."

"I don't know," said Flanagan, "I fell for you, didn't I?"

"Wow," said Deja. "What a sexist compliment. How lovely it is to be objectified."

"I love you for your brains first, as best expressed in your hostile sense of humor," said Flanagan, knowing he was treading on thin ice. "But I'm not going to act like I don't think you're beautiful or that I'm not attracted to you."

"Me and every other woman who crosses your path."

"Only you receive gifts and bad poetry from me."

"Aren't I the lucky gal," said Deja.

"Can I start seeing you regularly?"

"Are you going to be seeing anyone else?" asked Deja. "Those Pisano sisters can be very tempting and even more needy."

"No," said Flanagan, repeating as if to convince himself, "no, I want to be exclusively with you." As Deja eyed him suspiciously, he became more desperate. "You have to understand the influence of you and my daughter and the documentary on me. I am becoming more socially conscious. I am planting trees and shrubs in the neighborhood." Deja arched her right eyebrow, only nominally impressed. "I'll tell you what. Why don't we become pescatarians together? I don't even like fish, but I'll do it to show you I'm serious about becoming someone you can tolerate day after day."

"I already am a pescatarian," said Deja.

"That's perfect," said Flanagan. "I'll be the one bending toward you." In the back of his mind, he considered how his offer could align nicely with the vegetarian request from Michelle. His jump to being a pescatarian would be major shift from his three squares of pork and beef. Yes, with Kartik's advances he might be having more lobster than his daughter or his new girlfriend (could he make that claim yet?) would envision, but hey, both of them know what a flawed man they are trying to reclaim. Flanagan could tell in Deja's eyes that she was softening to the idea of their becoming steadies.

"No wonder you were shoving that fried chicken down your throat like there was no tomorrow," said Deja, "because you'd already had in the back of your mind that there would not be a tomorrow for Artie the Carnasaurus. I'm surprised you didn't order some ribs and brisket too."

"That might be my dessert ... unless they have meat pies."

Deja smiled. "Do you think it's a good idea to change who you are just to be with me?"

"No, I think it's an absolutely terrible idea," said Flanagan, "which is why I'm going to keep telling myself I am becoming a pescatarian for me. I'll eventually figure out if I am lying to myself."

"How long does that usually take?" she asked.

"Many years," Flanagan answered.

Deja lifted her glass. "Here's to years of deception."

"To deception," said Flanagan, "may it serve us well." He put down his glass and added, "Hey, you don't expect me to stop drinking, right?"

Deja just rolled her eyes.

"I mean this new diet will be hard enough," he continued. "I'm going to need a bourbon or two to wash down all of that cod and sole and tilapia."

"And so it begins ..." said Deja.

The next morning Flanagan did not wake up ruminating what he would send to Deja for breakfast and what pathetic rhymes he would concoct to accompany the delivery. Instead, he contemplated just what meats he would not eat today or tomorrow or the day after that.

CHAPTER 31
THE INTERVIEWING OF THE STAR WITNESS

For weeks, Suzie and her lawyers had been trying to crush Flanagan. Now she insisted he meet her at her mansion poolside and bring his camera. He knew the invitation must have come after Kartik engaged in many hours of negotiation that included exchanges about profit margins and promotion of *Peepin' on the Pisanos*. The temperature was the hottest November day on record: 81 degrees. Yes, the fall had been the warmest in recorded history. However, he could not help but suspect that Suzie had willed this sultry weather to meet the wardrobe demands of her family. She had turned New York into Southern California.

Suzie waited for Flanagan. She was stretched out on a lounge chair in a thong bikini, a 60-year-old woman with adolescent plastic surgery. She insisted he take a few shots of her from across the pool and then zoom in. "For atmosphere," she said. Then added. "Arthur, do be a dear and don't miss anything. Don't be shy. Get right in there." Suzie made certain he continued filming as she slowly turned over and stretched for a towel.

Flanagan tried to figure out what new angle she was working. He would find out soon enough. "Where do you want to shoot?" he asked.

"Right here. I'll stand. Why don't you frame me from head to toe?"

"You want to put on a wrap or anything?"

"No, why would I want to do that?"

He was tempted to suggest, "Modesty?" but didn't wish the conversation to dissolve into laughter just yet. "Anything off limits?"

"Suzie Wall has no limits," she pronounced.

After Suzie fluffed her deeply dyed locks and glided her fuchsia fingertips lovingly to her hips, Flanagan reframed the camera, pressed record, and started the discussion back in the 1980s. "What do you know about the death of the legendary basketball player and Senator Jimmy Doherty?"

"Well, I know he died in a car accident."

"Were you lovers at the time?"

Suzie stared more intensely at the camera like she was confessing to her best friend. "Yes, we were."

"Correct me if I am wrong, you had already been married for a couple of years to Frankie Pisano by then, right?"

"Yes, I was, but I had been with Jimmy before Frankie, and no matter how hard I tried, I couldn't stay away from Jimmy."

"But wasn't Jimmy also engaged at the time? His fiancé, the supermodel Cheryl Wood, says they were deeply in love."

Suzie arched her eyebrows and spoke confidently. "She would say that. What else could she say? But she knew she couldn't give him what I could give him?"

Flanagan wanted to get back to his investigation, but with his old reality show instincts kicking in, he had to ask, "And what could you give him?"

She smiled in a manner that the generous might describe as blushingly. Then she vibrated involuntarily, "Well … you know."

Flanagan let the pause play out. "Do you think Jimmy Doherty's death was really an accident?"

"An accident? I don't know. The timing seemed suspicious."

"You mean right after he gave the famous speech on global warming and lined up a coalition on a carbon tax so formidable that it seemed like President Bush might bend a bit to forge a compromise?"

Suzie laughed. "Global warming? Is that what you think this about?" She threw up her hands and frowned at the camera as if she might be speaking to the dumbest man on the planet.

"Well, there were many forces against it, and there were hundreds of millions of dollars on the line. The American Henry Center was willing to put a lot of resources behind destroying him. And he wouldn't be the last climate change advocate to die in an accident."

Suzie waved her hand dismissively. "No wonder this case has never been solved. You fools kept thinking about this global warming connection when things were really heating up in the Pisano household."

"What do you mean?"

"You know after Jimmy gave that speech he came by my house to celebrate," said Suzie. "Frankie was meeting with clients. Well, Jimmy was exuding all kinds of virile energy from the adoration of the crowds. He was irresistible."

"You slept with Jimmy in your house that night?" asked Flanagan.

"Neither of us could help ourselves," said Suzie. "We didn't even hear when Frankie came in."

"What did Frankie do?"

"He charged at Jimmy with a baseball bat," said Suzie.

"Did he hurt Jimmy?" asked Flanagan.

"Jimmy had eight inches on Frankie and was still in great shape. That I can tell you. It didn't take long for him to get the bat out of Frankie's hands."

"Do you think your husband was involved in the death of Jimmy Doherty?"

"I think it's a possibility," said Suzie. She drew closer to the camera in what Flanagan could only describe as a strut. "What do you think?" she asked more to the camera than to Flanagan, leaning in. If someone has to put in 10,000 hours to make a behavior natural, then Suzie clearly had put in the time to properly display a cleavage that had been properly enhanced. "Do you think I am so desirable that someone would kill for me?"

Flanagan was struck how she asked her question in the present tense. Another woman in her place in life might have asked, "Would you believe that I was once so desirable that someone would have killed for me? Would that be so hard to believe?" Flanagan now understood that Suzie was betting that this interview could revive her fame. Indeed, he understood she liked the idea of her dead husband being the killer of her former lover. Man, oh man, it was hard to draw the truth out of a reality television star.

He decided to turn the questioning directly on her. "Jealousy does go both ways, and Jimmy Doherty was indeed engaged to a supermodel who many considered one of the most beautiful women in the world."

"So what are you asking me?"

"Did you kill your lover Jimmy Doherty?"

Suzie could recognize good footage while it's filming and wasn't going to ruin it by dissembling or taking offense. "I did not kill my lover Jimmy Doherty."

"Did you kill your husband Frankie Pisano?"

"I did not kill my husband Frankie Pisano."

"Are you responsible for the accident that has left your husband Dirk Wall paralyzed?"

"I am not responsible for the injuries suffered by my husband Dirk Wall."

Flanagan paused to let the drama wash over and to zoom in to a close-up of Suzie's enigmatic expression.

After about thirty seconds, Suzie jumped back in. "Do you have anyone else you'd like to ask me about? Jack Kennedy? John Lennon? It can be whether I killed them or maimed them. I'm good with either."

Flanagan came to understand that he was just disembodied accusations behind the camera. He was nothing. The 60-year-old impressively renovated *femme fatale* was everything. As she played her role more broadly, Flanagan could sense his continued diminishment.

At that moment, Heather came poolside in a business suit; the outfit was form-fitting but not characteristically inappropriate. In the current context, she dressed like a Mennonite compared to her mother.

"Hi Mom," said Heather casually. "I just found out that Jimmy Doherty is my biological father. Did you know anything about that?"

Flanagan did not like the way the topic was introduced. On this occasion, he regretted that he was no longer writing the scripts for the Pisanos.

Suzie put her right hand to her lip to indicate deep thought. "I always considered it a possibility," she said. "But I was always afraid to find out."

"Why's that?" asked Heather, like it was not a major issue whichever the case.

"I thought it might be messy, with me being married to Frankie and all," Suzie explained. "It would have been a bigger problem to discover the identity after Tiffany was born."

"You could have warned me," said Heather. "All those years I thought Frankie was my father. He certainly acted like my father."

"That was exactly it," said Suzie. "I wanted you to have a father, and I was married to Frankie. There was no other way."

Heather picked up a glass of ice water in a colorful tumbler on the end table next to the chaise lounge and walked up to her mother. "There is always another way," she said and tossed the water in her mother's face.

Looking impressively surprised, downright shocked, Suzie breathed heavily and said, "God, that's cold."

Heather walked away, defiant and angry. Still, as she departed, Flanagan couldn't help but notice that Heather gave herself a round of applause. Suzie shook her face and hair slowly, the way she had been taught many years ago in modeling classes, allowing the drips of water to make rivulets along channels of her body.

Flanagan turned off the camera and thanked Suzie.

"Don't you want to ask me any more questions?"

"Not today," said Flanagan. "You are so honest I don't know what to ask next." When it came to the Pisanos, he knew lying was always the best policy in answering them.

"That's because I'm so real," said Suzie.

"Nobody could be more real," lied Flanagan one more time, knowing he had to get out of there before he slammed his head into the pool wall.

CHAPTER 32
THE DECODING OF A MURDER

Flanagan had sent former Detective Murphy the deathbed confession of Rusty Sansone hours after he recorded it. Murphy took two days to call him back.

"So what do you think?" asked Flanagan.

"I think it's possible," Murphy said.

"Last week, you said you couldn't figure out how the car could accelerate into the canal," said Flanagan. "Does Rusty's explanation about the throttle mechanism being tampered with sound kosher?"

"At first, I wasn't sure," said Murphy. "I had never heard about anyone doing that before. Then I started looking into it. That's what took me so long to get back to you. Yesterday, I read about a case a few years ago where a husband wished his wife dead because he didn't want to get hosed in the divorce. She got into an accident soon after. Investigators discovered that the husband had jammed a wooden shim into the throttle mechanism of her car."

"That' telling, right there," said Flanagan. "Can you send the information to me?"

"Sure," said Murphy. "Why not."

"So what happened to the wife?" asked Flanagan.

"She crashed into a couple of lightpoles, but survived," Murphy said. "Then she filed for divorce."

"So now you could buy that somebody messed with throttle mechanism," said Flanagan.

"It's funny," said Murphy. "Until I read about this case with the husband, I couldn't wrap my head about the tampering. I get pretty skeptical about theories when no one has ever done such a crime before."

"That's interesting," said Flanagan, "since this angry husband did his tampering about 30 years after whoever messed with Jimmy's car."

"Still," said Murphy. "Now that I know it happened, I know it's possible."

"Are you going to ask your detective buddies to reopen the investigation?" asked Flanagan.

"I was planning on it," said Murphy. "That's why I called you. I thought you might want to know that for your documentary."

"Could you tell them to be discreet about it?" asked Flanagan.

"I thought you'd want to make a big deal," said Murphy.

"I do," said Flanagan, "but I want it to be a big deal in a month when the documentary comes out."

"You're not exactly trying to speed up the cause of justice," said Murphy.

"I'm not saying the investigation shouldn't proceed aggressively," said Flanagan. "I am just hoping they could do it without any press for a while. I thought you guys liked when no reporters were poking their noses into your investigations."

"We do," said Murphy. "I guess I can see what I can do under one condition—"

"What's that?" asked Flanagan.

"You make us look good," said Murphy. "I can't have us looking like a bunch of dopes."

"First of all, I will come back and record another interview with you," said Flanagan. "You will be able to tell by my questions that I will make sure you sound smart and thoughtful. Second of all, I will make abundantly clear that Rusty Sansone's cover-up of the tampering undermined the entire investigation. Finally, the footage we shot by the Gowanus will further confirm that after all these years you were still considering all of the angles of the case."

"That will be helpful," said Murphy. "Don't forget to include what I uncovered about those two thugs Fratiani and Hoffman."

Flanagan laughed. "You mean Tony 'the Elbow' and Karl 'the Sausage'? I just love saying their names."

"Yeah," said Murphy. "They don't make nicknames like they used to."

"We are working on a chart linking the major players from the American Henry Center with not only Fratiani and Hoffman, but of course with Frankie Pisano," said Flanagan. "We're even investigating the Otis Freeman angle with all of his gambling debts." When Flanagan said "we," he really meant Mehnuma would be sorting and fortifying these lurid connections. After Kartik heard that a big athlete like Freeman could be linked to the documentary, he pressed Mehnuma harder.

"Good," said Murphy. "Make sure to investigate the falling out Fratiani and Hoffman had with Frankie in the late nineties, which is just about the time of Frankie's accident."

"I'm not sure we'll get to that one," said Flanagan. "We'll probably save it for next season."

"Next season?" asked Murphy. "Jesus, Flanagan, you're a bigger whore than any of the Pisanos."

Flanagan paused, deciding not to respond. "So can I come over now and record you."

Murphy laughed and then took a deep breath. "Yeah, why the hell not."

During his time with Murphy, Flanagan could not get himself to tell the retired detective that he had set up a visit with Karl the Sausage Hoffman. Murphy had warned Flanagan that Karl kept his mouth shut tighter than a clam in the Gowanus Canal. Still, Flanagan knew he would regret not trying to visit Karl at the prison in person, especially since the convict had stopped answering his Emails.

The next morning he rented a car and drove six hours across most of New York State to the mighty walled jail of Attica, where turrets greeted him, promising perches to shoot in every direction. Even though he had filled out his fair share of forms online, Flanagan found himself moving from form to form and door to door until, after an hour at the jail, he stared through the glass at Karl Hoffman. Now he understood why Karl was nicknamed "the Sausage," given his tubular shape filling out his orange uniform. Karl's thick German head directed its energies intensely at Flanagan, who spent much of the hour before the lifer wondering if he had ever peered into a murderer's eyes before.

True to Murphy's warning, Flanagan did all of the talking, asking Karl questions about Doherty's Honda Civic, about Frankie Pisano's connections to him, and especially about the vexing Emails he sent. Karl stared at Flanagan. It was not a menacing stare; instead, it indicated that Flanagan was not worth strangling.

Flanagan continued to talk and wait, eventually filling in Karl's silences with questions about the American Henry Center and Tony "the Elbow" Fratiani.

After an hour of his monologue, Flanagan had enough and bid farewell. As Karl was walking toward the door which led back to his endless incarceration, he yelled out to Flanagan, "I Emailed you."

Then, Karl's tubular orange presence disappeared far behind the glass.

As he headed in the opposite direction, Flanagan said to himself, "You did, you frustrating prick."

The ride down Route 390 and over to Route 17 along the state's southern tier seemed considerably longer than the ride there. Flanagan stewed. He had committed Karl's three short, obtuse Email responses to memory:

"You must be stupid if you'd think there'd be a situation where Frankie told us what."

"You must be an idiot to think we'd ever want a car to make go."

"You must be the dumbest man on the planet to think we'd care so Doherty'd be gone."

Each reply suggested ideas, but stubbornly refused to offer insight. He said the three messages aloud as he raced past Binghamton. They made no more sense than the 20 times he studied the Emails. Everything about the messages was off, down to the subject line: "In the End, just Four You." Karl couldn't even spell "Four" right. He remembered Murphy's comments about Karl being crazy but brilliant. All the time he peered at Karl through the glass, Flanagan understood the convict's intelligence was far beyond him. That each of the Emails opened with a mocking comment about Flanagan's stupidity drove the point home.

As he rode over a ravine, Flanagan suddenly understood that Karl would not have spelled "Four" in that way without a purpose. It was a clue. He muttered the subject line "In the End, just Four You" enough times to conclude that Carl had sent him a code. Not being able to organize the words and letters in his head, he stopped at the Roscoe Diner with paper and pencil in hand. He ordered pancakes and, in honor of Karl, some sausage. He wrote down Karl's Email responses and sipped coffee. At first, he tried looking at the letters of the messages in increments of four, but that soon led to words like *pfdne*, so he quickly abandoned that effort. He toyed with more elaborate ciphers and underlined words compulsively to no effect.

By the time his pancakes and sausage arrived, Flanagan realized he just wasn't bright enough to figure out the code. Flanagan offered a soft laugh in acknowledgement about how right Karl was about his brainpower. But if Karl was smart enough to realize Flanagan's limitations, he had to make the code simple enough for any moron to figure out. With that recognition, Flanagan returned to the word "Four." Every Email must have four useful words, but which four? Dense as he was, Flanagan had to read the subject line three more times ("In the End, just Four You") to conclude that the four had to be the last ones of each message: "In the End."

He wrote out the list of the last four words of each Email consecutively: "Frankie told us what car to make go so Doherty'd be gone."

And just like that, Flanagan had another piece of useful evidence. Karl had told Flanagan more than he could have hoped. No, the evidence would not hold up in a court of law, but in a documentary, it would be beautiful. He could already imagine the magic Mehnuma would make from it. She'd have the words of the three separate Emails swirling and blurring until they all lined up for the big reveal. In terms of the documentary, Karl Hoffman managed not to admit to his crime, yet tell the audience what had happened.

Flanagan enjoyed the remainder of the ride back to Astoria much more than the first leg. His belly was warm with pancakes and sausage and his documentary was rounding into shape. Added to Rusty's confession and Murphy's confirmation, Karl's connections to Frankie and the accident presented a scenario that was much more credible than the ones Flanagan had conjured days earlier.

Yes, he knew he would surprise Kartik with the revelation, but, more importantly, Flanagan now stood on firmer ground than he had in all the years he had planted his feet on the Pisano compound.

However, that evening on his green futon, doubts crept into Flanagan's thoughts like billows of fog. Did he just will a confession out of those Emails, rejiggering the words until they suited his narrative? Sure, Murphy said Karl Hoffman was bright, but would the convict bother to create a code just difficult enough to make Flanagan struggle, but simple enough that even a dope could figure out? To embed a coded message in a series of Emails seemed more like something out of the bad shows Flanagan watched than the stuff of everyday life? Was he applying reality television standards to real world challenges? In other words, was Arthur Flanagan simply full of crap?

Flanagan sat up. He had no margin for this perseverating and dithering. No, Flanagan must assert with confidence that Karl Hoffman's message was indeed – "Frankie told us what car to make go so Doherty'd be gone." Under Frankie

Pisano's direction, Tony and Karl identified and tampered with Doherty's Honda Civic, so when Jimmy hit the accelerator, he'd end up in the Gowanus Canal. That must be Flanagan findings and he must stick with them.

And he would deliver his findings with the confidence of a Pisano.

CHAPTER 33
THE STRIPPING AWAY OF POWER

Heather Pisano promised a major pronouncement at her press conference, so the media arrived like she was announcing her engagement to LeBron James. As usual, she made the paparazzi wait an hour before she found her way behind a podium. Behind her was a closed red curtain. Dressed in the same suit as she had for her confrontation with her mother, she turned what would normally be a fashion *faux pas* into a statement about the new Heather: no longer would the public spot her in three outfits over the course of an evening – nine over the course of a day; she would be recycling her wardrobe. As she expressed in the press release, "Get used to seeing me in the same clothes."

Her hair was pulled back, her eyes were without shadow, and her lipstick color was so light she might not have been wearing any at all. She spoke clearly with no hint of seductiveness in her voice. Flanagan considered how he would contrast such footage in the documentary with her more prurient moments, some to which Kartik had procured exclusive rights.

"Climate change is the existential issue of our time," she said. "How important is it? I could lecture you, but that is not my style and I know a number of scientists who could do a much better job explaining what is at stake from rising sea levels to extreme weather events to environmental cataclysms to massive species die-offs. I will underscore its importance by giving one-tenth of my personal fortune, $150 million, to the Union of Concerned Scientists.

"When addressing how daunting the climate change problem is, The Union of Concerned Scientists has now come to the same conclusion that I did three years ago: nuclear power needs to be part of the solution. It must serve as a bridge to get us to wide-scale solar and wind power, those clean resources that need more time for further technological improvements and better battery storage. Because nuclear power has not received the governmental and tax relief support that the fossil fuel industry has been granted, it has become less and less profitable as an industry. Nuclear power plant closures leave a short-term vacuum for even more gas and coal plants to exploit. We cannot let this happen."

Flanagan and the entire press corps were stunned. Not because of what Heather was saying – her points were of mild interest – but because of how much Heather spoke. She said more in this one speech than she had said collectively in public over the last year. Heather generally communicated through smoldering glances, the aforementioned wardrobe expressions, and intriguing positioning in and out of that wardrobe. Now, she offered no such inducements.

Heather delineated the improved safety measures and trumpeted smaller modular units of nuclear power plants that could be strung together. As she became more technical and specific in her explanation, more cameras switched off and more eyes glazed over. Just when Flanagan thought that Heather Pisano had finally achieved something heretofore never found on her resume, boring the masses to death, she pointed to the curtain and said, "All of this explanation leads to my next announcement. Let me show you who else I am."

Heather walked around the closed curtain. Within a few minutes, triumphal music blared and fog rose about the stage. Then the curtain opened. Smoke billowed from what looked like the cooling tower of a miniature nuclear reactor. But as the mist lifted, the pink Nike-sneakered feet appeared where the base met the ankles, the bottom steadily and elegantly expanding. Soon, Flanagan and the rest of the crowd could discern the well-designed costume of off-white, faded in spots to give the impression that the reactor had been in use for a while. Rising to the top of the structure, a steady stream of steam emerged from the tower's neck. Above that neck, a face peeked through the mist, one covered with black hair, long and scraggly atop, thick mustache in the middle, mangy beard below. Indeed, the face belonged to one who had walked over many mountains and crossed endless streams to reach this very point.

"Some of you may know me," said the mouth of the hairy, misty face, a voice that Flanagan now realized had been deepened and distorted by audio technology. "I am NukeMan. I am here to join the cause in helping to save the planet."

Then a pair of well-toned arms rose from the neck of the tower and pulled off the beard, followed by the moustache, and then the wild hair. In an entirely different form of a stripping than the public was accustomed to, Heather removed these NukeMan layers to reveal her soft and lovely face below those piercing eyes. Her voice remained that of the superhero. "Now, you know my true identity."

Heather waited for this revelation to sink in. When she spoke again, the voice was her own. "Now you know who NukeMan is. Now, you know my little secret. It's now our little secret. It's time to share that secret with the world. I will be dedicating myself to the cause of nuclear power. I am deeply committed to climate change like many of us are, but too many of us have been afraid to embrace nuclear power. I am here today to say that I will be embracing it with all of my love and all of my resources. I encourage you to join us. For to save our planet, I ask all of you to be NukeMen."

With that, the curtain closed. Flanagan imagined Heather's two hands bravely clapping in the cramped confines of her nuclear tower costume.

Heading around the back, Flanagan tried to get near enough to talk to Heather, but he was blocked not only by her entourage, but by the gathering of the paparazzi around her. Flanagan got the sneaking suspicion that his access to Heather would no longer be what it had been of late. Instead, he returned to his basement apartment and followed Twitter to gauge the reaction to her big reveal.

Flanagan grumbled, remembering he had in his first act of pescatarianism ceremoniously tossed out his salami, his soppresata, even his frozen meatballs in front of an approving Michelle. He couldn't get out of his head the words of "encouragement" his daughter offered. "Dad, I can't believe you are making the right decision for once."

What is this "for once" crap, Flanagan thought then and again later and even later. "Right decision," he muttered as he took out the tofu from the refrigerator. He poured extra virgin olive oil in a pan and blasted the burner on high, waiting for the oil nearly to scorch before his dropping in the tofu, now coated in a spiced cornstarch. As the tofu crackled, he looked at his twitter feed, scrolling down, absorbing the reaction to Heather's press conference. He flipped over the tofu, one side of which was now crisp and brown, and read on.

While Heather was not going to be happy, Mama Suzie was really going to blow a gasket. The first Tweet he had read was a sign of what would follow. "A word of advice for Heather Pisano: Shut up and jiggle." As he scrolled down, he registered the highlights.

■ "And we thought the Pisano family was toxic before. Now Heather will have us all die of radiation poisoning."

■ "Heather must have spent too much time in the tanning bed. It's fried what little brains she had."

■ "I always suspected the Pisano family secretly wanted to destroy us all. With Heather's announcement, the four horsewomen of the apocalypse have finally galloped out of the shadows."

■ "Heather says she wants to save planet. Sounds more like she wants to wreck it."

■ "Heather now claims she's NukeMan, more like PukeWoman to me."

■ "Die, you bitch, die."

■ "I guess when she skipped school to make booty calls, Heather missed those lessons on Chernobyl and Fukushima."

The hits kept coming about a detached, clueless celebrity who was hurting the planet, and, more importantly, hurting her brand. The last Tweet Flanagan read circled back to the first. "Just shut up and strip." Then there were the memes, which Flanagan had to admit were funny. His favorite was an image of an alarmed, scraggly kitten with the caption, "Trying to understand Heather Pisano is like eating the factor of X."

Flanagan decided now was as good as any time to tuck into the ration of fried tofu. He did not spare the salt and poured out a bowl of teriyaki for dipping. The tofu wasn't terrible. Trying to ignore the awareness that he felt nourished but unsatisfied, he pondered the withering attacks on Heather. Flanagan had no idea how much people disliked, no, abjectly hated nuclear power. The reasoned discourse and objections at the Earth Institute to Professor Bowman's, and in turn, Heather's assertions could not have prepared Heather for the onslaught she had just endured. So caught up in the ratings of her own series, Heather had not realized the popularity of the many shows like *Chernobyl* about the horrors of nuclear power.

As always, Flanagan returned to the question of what will Heather's meltdown in popularity mean to his documentary. Initially, he thought Heather's falling fortunes would drag down his too. Then he started to consider how this fiasco would play out in the Pisano mansion. He imagined Suzie, the grand matriarch of the entire empire, walking into her daughter's bedroom and announcing, as if the cameras were still on, "If you did this to hurt me, to hurt all of us, then you succeeded. Think of what you have done to the Pisano name."

Flanagan then decided that the best hope for restoring the family brand was his documentary which, ironically, they had been trying to block during the previous months. While the nuclear controversy was intolerable (far too heavy and serious), a juicy scandal with sex and murder never hurt the family name. If they mixed in a bit of blueblood propriety from Doherty, the Pisanos might get some badass street cred – ala Martha Stewart – out of their sketchy behaviors.

In the past, Flanagan would have fretted that his documentary had no action-packed climax. Sure, he had unearthed many revelations. But he didn't have a confrontation featuring a crazed oil magnate with a gun. No gorgeous Pisano was dramatically saved or, better yet, had saved anyone. No one was shot. He didn't even have a stunning rescue like the one featuring the collapsing shack on the shoreline in last season's finale of *Peepin' on the Pisanos*. No, Flanagan was out of the climax business. Anyway, he was confident that Kartik and Suzie would manufacture a climax of shameless contrivance.

Still hungry, Flanagan opened a can of black beans and plopped them in a pot on the stove. He cut up some red onion as the beans heated. When the beans made it to the bowl, Flanagan sprinkled the raw onions on top. Eating more ravenously than usual, he polished off the beans in no time and immediately encountered turbulence in his belly. He knew his body would take time to adjust to this new diet of bean curd and even more beans, not to mention the raw onion. He clicked on the fans, knowing that new winds would be blowing and thankful that tonight only he would endure them.

CHAPTER 34
THE RUTTINGS OF THE JUNGLE

Taking a page from Mehnuma, Flanagan called on Grace Chen to connect the dots of his research. As Flanagan stepped into her midtown office, he noted that Grace's work as a lawyer and activist for numerous environmental lobbying groups must be lucrative. He visited Grace in her corner suite, framing his camera to capture the mighty books on the shelf behind her, a collection that indicated she was quite the scholar. Sheepishly, he handed her a script. He wrote down exactly what he wanted to convey in the final episode, hoping that Grace would provide this commentary. Sure, he figured Grace would have some objections or amendments, but he trusted she would at least suggest what conclusions could be drawn from his months of work. She perused the script, occasionally looking up at Flanagan to indicate she was thinking, and then returned to the page.

"O.K.," she said. "I'm ready for you to turn on the camera."

"Any questions?" asked Flanagan.

"No," said Grace with finality. She put on her pink lab coat, her signature garment for interviews. Considering her training and occupation, the lab coat made absolutely no sense, but Grace managed to make it work for her.

So Flanagan simply framed, hit record, and let Grace go.

"The problems of trying to solve a thirty-year-old crime are legion and obvious. However, that doesn't mean we should ignore the evidence. So what do we have? We have two individuals with really compelling motives. We have a ruthless oil magnate in Roy Crowne who would stop at nothing to prevent legislation on climate change. Jimmy Doherty happened to be the biggest threat to the petroleum industry at the time. We have Roy Crowne's friend and associate Frankie Pisano who has his own issues with Jimmy. Jimmy had bequeathed unto Frankie the shame and embarrassment of being a cuckold. And what's worse, not only did his wife Suzie cheat on Frankie with Jimmy, but they sired a bastard child Heather, someone who was a physical reminder of Frankie's humiliation every day of his life. Then you have the connection of two career criminals in Tony the Elbow Fratiani and Karl the Sausage Hoffman with deep ties to both Roy Crowne and Frankie Pisano. Karl Hoffman's Emails to our lead investigator serve as tacit acknowledgement of his involvement with Frankie Pisano in the death of Jimmy Doherty. And finally, you have the confession of Frankie's childhood friend Rusty Sansone that someone had tampered with the throttle mechanism on the Honda Civic that Jimmy Doherty drove right into the Gowanus Canal. Even though this all took place thirty years ago, I think we now know what happened to Jimmy Doherty."

As she continued her closing argument, Grace Chen did not look once at the script. Yes, she changed a few words here and there. Flanagan would never have used "bequeathed" and he certainly hadn't written "cuckold" – half the audience would have to look up what the word meant. Still, he was quibbling. He could not have asked for more from an interviewee. There's something to be said for writing scripts in documentaries instead of all that spontaneous question-and-answer nonsense.

Flanagan knew he should allow Grace to address the one qualm the critics might have. Behind the camera, he pointed out to her, "Most of the people you are talking about are dead."

"I know," answered Grace. "Isn't *that* interesting?"

As he put away the camera and left the midtown office, he walked back out onto the street frustrated and restless. Grace's comments wrapped a lovely bow around his trough of circumstantial slop. All that work for an outcome that sounded much better than it actually was. He was glad to be done with the entire business … well, almost …

As the last of the footage was being edited and the first installment of *Death Canal* was ready to premiere, Flanagan prepared to conduct one final interview. Sean Clarkin had been the most valuable of all of Flanagan's sources throughout the process, so it was no surprise that he managed to arrange a sit-down with Sir Kevin Doherty. Realizing that with this interview he would have given Kartik everything he had asked for, Flanagan considered how he could squeeze a few more beans out of his producer (he mused about the fact he counted his currency in terms of beans now that he was consuming more of them).

Sir Kevin had insisted that Flanagan interview him at his studio set where he produced *Planet Green*. Flanagan didn't mind, given his career of presenting "reality" from a series of well-designed stages. With the abundance of flora and a menagerie of taxidermied critters about the set, Flanagan felt like he had stepped into a diorama at a natural history museum. After Flanagan waited for a while, Sir Kevin appeared through the high grasslands like he just stepped out of the jungle. His thick shirt and trousers were of matching parchment color, the outfit marked by many pockets. The textures and odors of his clothes were designed to scatter bugs. His matching Panama hat framed a face that had become much more famous and recognizable than the permanently younger but always identical mien of his long dead brother.

When Flanagan turned on the camera and asked about his brother, Sir Kevin didn't answer the question. Instead, he spoke of exotic birds.

"Have you ever seen the mating rituals of the blue manakin?" Sir Kevin asked.

"I can't say I have," answered Flanagan.

Sir Kevin chuckled in a manner Flanagan read as condescending. "I guess that would be unlikely unless you have tramped around the eastern forests of South America." Sir Kevin did not have add "like I have," just like he did not have to add "countless times."

"I am not nearly as well-traveled as you are, sir," said Flanagan.

Sir Kevin furrowed his eyebrows as if to express wordlessly, "that, my dear fellow, is an understatement." But his interest in Flanagan immediately flagged in favor of his recollection of his fine-feathered friends. "Even you, who Sean tells me has spent many a year doing field work on the Pisanos, would be impressed by these mating rituals. It takes four males daily practice for weeks to seduce one female."

"I usually need years of practice, but I am generally on my own," said Flanagan.

Sir Kevin grinned. "These are quite beautiful birds," he said. Flanagan tried not to read anything into that distinction. "The blue that gives the manakin its name covers the torso and is stunningly bright; it's offset by black on the wings, the tail, and the neck. The red cap reminds me of the pompadours popular with rockabilly singers."

Flanagan knew less about rockabilly singers than he did blue manakins. "They sound quite spectacular."

"They are, and the lead male is the most exquisite of the bunch. He is joined by three mates, who are the truest of all wing men, as the four practice a dance. It requires tremendous flapping and chirping as each one hurtles over the other three in a flying leap. Kind of like so …"

Rising from his chair, Sir Kevin began twittering and frantically fluttering his arms. The display reminded Flanagan just why Sir Kevin was such a successful storyteller and showman. Though he knew the demonstration was for the camera rather than for him, Flanagan laughed indulgently until Sir Kevin returned to his seat.

After catching his breath, Sir Kevin continued. "The four males not only practice together, but they even recruit a young male still of dull plumage to serve as a substitute for the female. They practice their dance, twirling and quivering ever closer to the stand-in, until the synchronization is so sharp that the lead signals their readiness for prime time."

"I'm guessing if the males are this attractive, then the females are absolutely magnificent," said Flanagan.

Sir Kevin's chuckle reached new heights of condescension and his faux British accent became more prominent. "Unlike our species, the male blue manakins are the fairer sex, as is the case with many exotic birds. I'm afraid the female is rather pedestrian … except for the continuation of the species, hardly worth the trouble."

"I'm sorry to interrupt," said Flanagan. "Where you last left off, you were saying the males were now ready for the actual mating ritual."

"Oh yes," said Sir Kevin. "All four of them line up on a branch next to the female and the closest one does the aerial fluttering millimeters from the female before hurtling over the other three to land at the far end of the branch; then the new nearest one will do the same trick, landing at the end of the line, and so on as each cycle through on this rumba line of love. Then the lead male delivers a spectacular finale, twisting and turning and flailing and shaking and quivering."

"So what happens next?" asked Flanagan.

"Then the three wing males look on and wait nervously on the same branch of their dance while the lead male and the female perch on opposite nearby branches until the female decides whether she is sufficiently excited to let him on her. If she does allow him to proceed, the entire consummation lasts about a second."

Flanagan tried to steer the interview back on track. "Speaking of mating rituals, what do you know about your brother's relationship with Suzie Pisano, who I believe when he first knew her was Suzie Jansen?"

"Do you know that males make up about sixty percent of the diet of a female praying mantis during mating season," said Sir Kevin.

"No, I did not," said Flanagan.

"But for purposes of our conversation, I believe the mating rituals of the pufferfish are more relevant. To attract females, the male makes wonderful symmetrical patterns in the sand. He will spend days and days on it just crafting these rings that can be as wide as a couple of yards. If the female likes what she sees, she lays her eggs in the center. Like the pufferfish, a Doherty knows how to make circles."

Now, we're getting somewhere, thought Flanagan. "When you say Doherty are you referring to your brother Jimmy or yourself, Sir Kevin?"

"As you might know, we are identical twins, so when I speak of Jimmy, I speak of myself."

"But in this case," said Flanagan, "I am asking you about Jimmy's relationship with Suzie Pisano, nee Jansen."

Sir Kevin offered a roguish grin. "I think you might find what I have to say illuminating. Imagine a tribe rooted in hierarchical tradition, where the laws of nature demand a constant struggle for the alpha male and the alpha female. Imagine a scenario where the queen of the jungle has been astonishingly dethroned by her sister, who until then seemed happy as the queen of even grander territories. Now, when this sister, let's say her name is Barbara, finds a cozy seat by the king, this queen, let's say her name is Suzie, decides that she too will foray into distant lands, in this case across the sea to send a message to King Jimmy. Here, she bows her head with such ardor for Jimmy's distant brother, an equally worthy monarch who has conquered a grand old land, that he offers his services for her to be queen for a day."

Flanagan looked puzzled.

Sir Kevin shrugged and added, "Now wouldn't that be an intriguing scenario."

My God, thought Flanagan, everyone involved in this world is a corrupt performer. How could he pierce the truth through this salacious slop, this prurient pudding? "You were living in England at the time your brother Jimmy was having a relationship with Suzie."

"Indeed, I was," said Sir Kevin. "Funny thing about the Doherty boys and the Jansen girls. All fine, feathered friends, flighty types, tending to be migratory in nature. The chosen professions of my brother and me informed us that the world could come to an end at any moment – whether it was nuclear bombs in the 1980s or climactic annihilation in the 2020s. We always lined up and made our circles."

Flanagan continued to ask Sir Kevin questions, but his thoughts were preoccupied about whether it might be worth revealing to Heather that her father could as well be Sir Kevin as it could be Jimmy. He would ask Kartik for guidance, knowing that the producer would say to let Sir Kevin's interview be a final surprise in a season of surprises on *Death Canal*. Kartik might suggest that Heather is told the day of the finale, so she could be both shocked and prepared to perpetuate the intrigue right into the following season.

When they finished up, Sir Kevin straightened his Panama hat, rose from his chair, and ambled through the set's grasslands, looking like for all appearances that he was heading deeper into the bush, which Flanagan now realized might be more of a likely scenario than he had previously imagined.

On his way back to Astoria, Flanagan ordered a pepperoni pizza. After he picked up both Michelle and the pie, he remembered he had converted to a devout pescatarian yesterday. He dropped the pizza box on the stove. Michelle and he methodically plucked off the pepperoni slices and dropped them into the garbage. "I think we are adding to the destruction of the planet by wasting this fine pepperoni," said Flanagan.

"I think I will have an easier time doing this than you will," said Michelle.

"That's because you're trying to impress a couple of boys," said Flanagan. He took it as parental prerogative to omit that he became a pescatarian to impress Deja.

"I just have more will power than you do," said Michelle.

"What are you talking about?" asked Flanagan. "You saw me take the pepperoni off the pie."

"But the fact that you ordered it is a sign that you are purposely trying to sabotage your efforts."

Flanagan was in no mood to admit his daughter might be right on that count. He ate a slice and was incredibly happy that he could still taste the wonderfully spicy, porklicious grease of the pepperoni on the cheese. He decided he would order only pepperoni pies, hoping he possessed the inner strength to toss all of that glorious meat in the garbage before he bit in.

Just when he was feeling he could get through the night as a pescatarian, Michelle casually tossed out, "I am going with Rafael and Ramon tonight to see a film."

"Both Espinal brothers," said Flanagan. "Jesus."

"What's the big deal about them being brothers?" asked Michelle.

"Brothers are trouble," said Flanagan.

"From what I've been reading lately in online," said Michelle, "I've heard that sisters are the real trouble."

Knowing the last thing he wanted to do was to have yet another conversation with his daughter about Heather and Tiffany Pisano, Flanagan pivoted, "You're just saying that because you're an only child. What are you guys seeing tonight?"

"*An Inconvenient Truth.*"

"That's kind of an old film, isn't it?"

"It's been updated," said Michelle. "I was thinking Dad, why don't you do a documentary about Al Gore?"

"For many reasons," said Flanagan.

"Like …," coaxed Michelle.

"Well, let me see, first of all, he's not dead; second of all, he hasn't slept with anyone in the Pisano family; and finally, he is not the father of any of the famous Pisano supermodel daughters."

"But climate change," said Michelle, "he was ahead of most politicians when it came to climate change, and he was almost President."

Flanagan sniffed, "Yeah … but that's all he's got."

"A documentary on Al Gore might be something you could do to help the cause," said Michelle.

Flanagan was discovering that his daughter was really good at making him feel terrible about himself. "I'll think about it," he told her. "Maybe I can convince Heather to strike up a friendship with him. She could use all the support she could get with her NukeMan initiative."

"O.K.," said Michelle, "but if you make Heather the star of the documentary instead of Al Gore, I'll never forgive you."

Flanagan laughed. "Now that would be an inconvenient truth."

CHAPTER 35
THE ENDING OF THE DISCONTINUATION

"That's a hell of dress," said Flanagan.

"For once in your life, you're not lying," said Deja. "Why are we eating before the premiere?"

"Because the last thing I want to do is hang around after the premiere," said Flanagan. "I have already built in an excuse that I have to pick up Michelle from a Sweet Sixteen party."

"You really are trying to ruin your career, aren't you?" said Deja.

"I'm trying to have a relationship with you and with my daughter," said Flanagan. "I don't think that's possible if I keep myself so entrenched in this world."

"Does that mean I get to meet Michelle tonight?" asked Deja.

"If you're ready and promise to hang around for a while," said Flanagan. "Otherwise, she'll just think I'm a slut."

Deja laughed. "No, she won't," she said. "She'll think you're a loser, who can't keep a girl around for more than five minutes."

"That might be true too, but don't tell Flanagan," said Flanagan, "because that could really destroy his self-esteem. He is very fragile, you know."

"He's more manipulative than fragile," said Deja.

Flanagan and Deja ate their meal, drank their wine, argued about the timelines for new nuclear power plants to be operational in the West, discussed why they had never had a serious conversation about the Knicks or the Mets, and concluded that Deja's parents really should lift their house in Hamilton Beach one more time.

As they walked their way from Milos to the Paris Theater, Deja asked Flanagan, "Shouldn't we be pulling up in some fancy automobile if we're going to walk the red carpet?"

"I was speaking to my friend Clarkin about it," said Flanagan, "and he thought it would be funny if we just walked up to the red carpet," said Flanagan.

"Do you always listen to Clarkin?" asked Deja

"Clarkin is the only reason I was able to put together this documentary in the first place," said Flanagan.

"I don't know if I should thank him or curse him for that," said Deja.

"Definitely thank him, since without talking to him, I would have never found my way out of that world and would have never found my way to you," said Flanagan.

"Yeah," said Deja. "That still leaves me with the question of whether I should thank him or curse him."

Neither Deja nor Flanagan was prepared for the premiere of *Death Canal* to be such a scene. Thousands were gathered in front of the theater and huge lights peered down from all directions, illuminating the sidewalk. If Flanagan didn't spot Kartik's brawny nephew Arnav, he and Deja might have never had their chance to walk the red carpet, since so many of the onlookers and the paparazzi were blocking the way. "You should go after the first round of stars," said Arnav, "but before the Pisanos."

Flanagan nodded, surprised he got a spot later than some of the celebrities.

On this warm December night (and not a hint of snow in the 10-day forecast), the onlookers lined up along the red carpet for a glimpse of small-screen royalty. Mostly, the B-List crowd arrived early: a starlet from a Netflix show that had yet to gain traction, the third most important member of an afternoon talk show panel, a weatherman who achieved some fame for asking people how they felt about the rain, and a TikTok star known for falling during every dance she attempted.

Right after those figures passed through with many onlookers asking, "Who is that?" (they still snapped pictures just in case the strutter really was somebody or one day would become somebody), Flanagan walked his first red carpet. Tellingly, most of the whispers were about Deja, whose wild afro and tone figure garnered the attention. Her kanga dress, marked by quilt-like panels of orange and blue and punctuated by concentric circle patches that narrowed down to a bull's eye, sent murmurs through the audience about who was the fashion designer and where could they buy that dress. Nobody bothered to tell the crowd that the somewhat handsome man with Deja was the lead writer and principal interviewer of *Death Canal*.

If a moment of recognition did surface, it was immediately blown away by the armada of limousines that now lined up at the curb, signaling that the Pisano clan had arrived. Yelling out his patented call "Moooove," as he was lifted from the back seat, Dirk Wall rolled onto the red carpet in his wheelchair, receiving applause. No one had the coldness of heart to discern whether some of the smatterings were soaked in pity. To Flanagan's horror, his old boss scooted right over to him, signaling that he should lean an ear down to Dirk's mouth.

"Remember, it's not too late," said Dirk.

"Too late for what?" asked Flanagan.

"To crash your car into a wall," said Dirk, his tightened fist opening, mimicking an explosion.

Flanagan was going to remind Dirk once again that he did not even have a car, but by then the wheelchair had rolled off and all that could be heard were gleeful giggles in the distance. The parade of family beauties followed, beginning with Nora Wall. She was only in the documentary in the most peripheral way – Kartik and Mehnuma slipped her photo shoots in wherever they could manufacture the slightest pretense – but even her half-sisters and her mother (to their chagrin) knew that Nora had become the celebrity of the moment. No matter how hard she fought it, Suzie became increasingly aware that her time was passing, which was why she practically had to wrestle the eye-rolling Nora into the limousine to give the premiere cross-generational appeal.

Suzie did indeed follow, her outfit more revealing than her youngest daughter's. Tiffany came next, as spectators and their camera lenses still tried to figure out just what they were ogling. As the surgery marks mellowed, she remained a woman at once gorgeous and off, a science experiment that was wildly successful, but barely so. Like Flanagan before them, the onlookers fell a little bit in love with Tiffany and had no idea why.

Never looking more beautiful, Heather was granted the final spot. Suzie hoped this appearance would be the beginning of her comeback after she damaged her brand with her incessant NukeMan rallies and her vexing appearances on news programs. Suzie had crafted Heather's image all of these years as a sultry, smoldering goddess. That persona demanded many intense gazes and few words. Now all Heather did was talk. Suzie arranged with Kartik that no interviewers would be permitted along this red carpet, requiring that the paparazzi once again soak in the sensual, silent Heather. As Suzie told Heather for the hundredth time in the past month, "the public likes to imagine you embracing them in the bedroom, not arguing with them around the dinner table."

For her part, Heather discovered that once she started talking about nuclear power and climate change, she couldn't stop. She also learned how desolate she felt from the absence of adulation in her life. Knowing she'd need a companion soon, Heather had kept her eyes open at both Goddard and the Earth Institute, asking for scouting reports from Deja about some of the scientists.

For his part, Flanagan was thrilled that he was no longer writing scripts for *Peepin' on the Pisanos*, since he sensed the once unified family was splitting off in many directions. As he watched the first two episodes of *Death Canal* before him on the Paris Theater's big screen, he tried to figure out how he was going to break the news to Kartik that he would not be involved in the upcoming season. For his next project, he considered writing a biography of Jimmy Doherty or maybe creating a documentary about the early figures of the climate change movement, getting to that story before the last of them were dead. At the moment, he was leaning in the latter direction, hoping that Heather still had enough juice so Kartik would agree to produce such a program. Flanagan understood that he might have to canvass younger celebrities for the documentary, perhaps even teaching them about the early movement, so they could regurgitate back quotes that would sound like they knew what they were talking about.

As Flanagan continued his musings near the closing of episode two, a shout came from the audience. "Climate Scammers! Oil Forever!" A figure rose out of a seat in the back of the theater, a thick dark jumpsuit protecting every inch of his frame, a hardhat over his skull, and a bandana covering his face. The burly man looked like he just moved a thick pipe in a Texas refinery. A pail in hand, he ran to the front row, yelling "Lubricate! Lubricate!" splashing oil on the two older Pisano sisters and their mother as the three screamed in horror. At the end of the aisle, the oiler spilled the remainder of his pail on Flanagan and proceeded to smash the galvanized steel bucket onto his head and shoulders. As Flanagan collapsed on the floor and Deja tried to block the attack, the burly oiler tossed Deja aside and slammed the pail down on Flanagan, giving him a couple of kicks before running up the aisle and out of the theater.

The tumult and commotion of the crowd was great, although the audience members were relieved on many fronts: firstly, that the oiler brandished a pail rather than a semiautomatic rifle; secondly, that the oiler did not attack the rest of them; thirdly, that the oiler had left the building. Deja lifted Flanagan's head, her kanga dress now too soaked in oil. She was happy to see he was neither bleeding nor dead. Meanwhile, the house lights came on and photographers were capturing images of Deja's oil saturated figure, not to mention a thousand clicks taken of the very lubricated Pisano family.

Soon, attendants carried the stunned and groggy Flanagan to a back room of the theater, placing him on a couch that had already been protected from staining by a multitude of blankets. Kartik checked on him, asking, "How are you doing, Artie?"

"I feel like a ton of bricks fell on me," said Flanagan "Is Deja all right?"

"We have her in the other room," said Kartik. "We're putting blankets on her, making sure she's O.K."

"That's good," said Flanagan. "Are the police coming?"

"Oh, no need for the police right now," said Kartik.

"But I think they'd want my testimony," said Flanagan.

"They will," said Kartik, "but there is no rush."

"There is a rush," said Flanagan. "Otherwise, the asshole who did this will get away."

Kartik laughed. "We want him to get away."

"Why the hell would we want him to get away?" asked Flanagan.

"Because I hired him," said Kartik.

"To beat me up?"

"Not to beat you up," said Kartik, "just to rough you up a little and throw some oil on the Pisano women."

Flanagan started to understand. It was just like Kartik to capture images of the stars of his documentary soaking wet in skimpy dresses. God, he hated this goddamn business. "So you're telling me that this was just a publicity stunt."

"Of course," said Kartik. "That's why you were the only one hurt. I figured anyone with a big problem with the documentary would go after the writer."

"Funny," said Flanagan, "I thought they'd go after the producer. That was awfully shitty of you."

"Oh, I told Arnav to go easy on you," said Kartik. "This will do wonders for your career."

"What career?" asked Flanagan.

Kartik laughed. He was in a joyful mood. "You'll thank me tomorrow."

"I doubt it."

Kartik chuckled. "You really are horrible at the promotional side of the business. I tried to give you so much publicity by delivering those dead animals to your doorstep, with the threatening notes, just to make sure you couldn't misread the intentions. And what did you do about it? Nothing."

Struggling to absorb the revelation Kartik just so cavalierly offered, Flanagan caressed his aching skull. Too weak to yell, he seethed, "You jammed those stinking things – the crow, the chipmunk, the pigeon, the squirrel – into my doorknob."

"Well," said Kartik, "not in that order, and I didn't do it personally. I'm a busy man, you know."

"You had Arnav do it, didn't you?" asked Flanagan. Kartik grinned. "No wonder the bastard was always smirking at me."

"You didn't make it easy, by not reporting any of these incidents to the police," said Kartik.

"I didn't want to jeopardize my investigation," said Flanagan.

"What you were really doing was killing the buzz I was trying to generate for the documentary," said Kartik. "A little danger would have gone a long way in making the press pay attention to what you were doing."

"Sorry," said Flanagan, who realized how ridiculous he was being by apologizing for not offering the proper response to the intimidation and harassment Kartik had hurled upon him. "I thought it would be better to tough it out. For a while there, I wasn't even sure there was going to be a documentary."

"There would have been a documentary," said Kartik, "with or without you. Anyway, after you didn't report the dead chipmunk with the note on the door, I made sure that Arnav took pictures of all of the dead animals with the notes attached. Normally, I would only have done three dead animals, but since the chipmunk wasn't recorded, I wanted a total of three to get out to the press."

"But I haven't seen any reports in the newspapers or on TV," said Flanagan.

"That's what tonight was about," said Kartik. "With you being so blatantly attacked, we can add this material to the intimidating harassment you received."

"From you," Flanagan noted.

"Only the people in the room know that," said Kartik. "And I would strongly advise that no one else find out."

Flanagan tried to imagine just what animals might be at his doorstep if he blabbed.

To make the situation more delightful for Flanagan, Suzie Pisano came to the back room. She asked Kartik, "How is the oil-drenched baby seal doing back here?"

"Oh, wonderful," said Kartik. "Could you stay with him for a few minutes?" he asked Suzie. "He probably should be kept awake, just in case he has a concussion. I've sent for the doctor to come back here to check him out."

"Sure," said Suzie, "I'll hang around to make sure no one lights a match near him."

"Thank you," said Kartik. "And may I say with your hair all slicked back from the oil and with the moistness of your toned skin that you look particularly ravishing."

"I had nearly forgotten what a charming conspirer you can be," said Suzie.

"There is wisdom and financial benefit in remembering that, my most lovely and profitable partner." With that combination of warning and compliment, Kartik left Suzie alone in the room with Flanagan. Flanagan knew he'd be safer in the presence of Arnav than Suzie.

As he rubbed his sore skull, he slowly came to the realization that Suzie's participation and her investment in *Death Canal* was greater than he had previously grasped. She sat there smirking at him as Flanagan made his best effort to not give her the satisfaction of hearing him groan. Heather and Tiffany stopped in, Tiffany dramatically asking whether he was O.K., hand on her hip, clearly happy how the oil had soiled her in just the right way. Tellingly, Heather had borrowed a jacket to cover herself up. "I hope you're feeling better," she said. "Deja gave me these Advil and a bottle of water. She told me you should take them. She said she ordered a car, which will be in here in a couple of minutes."

"Great," said Flanagan. "Thanks."

"I talked to Deja," said Heather. "I want to meet with the both of you tomorrow, if you're up to it."

Though dazed, Flanagan couldn't help but notice Suzie's scowl. Flanagan was not in physical condition to calculate whether Heather had made that announcement intentionally out in the open or because, given the circumstances, she had no other choice but to speak frankly in front of her mother. Whichever the case, Flanagan could tell that Heather was changing before his eyes. He struggled to recognize whether he was changing too.

Heather departed, clapping her hands on the way out, just another round of applause delivered to whom the hell knows. Then Tiffany slipped a pinch of clay in her mouth, gave Flanagan a muddy kiss on the cheek, and left him totally alone with Suzie, a sign that she really didn't care about him as much as she had occasionally intimated. In his head, he started to plot out Jimmy Doherty's biography, feeling the burden of writing a comprehensive and penetrating examination, something a more skilled researcher and author should have produced years ago. Even if he decided against writing directly about Jimmy's life and opted for the documentary on the early heroes of climate change, Jimmy would be part of the story, which meant ultimately Suzie would be part of the story. As his head throbbed from both a bucket bashing and troubling realizations, Flanagan became haunted by the inevitability of Suzie not leaving his life. He sure wished Deja would show up soon so he could get the hell out of there.

For a couple of minutes, Suzie had been speaking to him, but he wasn't listening. Avoiding rudeness, he didn't laugh when she strutted toward him, as proud as Tiffany with the effects of the oil, hands on her hips in a gesture so patented that Flanagan began to wonder whether it was a Pisano trademark. He decided against asking, "Did you learn that move from your daughter?" However, he did manage to tell her, "It's so nice of you to stay here with me, but really I'm fine. I'm sure the media is waiting for you to share your impressions with them."

Suzie answered by kneeling next to Flanagan on the couch and reaching over to give him the most intense of hugs: he could not figure out whether she wanted to love him or suffocate him. Even if it were the former, he knew the latter would inevitably follow.

As he pulled back from her blood warming embrace, Flanagan pointed out, "You know, Suzie, the best thing that ever happened was that I stopped working for you."

"Arthur, my dear boy," said Suzie. "Why would you ever think you stopped working for me?"

ABOUT THE AUTHOR

Michael Hartnett is the author of six other novels, including *The Blue Rat*. His everyday existence is a reality show with horrible ratings, but it is populated by wonderful characters.

NOTE FROM THE AUTHOR

Word-of-mouth is crucial for any author to succeed. If you enjoyed *Death Canal*, please leave a review online—anywhere you are able. Even if it's just a sentence or two. It would make all the difference and would be very much appreciated.

Thanks!
Michael Hartnett

We hope you enjoyed reading this title from:

www.blackrosewriting.com

Subscribe to our mailing list – *The Rosevine* – and receive **FREE** books, daily deals, and stay current with news about upcoming releases and our hottest authors.
Scan the QR code below to sign up.

Already a subscriber? Please accept a sincere thank you for being a fan of Black Rose Writing authors.

View other Black Rose Writing titles at www.blackrosewriting.com/books and use promo code **PRINT** to receive a **20% discount** when purchasing.

www.ingramcontent.com/pod-product-compliance
Lightning Source LLC
Chambersburg PA
CBHW010730100726
47899CB00009B/2997